JAILBIRD

CARO SAVAGE

Boldwood

First published in Great Britain in 2019 by Boldwood Books Ltd.

This paperback edition first published in 2020.

1

A CIP catalogue record for this book is available from the British Library.

Paperback ISBN: 978-1-83889-837-3

Ebook ISBN: 978-1-83889-438-2

Kindle ISBN: 978-1-83889-437-5

Audio CD ISBN: 978-1-83889-431-3

Digital audio download ISBN: 978-1-83889-434-4

Large Print ISBN: 978-1-83889-435-1

Boldwood Books Ltd.

23 Bowerdean Street, London, SW6 3TN

www.boldwoodbooks.com

For CPC

1

The clank sounded out of place.

Alice Jenkins stopped pushing the laundry trolley and lifted her head. She tossed her long reddish-blonde hair out of her face.

'Hey, who's there?'

She was answered only by the repetitive groaning of the huge industrial washing machines and dryers which lined both sides of the prison laundry.

She peered uncertainly into the shadows beyond the giant wire racks, which held folded piles of freshly laundered bedding and towels. Down here in the basement there were no windows and the overhead strip lighting flickered with a sickly insipid yellow which failed to illuminate the room properly.

Alice had only started her job in the laundry two days before. Normally there were other inmates working in here, but this afternoon she was all alone. That was because she'd volunteered to do some overtime, explaining to the laundry supervisor that she wanted to earn a little extra cash for her canteen account.

She hadn't been in prison for very long. Just a few weeks. She'd been sent down for benefit fraud. Not a major crime but enough to land her inside for a year and three months. But she seemed to be getting the hang of things. Like managing to get this job in the laundry.

There was still plenty of stuff that she was unfamiliar with though, so she wasn't totally relaxed by any means. In fact, she'd found that this place could suddenly put you on edge when you were least expecting it. Like now for example.

She glanced around nervously.

'Hey stop messing about!' she said.

Maybe some of the other inmates – her laundry colleagues – were playing a practical joke on her. She hoped so. Because if it wasn't them then maybe it was one of the dangerous-looking cliques she'd seen around the prison. Maybe they'd taken a dislike to her for some reason. Maybe they had it in for her.

'Haha. Try and creep up on Ally. Yeah that's hilarious. You can come out now.'

She tried to sound breezy but her nerves betrayed her, her voice instead coming out reedy and uneven.

There was no answer. Just the incessant rumbling of the machinery.

Her knuckles turned white as she tightened her grip on the handle of the trolley and squinted into the dim recesses of the cavernous laundry. A burst of excess steam hissed from a nearby pipe. She jumped and gasped, her heart thumping in her chest.

Her mind raced to think what had made the clanking sound. It might be a rat. The prison did have a rodent problem. Or maybe she was just spooking herself out unnecessarily.

'You silly girl,' she muttered, shaking her head and pulling herself upright.

She recommenced pushing the trolley, awkwardly manoeuvring its bulky weight towards one of the empty washing machines at the end of the room.

Then, out of the corner of her eye, she noticed a shadow pass behind one of the sheets that were hanging up, waiting to be folded and placed on the wire racks.

She let go of the trolley and spun around to look. Was there someone there? She could have sworn she was the only one in here.

No. It was surely just a ripple in the material caused by convection in the warm air currents generated by the dryers. She turned back to the trolley, taking hold of the handle once again.

But then in the darkness beyond the racking, just behind the dryers, something caught her eye.

A brief sparkle.

A shiny surface which captured the few photons bouncing around behind the stacks of machinery and reflected them back to her...

She stopped again, momentarily entranced by it as it twinkled in the shadows like a lone star aglow in the distant black depths of deep space. For a brief moment she forgot her apprehension as she tried to make sense of it floating there in the shadows like the needle of a compass... turning... pointing in her direction...

Then a depth charge of cold fear detonated in her gut as she realised what it was.

Long...

Thin...

Sharp...

A blade.

A shank.

Her heart began to hammer inside her chest. Her hands fell away from the handle of the trolley.

'Oh fuck,' she whispered.

They'd come to kill her.

They'd decided to come for her when she was all alone. She cursed her stupidity for making the mistake of being down here by herself.

Somewhere along the line she'd messed up and now she was going to pay for it with her life.

She felt a heavy nausea rise up inside her, the fear of impending death.

Slowly, she edged backwards around the trolley to put it between herself and whoever was behind the dryers. She again squinted to try and see more.

In the shadows, silence. A flicker of movement in the darkness. A shadow within a shadow. It was big. It was no rat. That was for sure. It was a person.

She gulped. Her mouth was dry. She glanced towards the doorway. It was at the far end of the laundry. That distant metal door had never looked more appealing. Nor had it ever seemed further away. She glanced back at the row of dryers.

Tensing, she took a deep breath... and bolted.

She sprinted through the laundry, heading towards the exit... weaving through the laundry bins... running away from whatever it was in the shadows... running away from the glitter of razor-sharp steel.

She ran faster than she had ever run in her life. As if something had taken her over. As if there was an animal inside her.

Her breath tore in her throat. Adrenaline coursed through her body. Her trainers hammered on the concrete floor, the slap of her footfalls echoing through the big room.

She ran and ran. The doorway getting closer. Her portal of freedom. If only she could get there. So close now. She panted. Her lungs working overtime to power her flight.

And then a laundry bin spun out in front of her and she tripped over it, crashing onto the floor amidst a cascade of dirty linen.

'Oh god!' she gasped. Her eyes filled with tears, blurring her vision.

She tried to scramble to her feet, but she got tangled in the sheets, the white material having wrapped itself around her ankles with an almost malevolent will of its own.

As she reached down to extract herself from the fatal web of dirty linen, she felt a hand grip her hair roughly from behind. The strands twisting into the fingers, winding tight like a winch.

With a sharp yank, her head was pulled back. She gasped in pain as she felt the roots ripping out. Literally one by one. Pop. Pop. Pop. Out of her scalp.

She tried in vain to twist her head to see her attacker but she couldn't, so tight was the grip. All she could see were her own hands clambering uselessly in the empty space in front of her.

'Oh god!' she choked. 'Please don't hurt me!'

But her words fell away unheard. Through tear-blurred vision she caught the flashing arc of the blade clutched in a black leather glove as it swooped down from above and sliced into the front of her scalp.

She screeched in agony as the cold steel carved the flesh away from her skull. The searing pain was beyond anything she'd ever experienced. A deluge of hot blood coursed down from the wound, transforming her face into a crimson liquid mask locked in a scream of terror.

With an audible rip, her partially severed scalp was savagely torn away from her head. Blinded by the blood in her eyes and paralysed by the shock of the assault, she was in no state to do anything about the knife as it came round again, this time to cut her throat.

2

Detective Constable Bailey Morgan studied the cryptic crossword on the desk in front of her. Technically she was supposed to be doing work – checking through a pile of witness statements – but it was one of those days when time seemed to be moving with the consistency of treacle and police paperwork just wasn't making it go any faster.

She glanced up, scanning the office to see if any of her colleagues had noticed what she was doing. It didn't appear that any of them had. But then it was a Friday afternoon and the place was relatively deserted.

Anyone meeting her gaze would have found themselves looking into a pair of eyes the colour of cold ashes, the dark rings around them under-scored by her pale complexion. They would probably have noticed that although her shoulder-length chestnut hair was tied up in a ponytail, there was a bit that she deliberately wore loose down over the left side of her face in a blatant, and not completely successful, attempt to conceal the thin white scar which ran from the top of her cheekbone down to the bottom of her jaw. They would hopefully at least have observed that she had good taste in clothes compared to the rest of her colleagues in the CID – whereas most of them, particularly the men, got their suits in Matalan, hers was a Donna Karan, cut to fit her lithe figure perfectly.

She fiddled absently with the lock of hair that hung down over the side of her face, curling it around her finger and letting it uncurl, as she was apt to do when she was lost in thought.

The good thing about cryptic crosswords was how completely they absorbed her. She could spend hours doing them, trying to untangle the mind-bending logic that went into their construction. And this one seemed to be doing the job very well. According to the clock on the wall, there were now just twenty-five minutes to go until she could officially knock off for the weekend and begin to concentrate on getting psyched up for the jiu-jitsu grading she was due to participate in the next day. If she passed, she'd move from green belt up to purple. For some people, moving up the belts was all about status, but for her the important thing was that it meant that she got to learn progressively more advanced and deadly ways of defending herself.

She curled her hair around her fingers and let it uncurl. She stared down at the cryptic crossword. There was one more word to fill in which she couldn't get. Twelve across...

_ _ _ e

The clue was 'Ceremony sounds correct'.

What the hell could it be?

Thinking laterally, it occurred to her that the hint probably lay in the word 'sounds'. A word for 'ceremony' that sounded like the word for 'correct'. It was on the tip of her tongue...

Her phone rang, loud in the quiet office. She jumped.

Her first thought was that it was her father. On Sunday she was supposed to have lunch with her parents, but earlier that week she'd had a big blowout with her dad, and those plans had fallen through. His phone call would either be an attempt to make up or an attempt to force home some point he'd made in their argument. She hoped it was the former rather than the latter.

Her parents lived in Bromley, not too far from where she lived in Crystal Palace, and she visited them on a fairly frequent basis. They were both in their sixties, and prior to retiring, her dad had worked for the local council as a health and safety inspector and her mum had been a teacher. She had always been closer to her father than to her mother, who was growing worryingly peculiar with age. However, her father was consumed with a very particular obsession, one that he and Bailey often argued about, to the point where they would sometimes end up not speaking to each other for weeks on end.

She sighed and braced herself as she fished her phone out of her bag. She looked at the number flashing on the screen.

It wasn't her dad.

An anxious tightness gripped her. She recognised the number immediately, even though she had deleted that person's contact details from her phone. It was her ex-boss, Detective Superintendent Frank Grinham. It had been almost six months since she'd last heard from him. Why was he calling her now, out of the blue?

She looked at the phone flashing, hesitating for a few moments, and then she answered it.

'Hello Frank,' she said.

'Hello Bailey.'

An uncomfortable pause.

'What can I do for you?' she asked stiffly.

'There's something important I need to talk to you about.'

'Go on.'

'I can't discuss it over the phone. Let's meet in person. Are you free tomorrow afternoon?'

There was something about his tone that put the wind up her, something ominous yet also compelling.

She opened her mouth to explain that she had a jiu-jitsu grading to go to tomorrow afternoon, but instead the words that came out were: 'Sure. I guess.'

'There's a pub called the Pig and Whistle just round the corner from my office. Know it?'

'Yeah, I remember.'

'Half past three?'

'See you there.'

She hung up.

Frank's phone call had been almost as cryptic as the crossword in front of her. But his enigmatic air didn't come as a complete surprise. After all, he was responsible for running undercover operations and secrecy was his stock-in-trade. She'd worked undercover for him on a variety of jobs over a two-year period, which had ended abruptly six months ago when she'd quit that line of work.

Working undercover had never been something she'd been intending to do when she'd joined the police seven years previously at the age of twenty-two. In fact, she'd barely been aware that that kind of thing even went on.

She'd started as a uniformed constable, doing the standard training at Hendon, followed by eighteen months on the beat. At the first opportunity, she'd transferred to the CID to work as a detective, eager to take a more proactive approach to catching criminals. And it was whilst she was there that she'd first become aware of Frank's operation.

Undercover work was where the danger and the kudos lay. And that was where she'd found her calling, running considerable risks on behalf of the law with the exhilarating feeling that she was really making a difference.

It had been great... until it hadn't been great.

And so she'd left, never to look back. That was why she'd deleted Frank's details from her phone. That was why she was sitting here in this office counting down the minutes until the end of the day.

But if she was so keen to put all that behind her then why had she agreed to meet him?

She knew his call could only mean one thing: that he needed her help. But whether she was ready to give it was another matter entirely.

She curled the lock of hair around her fingers and let it slowly uncurl.

She stared at the cryptic crossword.

The answer jumped out at her.

Rite.

The answer was 'rite'.

3

If she had a bad feeling about the meeting, Frank's choice of venue only increased her misgivings. Although she'd walked past it many a time, she'd never actually been inside the Pig and Whistle. It just wasn't her kind of place. It was a huge, brightly-lit sports pub with shiny fittings and a big TV screen on every wall blaring out the football highlights. She'd have much rather been in a dojo right now doing her jiu-jitsu grading, but she'd cancelled that to be here and it was too late to change her mind about it now.

She stood inside the doorway for a few moments and scanned the room from under the brim of her baseball cap, taking in the old men sitting by themselves staring vacantly at the football on the TV screens. She found the scene depressing and wondered why he'd chosen this pub when there were nicer and quieter places situated just as close to his office as this one.

Outwardly, it would have been hard to guess that she was a police detective, for she was just dressed casually in jeans and a suede-fringed cowboy jacket, her long brown hair tucked up under her cap, apart from the bit hanging down over the left side of her face.

The pub wasn't particularly busy and it didn't take her long to spot Frank sitting at a table in the far corner, his back to the wall, nursing a pint of lager. In his late forties, he had cropped red hair turning to grey and the kind of pasty countenance that made him look ill even when he wasn't.

With his grey suit and black Oxfords, he could have passed for some kind of sales rep sinking a pint after a business meeting in town. For him, Saturday was a workday, no different to any other. It was the nature of the work he did, and she knew just how committed he was to it.

He'd already noticed her and was watching her with a thin smile on his face, dashing any notion she might have had of turning around and leaving. She walked over to his table. He stood up and they engaged in a perfunctory and slightly awkward embrace. She put her bag down and sat in the chair opposite him.

His smile, just as she remembered, was purely a permutation of the muscles around his mouth. It didn't extend upwards to the rest of his face. His pale blue eyes were, as ever, dead, watery and penetrating.

'Vodka and blackcurrant?' he said.

'You've got a good memory.'

'It's only been six months.'

She watched him as he went to the bar to get her a drink, his profile illuminated by the blue light of the TV screens. Although his cold-fish demeanour could put a lot of people off, she felt a measure of affection for him as her former mentor. She'd learnt a lot from him, not least that you often had to think like an outlaw in order to catch one.

He came back from the bar and placed the drink down in front of her.

'How's the job?' he asked.

'Fine,' she said. 'Working towards my sergeant's exams.'

'You've got rings under your eyes.'

'I don't sleep so well these days.'

'I hear warm milk before bed is good for you.'

'I've tried everything.'

He nodded slowly and looked away.

They filled up the minutes with small talk, him asking her questions but seemingly only half-interested in her responses, his eyes flickering around the pub all the while.

She waited until they reached a natural pause in the conversation and raised her eyebrows at him expectantly. 'You were never one for casual chit-chat, Frank, so let's get to the point.'

He nodded slowly. 'I have some bad news for you. I thought it better to tell you in person.'

'I knew there was something wrong.'

'Alice is dead.'

A dagger of shock knifed through her. 'Alice Simms?'

'I know you two were quite close.'

She blinked and nodded stiffly. She felt like she'd been punched in the stomach. An unsolicited flood of memories and emotions threatened to overwhelm her. She bit them back. She didn't want to appear weak in front of Frank. She didn't want to break down in public and certainly not in a place like this.

Taking a deep breath, she steadied herself.

'We did undercover training together and you know how tough that is. We became really good mates.'

'I'm sorry to be the one who had to break it to you.'

'You could have chosen a slightly nicer place to do it in.'

He shrugged apologetically.

Alice had been one of Bailey's closest friends when she had been working undercover. The bond they had forged whilst operating in such a challenging environment had been particularly strong. They'd first met on the undercover training course and their friendship had rapidly grown beyond work to the point where they'd ended up sharing a flat together, an arrangement that had ceased when Bailey had quit that line of work. To hear that Alice was now dead left Bailey stunned.

'What happened?' she whispered.

'She was murdered last week. In the line of duty.'

'Doing what exactly?'

He glanced around. The TV screens blared. They were showing a replay of a penalty, the ball hitting the back of the net again and again from various angles. No one appeared to be paying the slightest bit of interest in them. She realised now that Frank had chosen this pub because it was big enough and noisy enough for them to chat without anyone over-hearing.

He turned back to face her and lowered his voice slightly. 'She was working undercover in a women's prison. She was going under the name of Alice Jenkins.'

Bailey raised her eyebrows in surprise. 'A prison? I've worked in some pretty dicey places but never anything quite like that. Which one was she in?'

'HMP Foxbrook. Know it?'

She nodded. 'I've driven past it a few times. Big old Victorian place. Public sector. It's pretty grim-looking, like something out of Dickens.'

'She'd gone undercover there to investigate a drugs ring. It's a very lucrative business, selling drugs in prison. It's a captive market. Quite literally.'

'Someone found out she was a cop?'

The very prospect of it filled her with horror. She could envisage all too clearly the reaction of a mob of prisoners suddenly discovering a copper in their midst.

'She was deep cover. Not even the prison authorities knew she was a police officer. And they still don't. And we want to keep it that way for the time being.'

'So what happened?'

'We don't know, but it's quite possible her cover got blown somehow. Maybe she slipped up in some way. But it's proving very hard to get to the bottom of it. The inmates are being extremely uncooperative, not surprisingly, and the staff aren't much better.'

'Forensics?'

He shook his head. 'Nothing of any specific value. And in the context of a closed environment like a prison, there's too much cross-contamination for DNA analysis to be reliable.'

Bailey shook her head. 'I can't believe it. Alice was good. She was always top of the class. I'm really surprised that something like this happened to her.'

'It seems she underestimated what she was up against. It was pretty brutal what they did to her. Her body was found in the prison laundry. She'd had her throat cut...' he hesitated for a moment, '...and she'd been scalped.'

Bailey sat there numbly absorbing what he was telling her. She finished her drink and placed the glass back on the table. She regretted not asking for a double.

'What about CCTV?' she said hoarsely. 'Surely that must have caught something.'

He shook his head. 'No cameras in the laundry. It's not considered to be a "high-risk" area. That's probably the reason why they chose to do it there.'

'They...?' she echoed.

He shrugged, opening his palms, welcoming an answer to her question.

'You want me to come back and work for you, don't you?' she said.

But it wasn't really a question because she'd known that this had been the whole point of the meeting all along.

'I want to find out what happened to her. I'm certain she was onto something and I'm pretty sure that was the reason she was killed. I want to know what she found out.'

He fixed her with his watery, penetrating gaze.

'Are you ready to come back, Bailey?'

4

'Spyros!'

Bailey wrenched awake, twisted in the sweat-soaked sheets, alone in her bed, gasping the name that she had been screaming in her dreams.

For a few moments, she just lay there, shrouded in the greyness of pre-dawn, her heart palpitating in her chest, and waited for the horror to slowly subside.

She'd tried prescription medication of all types – from sleeping pills to antidepressants. She'd gone for counselling. She'd even tried alternative medicine. Anything to make the nightmares go away. But none of it had been any good. Each and every night, a slightly different iteration of that last undercover job played out, and each time was no less horrific than the last.

She'd thought that quitting undercover work would make things better. But it hadn't. If anything, the nightmares had been getting worse.

Turning her head, she saw that the glowing digits of her bedside clock read 4.05 a.m. She knew that she would be unable to get back to sleep.

Pulling aside the sheets, she got up out of bed and stumbled to the bathroom. She switched the light on. Blinking in the harsh unflattering glare, she looked at herself in the mirror of the bathroom cabinet.

Jesus she looked like shit. Like some kind of zombie. Her skin was grey. Her eyes had dark rings around them. She couldn't remember the last time she'd had a good night's sleep.

She ran a hand through her hair, spotting yet another white strand amongst the brown. She was only twenty-nine and she already had white hairs appearing on a regular basis. Damn nightmares. She pulled the offending strand out with a snapping sound and dropped it in the sink.

Opening the cabinet, she took out a box of beta-blockers. She popped two of the tablets out of the blister pack and tossed them back with a mouthful of water directly from the tap.

She wasn't planning on going back to bed. No point lying in the darkness ruminating over things. She decided to go into the living room to watch whatever crap was showing on TV at this time in the morning, anything to distract her from the bad dreams, the stupider and more mundane the better.

Wandering into the living room, she sat down on the sofa and switched on the TV. It was showing a long American infomercial advertising an ultra-intensive workout programme that promised to transform flab into rippling muscle. She'd seen this one many times before. It was on most nights, most of the time, on most of the channels so it seemed. But she sat there and watched it again.

As she slouched on the sofa in the flickering light of the TV screen, she thought again about the decision she'd made the previous day. She'd said yes to Frank because of Alice. And later that evening she'd mourned alone for her friend in the privacy of her flat, resolving through tears and gritted teeth to find out what had happened to her. But now, after awakening from the nightmares, she wasn't so sure about her decision any more. Had it been a really bad idea?

Surely, she had to be crazy to want to plunge herself back into that same world which had chewed her up and left her like this.

A surge of black panic suddenly overwhelmed her.

It had been the wrong decision. She couldn't do it.

She picked her mobile phone up off the coffee table. The small screen glowed as she activated it. She dialled Frank Grinham's number. It began to ring.

Brrring... Brrring... Brrring...

She ended the call before he could answer. Switching off her phone, she tossed it aside, angry at her brief lapse in resolve. She realised now that her mistake had been quitting undercover work in the first place. It had left her too much time on her hands to think about stuff.

And some things it was just better not to dwell on.

5

Considering that it was the nerve centre for some very delicate and high-stakes undercover operations, the office came across as kind of poky and a bit disorganised, with messy stacks of papers lying everywhere on the desks next to the computers. However, despite the apparent disorder, Bailey knew that there was a system of sorts in place.

'It's been a while since you've been here,' said Frank over his shoulder as he led her through the desks towards one of the side rooms.

It was true. Previously, when she'd been working undercover, she'd seldom needed to come to headquarters, apart from the occasional briefing for the bigger or more sensitive jobs. More often, a job would just come through directly on the mobile phone she'd been issued with especially for that purpose and she'd take it directly from there.

Numerous black filing cabinets lined the sides of the rooms, containing files going back years relating to past cases. Noticeboards on the walls were adorned with mugshots linked together by lines tracing the connections between the various individuals within criminal organisations who were the subject of ongoing operations. There were several maps of the UK, including a big one of London, which were dotted with a plethora of coloured pins. All in all, it wasn't as slick or as high-tech in appearance as people might have expected. But then, at the end of the day, undercover work was primarily about human beings rather than technology.

She followed Frank through the office into a side room that contained little more than a table and two chairs. Through the window, she could see that it had started drizzling outside, the London skyline receding into a grey foggy murk.

He closed the door. They both sat down and he scrutinised her in silence for a few moments.

'I got a missed call from you the other night. Is everything okay?'

'Everything's fine.' He didn't need to know about the nightmares.

'Are you sure you're up to it? You know, I didn't actually check the records to see if you'd been signed off as psychologically fit to return to undercover work.'

'The shrinks all said I was fine.' But she hadn't told them the half of it. She just hadn't been able to bring herself to.

He smiled and nodded slowly. 'You miss the rush, don't you? There's nothing quite like it.'

She knew he spoke from bountiful experience. Frank had worked in undercover roles on countless operations over the years before eventually taking over the reins. He had an ex-wife and a kid he never saw who were casualties of his relentless dedication to the job. And to that end Bailey knew first-hand what a hard taskmaster he could be.

He was right, though. She did miss the rush of working undercover. It made her feel alive like nothing else, especially when normal life made her feel as if she was dying inside. But the buzz wasn't the only reason she was here. Not by a long stretch. Alice was the main reason.

'So what's the deal?' she said.

The smiled faded. He cleared his throat.

'As you may already be aware, drugs in prison are a major social issue and a political hot topic. They're worth up to four times their street value inside and it's estimated that the drugs trade in the UK prison system is worth around a hundred million pounds a year.'

'Big business,' she murmured.

'We've been aware of the problem at HMP Foxbrook for a while now and this operation forms part of the Government's overall initiative to clamp down on drug use and drug dealing within the wider prison system.'

'So just how big is the problem at HMP Foxbrook?' she asked.

'Well, we know that drugs get into the prison through all kinds of means. Visitors smuggle stuff in. Corrupt staff smuggle stuff in. Stuff gets chucked over the wall. Stuff gets hidden in packages posted to prisoners. Stuff gets flown in by drone. But that's all small fry. What we're concerned about here are much larger quantities. We suspect the existence of an organised drug smuggling and distribution ring who are working at scale.'

'Where's the budget for this operation coming from?'

'The operation is being funded by the Metropolitan Police, more specifically the Basic Command Unit which covers the borough that the prison lies in. Drugs detectives from that BCU will be overseeing the operation and they're also in charge of the budget. They're the ones I'll be reporting back to with any intelligence that you gather.'

The Metropolitan Police was divided up into a number of Basic Command Units, or BCUs, each assigned to a specific geographical area of London.

'So basically the whole thing's being run by the local drugs squad,' said Bailey.

'That's more or less correct,' Frank agreed. 'They want you to uncover how the drugs are entering the prison and they want to identify the key players involved. Once we've nailed the perpetrators, we should be able to find out who on the outside is behind the supply of drugs to the prison. We think that a major organised crime group is responsible. When we reach that point, the NCA will probably want to step in, so they're very interested in the outcome of this operation.'

The National Crime Agency, or NCA, were responsible for tackling organised crime on a variety of fronts, but they only dealt with really large and significant cases, underlining to Bailey that this operation could potentially lead into a major investigation.

'And Alice?'

'I want to make it clear right now, Bailey, that your priority is uncovering the drugs ring. Alice's murder is being investigated by the police separately. Do you understand?' He fixed her with a stern look and a raised eyebrow.

'Sure,' she said. 'The drugs ring is the priority. But I do also intend to find out who killed Alice.'

'Well, as I was saying before in the pub, I think her murder was probably connected to her investigation of the drugs ring, so unlocking the identity of her killer is likely to be a key element in cracking this case and securing some serious convictions, and finding out who did it will probably form an integral part of your investigation anyhow.'

'I figured as much. She must have been onto something serious.'

'In case you're not already aware, all murders in custody have to be investigated by the police, the Prison and Probation Ombudsman, the employer and the coroner. But, like I mentioned before, not a great deal of progress has been made in terms of finding out who killed her. But that's where you, in your undercover role, might be able to shed some light on matters. However, the murder investigation team who are currently investigating her death will not be made aware that you are a police officer and you will not make direct contact with them in any way. Everything goes through me. Do you understand?'

'That suits me just fine. So when do I start?'

'The budget's been signed off so you can start right away. We can get you in there almost immediately. I've already obtained the authorisation from your CID detective sergeant to get you released.' He paused. 'How's this Thursday?'

'The sixteenth of May?'

'Can you be ready by then?'

It was only three days away. Quite often in the past, undercover jobs would come up at short notice and Bailey had become used to rapidly dropping everything in order to accommodate them. Working undercover wasn't a permanent job and it never had been. Whenever she'd gone on an undercover operation her regular casework had merely been put on hold until she had finished or had been redistributed to others to do.

A thought suddenly crossed her mind. 'When's Alice's funeral?'

'I don't know at the moment. They've done the autopsy, but her body hasn't been released to the funeral home yet. There's got to be an inquest at some point and that always holds things up.'

She sighed. 'Okay, well I guess this Thursday's fine then,' she said. 'No point in delaying things.'

'That's what I like to hear,' he said. 'You know you'll probably make a decent bit of overtime from this job.'

'I'm not doing it for the money.'

'Do you have a cover story you can use?'

She nodded. She knew the drill. Her cover story was her responsibility. Quite often, there was never any need to resort to it, as a lot of people just weren't that concerned with hearing about your life. But then, other times, when infiltrating a criminal organisation, you encountered those who wanted to know every conceivable detail about you. So it was always best to have a solid background explanation to hand. 'What about my exit from the prison when the operation's over?' she asked.

'We'll find a reason to have you "transferred" to another prison, so it'll seem realistic when you suddenly have to leave. No one will ever need to know that you were a police officer.'

She nodded in approval.

'We've done our best to keep it out of the news that Alice was an undercover police officer,' he said. 'To all intents and purposes, she was just an inmate who got murdered. That's not to say that someone, somewhere in the prison, might have been aware of her true identity, which could be the reason she got killed. Either way, this time we don't want to take any chances. So, to keep security really tight, I'll be working directly as your handler. No one in the prison, not even the Governor, will know who you are. We can't risk any kind of leak, especially considering that you'll have no backup whatsoever.'

Part of what she liked about undercover work was not having someone looking over your shoulder, telling you what to do all the time. She liked the freedom of working on her own. Conversely, it meant that there was often no one to fall back on if things took a turn for the worse. You had to rely on your initiative and be able to think on your feet, and that could be scary, but it could also be exhilarating.

'How will I contact you?' she asked.

'I'll give you a number that you can call me on. It'll be routed through to the switchboard here. Once you get through to Rita, she'll put you through to me.'

In a soundproofed room off to one side of the office was the switchboard, operated by a civilian police worker called Rita. A former flight attendant from Essex who was now in her early fifties, she sounded like a generic secretary with her nasal sing-song voice and her brisk efficient tone. But her role was crucial, for the switchboard was the primary point of contact for all the different undercover police officers who were operating at any given time. When a call came through, Rita would answer with the name of whatever false company or organisation had been set up to provide a cover for that particular officer.

'Is that how it worked with Alice?'

'That's how it was supposed to work with Alice. But, being Alice, she managed to get hold of a mobile phone, even though they're illegal inside.'

'That doesn't surprise me. She was always very resourceful.'

'She would use it to call and text me with updates. We recovered it along with her body. She must have been pretty panicked if she didn't even have time to use it to call me for help. We downloaded all the data from it, but there was nothing on there of much help.'

'I'll see if I can get hold of one once I'm in there.'

Frank shook his head. 'Uh-uh. I don't want you doing that, especially in light of what's happened to her. If the phone is stolen or confiscated, the information on it – the sent texts and numbers called – could compromise your security. So no mobile phones. Got that?'

'Sure.'

'You'll call me via the public phones in the prison. We'll set up a fake law firm to take your calls, so it will seem like you're phoning your solicitor. It'll provide an element of plausibility and it'll also make it easier to clear the number with the prison as they have to approve all telephone numbers. Crucially, it also means that they're not allowed to listen in on the calls like they can with normal numbers. We want to maintain maximum secrecy.' He paused and tilted his head. 'I'll also come in and visit you from time to time,' he said. 'Just so you don't get too lonely.'

'As my lawyer?'

He shook his head. 'It'd be too risky for me to pretend to be a lawyer in case I bumped into a real one in the waiting room. He'd soon clock that I was a fake. No, it'll look better if I'm a family member. Like your brother or something.'

'You don't look anything like me. Your nose is too big for one thing.'

He snorted at her response. 'I'll be your half-brother. Same father, different mothers. That can explain the age difference as well.'

'Am I expected to wear a wire?'

He shook his head. 'It'd be too difficult getting it into the prison. And then you'd have to conceal it from your cellmate and also from the guards. There's too much risk that it could get found.'

'That's a relief. I never liked wearing those things anyway.'

'Your role, therefore, will be primarily to gather intelligence and to inform us about anything that might be going down. You'll be our eyes and ears on the inside.'

'And presumably at the critical point you'll swoop in and make arrests.'

'That's right.'

'So what kind of intel had Alice gathered so far? Do I have anything to go on?'

He grimaced and shook his head. 'She hadn't been in there long enough to identify any specific individuals or groups associated with the drugs ring. She'd been in there barely a few weeks before she was murdered.'

Bailey frowned. 'Yet you said you thought that she was onto something big. And that's why she might have been murdered.'

'I can only think that she found something out very suddenly and was murdered before she had the chance to properly tell me about it. The last communication I had with her was a text message in which she refers to the source of the drugs. She says it's well concealed, or not immediately obvious at any rate.'

'Can I see it?'

He took out his own mobile and tapped on the screen a few times. He pushed it across the table to her.

She picked it up and looked at the message on the small screen. It was tantalisingly brief.

Source well concealed in prison. Investigating today. Will update later.

'She never got to update me later,' he said. 'She sent this on the day she was killed.'

'Do you think the source of the drugs is a member of staff, hence the "well concealed" reference?'

'Could be. That's why I want to make sure that nobody in the prison authorities suspects that you're an undercover police officer. But then no one was supposed to know that Alice was a cop either, and that didn't prevent her from getting murdered.'

Bailey sighed. 'So no leads and very little information. I'm going in almost completely cold.'

'Oh yeah, I forgot to mention. There is one possible lead. The murder investigation team interviewed Alice's cellmate – a girl by the name of Melanie Clarke. But, by all accounts, she was a fruitcake and they couldn't get anything coherent out of her. But I suppose you could always give it another shot.'

Bailey nodded and filed the name away for future reference.

Frank observed her gravely.

'You're going to have to be really careful on this one, Bailey. This is a dangerous job.'

'What's new.'

6

Amber White had only started working as a prison officer a few weeks previously and already she was finding out that the job was proving to be much more challenging than anything she'd covered in the role-plays and written exercises she'd done during training.

She was sitting in the meeting room in the administration block with the rest of the other prison officers waiting for the Governor to arrive and begin their daily morning briefing.

'How long is it going to be before one of us gets murdered?' Terry was saying. 'That's what I want to know.'

Terry Brinkle was one of the longer-serving prison officers and he also functioned as the staff union rep. A big man with an acne-scarred face and lidded eyes, he gave the impression that he was perpetually half-asleep, but Amber had soon realised he was an unusually alert and calculating individual.

As staff union rep he always seemed to have something to gripe about in the morning briefings, but in this particular case his concerns appeared to be justified. The other prison officers seemed to think so too, as there was a general murmur of accord in the room.

'Yeah I don't want to get stabbed up,' she heard someone say.

'They did more than just stab her up!' someone else said.

'We don't get paid even remotely enough to face those kinds of risks.'

The murder in the laundry had happened not long after Amber had started and it had proved to be a particularly unpleasant introduction to life in the prison.

She swallowed nervously and adjusted her large thick-rimmed spectacles. She located a few loose strands of blonde hair which had escaped her tight bun and tucked them behind her ear.

'Try not to let it scare you,' whispered Maggie in her ear, attempting to reassure her. 'This kind of thing is quite unusual and hopefully it's just a one-off. Although, I have to say, it is a nasty one. No doubt about that.'

Maggie Cooper had been working in the prison system longer than Amber had been alive. Her face was etched with a multitude of deep worry lines around her mouth and eyes, and Amber had a horrible feeling that if she stayed in this job long enough she'd end up with a face like Maggie's. But what Maggie lacked in the looks department she more than made up for with an abundance of seasoned experience and wisdom.

Amber had heard about how gory the killing had been. About all the blood everywhere. And apparently it had entailed some kind of horrible mutilation, the exact nature of which hadn't been made clear yet. She'd done a control and restraint course as part of her prison officer entry level training at the Prison Service College near Rugby, but she was beginning to have doubts that it would be sufficient to cope with this level of violence.

'So who do you think did it then?' she asked apprehensively.

Maggie shrugged. 'Could be gang-related. Could be personal. It's hard to tell at this stage. I just know that in all my years here I've never seen anything like it.'

Terry had now moved onto one of his favourite topics – government cost-cutting. 'As I keep saying again and again, this prison is horribly overcrowded, yet government cost-cutting means that we're desperately understaffed, which means we're expected to work excessive hours, yet when anything goes wrong we're the ones who have to carry the can. No doubt we'll end up getting the blame for this murder.' He made each point with the blade of one meaty hand chopping into the palm of the other.

Amber hadn't quite worked out if Terry griped because he was a union rep, or if he'd become a union rep in order to legitimise his need to gripe. He exerted a certain amount of influence over the other prison officers and relished any opportunity to whip up discontent whenever he could. But underneath his reactionary facade she suspected that he was basically a malingerer.

It still surprised her just how fractious the prison staff were, let alone the inmates. She was still on her probationary period as a New Entry Prison Officer and wanted to make a good impression by looking smart and professional, and she was determined not to succumb to the kind of cynicism which enveloped some of the more seasoned members of staff like Terry.

'Don't let Terry get you down,' said Maggie. 'There's obviously a lot of truth in what he says, but this job is largely what you make it.'

'I guess I should take a leaf out of Dylan's book,' murmured Amber, glancing over at Dylan Prince, who was sitting there with his foot up on his knee, whistling softly to himself, projecting an unconcerned easy-going demeanour. He noticed her looking at him, flicked back his sandy-coloured hair and shot her a wink. She smiled and looked away.

One of the other things that had surprised Amber, as a newcomer, was the relatively high proportion of male staff here, more than she would have expected in a women's prison. Probably just under half of the staff were men. And that included the Governor.

As soon as he entered the room, the conversation subsided into a resentful silence and Dylan's whistling petered out.

The Governor was a large man in his mid-fifties who, unlike them, was dressed in a suit rather than a uniform. He stood there in front of them and fiddled with his cuffs, confronted with a tone of sullen obedience; he might be their superior, but he wasn't one of them and never would be.

He cleared his throat, his jowls shaking slightly, and spoke in his well-modulated Home Counties accent, looking at them uneasily, not wanting to meet their eyes. 'Today you are going to carry out a full prison cell search in relation to the recent... uh... murder.'

A murmur of dissatisfaction rippled through the room. A full prison cell search would take a whole day to complete. It would mean no end of aggro from the inmates. All their contraband would be found.

A full prison search was usually not announced in advance. This was so that the inmates didn't have time to hide or get rid of anything incriminating. It also ensured that any guards with loose tongues wouldn't let on about it, for in her short time here Amber had quickly come to realise that gossip formed an intrinsic part of life in the prison, both for the staff and for the inmates.

Normally, the Deputy Governor would have handled the logistics of a prison search, but she'd recently gone on maternity leave and apparently they'd had problems finding an interim replacement. In the meantime, the Governor himself was dealing with everything.

'This is a full lockdown,' he added. 'Only essential services will continue – the kitchen and the like. Any inmates involved in those activities will need a full cell search beforehand. You'll be looking for anything suspicious, anything out of the ordinary. It's imperative that you keep an eye out for any weapons. The murder weapon has still to be recovered. All areas of wing accommodation will also need to be searched.' That meant TV rooms and bathrooms in addition to cells.

'This should have been done last week,' whispered Maggie. 'Probably too late to find anything by now. They're closing the stable door after the horse has bolted.'

Amber could see Terry puffing up, ready to say something.

'A murder weapon,' he began. 'By all accounts, this murder was particularly savage. Surely it is indicative of the rising levels of violence in the prison, no doubt exacerbated by overcrowding and spending cuts. Can I remind you that protection of staff should be paramount here? We need proper protection where use of force is necessary. Basic control and restraint procedures are just not adequate. As I've said many times before, what we need are side-handle batons.'

The Governor had adopted that pained look which he always took with Terry, who constantly seemed to find something to have a go at him about.

'Look, we've covered this before,' said the Governor. 'It's not going to happen. You'll just have to make do.'

'Just like we always have to make do?' Terry shook his head in disgust. 'The police have them.'

'You're not the police.'

'Exactly. Our job is so much tougher than theirs is, yet we get treated so much worse. Every minute of our working day consists of dealing with violent, suicidal, mentally ill and substance-addicted criminals. All they have to do is arrest them. In terms of contact time, we have to interact with these people on a much more frequent basis.'

'While I understand these objections,' said the Governor, 'I don't want them to be getting in the way of the current police investigation. I want you to give the police your fullest co-operation.'

Since the murder, police detectives had been in the prison conducting an investigation, but as far as Amber had heard, they hadn't made much headway into solving the case.

'Bloody coppers,' muttered someone behind her. 'Coming in here. Walking around like they own the place, like they deserve some kind of respect. Well, we're the ones who deserve respect. More than them.'

There was another disgruntled murmur of assent among the assembled prison officers.

'That's enough whinging,' snapped the Governor. 'The sooner you help them clear it up, the quicker they'll be out of your hair. And the sooner they're out of here, the better because it's not the kind of thing that looks good in the newspapers.'

Amber knew how much the Governor cared what people thought of him. She'd been in his office one time when she'd first started and remembered seeing a big framed photograph on the wall depicting him standing next to the current Home Secretary with a proud grin on his face.

'One more thing,' said the Governor. 'I should also remind you that with this murder the inmate was mutilated... scalped. The scalp was missing from the crime scene and still hasn't been found. This is also something you need to look for when you carry out the cell search.'

There was a chorus of groans and whistles of disgust.

'Scalped?' whispered Amber. 'Why on earth would someone do something like that?'

Maggie shuddered. 'Beats me.'

'Let me get this straight,' said Terry. 'We're looking for a human body part?'

'That's correct,' replied the Governor uneasily.

'It's not part of our job remit to be looking for human body parts,' huffed Terry. 'There are hygiene issues for one thing. We haven't received adequate training to deal with this kind of situation. We'll see what the union has to say about this.'

'Just get on with it!' snarled the Governor and turned and marched out of the room.

7

The cell was fitted out in exactly the same way as almost all of the other cells in the prison – two metal-framed bunks, a stainless-steel sink, a mirror, a toilet, a small table in the corner and a single barred window seemingly designed to let in only the most miserly amount of light.

Sharon Finn lay on her bunk looking up at the springs of the empty bed above. Her cellmate had been released two days earlier. Sharon had had a number of cellmates over the past few years and she knew she'd probably have quite a few more as she still had another three years to serve. Three had been released, two had been transferred, one had escaped and one had died of cancer. She wondered what the next one would be like and how long they'd be hanging around.

Sharon was an addict of sorts and her addiction had got her into trouble. She wasn't addicted to substances. No, nothing as crude as that. She was addicted to secrets. Other people's secrets. And that was why she had been locked up.

In her mind, she hadn't committed a crime. In her mind, an injustice had been done by locking her up in here. Sure, someone had ended up killing himself as a result of her actions. But that had been his decision. He shouldn't have got himself into that kind of situation in the first place. She'd merely discovered that he'd been having an affair. She'd merely threatened to tell his wife. Everything would have been fine if he'd merely agreed to pay her the money she'd asked for.

She hadn't expected him to kill himself.

He had implicated her in his suicide note, and that, plus subsequent evidence of their correspondence, had been enough for the court to convict her.

Making unwarranted demands with menaces with a view to making a gain. That was how the judge had phrased it.

Blackmail. That was the shorter way to describe it.

Still, nine years seemed a bit excessive in her opinion.

The fact that her victim had been a high court judge might have had something to do with her heavy sentence now she thought about it. He'd probably had friends in high places. He'd probably been private-school chums with the judge who'd sentenced her.

She sighed and shifted on the bunk. Life just wasn't fair. She'd launched a number of appeals, but they'd all been unsuccessful.

Anyhow, prison wasn't quite as bad as people made out. In fact, she'd found that she actually quite enjoyed it. The main problem that most inmates suffered from in here was boredom. But that was only because most of them lacked the internal resources to amuse themselves. She, on the other hand, found the inmate population to be an almost inexhaustible source of entertainment. There were more than enough dark and dirty secrets in here to keep her occupied for a lifetime.

A metallic clank jerked her out of her reverie as the door to her cell opened. She looked up. A prison officer was standing there accompanied by an inmate she hadn't seen before who was holding a pack of sheets and prison-issue clothes and her plastic cup, plate and cutlery.

She suddenly remembered that today was when her new cellmate was due to arrive.

The prison officer was called Maggie Cooper. She was a big, lumbering woman. Solid, sensible and honest. Boring, in a nutshell. If people were books to read, Maggie would be the equivalent of the telephone directory.

The inmate, by contrast, looked like she had potential.

Sharon immediately sat up, like a hungry animal sniffing out the possibility of new food. She was pleased to have a new cellmate, to have someone to talk to, to find out about.

Maggie cleared her throat before speaking. 'Sharon, this is your new cellmate. Her name's Bailey Pike.'

Sharon's first impression was that the inmate was shy and wary, half hiding behind the fringe of hair which hung down over one side of her face. Mind you, a little apprehension was to be expected on her first day in prison.

With that brief introduction, Maggie left the cell. Sharon lay there and openly watched Bailey as she began to settle in. She took in her details. Brown hair. Some freckles scattered across the nose. Fairly slim. Looked like she kept herself in shape. Nothing out of the ordinary. Sharon had almost formed the opinion that Bailey was quite pretty, but then she noticed the scar.

As Bailey was placing her stuff on the bunk, her fringe fell back as she lifted her head, revealing a nasty jagged white scar which ran down the side of her face and neck. It definitely marred her looks.

Sharon realised then that Bailey's reticent demeanour wasn't so much due to shyness as a desire to conceal the scar behind the lock of hair which she evidently wore loose for that very reason. She obviously felt self-conscious about it.

Sharon was instantly intrigued. Her enquiring mind began to whir like clockwork as she wondered how Bailey had acquired the scar. Had it been an accident? Had she been the victim of some form of violence?

'So why are you in here then?' Sharon asked by way of greeting. After all, in her mind it was one of the most important questions you could ask in here.

'Fraud.'

'What? Like stealing money?'

'Yeah. I embezzled some money.'

She seemed a bit cagey. Sharon wondered if she still felt guilty about her wrongdoing even though she'd already been caught for it.

'A lot of money?'

Bailey paused unpacking her items and looked down at Sharon. Sharon found herself staring into an intense pair of grey eyes.

'Enough to put me away for four years.'

'Four years huh?' Sharon nodded, impressed. 'Must have been a decent wad. Who'd you nick it from?'

'I'm...' Bailey checked herself. 'I was an accountant. I stole the money from my employers.'

Fiddling the books. A fairly dull crime, thought Sharon. But she was a little puzzled nonetheless. The girl didn't quite look how Sharon imagined accountants to be. She didn't look boring enough. And she was certain that she could detect a seam of hardness just beneath the surface, a steel which she wouldn't have expected in a mere accountant. Or maybe she was imagining it.

She stared at the scar. It compounded her growing sense that there was more to Bailey than met the eye. How did she get that scar? Sharon would find out sooner or later. Over the course of the long hours spent in the cell together, you found out virtually everything there was to know about your cellmate. And, who knew, there might even be something to gain out of it.

Sharon lay back down on her bunk, smiled like a shark and flexed her fingers, cracking her knuckles one by one.

'So why are you in here?' asked Bailey.

Sharon sighed. 'I'm just too inquisitive for my own good.'

Bailey nodded and continued arranging her items on the bunk. Sharon continued to observe her. She could tell that Bailey was slightly ill at ease under her blatant scrutiny, but she didn't care. She'd found that the longer you stared at people, the more you noticed those little cracks that revealed who they really were.

'You know, Bailey, I'm glad to have your company to be honest.' She paused for effect. 'What with the murder and everything.'

Bailey froze. She turned to look at Sharon once more. 'What murder?'

'You haven't heard about it? Silly me. Of course you haven't. It's your first day. Well, I didn't see it or anything. But I heard all about it. Everyone's talking about it. Really vicious. Lots of blood. Bits cut off. That kind of thing. They did a big cell search yesterday. Looking for the murder weapon. But I overheard them saying that they were also looking for...' she dropped her voice to a conspiratorial whisper, '...a human body part.'

Bailey's face screwed up in disgust and alarm. Sharon was enjoying shocking her on her first day. It gave her a pleasant sense of superiority.

'Who got murdered?' said Bailey.

'Some girl. I never met her. Never even knew about her until she ended up dead.'

'Who murdered her?'

That was a very good point, thought Sharon, frowning to herself. She hadn't really thought about it up until now, and now she did think about it, it did somewhat bother her that whoever had done this was still around. Sharon wasn't the type who scared easily, but there was something about this particular murder that kind of got to her.

'I have no idea who did it,' she said. 'And I guess that means you want to be watching your back.'

Night had fallen and Bailey lay awake on her bunk in the dimness listening to the sounds of the prison – muted sobbing, a distant clang, the gurgling of pipes, a solitary shout, the creak of springs as her cellmate shifted position on the bunk below.

She was knackered, but she couldn't get to sleep as her buzzing mind was still processing her first day in prison.

The whole procedure had begun eleven hours earlier in the local Crown Court. She had been taken in handcuffs to a holding cell underneath the courtroom to make it seem as if she had just come directly from being sentenced. After spending three hours in the holding cell, she had been transferred to a prison van to be taken to HMP Foxbrook.

The drive to the prison took just under an hour, and as the van lurched into the prison complex, she caught a glimpse through the tinted window of the huge perimeter wall looming up, cold and forbidding, topped with thick coils of razor wire.

Stepping out of the van, she had looked up at the four huge house-blocks towering above her, their grey Victorian brickwork peppered with hundreds of tiny windows, each one denoting a cell. Whether it was just her imagination or whether it was real, she felt as if hundreds of eyes were watching her from the windows, judging her, forming opinions, already making decisions about her. An edging fear had begun to gnaw at her for she was only too aware that somewhere behind those walls was the person or persons who had killed Alice and that very soon she would be trapped in there with them.

Once inside the prison, she had been moved from room to room for each step of the processing and induction procedure. First, her details had been taken by the prison officers and her personal items had been taken away, logged and put in plastic bags, to be returned to her when she was released. Then she had been strip-searched and issued with prison clothes – a grey tracksuit – and a reception pack, consisting of blankets, soap, toothpaste, basic toiletries and a plastic cup, plate and cutlery for when she needed to eat anything in her cell. She had undergone a brief health check by the prison doctor and asked about any allergies she had that might need special requirements. Then she'd been given some psychometric questionnaires to fill out for the benefit of the prison psychologist. Finally, she'd been assigned a six-digit prison number and allocated a cell.

Naturally, she'd had very little say in anything during the whole procedure. The tone of it had been slightly shambolic, with the staff appearing bored and inattentive, which was perhaps unsurprising seeing as they did it day in day out. No one volunteered much in the way of information, after all she wasn't one of them, and she got the impression that she'd have to pick it up herself in due course.

After she had been processed, they had taken her to her cell. And that was when she got her first taste of what the prison was really like on the inside.

The four house-blocks of HMP Foxbrook were arranged like the spokes of a wheel around a central hub and atrium area. It was the classic panopticon layout, designed by the Victorians for optimal surveillance in an era before the invention of CCTV. They were five-storey galleried wings, the tiers of cells towering up above her, reaching almost to the ceiling high above. The green paint flaking off the ancient brickwork combined with the feeble daylight filtering through the distant, grimy skylights gave the place a dingy claustrophobic feel.

The whole place echoed with the noise of chatter, the clump of feet trudging up the flights of cast-iron stairs and the clank of doors opening and closing, and beyond the disinfectant smell lay the faint whiff of illicit drugs.

In the central atrium, inmates of all ages and ethnic backgrounds, dressed mostly in prison-issue grey tracksuits and trainers, were standing and sitting around in small groups on the plastic benches and tables, which she noticed were bolted to the floor.

Accompanied by a female prison officer, she was marched through the atrium and up the metal stairs to her cell, passing the inmates as they lounged on the landings and leant on the banisters, chatting and watching each other, some of them breaking off their conversations to observe her as she walked by. Most of the gazes were flat and impenetrable, others were curious, some were downright hostile. As she passed by one group of inmates, she heard one of them mutter something she couldn't quite make out, which got some sniggers in response. She knew it had been directed at her, but she kept her head down and avoided eye contact.

She felt that familiar gut-twisting fear return, that they would somehow see through her and see her for what she actually was – a serving police officer. But despite that, she found herself falling back into her undercover role with an ease she hadn't been expecting, especially considering what had happened on the previous job. And, what was more, on the crest of the fear, she felt that old buzz, the reason she'd started working undercover in the first place. Only now, after her extended absence from this kind of work, did she realise just how much she craved it.

As for her cellmate, Sharon, her cover story seemed to have done the trick for the time being. Sharon seemed affable enough, but Bailey didn't trust her one inch. She had that familiar animal cunning that so many criminals seemed to possess. As a policewoman, Bailey had encountered it innumerable times. Although not necessarily intelligent as such, these people had an innate deviousness that it was well to be wary of and fatal to underestimate.

The undercover training course had emphasised that it was always best to try to keep your cover story as true to life as possible. The more you lied, the more you were at risk of holes showing in your story. And the more you tried to be what you weren't, the more likely people were to see through you. Criminals were paranoid people by their very nature, and often on the lookout for anything suspicious. So it had been no lie about the accountancy. Bailey really had once been an accountant. For about five minutes. She'd studied it at college, thinking that it would make a good solid career. But as a job, she'd found it so boring that she'd quit after two months and applied to join the police instead, something she'd wanted to do ever since she was a kid. The upshot of this, however, was that when it came to financial records and bookkeeping, spreadsheets and payroll, she could talk with some authority and sound natural.

And that was important, because maintaining a cover story required discipline and the ability to stay on the ball all the time, however tired you were. One thing the training course had emphasised was that the effort of sustaining a facade, the pressure of having to lie, and the consequences of making mistakes could take a heavy psychological toll, especially over an extended period of time.

But the central tenet that had been drilled into them incessantly was that, whatever the circumstances, you had to maintain your cover, however tempting it might be to reveal the truth, however much someone might claim that they knew you were a police officer.

Never break cover.

Never admit that you're a cop.

Never. Break. Cover.

9

Bailey stood under the jet of water, her eyes closed, massaging the prison-issue shower gel over her body, working up a lather. The shower gel smelt cheap and harsh and left her skin feeling dry and sensitive and she made a mental note there and then to check if the prison shop stocked anything of a slightly better quality.

She didn't particularly enjoy communal showering and had been apprehensive about exposing her scars but knew that she would have no choice in the matter. She was self-conscious about them at the best of times, and in here she didn't quite know what reaction they would elicit.

The one down the side of her face was what most people saw, if they noticed it beneath her hair, but that was the least of them, for they stretched in an extensive zigzag lattice down across her breasts, shoulders and back, interspersed here and there with a number of small round burn marks.

As it turned out, in the shower she'd got a few glances of interest and several double-takes though no one had actually said anything. Maybe in an environment like prison, scars weren't such a big deal. If anything, the other inmates had given her a slightly wider berth, and she realised that her disfigurement constituted a useful asset as it seemed to confer on her an aura of criminal credibility that she wouldn't otherwise have had.

Looking around her, she was amazed by the number of tattoos. She'd never seen so many in one place. Some of the artwork was quite impressive, but for the most part it was pretty tacky, the kind of thing she'd seen on sex workers she'd encountered in the course of upholding the law.

Bailey herself had no tattoos. She'd never seen the point in getting one. Once upon a time, if anyone had asked her why, she'd have responded by saying that tattoos were an identifying feature – not necessarily a good thing if you were an undercover police officer. People remembered things like tattoos, and at some point down the line, on a different job, under a different cover, you might bump into someone from a former job who might otherwise not have recognised you were it not for your distinctive tattoo and who might then realise that you weren't who you claimed to be. But now she had the scars, all of that seemed immaterial, for they were probably even more of an identifying feature than a tattoo.

The girl next to her, slim and boyish, ran her hands through her bleached blonde hair, slicking it back, and as she did so, Bailey noticed the track marks running along the insides of her forearms. The ugly puncture wounds dotted along the paths of the veins were clear evidence of intravenous hard drug use and they looked recent.

'What are you looking at?' said the girl, fixing Bailey with a hostile glare.

'Oh nothing,' said Bailey, backing off with a placatory smile. Although she was curious to find out more, the shower probably wasn't the best place to start asking questions.

She hurriedly finished up, towelled off and headed back to her cell, reminding herself to pick up some decent shower gel from the prison shop.

* * *

In the reflection of the small plastic mirror above the sink, she could see Sharon lying on the bunk behind her, engrossed in a Mills & Boon novel.

Bailey had just finished drying her hair, and she now started to apply some moisturiser to her face. As she was doing so, she couldn't help but notice the beginnings of crow's feet around her eyes. Age crept up on you. A wrinkle here, a wrinkle there. She thought wistfully of the Clarins eye serum she kept in her bathroom cabinet at home. She couldn't imagine the prison shop stocked it.

Despite these small vanities, she had never been a big one for make-up. A bit of lip gloss was the most she'd stretch to if she wanted to do herself up. And, what with the scars, there seemed even less of a point bothering with that kind of thing these days.

She noticed Sharon watching her from her bunk. Her cellmate had put her book down and was looking at her curiously.

'Have you got a boyfriend?' Sharon asked.

Bailey shook her head.

'Surely there must be someone?'

'Yeah... there was. But it didn't work out.'

'Why not?'

Her last boyfriend had been called Mark. He was a detective in the CID. She'd lived with him for just over two years. He had wanted to settle down, get married and start a family. He'd seemed more concerned with her biological clock than she was. But she wasn't interested in having children. She valued her independence too much. So it had fallen apart.

More than that, she feared the quiet oppression of suburbia. A pebble-dashed house. Kids. A normal life. A suffocating prison. Worse than a real prison. She'd rather be here than there. And here she was...

'I guess we wanted different things,' she said.

'You probably had incompatible star signs,' Sharon replied knowledgeably. 'I'm a big one for star signs. I'm a Virgo myself. What sign are you?'

Bailey met Sharon's eyes in the mirror. 'Aren't Virgos supposed to be intuitive by nature? Why don't you try and work it out?'

Sharon smiled at the challenge. She scrutinised Bailey's meagre collection of belongings. Bailey had brought little into the prison – a few books of cryptic crosswords and Sudoku, and an iPod full of eighties power ballads, her one guilty pleasure.

'Mmm...' Sharon stroked her chin. 'Not a lot to go on. You like puzzles. That means you're analytical. Probably good with numbers. I'd say you were... a Capricorn.'

Sharon was correct.

'Well done. Not bad at all.'

Sharon grinned proudly. 'So what kind of guys do you like? Tall, dark and handsome?'

Sharon held up her romance novel for Bailey to see. Bailey glanced over her shoulder to look at it – the cover depicted an airbrushed picture of a tall, dark handsome man with a glistening muscled torso. The novel was called *The Billionaire's Secret Cinderella*.

Bailey snorted a laugh.

'Actually, I prefer blonde hair and blue eyes.'

'You like the Teutonic look, eh? I've got one over there called *Seduced by the Surgeon*. The bloke in it is this rich blonde doctor. You can borrow it if you want.'

'No thanks.'

'Suit yourself. So have you been getting much action since... what was his name?'

Since the end of that relationship, it had been a case of going out every once in a while when the mood took her – putting on a bit of lip gloss and her favourite suede-fringed cowboy jacket, going to a bar, hitting on some guy, bringing him back to her place, and then ejecting him once business was done.

But then she'd got the scars and they had put an end to that. Intimacy was no longer something she felt comfortable with in the wake of that last undercover job. More than that, the wounds from the violations she'd been subjected to went far deeper than any physical injuries she'd suffered, and unlike the scars they were still raw and painful. No – she couldn't see herself getting intimate with anyone again anytime soon, and perhaps not ever.

Bailey snapped the lid closed on the bottle of moisturiser and placed it back on the shelf by the mirror. She turned around and forced a smile at Sharon.

'I've got some stuff to get done.'

And she turned and left the cell.

10

She walked out onto the landing. There were plenty of inmates hanging around, some by themselves, many in groups, and the air was filled with their murmured conversations.

It was free association time and the inmates could move around the prison as they wished, although many just remained in their cells, watching TV or playing computer games.

Free association seemed to work out at around two to three hours a day and inmates were legally entitled to spend one hour of it outside in the fresh air in the yard if they chose. The actual times for free association varied from day to day. Bailey had realised that this time provided the best opportunity for her to conduct her investigation and she was determined to make the most of it. Her plan was to keep herself to herself and conduct her activities as discreetly as possible.

She figured that at some point she should probably try and track down Alice's cellmate, Melanie Clarke, to see if she could extract any useful information from her, but at the moment she was unsure of the best way to go about finding her. She definitely wasn't going to ask Sharon. Sharon was way too nosey and she was already asking too many questions. Not to worry. Bailey was confident that she'd locate this Melanie Clarke eventually. It was just a matter of time. Meanwhile, she had other avenues in mind.

She made her way down the landing, heading for the stairwell that was situated halfway along, consciously veering wide of the various clusters of inmates, hoping that no one would pay her too much attention.

Talk broke off as she passed by. Cold suspicious looks over the shoulder, followed by furtive whispering. Gossip was the lifeblood of a place like this where people had too much time on their hands. If only she knew what they were talking about. Judging by the general vibe, she was certain Alice's murder wasn't far from their lips.

Her efforts to remain inconspicuous proved to be in vain. Ahead of her, she saw that a group of eight or so inmates had noticed her approaching. It was probably because she was new and they didn't recognise her. A preliminary pang of anxiety shot through her.

It was becoming apparent that the prison was full of different cliques, formed for the purposes of company and mutual self-protection. This particular group looked like they'd come straight off some particularly grim council estate: hard eyes, hard faces, hard lives. They were watching her and conferring amongst themselves and it didn't look like they were saying nice things.

She put her head down and increased her pace slightly as she passed by them...

And suddenly she found herself sprawled face-down on the cold concrete surface of the landing, the palms of her hands stinging with the impact of the floor.

She lay there stunned and bewildered for a few moments before it sunk in that one of them had deliberately tripped her up. She turned her head and saw the culprit – a slight, skinny girl with carrot-coloured hair, who was grinning at her unpleasantly.

'Whoops!' said the girl, looking to her companions for approval.

They all sniggered.

Bailey felt a cold anger consume her. How dare they? She pulled herself to her feet. *Stay calm*, she thought, taking a deep breath. *No rash actions.*

She shot a long hard look of contempt at the one who'd tripped her up. She was clearly the smallest and weediest of the group, the kind of pathetic hanger-on who would have sucked up to the bullies at school.

The girl puffed her chest out aggressively.

'What are you gonna do about it?' she sneered.

If she'd had the inmate to herself, Bailey could quite easily have subdued her and taught her a painful lesson in why it was important to be nice to people; but, like any true coward, the girl was operating from within the safety of a group. A confrontation would thus be risky. Anyhow, Bailey had more important things to focus on.

She turned away from them and continued on her way, ignoring their jeers.

She was glad to reach the stairwell and get away from them. As she descended the metal flights of stairs, it occurred to her that perhaps she should have made more of an overt effort to stand up for herself. Because she hadn't, they might try it on again. Too late now though.

When she reached the ground floor, she began to head towards the atrium. As she did so, she felt something wet splat onto the top of her head. She stopped and reached up to check, a sense of revulsion coming over her as she felt sticky strands of what she realised was saliva in her hair.

She looked up to see the carrot-haired girl leaning over the balcony, leering down at her with her friends. They all cackled with laughter.

Bailey wiped the saliva from her head, flicking it away in disgust. She moved underneath the cover of the first-floor landing so they couldn't spit on her any more and continued on her way.

How mindless, she thought angrily. To pick on her for no other reason than that she was by herself and they thought they could get away with it.

But then what was she expecting? This was prison. People generally didn't end up in here because they were nice.

11

The central atrium was where the four house-blocks converged. She stood there in the middle and slowly gazed around. In all directions, vaulted tiers of cells stretched away into the gloom. She tried to remember what she'd been told during her induction about where everything was located.

As she recalled, the four house-blocks were known as A-Wing – which was her wing – B-Wing, C-Wing and D-Wing. Within the perimeter wall, besides the house-blocks, there was the prison exercise yard, an administrative complex, a medical facility, a chapel and the segregation block. The administrative buildings included the staff mess room and facilities, and that was also where the Governor's office was situated. The gatehouse, fortified in the tradition of a medieval keep, was located midway along the eastern wall of the prison, next to the main road, and provided the only point of access to the prison. And if she wasn't mistaken, the stairwell on the other side of the atrium led down to the basement level of the prison, where the laundry was located, somewhere underneath A-Wing.

Doing her best to avoid any further hostile encounters, she made her way across the atrium and descended the flight of stairs.

The place where Alice had been murdered seemed as good a place as any to start her investigation, even though the crime scene had long since been cleaned up. The police often retraced the steps of victims in order to trigger associations in the minds of potential witnesses, but for her she hoped that it might provoke some insight into Alice's thought patterns in those final few hours that she had been alive.

The basement corridor appeared dingy and deserted, the overhead strip lighting flickering uncertainly. Down here, there was a more pronounced sense of dilapidation than elsewhere in the prison. Paint was peeling off the ancient brickwork, the flakes scattering the flagstones amidst the dry husks of long-dead bugs, and bits of cladding hung loose from the pipes which ran along the sides of the walls.

Bailey wasn't entirely sure if she was even allowed to be down here, but seeing as no one had stopped her, she saw no reason not to continue.

As she walked along the corridor, she reflected that she knew little about the history of HMP Foxbrook, only that it had been built as a prison in Victorian times when penal attitudes had been much harsher. And, as such, the fabric of the building was still permeated with the dank oppressiveness of that era.

Preoccupied by those thoughts, she almost walked right past the entrance to the laundry – a heavy iron door with a metal plaque riveted onto it which said 'WATER SUPPLY ROOM'. There was a small glass panel set into the door, through which she noticed what appeared to be a row of washing machines or dryers stretching down the length of the large room that lay beyond.

Standing outside, peering through the glass panel, she could see inmates at work inside – pushing trolleys, loading washing machines, emptying dryers, folding sheets.

She debated with herself for a few moments whether to enter.

Act like you work here, she told herself. *Move with a purpose and people will be less likely to doubt you.*

She took a deep breath, pushed the door open and strode confidently into the laundry.

A few of the inmates glanced up, but then went back to their tasks, indifferent to her. They probably assumed, as she'd intended, that she had come here to work, just like them. The overall atmosphere was one of subdued industriousness.

The laundry was a long cavernous room, the farther edges of which lay beyond the reach of the weak light emanating from the bulbs hanging down from the ceiling. It was warm down here, stuffy even, and the air was suffused with the acrid smell of detergent.

The floor of the laundry was filled with large yellow trolleys made of canvas. Along one side of the room, a row of huge stainless-steel washing machines groaned as their massive drums rotated, churning the items inside, washing the filth of the prison off them. A bit further along, big industrial dryers rumbled at a different frequency, the hot air carried out of the room through an overhead aluminium ventilation duct. On the other side were the industrial folders and the steam presses, and giant wire racks stacked with folded piles of freshly laundered items. Sheets hung up next to the racking, the white material billowing softly.

She remembered from her induction that the individual inmates' laundry was sent down here in numbered mesh bags which were never opened. The bags went straight into the machines, and then into the dryers, and then back to the inmates.

She stood there amongst the trolleys and did a slow three-sixty, scanning the room for any possible clues or insights. Nothing jumped out at her, apart from the lack of CCTV cameras, just as Frank had mentioned.

According to him, Alice had obtained a job in the laundry and had been down here alone when she had been murdered. The question was whether there was any special significance to the laundry beyond the fact that it was secluded enough to commit a murder away from the eyes of the prison authorities and the other inmates. Either way, it sounded as if Alice had been very close to identifying those responsible for bringing the drugs into the prison, and it seemed that they'd murdered her before she'd had a chance to report back to Frank.

Her attention snagged on the white shirt and black epaulettes of a prison officer's uniform. The female officer – stern and masculine-looking – had just emerged from behind the racking and was slowly patrolling the other side of the room. Bailey didn't know her name.

Bailey hurriedly turned away and took hold of the nearest trolley and began to push it along, keeping her head down as she did so. Her trolley appeared to be piled with used cleaning rags and mop ends and it didn't smell too good.

She walked along, feeling the crunch of spilt washing powder on the tiled floor beneath her feet and eventually found that she had reached the far end of the laundry.

Glancing around, she decided to buy a little more time by pretending to do some work. She manoeuvred the trolley in front of a washing machine, an old top-loader standing up against the wall, and picked up a handful of rags, wrinkling her nose at the horrible smell which emanated from them. Holding them in one hand at arm's length, she started to lift up the lid of the washing machine.

'Can't you read the sign?' said a voice with a hint of alarm.

Bailey turned around. A small tubby inmate was standing there. She had pale blotchy skin and the kind of cheap glasses which made her eyes look huge.

'What sign?'

'That one.'

The inmate was pointing to a piece of A4 paper taped over the washing machine's control panel. Written on it in crude felt-tip pen were the words: 'OUT OF ORDER – ELECTROCUTION HAZARD!'

Bailey jerked away from the machine, letting the lid drop shut with a clang.

'Thanks,' she muttered.

The inmate squinted at the handful of rags she was holding. 'You shouldn't be washing that stuff anyway. We're leaving all the mops and rags until Friday. Today it's sheets, pillowcases, towels and blankets.'

Bailey looked at the stinking handful of rags.

'Oh right. Sure.' She dropped them back into the trolley and watched the inmate trudge away, dwarfed by the huge trolley she was pushing.

Bailey left the trolley full of smelly rags where it was and stealthily made her way around the back of the laundry so she could walk along the other side of the racking.

As she did so, she noticed an odd contraption standing next to the wall. It had a large cast-iron frame and two thick wooden rollers. It took her a few moments to realise that it was an industrial mangle, a relic from Victorian times. Surely they still didn't use this to dry clothes? She smiled to herself at the thought of it. More likely they'd just never got round to moving it – it looked like it weighed a ton.

'Who are you?'

Bailey spun around, her heart thumping in surprise.

The stern-looking prison officer she had seen a short while earlier was standing there, arms crossed, eyeing her suspiciously. She was short and heavily built, like a female gorilla, and she didn't look like the kind of person who brooked any messing around.

'I don't recognise you,' said the prison officer. 'You weren't in here ten minutes ago.'

'Oh hello...' said Bailey, smiling affably and clicking her fingers in attempted recall. 'Sorry what was your name again?'

'Shelley Foster,' the officer replied without smiling. 'And you are...?'

'Bailey Pike.' Bailey smiled and held out her hand. Shelley made no attempt to shake it.

'You haven't answered my question,' said Shelley. 'What are you doing in here?'

'I was just... er... admiring this antique mangle.'

Bailey cringed inside at her excuse. Surely she could do better than that. What had happened to her ability to think on her feet? She must be rusty.

Shelley curled her lip in a sceptical sneer and tapped one of her chunky black shoes on the floor impatiently.

'Do you work in here?' she asked.

'Um... No.'

'Then you shouldn't be in here. The laundry is off limits to anyone who doesn't work here.'

'I guess I'll be going then.'

'Inmates need to stay in the right areas. If I see you out of bounds again, I'll put you on the nicking sheet.'

'I'm sorry. I'm new here. I didn't know the rules.'

'You should have been paying more attention at induction.'

Bailey nodded meekly and rapidly made her way out of the laundry, disappointed that her investigation had yielded no useful information so far.

When Bailey got to the phones, she found a large noisy queue. The opportunity to make phone calls was limited to a few hours a day during the association period, and everyone wanted to make calls at the same time – off-peak and out of office hours.

She joined the end of the queue and stood there eavesdropping on the conversations going on around her, listening out for any nuggets of gossip which might concern Alice. But she didn't pick up anything about the murder. The inmates' talk seemed to revolve mainly around their lawyers and their appeals, their kids and what to get them for their birthdays, and their husbands and boyfriends and whether they were cheating on them whilst they were in prison. The lives she was hearing about put the prison demographic firmly at the lower end of the socio-economic spectrum.

Standing there in the queue, she reflected that she would have liked to have called her parents, particularly her father. She'd talked to him briefly on the phone before entering the prison, in an attempt to clear the air, but he hadn't really been very receptive to her overtures and she was now going to have to wait until this job was over before trying again. For the period that she was incarcerated in the prison, she would be unable to conduct any kind of communication with them for security reasons. It would just be too risky. Her parents knew about her undercover work and that she could never reveal any more than the vaguest details about whatever job she was working on. All they knew was that she could be out of touch for indeterminate periods of time and she always tried to warn them in advance when it looked like this might be the case so they didn't get too worried about her. On this occasion though, she hadn't had the chance to properly inform them before her father had ended the call in a frosty huff, making her remember once again that it was pointless trying to communicate with him when he was in one of his moods.

Finally her turn came and she ducked into a booth. She punched her PIN number into the metal keypad of the phone and then dialled Frank's number. The phone rang for a few rings, then Rita answered it in her characteristic Essex accent.

'Hello, Sullivan Knight Solicitors. How can I help?'

It sounded pretty authentic, Bailey had to admit. Rita did indeed come across exactly like a secretary in a law firm somewhere.

'It's Bailey Pike speaking. I'd like to talk to Mr Knight please.'

'Just putting you through.'

Some holding music came on – a sorrowful and hypnotic piano melody that she'd heard before but which, like most classical music, she couldn't put a name to.

It stopped abruptly as Frank came on the line.

'Hello Bailey.'

'What's the holding music? It sounds familiar.'

'Beethoven's 'Moonlight Sonata'.'

'A personal choice?'

'It's one of his most popular pieces.'

'It's kind of... funereal-sounding.'

'I'm sure it'll grow on you.' He paused. 'Are you okay to talk?'

She glanced around and pushed herself further into the booth. There wasn't a lot of privacy, but the general background noise would help to drown out her conversation.

'It's fine,' she said. 'No one can hear me.'

'What's the status of your investigation?'

'I checked out the laundry. Looks like it's a dead end. And so far I haven't heard anything to suggest that Alice's cover was blown.'

'What about the drugs ring?'

'Nothing yet. But then I've only been in here two days.'

'Maybe it's time you started making some friends.'

'You don't need to tell me how to do my job.'

'Sorry. I don't mean to rush you. It's just that I'm certain someone in there must know something. Have you managed to talk to her cellmate?'

'I'm working on it. If someone in here knows something, I'll find them and I'll find out what they know. But I'll do it my way.'

There was a pregnant pause on the other end of the line.

'A slight complication has arisen that you should be aware of,' he said.

'What's that?'

'Alice's family are unhappy about the fact that her death's been covered up. They want to know what happened to her and they've threatened to go to the newspapers.'

Bailey let the news sink in. She tried to get her head around the potential ramifications of what he'd just told her. 'What's the official version of events?'

'They were told that she died in the line of duty on an unspecified undercover operation.'

'And they want to know the specifics?'

'Yeah. We've told them it could jeopardise ongoing operations and even the lives of people involved, but they're pretty persistent. They're upset and angry. Understandably.'

'Hold them off for as long as you can. I don't think there's any need to panic just yet.'

'Glad to see you're keeping cool.'

'I used to do this for a living, remember?'

She hung up the phone and went back to her cell, already feeling an acute sense that the pressure on her was starting to ramp up.

'And that's why it's called Foxbrook.'

'Eh?' said Amber. She had momentarily switched off whilst Maggie had been explaining the etymology of the prison's name.

'Because of the Foxbrook.'

'Oh right,' said Amber, collecting herself. 'The river yeah? The one that used to flow nearby.'

Maggie nodded and smiled, satisfied that Amber had been paying attention to her.

They were walking together at a leisurely pace along the upper landing of C-Wing. It was mid-morning, the cells were open and most of the inmates on this wing were out in the yard, ostensibly to take exercise although it seemed to Amber that most of them just stood around out there smoking and talking.

Maggie had been at the prison for donkey's years and seemed to know everything there was to know about it. How it was named after a nearby river. How there had been a gallows here at one time in the north end of the yard. How the prison used to hold men but had switched to women just after World War Two. How in Victorian times the prisoners used to have to go on treadmills as a form of punishment. How the whole reason that prison officers came to be known as screws was because they were the ones who'd tighten the screws on the treadmills to make them more difficult for the prisoners to walk on.

She liked to regale the inmates with these anecdotes and facts, and Amber would often notice them glancing at one another, not quite understanding why she was boring them with trivia. But Amber could see that Maggie was actually being rather clever. The prison's history was a neutral topic through which she could engage with the inmates without overstepping any kind of personal boundaries. And, who knew, perhaps some of them even came to appreciate the place a little more with a deeper understanding of its historical context.

Maggie did go on a bit, but Amber was grateful for her protective guidance. Maggie had taken Amber under her wing, so to speak, and had certainly helped to accelerate her learning, letting her in on all the little tips and shortcuts that they didn't teach you in training.

Today, they were both on general duty as landing officers. This meant that first thing in the morning they would unlock the landings of the various wings and let the inmates know that they had an hour for exercise. Whilst the prisoners were on exercise in the yard, they would remain on the wing and check the LBBs – the locks, bolts and bars – and carry out any individual cell searches that needed to be done. Once the inmates were back on the wing, they were free to patrol the prison as they wished, keeping a general eye out for trouble, sorting out any petty problems and lending a helping ear if need be.

Out of all the roles that the guards had to perform, this was the one that Amber enjoyed the most. It meant that she could get out and about and have a chat. She liked to chat. Perhaps not quite as much as Maggie though.

As they walked along, she nodded to the inmates who were returning from the yard. Some of them nodded back. Some of them ignored her. The odd one scowled at her. Generally, they were fairly closed when it came to communicating with the guards, except when they wanted something like an extra privilege such as cigarettes or additional visiting time.

'Well they mostly seem in a good mood today,' said Amber. 'It looks like it'll be a day without friction.'

Friction meant trouble.

Maggie smiled in a knowing manner and looked at her watch. 'It's nine thirty now. Let's hope it's still that way by twenty-one thirty.'

'Are there many fights in here?' she asked.

Amber hadn't seen any serious occurrences since she'd started, something she was quite grateful for, but she knew it was only a matter of time before something did happen and she was kind of dreading it, especially if it entailed anything approaching the kind of viciousness that had been seen with the murder.

'You should always be prepared for a slam,' said Maggie matter-of-factly.

'A slam?'

'A fight. They're much less of an occurrence in female prisons than they are in male prisons… but when something does kick off you never know what might happen.'

As prison officers, they weren't allowed to carry batons and thus had to rely on techniques of unarmed physical restraint, and on each other. That was why it was so important to be able to trust your fellow officers. The personal safety of the guards was something Terry was always sounding off about amongst other things.

'Any trouble that kicks off mostly boils down to their routines,' said Maggie.

'I don't understand.'

'Time passes slowly in here and the only way most of them stay sane is to have a routine of some sort. Most problems start when the inmates mess with each other's routines.'

Maggie paused and nodded politely to a passing inmate, then she continued.

'The same goes for us. We need to respect their routines as well. If you respect their routines, they're much more compliant, much easier to get along with, and that's so much better for everyone in the long run.'

'Sometimes it's hard to know how friendly to be. I feel that we're not supposed to be too friendly. But I want them to like me.'

'Be friendly but don't be friends,' said Maggie. 'Respect them and they'll respect you. But remember there's always a line between us and them.'

'There's just so much to learn here that isn't in the book.'

'The book will only get you so far. You'll be fine just so long as you remember the following things.' Maggie counted the points off on her fingers. 'Always help an officer in trouble. Always back up an officer in an argument with the inmates. Never rat on an officer. Never make an officer look bad in front of the inmates. And, most importantly, don't let yourself get corrupted by them. The main thing is that your fellow officer always comes first. Above this lot. Always.'

Amber gritted her teeth and nodded. She was rapidly learning that hard experience was the only thing that could truly prepare her for the reality of this job.

14

Bailey stood in the lunch queue scanning the inmates sitting in the canteen, wondering if Alice's killer was sitting somewhere among them right now. Much as Alice was the reason that she had elected to come in here, she had to remind herself that her operational priority was to find out about the drugs ring, and if she didn't do that then Frank would be unhappy and the pressure on her would only increase.

Her best bet, in terms of finding out useful information, was to start talking to her fellow convicts. But where was the best place to start? Where was the best place to sit? Which one of them was Melanie Clarke? Bailey had no idea what she even looked like.

She glanced from table to table, trying to spot the right opportunity. She ruled out the table of butch-looking dykes sitting together whispering furtively amongst themselves. They looked too cliquey to break into. Likewise with the group of black inmates over by the window. As she'd already found out, by its very nature prison was cliquey and inmates tended to gravitate towards groups formed of their own types. Bailey had known that this would present a challenge for a new lone inmate such as herself.

Then she noticed the girl she'd seen in the shower, the one with the track marks on her arms. Her bleached hair, shaved at the back and sides, was tied up in a distinctive topknot, and she was wearing a long-sleeved jogging top which concealed her punctured forearms. As luck would have it, she was sitting by herself.

As soon as she got served her food, Bailey headed over to the girl's table, and stood there, her tray poised.

'Mind if I sit here?'

The girl looked up at her with pained dark-rimmed eyes. Her pale skin glistened with a faint sheen of perspiration and she appeared to be shivering slightly.

'Fuck off,' she muttered.

Okay, maybe some other time, thought Bailey.

She shrugged and looked around for somewhere else to sit. She spotted an empty table in the corner. She headed over to it and placed her tray down. Maybe it would work the other way round. Hopefully someone would come and sit down at her table and start a conversation with her.

She started eating. She'd opted for the chicken chasseur and it tasted surprisingly good. In between mouthfuls, she began to notice other people in the canteen staring at her. The table of dykes were murmuring and looking in her direction. She wondered what they were saying about her. She was starting to get a bad feeling. Something wasn't quite right.

She got her answer a short while later, but not quite in the way she was hoping.

'You're sitting in my seat,' said a harsh, rough voice.

Bailey looked up. Standing over her was a blonde inmate with short spiky hair. She was accompanied by several others who all had the same hard, sinewy look about them. There was a black one, an oriental one who appeared to have a squint, and a huge one, looming up behind them, who looked like she'd been hewn from a large block of concrete.

'I didn't realise reservations applied here,' said Bailey.

'You trying to be clever?' The blonde inmate drew her lips back in an aggressive sneer, revealing a gold tooth set in her upper jaw.

Bailey instantly regretted the quip. She realised that she had to strike the right balance between not drawing too much attention to herself and not appearing to be a weakling.

The rest of the canteen had suddenly gone quiet and all eyes were now on her table.

'It's okay. I'll move,' she said. Better to keep a low profile for the time being rather than rile anybody.

She stood up and picked up her tray. But the gold-toothed inmate knocked it out of her hands. Her lunch splattered all over the table.

'Now look what you've done, you clumsy bitch,' said gold-tooth. 'You've gone and knocked crap all over our table. Clean it up. Now.'

'Maybe she should lick it up,' said the oriental one with a smirk.

The others sniggered.

'Good idea,' said gold-tooth. 'Lick it up.'

Bailey stood there looking at the remnants of her meal. She'd hardly begun to eat it.

The group of inmates crowded around her in a menacing fashion. The big one towered over her, no glimmer of emotion in her dead piggy eyes.

Bailey's heart was beating hard, adrenaline pumping through her system, as she tried to determine the best course of action. Everyone else had paused eating and was now transfixed. This was prime entertainment.

'Well, what are you waiting for?' said gold-tooth.

Bailey slowly clenched her fists. They could forget it. Submitting to their humiliation wasn't an option. To do so in front of everyone else in here would open her up to all kinds of abuse further down the line.

Instead, her jiu-jitsu training kicked in and she moved into the basic defensive *yoi* stance: her body positioned side-on so it formed a narrower target, her knees slightly bent to give her a lower centre of balance, one foot positioned in front of the other to ensure maximum stability, her arms raised up in front of her, poised ready to parry and strike. She marked their positions, eyed them individually in turn, took a deep breath and prepared to go down fighting.

'That's enough of that,' said a firm voice.

She looked around to see one of the prison officers standing there. A tide of relief rolled over her. The prison officer was young, with a somewhat prim and starched appearance. Her blonde hair was tucked into a tight bun and bright blue eyes looked out from behind a pair of large thick-rimmed glasses.

Gold-tooth scowled at her. 'She's dropped her food all over our table.'

'You can find somewhere else to sit today, Toni.'

They all stood there for a few moments, glaring at the prison officer. Bailey wondered what would happen. But the prison officer stood her ground, her hands on her hips, fearlessly staring them down.

'Your lunch is getting colder the longer you stand there,' she said.

The gold-toothed one called Toni turned to Bailey with a sneer. 'Next time,' she hissed.

Then she and her associates swaggered over to another table and sat down, hunched over their food, throwing her the occasional dirty look over their shoulders.

'Thanks,' said Bailey.

'Don't mention it.' The prison officer scrutinised her. 'You're new here, aren't you? I haven't seen you before.'

'I just got in the other day.'

'I'm Amber.' She held out her hand for Bailey to shake.

Bailey hesitated. She was wary of appearing to look too friendly with a prison officer in case she got mistaken for a snitch. She knew all too well how criminals felt about snitches.

Amber seemed to sense her reticence and withdrew her hand with a light shrug.

Bailey reflected how ironic it was that this prison officer looked just the type of person she would have got on with on the outside. But in here she was forced to keep a distance for the sake of maintaining a realistic cover.

'Get yourself another tray of food,' said Amber. 'I'll arrange for this to be cleared up.'

'I'm not hungry any more.'

It was true. She wasn't. The confrontation suddenly seemed to have robbed her of her appetite. She left the canteen to go back to her cell.

With each passing moment in this place, Bailey was starting to question what she'd got herself into.

15

Bailey lay on her bunk and reflected on the altercation in the canteen. That had been the second run-in she'd had with a hostile group of inmates since she'd been locked up. First the carrot-haired one and her friends, and now this other group led by the one with the gold tooth.

What was that old saying? You've made your bed, now lie in it. She'd chosen to be here and, at the end of the day, these kinds of situations were all part of the job.

Despite her short ill-advised detour into accountancy, all she'd ever really wanted was to be a policewoman. She'd wanted to be one ever since she was very young.

Growing up in the outer London suburbs, she and her sister Jennifer had had a happy early childhood, their plain semi-detached house forming the scene for countless games of make-believe. They had been close despite their considerable differences. Jennifer, two years older, had been the demure girly one, and Bailey had been the scrappy little tomboy who'd looked up to her.

Then, one day, at the age of eight years old, Jennifer had gone missing, abducted on the way home from a friend's house just a few doors down the street. She had never been seen again. An extensive police investigation was launched but no witnesses were found, there were no records of any suspicious vehicles being seen in the area, and the detectives were unable to identify any potential suspects. No similar occurrences appeared to have taken place in the vicinity and it seemed like her abduction was just a random, opportunistic one-off. Her disappearance featured on *Crimewatch* and there was a reconstruction, but that too yielded no useful leads. It was as if she had just vanished into thin air.

For six-year-old Bailey, the loss had been extremely hard to comprehend, even harder for her parents to convey to her, devastated as they were. The word 'dead' was never said aloud in the house. But that unspoken likelihood constantly hovered there, grew ever more pronounced as time passed.

Later on, when she was older, Bailey came to understand the kinds of things that happened to children who were abducted and the kind of sick people who did those things. It had instilled in her a strong need for justice. And what better way to see justice done than to join the police?

As a result of Jennifer's disappearance, her parents had become extremely protective of Bailey, oppressively so. She had reacted against it, especially as a teenager, actively seeking out risky situations. That tendency had continued into adulthood, eventually drawing her into the most dangerous area of policing – undercover work.

But her choice of profession was also a point of contention with her father. Over the years, her parents had become affected in different ways by Jennifer's disappearance. Her mother had turned increasingly religious and had grown potty, to the point where Bailey was beginning to wonder if she was suffering from some kind of premature dementia. Her father, on the other hand, was haunted by the conviction that Jennifer was still alive and he maintained a dogmatic obsession with finding her. He still clung desperately to some shred of hope that she was out there somewhere and that she would come home someday, if only he could locate her. He kept a large scrapbook full of yellowing newspaper clippings relating to her disappearance and he insisted on keeping her bedroom preserved exactly the way it had been the day she had gone missing – the walls covered with her crude felt-tip pictures, her stuffed toys lined up along her bed, her clothes hanging in the wardrobe, her dinosaur-themed mobile still suspended from the ceiling. Bailey found it kind of creepy and she did her utmost to avoid going into Jennifer's bedroom whenever she was at her parents' house.

Her father was forever claiming that he was on the verge of finding Jennifer. It would usually be something or other he'd found on the internet – some vague clue alluding to her existence. He'd get all excited and call up Bailey to tell her about it. But, of course, it always turned out to be groundless, a mere concoction of wishful thinking. She understood that this was his way of coping. It was the only thing that kept him going. He was in denial and she didn't have the heart to tell him to snap out of it.

But sometimes it would erupt, like the argument they'd had the last time they'd met. He'd had a go at her, demanding to know why she wasn't doing more, as a policewoman, to find out Jennifer's whereabouts. It wasn't like she hadn't tried, of course. Not long after becoming a detective, she had taken the opportunity to examine the original case files. However, she had soon realised that with no evidence, no witnesses and no body, it would have been futile to try and reopen what was essentially a cold case that was now over twenty years old. She was a realist and, as a policewoman, she had become familiar with enough cases of a similar ilk to know the unpleasant truth about what had probably happened to Jennifer.

Despite the fact that she believed Jennifer was long dead, it didn't mean that she'd forgotten her sister. Quite the opposite. Jennifer was there every day in the back of Bailey's mind, crying out for redress, pushing her ever onwards to do her job the best she could. Jennifer, as well as Alice, was the reason she was here right now, endangering her well-being for the sake of making some kind of difference.

Not that it would ever bring either of them back...

16

Pushing the memories away, she rolled into a sitting position and tried to think of what to do next. She was itching to make progress, but she felt stuck already. Curling her free-hanging lock of hair around her fingers and letting it uncurl again, she contemplated her options.

She looked at her watch. There were forty-five minutes of free association time left before she was locked in her cell. Hoisting herself off the bunk, she left the cell and walked out onto the landing. She scanned her surroundings.

Her gaze settled on a female prison officer standing around ten metres away, sturdily built, with a face like old leather. She tried to recall her name...

Maggie. That was it. Maggie Cooper.

She looked like she'd been working here for a while, long enough to be familiar with the whereabouts of any given inmate. And from what Bailey had observed of her in the short time she'd been here, she appeared to be relatively approachable.

Bailey eased up to her.

'I'm looking for Melanie Clarke,' she said with a polite smile. 'Do you know where I can find her?'

Maggie gave her the once-over with a steely professional flick of the eye. 'Any particular reason?'

'Uh... just wanted to have a chat,' said Bailey innocently.

'Just a regular conversation, huh?'

Bailey nodded earnestly.

Maggie sighed and raised one eyebrow.

'Well... good luck with that,' she said in a manner that suggested that having any kind of conversation with Melanie Clarke would prove to be most challenging. 'She lives on B-Wing. Cell number one-one-three.'

'Thank you,' said Bailey and headed off along the landing.

After having given it some thought, Bailey had come to the conclusion that asking a guard about Melanie Clarke was a safer bet than asking the inmates whose affiliations at this stage she was still uncertain of.

At the end of the landing, she descended a flight of stairs and eventually reached the junction of A-Wing and B-Wing. She turned and began to walk along one of the lower landings of B-Wing, passing by the cells, moving carefully through the groups of inmates leaning on the balconies. This was deep within the heart of the hive. It was an unfamiliar area to Bailey and she was on edge.

Once again, she was shocked by the general air of neglect in the prison and the distinct lack of modernity. Although she knew that these were criminals and this their place of punishment it was still worse than she'd anticipated. The antique architecture made no concessions to light or space, instead suffusing the place with a dark labyrinthine feel. She got the sense of things happening unseen, things being got away with...

She walked past cells where inmates sat entranced by the flickering lights of TV screens or computer games. In other cells, they just lay there immobile on their bunks plugged into headphones listening to music or reading magazines.

To an outside observer, it might have seemed an easy life, but she sensed that it was all part of a desperate quest for distraction from the tedium and boredom of life in the prison. And more than that it was a way to avoid having to think too much about what they had done to end up behind bars in the first place.

As she walked along, she wondered how best to frame her approach to Melanie Clarke, how to broach the subject of Alice without sounding odd or raising suspicion. After all, she and Alice weren't supposed to be connected to each other in any way whatsoever. In the end, she decided that she'd just play it by ear.

She reached cell number 113 and stepped into the open doorway. A white inmate with long brown hair was sitting cross-legged on the floor with her eyes closed in what appeared to be a meditative yoga position.

'Melanie Clarke?' said Bailey.

The inmate opened her eyes and looked at Bailey with a slightly miffed expression. She shook her head and nodded to her right. 'She's with her mates. Cell at the end. Follow your nose.'

She closed her eyes again.

Bailey stepped back onto the landing. She sniffed the air. The odour of illicit drugs was always present, but the distinctive smell of marijuana seemed to be particularly pronounced down here. She continued walking along the landing. As she drew closer to the cell at the end, the pungent smell of dope grew even stronger. As did the sound of music. She recognised the bass thump and reverb of heavy dub. It resembled some psychedelic form of reggae.

She stopped outside the last cell. The door was open. She peered in warily but it was hard to see anything through the thick layers of marijuana smoke. As her eyes adjusted to the dimness, the first thing she made out was the glowing tip of a joint as it flared and was passed around the three inmates occupying the cell.

Beneath a large poster of Jean-Claude Van Damme flexing his oiled muscles was a white inmate sitting on a chair at the desk rolling a joint. She had a nose ring and her dark red hair was twisted into crude dreadlocks. On the bunk was a mocha-skinned Asian inmate who was nodding her head hypnotically to the music emanating from the cheap portable stereo that was sitting by her feet. And slumped next to her on the bunk was a mixed-race inmate with her frizzy hair poking out in all directions. She was just staring vacantly into middle space.

Bailey wondered which one of the three was Melanie Clarke.

For some reason, there was a colourful profusion of small origami animals scattered around the cell. With a single glance, Bailey could distinguish a crane, a horse, a tortoise and what even appeared to be a spider.

She hung around outside, doing a good imitation of casually lounging, all the while attempting to eavesdrop on the conversation of the inmates in the cell.

'*Bloodsport* without a doubt,' the Asian one was saying. 'It's an instant classic.'

The white one was shaking her head, without looking up from the joint.

'*Hard Target*. Has to be. He'd matured by that stage. He was at the height of his powers. Couple that with a top-drawer action director like John Woo and you've got a masterpiece.'

'Nah. It's got too much shooting and not enough kickboxing. Van Damme is a kickboxer first and foremost. His best films are the ones that fully showcase his kickboxing talent.'

Bailey hovered on the threshold, wondering how she could interject. She trawled her mind. A piece of trivia floated to the surface. As an undercover cop, she had fallen into a habit of storing any bits of information that she could later retrieve to buttress a cover story or insinuate herself with people. However useless a bit of trivia might seem, you never knew when it might come in handy.

She sidled into the doorway. At first, none of the three figures in the cell registered her presence.

'I think you're forgetting *Cyborg*,' said Bailey.

The white one was the first to look up. Then the Asian one. And, finally, the mixed-race one.

They all stared at her blankly through the thick haze of smoke. She moved just inside the doorway to the cell. She stifled a cough and blinked. The smoke was dense enough to make her eyes water.

'Who the fuck are you?' said the white one, her face creased in suspicion.

The Asian one squinted at her as a thought seemed to occur.

'*Cyborg*? Of course.' She turned to the white one. 'Kay, I totally forgot about *Cyborg*. Totally underrated. Kind of a low-budget masterpiece.'

The white one called Kay turned to her. Her face morphed into an expression of disgust. 'Seema, you cannot be serious! *Cyborg* is worse than *Nowhere to Run*. It's a substandard *Mad Max* rip-off. It's one of his early ones you want to forget about.'

If the white one was called Kay and the Asian one was called Seema, then Bailey deduced that the frazzled-looking mixed-race one had to be Melanie Clarke.

Seema was shaking her head vigorously in disagreement with Kay. '*Cyborg* was a massive straight-to-video hit. So successful that they made two sequels.'

'Neither of which had Jean-Claude in them. So they don't count.'

Bailey judged that now was the time to drop her nugget of useless trivia. On one of her many sleepless nights, she'd found herself watching *Cyborg*, the type of low-budget sci-fi thriller which occupied the late-night slots on lesser-viewed channels. It wasn't exactly her kind of film, but she'd noticed something faintly odd whilst watching it. 'Did you know that the main characters in *Cyborg* are named after guitars?' she said.

'Guitars?' sneered Kay. 'I have never heard such a load of crap in all my life. Anyway, you still haven't answered my question. Who are you and what do you want?'

But Seema was staring up at Bailey with an expression of wonderment verging on awe. 'You know she's right,' she murmured. 'Jean-Claude's character is called Gibson Rickenbacker. Gibson is a type of guitar and so is Rickenbacker. And the baddie's called Fender. Another guitar!'

Seema shook her head in stupefaction.

'Guitars! Fuck me! All these times I've watched it and I've never noticed. Man that totally blows my mind. What do you think, Mel?'

Mel had been sitting there vacantly, her eyes half-closed and her mouth half-open, taking a pull from a spliff every so often, a long head of ash building up at the end. She didn't seem to have heard Seema.

Seema whacked her on the upper arm to get her attention. 'Mel, I asked you a question.'

Mel blinked and looked around at them as if for the first time. The head of ash fell off the spliff into her lap. She didn't seem to notice.

'Uhh... yeah... rich tea biscuits... yeah.'

Kay screwed up her face in disgust. 'Mel, get with the picture! We had the biscuit conversation over twenty minutes ago.'

Mel looked confused. With a faint sense of dismay, Bailey could see that extracting any kind of useful information from this inmate would require an effort of the first order. And that was if she actually even had anything useful to say, which Bailey was beginning to seriously doubt from looking at her. Either way, she judged that now wasn't the time or the place to start grilling her. Still, at least she knew what she looked like and where she hung out.

Mel turned to face her. Bailey looked down and realised that Mel was holding out the spliff.

'Don't give her our weed!' said Kay. 'The only reason she butted in just now was so she could weasel a smoke out of us. We don't even know her name.'

Bailey held up a hand to refuse the spliff. It was a good excuse to avoid having to smoke any. As an undercover police officer, she was technically forbidden from taking drugs, although sometimes situations arose when it was difficult not to participate without appearing suspicious.

Evaluating the situation, she saw an opportunity to provide an excuse for her intrusion and also hopefully gain some understanding of how the drugs were distributed in this place.

'My name's Bailey. I just happened to be passing by and I smelt your gear. If you'd just be nice enough to tell me where I could buy some, I'll get out of your hair.'

Seema looked her up and down, then conceded, 'Keisha. She stands on the third floor at the end of C-Wing. She'll sort you out.'

17

'Spyros!'

Bailey jerked awake, breathing hard, soaked in sweat, sheets tangled around her, repeating the name over and over.

The grey light of pre-dawn filtered through the small cell window. She guessed it was about 4 a.m., but in here she couldn't get up and watch TV to distract herself from the bad dreams like she could at home.

Slowly, the palpitations subsided and she lay there listening to Sharon snoring softly beneath her, apparently deep in peaceful slumber. Lucky her.

The worst thing about the dreams was their inevitability. It instilled in her a sense of dreadful anticipation each night before she went to sleep. The dreams were really just one dream, recurring in different permutations of the same scenario, but always with the same awful outcome.

Her fingertips semi-consciously traced the latticework of scars across her body. Unable to get back to sleep, all she could do was lie there and try not to think too hard about how badly that last job had turned out.

It hadn't always been this way, of course. It had all started out just fine...

The undercover training course – that's where it had started. That's where she had first met Alice.

The course had been an incredibly challenging undertaking, going from 7 a.m. to 4 a.m. for two full weeks. It had a notoriously high drop-out rate and, out of the original twelve students who had enrolled on the course, only five had made it through to the end. She and Alice had been among them.

They'd learnt everything about working undercover, from the basic stuff like how to interpret body language and how to dress in the right way, through to the more advanced things like how to do drug deals, how to run informants and how to conduct surveillance.

They'd subsequently worked together in Frank's undercover unit, sometimes on the same jobs, more often on separate jobs, growing ever closer as they did so. Nobody but another undercover understood the unique stresses of the job, the constant peril within which you operated. It wasn't always easy to cope with, so they'd relied upon each other for emotional support. They'd even gone to jiu-jitsu classes together, figuring that a bit of self-defence training could be helpful in a tight corner.

Bailey remembered how much they'd both revelled in the maverick glamour of working undercover and the satisfaction they'd gained in taking down dangerous and powerful villains...

...but then it had all gone so horribly wrong.

After the trauma of that last operation, Bailey had quit undercover work, had moved out of the flat she'd shared with Alice and had temporarily moved back in with her parents. She had almost quit the police force completely, only deciding against it after realising that there was nothing else she felt inclined to do. So she had retreated back to her safe, boring desk job, doing paperwork, transcribing recordings of interviews, checking witness statements, and numerous other tasks which kept the past at bay.

She had decided to concentrate on passing her sergeant's exams in order to work her way up the police hierarchy, something she hadn't had much opportunity to do when working undercover. Her plan was to try to get promoted and put it all behind her. But normal life had proved harder than she'd bargained on.

Alice had reached out to her, offering the kind of understanding, as a fellow undercover, and as a friend, that no one else would have been able to. But in her messed-up state, Bailey had shunned her help, not wanting to have anything more to do with any of them. She'd eventually relented and tried to contact her, hoping to heal the rift, but Alice had been incommunicado, working undercover in this prison as it turned out. And then all of a sudden Alice was dead. Bailey had been too late in trying to make up with her friend and she would always regret it. But she was here now and determined to make amends. If there was one last thing she could do for Alice it would be to find her killer and make them pay.

18

Poodle let out a soft moan of relief and sank back against the wall, her aches and chills instantly dissipating in the sublime rush of the narcotic flowing through her system. All of her troubles and concerns melted away into nothing. Suddenly being in prison no longer bothered her like it normally did. Three square meals a day and a roof over her head. Who could want for more? And the other inmates – maybe they weren't such a bad bunch after all.

She lay slumped in the shadows with the hypodermic syringe still poking out of her track-marked forearm, her drug-taking paraphernalia scattered on the ground beside her.

She was in her favourite place – the Old Tread-Wheel House, known as such because it was where the treadmills had been located back in Victorian times. Or at least that's what Maggie had told her one time when she'd been standing out in the yard. But the treadmills were long gone, leaving only large square bracket holes in the crumbling brickwork to indicate where they had once been fitted. In their place lay sheets of timber stacked against the walls, several piles of concrete blocks and some scaffolding poles scattered on the ground. That's all this place was used for these days – storing building materials and other bits of old junk. It was technically kept locked, but Poodle had found a missing panel on a side door through which she managed to squeeze in.

The building was located over on the far west side of the prison complex and no one ever really went there, which meant it was the perfect place to keep her stash safe from the greedy prying hands of other inmates and the random cell searches by the prison officers.

It was comfortably dim, the small narrow windows emitting only a meagre amount of light. It might have been mouldy and musty and full of spiders, but it was quiet, there were no cameras, and no one would disturb her while she was shooting up, and that was the most important thing.

She lay there cocooned in the warm afterglow of the hit with her eyes closed and a drowsy smile on her face. Wrapped in the cosy darkness, she wished she could lie here like this forever.

But eventually the heroin daze began to recede as it always did, leaving her feeling pleasantly mellow. She sat up and looked at her watch. It was time to be getting back to her cell. Gathering up her drug paraphernalia, she placed it back in its plastic bag, rolled it up and concealed it once again in its hiding place behind a loose brick in the wall.

She stood up slowly and began to walk back towards the door with the missing panel.

And that's when she heard the noise.

A faint scraping sound.

It came from the shadows down the other end of the room.

Poodle stopped, motionless for a moment. She scanned the murk.

Something wasn't right.

She could feel the hairs on the back of her neck standing up. She could sense another presence in the room.

In the dinginess, in the shadows, among the stacks of debris, someone or something was there. She knew she wasn't hallucinating. She'd taken more than enough heroin to know that it didn't make you hallucinate.

She stared intently into the gloom at the far end of the room, but she couldn't make out what lay in the depths of the shadows.

Small tendrils of fear began to impinge upon her chilled-out mood and her heart began to beat a little faster. Was it a guard? Was it another inmate? Most importantly, was her stash in danger?

'Who's there?' she whispered hoarsely. Her voice seemed to echo around the room like the ringing of a huge bell.

Her only answer was silence.

'Who are you?'

Still no answer.

'What do you want?'

Nothing.

She began to walk forward in the direction of the door, but with each step that she took, the more the sensation increased of someone in the shadows looking directly at her, their eyes boring into her.

She stopped, unable to proceed any further. She swallowed, her mouth dry all of a sudden. Then she began to back slowly away from the blackness in the further reaches of the room because that's where it was.

She could sense it moving towards her. Soon it would emerge from the shadows.

She suddenly remembered now. The gossip. About that murder in the laundry. How horrible it had been. How they still hadn't caught whoever had done it. She hadn't paid much attention to it. She'd had more important things on her mind. Like her next shot of smack. But now it hit home with a sickening dread... that maybe, just maybe, there was something that she should be very scared about.

'Please don't hurt me,' she begged, imploring the mute shadows. 'You can have my stash. Take it all. Just please don't hurt me.'

She stumbled backwards, her feet scraping the rough floor...

...And bumped into something.

She gasped and spun around.

A pile of concrete blocks. She had backed into a pile of concrete blocks.

She let out an exhalation of relief and smiled to herself. Maybe it was nothing. Maybe she was just jittery. Maybe just...

SCHWIPPP...

Poodle's ears perked up and she tensed. The noise had been very close to her. It had been accompanied by a strange tight feeling in her chest. She tried to swallow but found that she couldn't.

She looked down.

Protruding from the centre of her chest was a long glistening metal blade. A globule of her blood ran along the blade and came to the end. It hung there, crimson and viscous.

She watched it, entranced, as it swung there, hanging by an ever-extending thread, which then snapped.

The drop of blood fell to the floor in what seemed like slow motion. It seemed to take forever to hit the floor. As it fell, it assumed a circular shape, revolving and rotating, the light reflecting off its pulsating surface. Then it hit the floor and disintegrated with an audible splat.

Poodle reached up slowly with her hand to touch the blade, to see if it was real. Her slender fingers brushed the razor tip of the steel.

It was real.

SCHWURP...

The blade disappeared, sucked back into her chest. Gone, as if by magic, as if it had never been there.

Poodle coughed.

Inside her throat there was a surge of hot iron-tang flavoured blood. She coughed and tried to swallow to force it back down but the eruption was too much.

Her punctured lungs spasmed and she coughed again and this time the blood escaped her mouth, spraying outwards in a fine mist, landing on the pale flesh of her face and on her hands.

She coughed again, blood now pouring uncontrollably from her mouth.

She took a step forward but found that her legs seemed to be only partially under her control. They felt as if they were made of lead.

She took another step, weaving uncertainly. Heading towards the door. Maybe she could get to the door, get out through the panel. If only she could get into the yard...

In her peripheral vision, she saw something moving in the shadows, past her towards the doorway, cutting off her route of escape. In the darkness, she glimpsed the flash of steel.

Poodle walked towards the door, the hardest walking she had ever done in her life, the hardest walking she would ever do in her life.

Almost at the door now. She just needed to get to the door.

But then a figure stepped forward, its upper half cloaked in shadow.

Poodle gasped and staggered back two steps. She opened her mouth to scream, but instead she gurgled and more blood came out of her mouth.

Out of the darkness, the glinting blade came around horizontally, clutched in a black leather-gloved hand, the razor edge turned towards her. She noted mathematically that the intersection point of its trajectory was precisely where her throat was.

And then the blade made contact, although it did not halt. Its arc continued and terminated, having travelled almost one hundred and eighty degrees from its starting point.

The figure stepped fully out of the shadows to reveal itself as a jet of hot arterial blood gushed up the side of Poodle's face.

19

They'd been locked down for over two hours now with no explanation as to the reason why. Bailey had been spending the time lying on her bunk plugged into her iPod, listening all the way through her entire collection of eighties power ballads. She'd come to the realisation that Whitesnake's 'Is This Love' was actually a much better track than she'd given it credit for up until now, although it was still nowhere near as good as her all-time favourite, 'Kayleigh' by Marillion, which she could listen to endlessly on repeat.

She unplugged herself and stood up and stretched. She walked over to the small window of the cell and gazed out across the yard at the huge grey walls topped with multiple coils of razor wire, the tiny vicious blades sparkling orange in the light of the setting sun. Sharon lay on her bunk, engrossed in a women's lifestyle magazine.

'Did you know,' said Sharon, reading from the magazine, 'that in Cambodia they eat deep-fried tarantula as an aphrodisiac?'

Bailey shook her head. 'No. I can't say I knew that.'

'There's a whole list of weird aphrodisiacs here. I think I'll just stick to asparagus though. Apparently that does the job just as well.'

'Really? I heard it makes your wee smell bad.'

'Yeah, but that doesn't matter, does it? Not unless you're into water sports of course.' Sharon sniggered.

Bailey's attention was captured by some sort of commotion in the yard.

A group of prison officers had suddenly appeared and were standing there gesticulating to each other, engaged in some sort of heated debate.

'Are you?' said Sharon.

'Am I what?' murmured Bailey absently. She was no longer paying attention to Sharon.

'Are you into water sports?'

Bailey craned her head to peer down into the yard, trying to work out what was going on. Then, from around the corner of B-Wing, a group of SOCOs – scene of crime officers – appeared, marching in a procession across the yard, dressed in paper suits, overshoes and masks, looking like astronauts, probably sweating in the warm weather. They were accompanied by uniformed police officers and detectives in suits, as well as a number of prison officers.

The police were here and the presence of SOCOs meant one thing.

A murder.

The SOCOs were supposed to ensure that the crime scene forensics remained as uncontaminated as possible. That's why they wore those strange outfits.

Sharon looked up from her magazine, noticing that something had caught Bailey's eye.

'What's going on?' she asked.

'Looks like trouble,' Bailey replied. 'That's why we've been locked down. Police everywhere.'

Sharon tossed her magazine aside and jumped off her bunk to join Bailey next to the window.

'Fucking pigs,' she muttered. 'Wonder if someone else has topped it.'

She stood there for a few moments, then yawned and went back and sat down on her bunk and picked up her magazine again. Bailey continued to stand by the window looking down at the yard.

Eventually her conjecture was confirmed when the SOCOs re-emerged from across the other side of the prison yard wheeling a metal trolley on which lay what was unmistakably a black body bag. Bailey wondered who indeed was zipped up beneath the black plastic.

It was frustrating not to be able to know more. She wished she could just go and ask the homicide detectives who were down there right now. But, obviously, in her undercover capacity she could do no such thing.

After another hour or so, the lockdown lifted and their cell was unlocked. Bailey noticed that it was Amber who unlocked the cell, the prison officer she had encountered in the canteen. She seemed like the approachable type.

'It's Amber, isn't it?' said Bailey.

'That's right,' smiled Amber.

'What happened?'

Amber hesitated a few moments, her face becoming serious. 'Dead inmate. One of the building contractors found her in the Old Tread-Wheel House.'

'Who was she?'

'Her name was Sarah Prebble. She had a little blonde topknot. You might have seen her around.'

'You mean Poodle?' said Sharon from her bunk.

Bailey remembered her distinctive hairstyle. She realised Poodle must be the nickname for the girl with the track marks that she'd noticed in the shower, the one who'd told her to fuck off in the canteen. The junkie.

'She was murdered, wasn't she?' said Bailey. 'That's why all the police were here.'

Amber looked around uneasily. 'We haven't really been told anything yet, but yes, it looks that way.'

'Poodle got murdered?!' said Sharon. 'No way!'

'What happened?' asked Bailey.

'We're not supposed to talk about it.'

'Oh come on. You must know something.'

'Yeah give us the juicy details,' said Sharon.

Amber sighed. 'Well,' she said. 'From what I've heard, it was pretty unpleasant. And that's all I can tell you at this stage.'

Bailey watched her walk off along the landing unlocking the cells.

Unpleasant. What did that mean exactly?

20

'What it means,' said the Governor, surveying the roomful of prison officers, 'is that you all need to keep an extra-special eye out for anything which appears in the least bit suspicious.'

'But you still haven't answered my question,' said Maggie. 'Is this murder linked in any way to the one in the laundry? By all accounts—'

'We won't know anything for certain until the autopsy's been done,' said the Governor firmly. 'So there's no point speculating about it. Anyhow, it's not your job or my job to be thinking about such things. That's the job of the police. That's why they're here.'

At the mention of the police, a low series of resentful groans rumbled across the room.

'Your job,' the Governor continued, 'is to maintain security and order within the prison.'

'But how can we do that if the tools that we have at our disposal are inadequate?' Terry griped. 'We can barely protect ourselves, let alone the inmates. Not to mention the fact that we're seriously understaffed and seriously overstretched. Is it any wonder that this kind of thing is happening?'

He crossed his arms and stared defiantly at the Governor. The Governor glared back at him. The room fell into a tense silence at their stand-off.

Amber glanced around. Dylan was sitting a few seats away. As usual, he was looking bored and faintly amused by it all. He raised his sandy-coloured eyebrows at her in mock alarm. She couldn't help but smile. The daily morning briefings never seemed to go by without some kind of confrontation between Terry and the Governor.

The Governor pulled his attention away from Terry to address them all. 'I had a meeting with the lead detective on the case. And if there's one thing we both agree on, it's that we want to do our best to keep all of this out of the media. From the police's perspective, they don't need loads of journalists clogging up their investigation. And from our perspective, a media frenzy could create unnecessary panic and disorder inside the prison, and that's one thing we definitely don't need.'

Amber observed him cynically. She and the rest of them knew very well that what the Governor was really concerned about was looking bad in front of his superiors in the Home Office.

He scoured the room. 'So I don't want any of you talking to any journalists,' he said. 'And I don't want you discussing any of the details of these murders with the inmates; the less they know the better. Understood?'

21

It was visiting time and the cries and laughter of children rang through the air. Bailey stood in the doorway of the visit hall and scanned the crowded room. Apparently a good third of the inmates in here had children. There was a mother and baby unit in D-Wing for inmates who were admitted when pregnant, but for most of them this was the only opportunity they got to see their kids.

Bailey herself had never felt the maternal urge. At least not yet, and she figured that if it was going to happen, she probably would have done something about it by now, going by what her friends and contemporaries from school and college were up to. Most of them were now married and in the process of starting families, and she'd grown sick of going round their houses to coo over yet another new baby. That was probably why she had got on so well with Alice. They had shared much the same attitude towards relationships and kids. Birds of a feather...

She spotted Frank sitting over in the far corner of the visit hall, as far removed from the other visitors as he could manage in the busy room. She navigated her way through the tables and sat down opposite him. He smiled at her, his watery eyes cool and emotionless as usual. He was wearing casual clothes – a black leather jacket and faded jeans – and she was relieved that he didn't look too much like a policeman. She wasn't too worried about anyone in here recognising him from his undercover days as those were long behind him and he was now mainly office-based.

She glanced at the table next to them, concerned that they might be in earshot. It was occupied by a young couple who were barely in their twenties. On his knee the man was balancing a vacant-looking toddler that had strings of drool coming out of its mouth. Both parents were talking intently to each other, stroking hands, gazes locked, clearly still in love and very much oblivious to anything going on around them.

'So how's Dad?' said Bailey in a slightly louder voice than she needed to. 'Is his back still playing up?'

'Yes, now and then,' said Frank, a completely fake smile frozen onto the lower half of his face. 'He misses you, you know.'

She nodded to herself, satisfied that the young couple weren't paying them the slightest bit of interest. She fixed her attention on Frank and lowered her voice.

'I've only been in here a week and someone's been murdered already. A junkie by the name of Poodle.'

Frank's fake smile dissolved away, his face reverting to its usual cold and impassive expression. 'Poodle?'

'I mean Sarah Prebble. Her nickname was Poodle. Because of her little blonde topknot.'

'Oh right. Well, she doesn't have that any more.' He glanced around to check no one was listening. 'Preliminary autopsy results strongly indicate that she was scalped.'

Bailey nodded slowly, a strange tingling feeling coming over her.

'Exactly the same signature as with Alice's murder.' She paused. 'Are you going to tell me Poodle was an undercover cop as well?'

'No, she most certainly wasn't. But I'm guessing that there must be some kind of connection between the two murders. Same perpetrator or perpetrators.'

'How much do the press know? It's the kind of thing they'd jump on in an instant.'

'For the time being, we're withholding specific details of the mutilations. Standard procedure with this kind of thing.'

'I'm sure it'll get out eventually. For one thing, the inmates can't stop talking about it. It's the kind of thing that spreads like wildfire in here. One was bad enough. But two? I think they're getting kind of scared now.'

He shrugged and fixed her with his cold watery gaze. 'Any leads on the drugs ring? Remember your priorities.'

At that very moment, a prison officer walked slowly past them, eyeing them vigilantly as part of his duty to make sure that no visitors were attempting to transfer illegal contraband to the inmates.

'I hear Uncle John's just bought a new lawnmower,' said Bailey.

'That's right. It's got a cylinder blade instead of a rotary blade, which means he can cut his lawn in these neat little light- and dark-coloured strips.'

They both tracked the movement of the prison officer who had now wandered out of hearing range, then leant in to face each other once more.

'I found the cellmate. Melanie Clarke. But like you said, she didn't seem all that coherent. I don't think I'm going to get much out of her.'

Frank sighed. She could tell he was disappointed with her progress.

'But...' she said, 'her mates did tell me where I could buy some drugs, so I'm going to try and get hold of some tomorrow. Hopefully it'll lead to something specific.'

'Time is money, and money only lasts so long. If you don't find out something soon, the drugs squad will pull the plug on the operation.'

She paused and looked around the visit hall at all the inmates chatting to their friends and relatives.

'You know... just because Poodle was a junkie and an inmate, she was still a human being. Try not to lose sight of that fact with your government drugs targets. I mean, surely her family must be pretty upset about it.'

'Sadly it's proving hard to find someone who actually gave a shit about her. She spent most of her life in care and what family she does have look to be even bigger junkies and wasters than she was. Listen, the murder investigation team are doing all they can. The prison authorities have searched this place from top to bottom twice now and come up empty.'

'I'm not surprised. It's like a maze in here. Too many dark corners. And security's a shambles. Too many inmates, not enough staff.'

'I hope you're not trying to make excuses. You know how much I hate excuses.'

22

Bailey lay on her bunk in the darkness, eyes open, looking up at the ceiling. The lights were now off and they had been locked in for the night. The springs creaked as Sharon shifted position on the bunk below.

Wide awake, Bailey was contemplating her next move, trying to work out how Poodle's murder fitted into the wider picture. Did it simplify things or did it complicate them?

Sharon's voice drifted up from below.

'Who was that visiting you today?' she asked.

Bailey felt a small pinch of anxiety. She hadn't noticed Sharon in the visit hall. It just went to show that you never knew who might be watching you when you weren't aware. You couldn't afford to let your cover slip for one moment.

She resisted the urge to tell Sharon that it was none of her business.

'He's my brother,' she answered.

There was a brief pause.

'You don't look alike. His nose is way bigger than yours for one thing.'

Bailey sighed inwardly. This inmate was too inquisitive by half.

'He got his mum's nose. He's my half-brother. Same father, different mothers.'

'Oh.'

Sharon went quiet. Bailey hoped that the explanation was sufficient.

Not being able to see Sharon's face, it was hard to know what she was thinking.

There was no noise from the bunk below for a few minutes. Hopefully she had gone to sleep.

'How did you get those scars?' said Sharon.

No such luck.

'I'd rather not talk about it.'

'Sorry I asked.'

'No problem.'

Another pause. Just long enough for Bailey to think that she actually had gone to sleep this time, when she spoke up again.

'What did you do with the money?'

'What money?' Bailey was confused.

'The money you stole when you were an accountant. You told me you stole a load of money, right?'

Bailey cursed herself for her slow uptake. 'Oh, that money.'

'Yeah. That money. Did you give it back?'

'Yes. I had to.'

'You must have spent some of it surely? Why steal it otherwise?'

Bailey paused. She wasn't enjoying this interrogation. Why couldn't Sharon just go to sleep?

'Yeah, of course I spent some.'

'So what did you buy then?'

'Oh... handbags, shoes, that kind of thing. Stuff I couldn't normally afford. Louis Vuitton, Kurt Geiger, y'know.'

'Nice. How much did you nick?'

Bailey couldn't work out if Sharon's questions were innocent curiosity or if she was angling for something somehow. Either way, she knew she had to be careful.

'It was in the thousands.'

'Tens of thousands or hundreds of thousands?'

'Enough to put me away for four years.'

'Keeping it close to your chest, huh?' Sharon laughed. 'I bet you squir-relled some of it away somewhere. Some cash buried in the woods wrapped in plastic?'

'No. I told you, I had to give it all back.'

'If I'd been in your situation, I would have invested in property.'

'They would have confiscated it.'

'Not if you'd bought it in Northern Cyprus. That's the place to buy property with illegal cash. And there's no extradition treaty either.'

'Thanks for the tip.'

'Remember it for next time, eh?'

23

Amber gazed idly at the three multiplexer monitors which filled the entire span of one wall of the CCTV control room. Each monitor was subdivided into twelve mini-screens, each of those in turn connected to a camera somewhere in the prison complex. There were no windows in the control room, and this gave it a vaguely claustrophobic feel, but with so many things to pay attention to on the screens, they would have presented an unnecessary distraction anyhow.

All of the prison officers were required to work shifts in the control room. Some of them enjoyed it, seeing it as a cushy job, the opportunity to watch television for several hours. Amber had initially found it quite intriguing from a voyeuristic perspective, however the novelty had soon dulled. When you watched normal television, there was usually a story of some sort to maintain your interest. In here, however, much of the activity displayed on the screens was incredibly mundane and repetitive. And it got boring pretty quickly.

From her vantage point in her swivel chair, she could see what was happening all over the prison at that exact moment in time. A group of inmates loitering around on one of the landings, laughing and joking amongst themselves. Two of her colleagues leading a nervous new inmate from the back of a prison van. A brood of crying children being scolded by their incarcerated mother in the crowded visit hall. A chaotic and argumentative game of football in the prison yard. And so on. And so forth.

Directly in front of her was a spot monitor where she could view the feed from a specific camera in larger detail. Using the keyboard on the desk, she could switch between cameras and different locations within the prison, and she could also operate the cameras, tilting, panning and zooming them as necessary. That was perhaps the only fun bit – being able to zoom in on people without them knowing that you were doing so.

During her induction a few weeks previously, Maggie had brought her in here and explained how it all worked.

'The cameras give real-time coverage of what's going on in the prison, and all of it is recorded onto this hard drive.' She'd gestured at the computer terminal on the desk. 'We archive the footage for twenty-eight days, then it's overwritten automatically. It's time-stamped and it's admissible as evidence in court, so it's good if you want to check back on a particular incident, and it's also handy if an inmate accuses you of something you didn't do.

'Obviously, we can't hope to monitor every square inch of the place. That would be impossible in a huge old Victorian building like this with all its millions of nooks and crannies. Anyhow, it would be counterproductive to try and see everywhere as there are a limited number of screens in here and there's only ever one person manning them at any particular time. So we stick the cameras in places where we think incidents are most likely to occur, and also in places where overall security is particularly important.'

She'd pointed to various mini-screens as she spoke.

'The gatehouse and the reception area – so we can see who's coming in and out of the prison; the landings and the common areas, such as the atrium, the canteen and the yard – to cut down on general misbehaviour and to increase safety for the inmates and for us as well; the main corridors, walkways and stairwells, as well as all the major entrances and exits – to monitor inmates' movements; the visit hall – to deter visitors from passing over contraband; the segregation block – to monitor dangerous or vulnerable inmates; the perimeter wall – to prevent people from escaping; and the medical unit – as those who are at risk of self-harm or suicide are often kept there.

'Of course, there are plenty of blind spots. There always will be. I'm sure the more wily inmates are aware of those. But, generally speaking, we've got most of the important locations pretty well covered.

'The bits of the prison which don't have any surveillance, or which have very limited surveillance, are those areas where we think incidents are less likely to occur, either because they're normally quite well-staffed or because the inmates are engaged in structured activities which keep them occupied and out of trouble.'

Since the murder of Sarah Prebble, a.k.a. Poodle, the Governor had specified that all of the prison officers, especially those working in the control room, maintain an increased vigilance for anything appearing remotely suspicious.

Amber dutifully scanned the multiple mini-screens – up, down, left, right – skimming back and forth across the entire prison complex. How would she know 'suspicious' when she saw it? Everything looked normal. Monotonously so.

Her attention paused on one of the mini-screens at the bottom left of the central multiplexer monitor. It was displaying several inmates standing around on one of the upper landings at the central point where the four wings of the prison converged. She squinted at it more closely. She recognised one of them as Bailey Pike, the inmate who'd been victimised in the canteen, the one who she'd intervened to help.

She was leaning on a balcony and appeared to be doing very little else apart from that. She was probably as bored as Amber was. She seemed like a decent sort, relatively speaking, and Amber didn't like to see nice people getting picked on. If it had happened once, it could happen again. The bullies were like that. If you weren't part of a group, then you were fair game. She made a mental note to keep an extra eye out for Bailey's well-being.

Amber reached forward to the keyboard and switched that particular camera to the spot monitor. She tilted the camera towards Bailey and zoomed in, studying her face, observing her with mild interest, realising that she had no idea why Bailey was even in here...

24

Bailey stood on the landing doing what most of the inmates did best –
lounging. It ranked as one of their top activities. There was an art to it,
she'd discovered, to be able to stand around and be casually engaged in
nothing in particular.

But she was lounging with a purpose, using the architecture of the
prison to her advantage. From her position at the centre, she could see
down all four wings.

She was propped nonchalantly against a metal balcony, the cold iron
surface beneath her hands worn smooth by generations of inmates who'd
been doing the same kind of thing. She craned her head slightly to peer
downwards.

It didn't take her long to identify Keisha standing on the landing below
at the far end of C-Wing, just where Seema had said she would be. It
wasn't hard to spot a drug dealer when you knew what you were looking
for. As a police officer, Bailey'd had plenty of experience in that area.

She watched as a string of different inmates approached Keisha, smiled
and greeted her with a handshake. And always something passed between
them, transferred via the handshake, so subtle and fast that it would have
been easy to miss if she hadn't been paying attention.

Keisha was putting on a pretty good act of lounging, her hands tucked
in the pockets of her jogging top, but Bailey knew that those pockets
contained more than just a pair of hands.

Bailey pushed herself off the balcony and moved along the landing to get a closer look. She'd learned covert surveillance techniques as part of her undercover training. Really, though, all it came down to was being as observant as possible whilst remaining as inconspicuous as possible. Fortunately for her, the inmates' general predilection towards lounging made it much easier for her to blend in and disguise her actions.

She observed another inmate walk up to Keisha, exchange a few inaudible words and a handshake. Watching closely, she saw the inmate casually palm something into her pocket, most likely a small package of drugs that had been concealed within the handshake. The exchange was quick and furtive and over in less than five seconds.

Bailey marvelled at Keisha's audacity. She was blatantly dealing drugs under the noses of the prison officers, although, admittedly, there were only two per landing.

More interestingly though, when it came to putting a face to the name, Keisha's face belonged to one of the inmates in the group of bullies who had harassed her in the canteen a few days earlier. She was the black one in the group. As Bailey was learning, it was a small world in here.

She waited until Keisha had finished dealing with the inmate before deciding to act. Pushing herself off the balcony, she walked to the end of the landing and descended the metal staircase to Keisha's level. Looking around, she saw a male prison officer approaching, his shiny black shoes clumping along on the concrete floor. She waited until he had passed her and then made her move. She trotted up to Keisha and leant on the balcony next to her.

Keisha looked her up and down suspiciously with her hard cold eyes. If she recognised Bailey from the altercation in the canteen, she didn't show it.

'I want to buy some weed,' said Bailey quietly.

'How much?'

'An eighth.'

'Ninety quid.'

'Ninety quid!'

Bailey was stunned. That was more than four times the street price for an eighth of an ounce of marijuana.

Keisha shrugged and looked away as if to say take it or leave it.

'All right,' said Bailey.

'Have you got cash?'

She shook her head. 'It's not allowed, is it?'

Keisha snorted in contempt as if she had said something stupid. 'Cigarettes then. From your canteen account.'

'It'll take me a while to get that many.'

'You can have it on credit.' Keisha's face twisted into a mean-looking sneer. 'But if you lose it or get it confiscated, you still have to pay. Just remember... when it comes to paying, you always pay, because there's nowhere to hide in here and it won't take us long to find out where you live.'

Bailey was in no doubt that this would be the case. She smiled at Keisha, shook her hand, pocketed the weed and walked off.

25

Bailey stood beneath the showerhead and let the streams of hot water wash the grime of the prison off her. She had finally got some decent shower gel from the prison shop and it made the uncomfortable experience of communal showering marginally more tolerable than it had been before.

She blinked the soap out of her eyes and glanced casually over her shoulder at Keisha, who was standing just a few metres away.

Since buying the drugs, Bailey had been surreptitiously shadowing Keisha, gathering intelligence on her movements, the people she associated with and what she got up to on a daily basis. It transpired, as she'd suspected, that her core associates consisted of the group that she'd encountered in the canteen – the gold-toothed one, the oriental one and the big lumbering one.

Their primary activities appeared to consist of selling drugs and collecting debts, with some intimidation thrown in for good measure. As far as she could ascertain, the gold-toothed one seemed to be in charge of this illicit enterprise.

She was standing over there right now, next to Keisha, facing away from Bailey, soap suds running down her firm, boyish form. They were chatting furtively about something and Bailey was curious to know what, but she couldn't make out what they were saying under the roar of the water and she didn't want to get too close in case the gold-toothed one spotted her and decided to pick on her again.

She flicked the excess water from her hair and was about to leave the shower room when she noticed something unusual about the pair of them. The gold-toothed one had a distinctive tattoo etched at the base of her spine, and Keisha had an identical design in exactly the same place.

It consisted of three playing cards fanned out. The one on the front was an ace of spades, with a black A in the top right corner and an inverted A in the bottom left corner. The spade in the middle of the playing card was depicted in the form of a dagger clutched in a skeletal hand, behind which leered a malevolent grinning skull. The top right corners of the other two cards showed only the letters B and C respectively, drawn in the same font as the letter A.

A, B, C...

The workmanship was clean, intricate and masterful. With all the tattoos in here, it would have been easy to write it off as just another tramp stamp, but the longer Bailey looked at it, the more certain she became that it carried some sort of significance.

A.B.C.

The letters evidently formed some kind of acronym, but what did it stand for?

She snapped out of her trance, realising that she'd been staring at them a little too long. Thankfully they hadn't noticed. She left the shower room, turning the letters over in her mind, analysing them like a cryptic cross-word clue. If they contained an answer she was determined to find it.

26

The soft pulse of dub emanated from the stereo, the air was thick with layers of marijuana smoke, and origami animals littered the cell.

Bailey stood in the doorway and surveyed the three stoners sitting slumped in the smoky gloom. After a few moments, Kay noticed her, squinting up at her with red-rimmed eyes through the grey miasma. There was a look of blankness, then slowly recognition seeped in.

'It's you again,' she said. 'The one with bad taste in Jean-Claude Van Damme films.'

Seema looked up. At the sight of Bailey, her face broke into a smile.

'Got any more interesting film facts?' she asked.

'No,' said Bailey. 'But I do have some weed if you want a smoke.'

She pulled the ninety quid bag of weed out of her pocket and dangled it in front of her. Kay eyed it hungrily. Bailey tossed it onto the table and Kay scrambled sharply for it, pulled it open and took a deep sniff.

'Mmm... sensimilla...' She looked up at Bailey. 'You arrived at exactly the right time. I was just about to skin up.'

She held up some rolling papers which had already been stuck together to form the basis of a joint. Shovelling a large pinch of Bailey's weed into it, she added a few token strands of tobacco from a pouch of Golden Virginia, rolled it up, licked the gummed edges of the paper and sealed it into a tight cone-shaped joint which she then held up for the approval of the other two.

'Seven out of ten,' said Seema.

'An eight surely?' said Kay. 'What do you think, Mel?'

'Uh?' Mel didn't appear to be paying attention. She blinked and looked at them vacantly, scratching her frayed afro.

'Forget it,' said Kay, placing the joint in her mouth and sparking it up. She took a deep drag, then passed it to Seema, who took a drag and then passed it to Mel. Mel took a drag and held it up to Bailey.

Bailey looked at it. She couldn't very well refuse it, seeing as she'd come here with a bag of weed to a cell full of people who spent most of their day smoking it. It would look odd, if not downright suspicious, if she didn't partake of it too.

So she plucked the joint from Mel's fingers and put the damp roach-end between her lips and took a large puff. But she didn't draw the smoke down into her lungs, holding it instead in her mouth and throat, blowing it out a few moments later.

It would have been both easy and fun to participate a little more wholeheartedly. But it was never a good idea to get strung out on drugs while undercover. If you were strung out, you could make mistakes, screw up an operation or even make an error that could turn out to be fatal to you or someone else.

'Want to see something funny?' said Seema.

Bailey shrugged and nodded.

Seema turned to Mel. 'Hey, Mel, did you know that the universe goes on forever?'

Mel's face slowly screwed up into a painful frown as she attempted to comprehend the fact. For a while, her eyes were stuck in an odd squint.

'That does my head in,' she said. 'Why would you say something like that?'

Seema and Kay collapsed into paroxysms of laughter.

'Aren't you worried the screws might come in here and catch us?' said Bailey. 'I mean, it's not exactly subtle... the smell and everything.'

They looked at each other and shrugged indifferently.

'You know what,' said Kay, 'I think the authorities turn a blind eye on us smoking weed because it makes us behave. You don't see us committing crimes or starting riots. We're just sitting here and chilling out, not causing trouble to anybody.'

She tossed the bag of weed to Mel.

'Roll us a joint, Mel.'

Mel picked up a pack of rolling papers and plucked out several sheets. Her long brown fingers manipulated the papers with a fluid dexterity as she fashioned the foundations of a large joint, her tongue darting out to lick the gummed strips to glue them together.

'She's the best joint roller in here,' said Seema. 'Papercraft is her forte. Hence all the origami animals.'

Bailey watched her skin up, silently impressed by her casual expertise. Here was a master at work, one whose vacant demeanour belied a genuine aptitude for the task at hand.

After she'd finished packing the dope in, Mel rolled it smoothly into a long tight cone, gracefully twisting the loose paper at the end into a neat point which sealed the joint. She tore a piece of cardboard off the pack of rolling papers and rolled it into a roach, which she inserted into the other end. She held the joint up for them to see.

'Nine and three-quarters,' said Seema.

Mel smiled proudly.

'I still think mine was an eight,' muttered Kay.

The first joint came round to Bailey again. There were now two joints circulating and the air was denser than ever with smoke. The poor ventilation in the cells, courtesy of the prison's outmoded design, didn't help the situation.

Despite attempting not to inhale directly from the joints, she couldn't help but passively smoke what was fairly potent marijuana, and she was starting to feel quite stoned. She had that distinct fuzziness at the edges of her consciousness, accompanied by a noticeable disruption to her linear thinking patterns. It was quite pleasant, she couldn't deny it.

The high quality of the marijuana was evidence that those importing the drugs into the prison had good contacts on the outside. Hopefully, her undercover operation would shed some light on who those contacts were.

'Talking of Van Damme movies, have you seen *Death Warrant*?' said Seema, blowing out a long stream of smoke.

Bailey shook her head.

'I can't believe you haven't seen it,' said Kay. 'I thought you were a Van Damme fan. It's definitely in his top five. Do you know what it's about?'

'No.'

'It's about this cop that goes undercover in a prison. Are you sure you haven't seen it?'

Bailey was seized by a sudden paranoia. They were all staring at her and they no longer seemed to be smiling. Did they suspect? Why would they suddenly mention that? Was it a coincidence or were they making a point? Did it seem obvious to them that she was an undercover police officer? Was this some kind of test?

Black tendrils of anxiety wormed their way through her thoughts as her stoned mind frenetically generated all kinds of unpleasant possibilities. Dope paranoia was like that; once the fear gripped you, it was extremely hard to get rid of it. She fought to stay calm, to not show any signs of panic.

Three pairs of red-rimmed eyes bored into her. Time seemed to dilate, slowing right down as it often did in a stoned state. Her heart was beating hard and her mouth was dry. Very dry. She needed water. Why were they all staring at her so intently? She then realised that they were still waiting for an answer from her.

'Uh... yeah, I'm pretty sure I haven't seen it. I think I'd have remembered.'

'Imagine that,' said Seema slowly. 'Being an undercover cop in a prison. You'd be fucked if people realised who you actually were.'

'What kind of person would want to do that anyway?' said Kay. 'You'd have to be a bit mad in the first place to want to try and pretend to be someone else. You'd have to be loopier than Mel. Isn't that right, Mel?'

Mel blinked and looked at them as if seeing them for the first time. Despite staring hard at Bailey, she'd actually been zoned out elsewhere. Kay and Seema laughed.

'We call her Crazy Mel, don't we, Mel?'

'Why's that?' asked Bailey.

'Because she's crazy,' said Kay, as if no further explanation was needed.

'Mel's not crazy,' murmured Mel.

'Then why do you talk about yourself in the third person?' said Kay.

Seema frowned. 'Stop being mean.'

'Yeah stop being mean to Mel,' grouched Mel.

Bailey began to relax again, her anxiety receding slightly now that she was no longer under the spotlight. The mention of *Death Warrant* had turned out to be nothing more than just an innocent film reference.

She glanced at her watch. Time was finite and she'd come here for a reason. Now that they appeared to be relatively at ease in her presence, she decided it was time to steer the conversation in a more productive direction.

'You know... I keep seeing this tattoo around,' she said. 'It's like these three playing cards with the letters ABC on them.'

Their smiles disappeared abruptly and the atmosphere in the cell instantly became cold and serious. Kay and Seema swapped glances. They looked frightened. Bailey had obviously touched on something.

'I just wondered what it meant,' she said.

'It stands for Ace Blade Crew,' said Kay quietly, looking around warily as if the walls had ears.

'Ace Blade Crew?'

'They're a gang. You sure don't want to mess with them. As the name suggests, they all carry shanks. They're psychos, especially that Toni, the one with the gold tooth. She's banged up for murder. Apparently it involved a machete.'

It sounded like they were more dangerous than she'd realised. A prison gang. Interesting.

'What do they do exactly?' Bailey asked.

'They run all the drugs in here,' said Kay. 'They have a monopoly on it. Anyone else would have to be stupid to start selling drugs, unless they had some kind of death wish.'

'The less questions you ask about them, the better,' said Seema.

'I just want to know who to watch out for, y'know, for my own personal safety,' said Bailey. She paused for a moment. 'I don't want to end up like Poodle.'

At the mention of Poodle, Kay's lip curled in contempt.

'Poodle had drug debts. She was always in debt. These junkie scum always are. I wouldn't be in the least bit surprised if they did it to teach her a lesson.'

Bailey nodded with interest. She remembered Keisha's warning about the consequences of not paying back debts. The Ace Blade Crew sounded like the kind of people who didn't shy away from violence. Had she already found Alice's killers?

'Fuck, man, but I heard she was like... all mutilated,' said Seema.

'Just like Mel's cellmate,' said Kay. 'What was her name again? Ally or something? She didn't last very long, did she?'

Bailey's ears perked up at the mention of Alice. She glanced at Mel. Mel had started to fidget uncomfortably.

'Yeah I heard about her,' said Bailey carefully. 'Did she die in the same way then?'

Kay nodded. 'Yeah. Scalped. Like what the Native Americans used to do. Puts the fear of God into your enemies. You do that to enough people, no one will fuck with you.'

Bailey scanned the three of them. 'Do you think this ABC gang killed her as well then?'

Kay and Seema once again exchanged nervous looks.

'Maybe,' said Kay. 'Maybe she crossed them. They don't mess around. You even just look at them the wrong way and you're in trouble.'

'What do you think, Mel?' asked Seema. 'Do you think they did it?'

Mel's fidgeting got more agitated and a muscle in her left eye began to twitch.

'Stop talking about killing!' she said, her voice coming out in fits and spurts. 'Mel doesn't like it.'

'Mel's been getting a bit jittery about this murder business ever since her cellmate got killed,' explained Seema. 'A bit too close to home, eh Mel?'

'What was she like?' said Bailey. 'This cellmate?'

She suddenly craved some morsel of detail about her deceased friend, something that would momentarily bring her back to life.

Seema shrugged. 'Never talked to her.'

'Kept herself to herself,' said Kay.

'Bit of a loner,' added Seema.

'Just like you,' murmured Kay, fixing Bailey with a curious stare. 'Loners don't always last too long in a place like this. You gotta have mates, y'know. Safety in numbers, know what I mean?'

Bailey nodded slowly, recalling all the different cliques she'd seen around the prison. It felt like a warning. She guessed it was.

'Ally was nice to Mel,' said Mel in a quiet voice. 'Mel liked Ally.'

Bailey looked at Mel. She was staring dejectedly at her feet with a melancholy look on her face.

That figured, thought Bailey. Alice had always been a compassionate person. She was the kind of person who would have had time even for a spaced-out headcase like Mel. She'd had time for Bailey when Bailey had been going through a rough patch, after she'd split up with Mark, and then later also, after that last undercover job had gone so wrong. That's what friends were for. They were there when you needed them. It was just a shame that Bailey hadn't been able to be there for Alice when she'd been in her greatest hour of need. Bailey felt like she'd let her down.

'Can you die from being scalped?' asked Seema, creasing her brow quizzically.

'I reckon the shock alone would kill you,' said Kay.

'I heard there was blood everywhere. Like, *every*where.'

'Scalp wounds bleed a lot. That's because there are more capillaries under the scalp.'

'But I heard she was stabbed as well. Like, properly carved up. Throat cut and all that. Like a frenzy. Poodle as well. Both of them done the same way. That's what I heard.'

'Stop talking about this!' screeched Mel suddenly, clapping her hands over her ears. 'Mel doesn't like it! It's horrible!'

Bailey recoiled at the outburst. They all went silent and their attention turned to Mel.

Kay smiled vindictively and leaned forward towards Mel and mimed the scalping.

'Yeah... all ripped off... rrriiiiipppp!!! Blood everywhere!!!! Uuuurr-rrgggghhhh!!! Cut her scalp right off!'

Mel screamed louder, clamping her hands tighter over her ears, shutting her eyes and banging her legs on the bunk.

Kay collapsed into stitches of laughter.

Mel's eyes popped open. She snatched the joint out from Seema's fingers and took a huge drag on it. The tip glowed orange and a big end of ash formed. The ash trembled dangerously before falling squarely in her lap. She didn't seem to notice.

Bailey tensed, concerned at what she might do next.

Mel turned to stare at her with big bloodshot saucers of eyes. Bailey shivered, transfixed by these twin whirlpools of torment. She wondered exactly what traumas Mel had undergone in her past to fracture her reality so.

'Stop talking about killing,' said Mel in a low voice. 'It makes me paranoid.'

Seema laughed nervously. 'You sure don't want to make Mel paranoid. We don't call her Crazy Mel for nothing...'

And with that, Seema suddenly leaned across to the table at the end of the cell and plucked a small square of coloured paper from a pile lying there. She thrust it out to Mel, who was still staring at Bailey.

'Here, Mel, calm yourself down,' she said.

Mel looked down and noticed the piece of paper. She suddenly seemed to snap out of whatever trance she was in. With a deft gesture, she swapped the joint for the piece of paper in Seema's hand and started folding it furiously.

Bailey exhaled in relief and then watched her in bemusement.

Mel's long brown fingers moved rapidly to fold and crease the paper. Bailey could see her visibly relax as she engaged completely with her task, now oblivious to the rest of them.

Seema nodded at Bailey and winked. 'Origami. It chills her out, y'know... eastern mind–body shit.'

It explained all the little coloured paper animals lying around the cell.

'Maybe she should just smoke less dope,' said Bailey.

Mel grinned happily and looked up at the rest of them. She proudly displayed her outstretched palm to Bailey.

Standing there was a small origami duck.

27

There were the customary large, noisy queues down by the phones. As she waited there, Bailey noticed Sharon join the end of the line. They made eye contact. Bailey smiled at her. Sharon smiled back.

After a few minutes, Bailey glanced over her shoulder again. Sharon was staring hard at her as if intensely curious. Bailey felt a pang of annoyance. One thing she didn't need was a nosey parker like Sharon marking her every move.

When her turn came, Bailey pushed herself into the phone booth, twisting her head away from Sharon's view, just in case she happened to be good at lip-reading.

She entered her PIN and then dialled the number. The phone rang for a few rings, then Rita answered in her nasal voice.

'Hello, Sullivan Knight Solicitors. How can I help?'

'It's Bailey Pike speaking. I'd like to talk to Mr Knight please.'

'Just putting you through.'

This brief exchange between Rita and Bailey took exactly the same format every time, the strict protocol decided in advance for the sake of security.

For a few seconds, Bailey enjoyed the sweeping melancholy tones of Beethoven's 'Moonlight Sonata', and then it broke off as Frank Grinham came on the line.

'So what have you got for me?'

'It appears that a prison gang who call themselves the Ace Blade Crew hold a virtual monopoly on drug distribution within the prison.'

'Ace Blade Crew?'

'ABC for short. They've got these distinctive tattoos. I noticed them in the shower. Apparently they carry knives and they're not averse to using them. People in here seem to be really scared of them. I think it's highly possible that they killed both Alice and Poodle. Alice because she was a police officer, Poodle because she owed them drug debts.'

'Good work. Now we're getting somewhere. But—'

'It's not enough. Yes, I know. We need something more tangible than say-so and conjecture.'

'So what's your next move?'

'I need to find a way in somehow.'

'Prison gangs are notoriously hard to infiltrate. It would be somewhat easier if we had an informant in place to vouch for you.'

'But we don't. And that's fine by me.'

He was quiet for a few moments. She knew he was well aware of how her previous job had panned out. The whole debacle had centred around an informant.

'Oh, yeah, and I'm going to need some more money in my canteen account to buy stuff like cigarettes.'

'You don't smoke.'

'They're used as currency in here. I made a small drugs buy the other day and it wasn't cheap, I can tell you that.'

'I'll see what I can do,' he said.

'Thanks.'

'By the way,' he said. 'I think it'll be okay with Alice's family. I think I managed to smooth it over with them and convince them not to go to the papers.'

'That's good news.'

There was a loaded pause. 'Bailey?'

'Yes.'

'Be careful.'

She nodded without saying anything, not that he could see her, and hung up the phone. She looked around. Sharon was nowhere to be seen and she guessed that was a good thing.

28

Bailey observed Toni through the anti-suicide netting that was strung between the balconies at an interval of every two floors.

Now that she knew Toni was the leader, Bailey had switched the focus of her surveillance onto her. Toni was walking along the landing below with her customary self-assured swagger, her lip curled in an expression of permanent disdain.

She glanced upwards and Bailey drew back behind the thin cover of a cast-iron balcony column. Her stomach turned over, for she feared that Toni might have spotted her. But peeking out from behind the pillar it seemed that she hadn't.

Bailey took off, moving parallel to Toni on the landing above, weaving between the inmates who were lounging there. Utilising her covert surveillance skills, she trailed her at a distance as she reached the end of the landing and descended to the floor below. It looked like she was heading for the house-block exit and the prison yard. Bailey moved rapidly, her heart beating hard as she skipped down the metal stairs, determined not to lose sight of her target.

She had been secretly observing the movements and activities of Toni and her gang for several days now, determined to generate some useful information. But she was careful to be very discreet and stay well out of their way. After all, she now knew that they carried weapons and had few qualms about using them.

Her observations so far confirmed what she had assumed – that Toni was the leader of the gang, for it was she who appeared to be the one issuing commands to the others. It seemed that her second-in-command, or lieutenant, was Keisha. The oriental one with the squint was called Rong, she'd overheard, but she still didn't know the name of the big one that looked like a bodybuilder.

Toni had indeed left the house-block for the yard and Bailey followed her outside. It was overcast and spitting lightly with rain. Scanning around, she spotted Toni walking towards the north end of the yard. Bailey cursed the bad weather. The rain meant that there weren't many inmates in the yard so she would be much more conspicuous in the large open space. Keeping close to the outside wall of C-Wing, she headed briskly after Toni.

Up this end of the yard lay nothing much besides the library and the chapel, neither of which were places she would have associated with someone like Toni. Bailey reached the end of C-Wing and stopped there, peering around the corner of the wall. She was surprised to see Toni enter the prison chapel.

She didn't expect Toni would have much respect for religion. Unless of course there was some other reason for her entering the chapel...

Bailey decided not to follow her directly in. Although she had never been inside the chapel, she imagined it was a fairly small place which would make her presence quite obvious. So she stood in the yard and watched while the spitting rain grew ever steadier, making dark blotches on her grey tracksuit.

She huddled, small and insignificant in the shadow of the huge granite walls, the leaden sky only serving to compound the bleak penal atmosphere.

After about ten minutes, the chapel door opened and Toni emerged. She looked around shiftily and then started to head back across the yard in Bailey's direction, back the way she had come. With a burst of panic, Bailey realised that she was exposed and that Toni would spot her when she came around the corner of C-Wing, which she would do in a few seconds. Why would she be out alone in the rain in the middle of the yard? It would look mightily suspicious. There was no time to run anywhere and it was too far to go back to the entrance to the house-blocks.

Toni was almost upon her. Looking around frantically, Bailey's eye was caught by the numerous cigarette butts littering the dirt by the wall. Thinking fast, she rapidly swooped down and picked one up. She then pulled her tracksuit hood up over her head and dropped her face to conceal her features. She slumped against the wall in an imitation of the junkie-style slouch that she had seen other inmates adopting, clutching the cigarette butt between her fingers, pretending as if she were part-way through smoking it.

Moments later, Toni strode by, passing her by a matter of centimetres, giving her little more than a cursory hostile glance up and down. Just another inmate out in the yard putting up with the rain for the sake of a smoke...

And then she was gone, heading back to the main entrance to the house-blocks.

Letting out a sigh of relief, Bailey flicked the cigarette butt away in disgust. She pulled her hood down and looked at Toni's retreating back. Then she turned and made her way quickly across the yard to the chapel. Pushing the heavy wooden door open, she entered it for the first time since she had been in the prison. Inside, it was cool and dark and it presented an oasis of tranquillity in the otherwise tense atmosphere of the prison.

A number of wooden pews lined either side of the aisle, hymn books lying here and there on them. The pews were empty and the chapel appeared to be completely devoid of inmates.

Dominating the front of the chapel was the altar. Resting on top of the altar block was a large wooden cross, upon which was a model of the crucified Jesus painted in full gory colour.

Also at the front of the chapel was a simple wooden lectern and to one side of that was an organ festooned with pipes and buttons. On the far left-hand side of the chapel were two carved wooden confessional booths, side by side, one for the chaplain and one for the confessor. On the right-hand side of the chapel, Bailey noticed a door which was slightly ajar.

She sat down on a pew and reflected on things. Why would Toni have come here, and only for ten minutes? There were no other inmates in the chapel, so she couldn't have been meeting anyone.

Perhaps she was being too cynical. Perhaps even a brutal bully like Toni was religious. Religion didn't always engender the most rational behaviour in people.

Bailey's own mother was a great example. Although she had always been religious, Jennifer's abduction had tipped her gradually into an almost fanatical devotion to the Christian faith, to the point where it had now become impossible to reason with her about anything which remotely contravened her very literal interpretation of its doctrines. She'd forced Bailey to attend Sunday school throughout the majority of her childhood, giving her a great knowledge of the Bible, along with a strong awareness of the fact that she couldn't bring herself to believe in God, however hard she tried. How could He let bad things happen to good people like Jennifer? She still felt much the same way today.

As she sat there, she slowly became aware of a strange snorting noise. She tilted her head to try and better ascertain what it was. Perhaps she wasn't alone in here after all. She stood up slowly and looked around, trying to locate its source.

After a few moments, she realised that it was emanating from the partially open door on the right side of the chapel.

She walked up the aisle and approached the door. She leaned in. The noise was definitely coming from the other side. Gently, she pushed the door and it silently swung open to reveal a small wood-panelled office. Sprawled in a chair by the desk, asleep, was the prison chaplain, Father O'Malley. The noise she had heard was that of his snoring, a horrible nasal, rasping sound.

During her induction process, she'd been informed about Father O'Malley and the spiritual services he provided. She had only ever seen him from a distance, but even then he cut a distinctive figure, lumbering along in his cassock, constantly muttering to himself. Up close here, she could see that beneath the receding tangle of grey hair he had the veined face of a heavy drinker.

Some part of him sensed her presence as he promptly twitched, then awoke. He looked up at her blankly and then started with a panic, sitting up sharply in his chair.

'What are you doing here?' he exclaimed, affronted. 'This office is out of bounds to inmates!'

'Sorry. I just heard a noise...'

'No respect! That's the problem with you lot. Not one of you harlots knows the meaning of the word "respect". That's why you're all in here.'

'You're drunk,' said Bailey in disgust.

'I am not!' he said indignantly.

'I can smell it on your breath. Even from here.'

He looked her up and down critically.

'For by means of a harlot a man is reduced to a crust of bread.' He nodded and smiled to himself. 'Proverbs, chapter six, verse twenty-six.'

'How about Proverbs, chapter twenty-three? As I recall, it's got a bit about those who "tarry too long at the wine".'

He stared at her sullenly with his glassy bloodshot eyes.

'Do you want to confess or not?' he slurred aggressively.

'To you? I don't think so.'

She backed rapidly out of his office, leaving him to rant to himself.

One thing seemed likely. Toni probably hadn't gone to the chapel to talk to Father O'Malley, because he'd been asleep in a drunken stupor.

So why had she gone there?

Normally, the way it worked was that an informant introduced the under-cover police officer to the criminal group that they were trying to infiltrate. This was usually arranged as part of some kind of deal that the informant had done with the police in order to avoid prosecution or jail time. Having an informant who was already a member of the group to vouch for the police officer was crucial in gaining their trust.

Once they were successfully infiltrated, the undercover police officer would subsequently introduce and vouch for another police officer and so on, so that it was harder for the criminals to trace the infiltration back to the original informant once the operation was over.

In here, however, for better or for worse, Bailey was all alone. She was going in cold. She had no informant to introduce her to the gang, so it was a much more challenging situation in terms of getting to know them and getting them to trust her, a relative newcomer to the prison. She needed to engineer an appropriate situation to facilitate her infiltration into the gang. And that was going to require a certain amount of creativity.

Based on her observations, she had ascertained that each member of the gang was allocated an area of the prison in which to sell drugs.

When it came to free association time, she walked methodically around each wing of the prison and along every landing until she had located Toni. As the leader of the gang, she knew it had to be Toni who she targeted.

Toni was leaning on an upper balcony of D-Wing, casually lounging, her hands in the pockets of her jogging top, sporadically conducting trans-actions with a succession of inmates.

By now it was late afternoon and Bailey knew that Toni probably had a good amount of both cash and drugs in her possession – more than enough illicit material to get her into serious trouble if she was searched. However, she had chosen her position well; from her perch at the end of the upper balcony, Toni had an excellent vantage point from which to spot any approaching prison officers.

After observing her from a safe distance for a short while, Bailey made her way to the stairwell and descended all the way down to the ground floor of D-Wing.

Earlier on, when she had been determining the locations of the gang members, she had made a mental note of where Shelley Foster had been patrolling. Shelley was the prison officer who'd reprimanded Bailey in the laundry, the one who resembled a female gorilla. She was known to be one of the most humourless, straight and stern of the prison officers, and that was exactly the reason that Bailey had chosen her for this next vital stage in her plan.

She was going to snitch.

This was a particularly risky venture as she could not afford to let the other inmates witness her communicating with Shelley. To be known as a snitch in prison was not a good thing. The comebacks were just as brutal as they were on the outside but a whole lot harder to evade. After all, you couldn't just skip town if things got too hot. And once your card was marked, it stayed that way even if you were transferred to another institution.

Bailey retreated into the protective shadows of the large stairwell on the ground floor in the middle of D-Wing, waiting for Shelley to walk past. She could hear her big heavy shoes clunking on the floor as she got closer.

As she walked past, Bailey whispered to her from the shadows. 'Hey! Psst! Shelley!'

Shelley halted and looked around. Her eyes narrowed in automatic suspicion as she sized Bailey up.

'What do you want?'

Bailey beckoned her into the shadows, but Shelley just stood there, hands on her hips, tapping her foot.

'It's important,' hissed Bailey, looking around urgently. Speed was of the essence.

Shelley sighed and stepped warily towards Bailey. She cocked her head to indicate that Bailey should come out with whatever it was she wanted to say.

'You know Toni, the one with the gold tooth?'

Shelley nodded, grinding her jaw slightly. Of course she knew Toni. Everyone in the prison knew Toni. She probably hated her. 'What about her?'

'She's up at the top of D-Wing, at the far end, selling drugs, right this minute.'

'Is she now?' Shelley raised her thick dark eyebrows.

She definitely looked interested. She also didn't look particularly surprised. Bailey guessed the prison officers probably had a fairly good idea what Toni and her gang were up to.

Shelley eyed Bailey one last time, marking her as a snitch with a certain amount of contempt in her eyes, but then she probably regarded most of the inmates in here as scummy people with their own scummy reasons for wanting to stitch each other up. She probably thought Bailey had some score to settle with Toni. But that was immaterial if Bailey's information was sound.

As a police officer, Bailey felt a similar way about snitches herself, but this was a means to an end. And, anyhow, if all went to plan, it wouldn't turn out like a normal snitching.

Shelley did an about-turn and headed towards the stairwell which would bring her out on the top landing closest to where Toni was situated.

Bailey glanced around, checking that no one had seen her talking to Shelley. She waited until Shelley had begun to climb the stairs and then she took action. She marched rapidly in the opposite direction towards the central atrium.

There were three main stairwells in each house-block – one by the central junction of the four wings, one in the middle of each wing and one at the far end of each wing. Shelley had taken the one at the far end of D-Wing. Bailey took the one by the central atrium, paralleling Shelley's ascent, going up two stairs at a time, as fast as she could without drawing too much attention to herself.

She reached the top floor at exactly the same time that Shelley did.

Peering along the landing, she saw Toni clock Shelley and rapidly begin to walk away, head down, trying to look as inconspicuous as possible.

'Hey you! Stop!' barked Shelley.

Toni continued walking, her hands tucked into the pockets of her tracksuit top, pretending she hadn't heard Shelley, making out like she thought Shelley wasn't talking to her.

'Toni!' shouted Shelley. 'Stop right there!'

Toni halted without turning around. She gritted her teeth and cursed.

'Where do you think you're going?' said Shelley.

Toni forced a smile onto her face. She turned around slowly, her hands still in her pockets. She smiled at Shelley. Shelley didn't smile back, her face like granite. She paced slowly up to Toni, almost leisurely, knowing she had caught her bang to rights.

'Just heading back to my cell,' said Toni.

Bailey rapidly advanced along the opposite side of the landing to where Shelley was confronting Toni. She kept to the wall, unobtrusive, scurrying in the direction of the stairwell that Shelley had just ascended. She looped around it and began to work her way stealthily along the landing so she was right up behind Shelley, just a few metres away.

'Empty your pockets,' she could hear Shelley saying.

'I don't have anything on me,' said Toni.

'I don't want to have to repeat myself. Now empty your pockets.'

'I haven't done anything wrong.'

'You're in big trouble and you know it. Dealing drugs'll get you an extra forty days in nick.'

'I don't know what you're talking about.'

But Toni was looking panicky now. Her eyes were darting around furiously, looking for some way out of the situation. But she was stuck and she knew it.

The landing had gone silent and all the inmates were now watching the show. They'd known exactly what Toni was up to. And they knew that if she emptied her pockets, which she would have to do in a matter of seconds, she'd be in big trouble. Bailey could feel the tension and anticipation in the air.

Bailey tiptoed a little closer towards them, her trainers silent on the metal floor, creeping up closer behind Shelley. She craned her head to peer over Shelley's shoulder and catch Toni's eye. She gave Toni a large exaggerated wink and nodded in the direction of the banister. An almost indiscernible frown of puzzlement flickered over Toni's face. But it was all the confirmation Bailey needed that Toni had acknowledged her presence.

Bailey grabbed onto one of the metal pillars and pulled herself up onto the banister. She stood balancing precariously, hanging onto the pillar for support. She looked down and could see the tiled floor four storeys below.

Toni's eyes widened. Shelley tensed as she realised something was up.

'I'm gonna jump!' shouted Bailey. 'I'm going to do it! I can't stand being in this place any longer!'

Shelley spun around. Her eyes widened. 'What the...? Get down right now!'

Bailey looked down. She wobbled a little. She had never been great with heights. She had no intention of actually jumping, but if she did go over she'd have two floors to fall before she hit the anti-suicide netting. She hoped it was attached strongly.

She glanced at Toni. Shelley was trying to negotiate both Bailey and Toni, her attention flicking frantically back and forth between them, desperately trying to keep an eye on both of them at the same time.

The moment Shelley's back was turned to her, Toni started furiously mouthing at Rong, who had appeared on the other side of the landing. Rong swiftly made her way around the landing to come up behind Toni.

Bailey saw that just a few more seconds were needed.

'I'm going to do it,' shouted Bailey. 'I'm going to jump. I can't bear it any longer.'

'You're going to do nothing of the sort,' barked Shelley, taking a step towards her.

'Don't come any closer!' said Bailey. 'I'm warning you!'

She released her grip on the pillar, so she was balancing with just her feet on the slippery metal surface of the thin banister. She stood there wavering, her arms going in circles one way and then the other in order to try and keep her balance.

She now had Shelley's full attention.

Out of the corner of her eye, she saw Rong finally catch up with Toni, who rapidly offloaded a pouch of contraband onto her. Rong folded the pouch of drugs and cash into her tracksuit top and melted away back into the crowds of inmates who had gathered to watch.

Mission successful.

Shelley spun around back to Toni, who gave her a wide smile, pulling her pockets inside out with an innocent look on her face.

'Look. Nothing.'

Shelley's eyes narrowed furiously. She knew she had been given the slip somehow.

Bailey suddenly felt the sole of her trainer slip on the smooth metal surface of the banister. Her balance was starting to go.

'Oh shit,' she muttered. She grabbed for the pillar, but her fingertips brushed it in vain, not quite able to get a grip on the glossy metal.

She saw Shelley's eyes bulge even wider as she reached out to try and grab Bailey's leg.

She saw Toni's smile transform into a grin of genuine amusement.

And then she was falling.

Down.

Down.

Down.

Past a landing full of inmates. Their faces watching in entertainment. Their mouths open, their jaws hanging slack.

And then she hit the anti-suicide netting, landing on her back. It creaked dangerously, the support springs stretching as they took her weight.

She felt the thin strands of the netting flexing elastically, biting into her back and shoulder muscles as they absorbed her impact.

And then she bounced up, like she was on a trampoline. Up in mid-air again.

And then she landed again.

And bounced back up again.

And landed again, finally coming to rest in the vibrating netting.

She lay there looking up at the ceiling, at the grimy skylights high above. At the faces of the inmates leaning over the banisters looking down at her. Among them she could see Toni.

Whoops and cheers echoed around the interior of the house-block.

It had been kind of fun.

Bailey got to her feet and walked unsteadily off the anti-suicide netting onto the landing. Shelley was standing there waiting for her. She looked pissed off in the extreme. She took a firm hold of Bailey's arm, her fingers biting like a vice into her biceps. She glared into Bailey's eyes and spoke in a low growl.

'I don't know what kind of game you're playing, but whatever it is, I don't like it. I'm putting you on the nicking sheet.'

30

The next day, Bailey arrived at the canteen for lunch as early as she could, got her food and headed straight for their corner table, which was, as she'd hoped, empty. She sat down, getting the expected looks and whispers from the other inmates, and waited for the gang to arrive.

After jumping off the balcony, she'd received a DIS1 form almost immediately from Shelley. The DIS1 form was what was informally known as the 'nicking sheet', and they had to give it to Bailey within forty-eight hours of the offence being committed. What it meant was that she would have to have an adjudication to discipline her for her actions. Although it was regarded as a negative thing by both the inmates and the prison authorities, it made her feel a little more comfortable in her cover because it made her feel that little bit more like a genuine inmate.

She noticed the gang file into the canteen. They queued up for their food, and she saw them look over at her and then talk amongst themselves.

Her heart was beating hard, thumping against the inside of her chest. She was too nervous to take even the smallest bite of her food. In fact, she felt like she was about to throw up. She could sense the eyes of the entire canteen upon her table. Sitting down here was a big gamble. If it paid off, fine. If it didn't... Best not think about what might happen if it didn't. She took a deep, slow breath and fought to keep her cool. It was all about keeping cool.

Their shadows fell across the table.

For a few moments, they stood there surrounding her, holding their trays of food. The entire canteen had gone silent. Not even the smallest clatter of cutlery could be heard. Everyone was waiting for something to happen. To her.

But, unlike last time, they didn't ask her to move.

They just sat down around her. She was sandwiched between the big lumbering one to her left and Keisha to her right. Toni sat directly opposite her, next to Rong.

Bailey breathed out slowly. So far so good...

Toni gave her a long hard look. Then she started eating, which was a signal for the others to also start eating.

They ate in silence, indecipherable looks occasionally passing between them.

Bailey also ate, forcing the food down even though she didn't feel like it.

The rest of the canteen ate and watched, waiting – perhaps hopefully – for the inevitable violent outcome.

But that didn't happen.

What happened was that Toni finished eating, put down her knife and fork, steepled her fingers and fixed Bailey with another long hard gaze with her pale flint-coloured eyes.

Bailey held her stare, forcing herself not to blink.

'So, you want to sit at our table, huh?' said Toni finally.

'Seems like the best seat in the canteen,' said Bailey.

Toni's eyes narrowed as she sized Bailey up. She nodded to herself, coming to some unspoken conclusion.

Toni glanced around the canteen. All eyes seemed to be upon them. Everyone appeared to be straining to hear what they were saying. She leaned in close to Bailey and lowered her voice so it was almost inaudible.

'Meet me in the yard. Half an hour. Corner of C-Wing.'

Then she stood up. The others followed suit. They left the canteen, leaving Bailey sitting by herself alone at the table.

She looked around.

The other inmates were looking at her with a certain amount of curiosity and even a little respect.

She couldn't help but smile to herself, pleased with how it had turned out so far. But a strong sense of trepidation also gripped her. What was going to happen next?

31

The yard was flat, bare, compacted dirt, encircled with wire fences topped with concertina coils of razor wire, beyond which lay the massive perimeter wall with its fortress-like crenellations and watchtowers. Inmates dotted the yard in ones and twos, some walking along, others kicking a ball to and fro, some sitting on the series of poured concrete picnic-style benches which lined one side. Mostly they just stood around and smoked.

Bailey trotted across the yard in the direction of her impending rendezvous. Although she felt a certain amount of apprehension, she was fairly confident she'd done a decent job of convincing them. After all she wasn't a complete rookie when it came to this kind of work.

Moments later, she spotted Toni, smoking a cigarette, leaning against the corner of the exterior wall of the house-block which formed C-Wing. Toni smiled at her and beckoned her over.

'Hey,' she said, looking around. 'Anyone with you?'

Bailey shook her head. Toni nodded slyly, flicked her cigarette away and motioned for Bailey to follow her.

'We couldn't really talk in the canteen. Too many ears, if you know what I mean.' She glanced around the yard, her eyes resting for a moment on the CCTV mast. 'Let's go round here a second.'

Bailey hesitated for a moment, then followed her around the corner, out of sight of the cameras...

Where someone suddenly slammed hard into the side of her. She crashed up against the wall. Stunned. Winded.

She found herself pinned against the wall by her neck. The big one whose name she didn't know was holding her with a giant meaty hand, staring at her with dead piggy eyes.

Next to her were Keisha and Rong. Rong was staring at her cross-eyed, one eye deceptively peering over Bailey's left shoulder. Toni stood there, hands on hips, nodding slowly to herself and smiling.

'I don't think you've been properly introduced. This is Muscles,' said Toni, gesturing at the big one who was holding Bailey. 'I think it's probably fairly self-evident why we call her that. She could rip you open like a bag of crisps. She doesn't know her own strength, you see. That's kind of why she's in here. But she's a gentle giant really. Except for the "gentle" part, maybe. And she does exactly what I tell her. Look...' Toni tilted her head at Muscles. 'Squeeze, Muscles.'

Muscles' thick fingers began to squeeze Bailey's neck.

'Urghhh...' choked Bailey. 'Let... urgh... let go.'

'A little bit more, Muscles.'

Muscles increased the force of her grip. Bailey flailed uselessly and started to feel herself going dizzy. She tried in vain to prise Muscles' fingers from her neck, but it was no good. She batted at her huge thick forearms to no avail. Muscles' face was expressionless.

'She's gone the colour of a tomato,' said Rong with a snigger.

'I think her eyes are going to pop right out of her head,' said Keisha in a tone of mild observational interest.

'Let go, Muscles,' said Toni.

Muscles relaxed her grip and Bailey collapsed to her knees on the ground hyperventilating.

'Pick her up, Muscles.'

Muscles gripped hold of Bailey's collar and yanked her to her feet. Toni gestured for her to step back and Muscles stepped back and stood there, her huge arms slack by her side.

Toni stepped forward, right up close to Bailey, almost nose to nose.

'Do you know what we call ourselves?' she said.

'You're the Ace Blade Crew,' said Bailey, fighting to keep her voice from stammering.

Toni nodded slowly, a thin smile spreading across her face as she reached behind her and pulled a home-made shank from her waistband. It was little more than a sharpened sliver of metal with the handle bound with tape, but Bailey could see that it was quite capable of inflicting serious damage.

Keisha and Rong both reached behind them and also pulled out knives. The three crudely fashioned blades sparkled in the sunlight. A thought flashed through Bailey's mind – was this the last thing Alice had seen before she was murdered?

The three of them pressed up against her, leaning in, their faces twisted in hostile grimaces. She felt the points of their knives digging into different parts of her body – her stomach, her chest, her neck.

'Who the fuck are you?' said Toni.

'Where the fuck are you from?' said Keisha.

'What the fuck do you want?' said Rong.

Bailey cowered beneath them, frozen, not daring to move for fear of puncturing herself on their shanks.

'We're going to fuck you up unless you start answering our questions,' said Toni.

Bailey could feel beads of sweat rolling down her face.

'My name's Bailey Pike, I come from London, and I want to hang out with you guys because...' she paused to think of a reason and they leaned in even closer '...because you're cool.'

She bit her lip, realising in retrospect that it sounded a bit lame, but it was the best she could manage under the circumstances.

'Because we're cool?' said Toni, her face morphing into an expression of absolute disdain. The three of them swapped derisory glances, shaking their heads in disbelief.

Toni drew back her lips, revealing her gold tooth, which glinted in the afternoon sun. It took Bailey a few moments to realise that it was a smile, but one that was devoid of any warmth.

'Well, that was a clever little move you pulled back there, jumping off the balcony. I suppose you think I should be thanking you. The thing is though... you could be a snitch for all we know. All that could just have been a set-up, just so you could ingratiate yourself with us.'

The three of them glowered at her, the sharp points of their knives pressing into her even harder.

'Tell us why you're really here,' hissed Toni.

Bailey's blood turned cold as fear seeped through her veins. Had she made a massive misjudgement? Had she underestimated their powers of perception? Had Alice made the same mistake? Was she about to end up the same way?

She gritted her teeth and held eye contact with Toni. Toni was clearly a sociopath – the mildly amicable front was a thin facade behind which dwelt a ruthless, highly intelligent and very paranoid individual. She'd encountered people like this before as a police officer and she knew just how dangerous and unpredictable they could be.

She took a deep breath, willing the steel from within. To reveal any sign of weakness right now would be fatal.

'Fuck you,' she snarled. 'I'm no snitch.'

Toni raised her eyebrows in surprise. 'Oh yeah? So why did you help me then?'

These were people who didn't help anyone. To them it was a pathological behaviour.

'Like you said, maybe I just want to sit at your table.'

Toni smiled and laughed softly. 'Not just anyone can join our gang. No, I'm afraid it's not going to be quite that easy.' She crossed her arms and smiled sadistically. 'No. First, you've got to prove yourself.'

'Prove myself how?'

'Blood in. Blood out. Know what that means?'

Bailey didn't know exactly what it meant, but she didn't like the sound of it.

'"Blood in" means that in order to get in, blood has to be shed,' said Toni. 'Either your blood or someone else's.' She pointed to an inmate slouching across the yard. The inmate had a thin wan look about her. 'See her? She's a snitch. A bit too matey with the guards. No moral compass, if you know what I mean.'

Bailey watched the hapless inmate walk across the yard puffing on a roll-up. She had seen her previously in the canteen, sitting alone with no mates.

'You're going to shank her with this blade.' Toni said matter-of-factly.

She looked down and saw Toni had flipped the shank in her hand so she was offering the handle to Bailey. She felt her policewoman's principles rise to the surface. There was no way that she could justify stabbing an innocent person, even though technically no one was innocent in here. At any rate, doing anything illegal undercover could risk destroying the entire operation if it surfaced later in court.

'You either shank her or you face a beating from us,' said Toni. 'Either way, blood has to be spilt if you want to get in. Yours or hers. What's it going to be?'

Bailey knew she only had one choice. And it wasn't looking good.

'You know what I think?' said Bailey.

'What's that?'

'You didn't say the magic word.'

Bailey took a deep breath and punched Toni in the face.

Toni staggered backwards but quickly regained her balance. She looked astounded that Bailey had actually hit her, as did the others. A small dribble of blood oozed from her left nostril. She slowly brought her finger up to wipe it off. She looked at the smear of blood on her finger. Then she looked at Bailey. A strange empty crazy look came over her face.

Bailey gulped and braced herself.

And then all four of them simultaneously laid into her. Their blows rained down on her, each impact sending shockwaves of pain through her body. She felt them punching her in the face, the ribs, the back, the stomach, and there was no way she could parry all of their blows at the same time.

She swung out blindly, making contact, hearing grunts of discomfort. But the force was overwhelming as they pummelled her into submission.

She crumpled down onto the ground, putting up her hands and arms to try and protect her head. And the last thing she remembered seeing was Muscles' huge trainer-shod foot coming towards her face.

And then blackness.

32

Bailey woke up and opened her eyes. Or at least she tried to, but the left one wouldn't open properly for some reason. Through her semi-blurred vision, she could deduce that she was lying in a bed in a whitewashed pristine room that was definitely not her cell. Where was she?

The sheets felt crisp and clean and the room smelt faintly of disinfectant and chlorine. It was quiet, apart from the odd sound of a door opening and closing, but there seemed to be something wrong with her hearing. The sounds appeared to be coming from a long distance away, as if she was standing at the other end of a tunnel.

Her thoughts were scattered and confused and she couldn't quite get them to gel coherently in her head in order to work out what was going on.

She looked down. Just that small movement of her head sent a sharp jagged pain through her neck. She shifted slightly in the bed and her entire body responded in the same way. It hurt all over.

What the hell had happened to her?

She noticed that the white sheets were stained with blood.

Now it was coming back to her.

Blood in...

She was in the prison hospital. That's where she was.

Bailey turned her head slowly from left to right, wincing as she did so. She was the only person in the ward. The other beds were neatly made and empty. The place seemed remarkably clean, lacking the signature grime and decay which marked the rest of the prison.

Concussion. That was the reason she couldn't think straight. That was the reason for the weird thing with the sounds.

She gingerly touched her eye with her forefinger. It was tender and sore. That was why she couldn't see through it properly – because it was all swollen up.

Bailey looked around for a mirror, but there wasn't one in the room, which was probably a blessing.

She ran her tongue around her teeth. They were all still there, thank god, but at least one of them was loose enough for her to wiggle it with her tongue.

Slowly, methodically, she checked the rest of her body. She appeared to have a cut lip, multiple bruises on her forehead, and her ribs... Jesus her ribcage felt like—

The door to the ward swung open. She looked up. It was Amber. As soon as Amber saw her, her jaw fell open with shock. Bailey had no need for a mirror – Amber's expression said it all.

'You look awful,' whispered Amber.

'I feel awful,' she said hoarsely.

Amber sat down gently on the side of her bed.

'I want you to tell me who did it,' she said, her eyes smouldering with fury.

Bailey knew that Amber had her best interests at heart. She was just doing her job and she meant well. But to reveal who'd beaten her up would be to undo everything that she had just worked so hard to achieve.

Bailey shook her head. 'Nobody. I just slipped and fell.'

Amber rolled her eyes in frustration.

'You slipped and fell?' She sounded very sceptical.

Bailey shrugged and nodded. 'What can I say? I'm just clumsy.'

Amber placed a caring hand on her forearm. 'Don't be afraid, Bailey. Don't be intimidated by the bullies in here. We can protect you from them. We can put you in segregation.'

'What? With all the sickos and the snitches?'

'There's no shame in being a snitch.'

'Maybe not to you, but on my side of the bars there is.'

Bailey had worked undercover long enough to know that criminals regarded snitches as the lowest of the low. Admitting to being one was tantamount to signing your own death warrant.

'I'm worried about you,' said Amber.

'I can handle myself.'

'Are you sure?' Amber didn't look convinced.

Bailey turned her head away to signal that she wasn't going to reveal anything more.

Amber sighed and stood up. 'Just remember, I'm around if you need me.'

She headed to the exit of the ward. Just as she got there, the doors swung open and Toni and Keisha swaggered in. Amber stopped and fixed them with a stern stare. They passed slowly by her, defiantly staring back.

Amber glanced back at Bailey with concern. She seemed to know it was them who were responsible. She must have recalled what had happened in the canteen that time she had intervened.

She stood there for a few moments. Bailey gave her a small nod to indicate that she would be fine. She sighed again and shot Bailey one last anxious look and then left the ward.

Toni sat down on one side of her bed. Keisha sat down on the other side.

Bailey swallowed, her body tense. For a moment she wondered if they were going to finish her off, lying here, vulnerable as she was. Toni could easily slide a shank into her right here in the hospital bed.

Toni held her head poised upright, listening for the sound of the outer swing doors to the ward closing, ensuring that Amber was well out of earshot. Then she looked down at Bailey and broke into a wide grin, her gold tooth glinting.

'Welcome to our little club,' she said.

Bailey forced a weak smile. A mixture of relief and joy surged through her, momentarily eclipsing the pain. She was in. Her ploy had worked.

'You took your beating well,' said Keisha, nodding in admiration. 'When I saw Muscles lay into you, I thought you were a goner, but it appears you're tougher than you look.'

Toni's smile dropped off her face and she went serious again. She leaned into Bailey, gazing deep into her eyes. 'Just remember what I said though. Blood in. Blood out.'

'You never told me what "blood out" meant.' Although she wasn't sure she really wanted to know right now.

'It means that, now you're in, you can't ever leave. The only way out is by dying, by spilling your blood. So if you want to leave, just let us know and we'll be more than pleased to help you out on that front.'

Bailey nodded, trying to look like it didn't bother her. What had she gotten herself into?

'Sounds pretty straightforward to me.'

Toni scrutinised her thoughtfully. 'It's kind of fortuitous that you joined us when you did,' she said. 'Seeing as we're shy of one member.'

A dirty look passed between Toni and Keisha. Bailey wondered what Toni meant, but she didn't ask them to elaborate. It was a bit too early to start asking questions, particularly as she had the feeling that the answers wouldn't make very pleasant listening.

33

All in all, Bailey spent three days in hospital recovering from her injuries before the prison's medical staff felt reassured that she had improved sufficiently to be released back into the prison population. All the while she lay in the ward, her mind was riven with concerns that she had been out of contact with Frank and was wasting valuable time, but she managed to assuage her worries to a certain extent with the knowledge that all of this was ultimately serving a valuable purpose in helping to insinuate her with the gang.

By the time she was released, her black eye had gone down considerably, the other bruises had started to fade and the multiple aches and pains had subsided to the extent that she could move around without wincing too much. It turned out, fortunately, that none of her ribs had been broken and her tooth was fine, but she had required several stitches for the cut in her lip; the stitches would apparently fall out of their own accord within the next few days as the wound healed.

On leaving the hospital, she made her way across the prison yard in the direction of the phones to call Frank. The sun was shining brightly and she welcomed its warmth on her face. She felt like she hadn't been outside in ages. The weather seemed summery and she recalled that the calendar in the hospital had read 31 May. Summer was indeed almost upon them. She worked out that she had been incarcerated for just over two weeks now, although it felt like much longer.

Bailey had got about halfway across the yard when the gang appeared out of nowhere to intercept her. They closed in around her in a menacing fashion, Muscles looming up behind them, blocking out the sun. Bailey held herself upright and tried not to look scared.

'It's not quite over yet,' said Toni.

Bailey's stomach turned over for fear of what might be next. She prayed it wasn't going to be a repeat of what they'd just put her through. Or worse.

'Yeah,' said Keisha. 'We've got to get you inked up.'

* * *

Poppy was a member of the gang Bailey hadn't met before – a biker goth with pale skin and large green eyes, her black hair cut in a ragged fringe with a shaved undercut. She wore a dark grey vest which revealed numerous tattoos of a particularly striking quality. A psychedelic Day of the Dead skull ornamented with multi-hued flowers dominated her upper left arm, while a rattlesnake coiled down the entire length of her right arm. She had a knuckleduster engraved on the side of her neck and Bailey could make out some kind of French writing etched in an antique font across the top of her chest. The writing looked elegant, pretty even, but Bailey suspected its sentiments didn't match its style.

She sat on the chair in the cell, one knee up under her chin, observing Bailey, while the rest of the gang filed out, leaving just the two of them in there.

Poppy's cell was situated on the very top floor of C-Wing at the far end of the landing. From this high up, it was possible to see over the prison wall, to see the countryside which lay beyond – a patchwork of fields and woods and the blue expanse of a nearby reservoir. The cell felt akin to an eyrie and Poppy some kind of exotic beautiful bird which dwelt there.

Poppy eyed Bailey up and down, scrutinising her body with the professional detached eye of a craftsman. She looked serious, stern even.

'Take off your clothes,' she said, unsmiling.

Knowing there was no easy way out of this, Bailey obeyed, pulling off her shoes, then removing her trousers and then her vest, until she was standing there just in her underwear.

'And the bra,' said Poppy.

She took off her bra and dropped it on the floor on top of her other clothes. She crossed her arms across her breasts. Bailey's modesty elicited a small glint of amusement in Poppy's eyes.

'Turn around.'

Bailey turned around slowly, three hundred and sixty degrees. She could feel Poppy's eyes on her, an intense penetrating gaze, inspecting every inch of her body.

Poppy raised her eyebrows. 'Mmm… no tattoos. Unusual.'

It was true – almost every inmate Bailey had seen in here had a tattoo of one form or another.

'I could never think of anything I wanted engraved on my body for eternity.'

Poppy gazed at the lattice of scars with interest. Bailey dropped her arms to reveal the scars in their entirety.

Poppy frowned. 'Did you do those yourself?'

'I'm not the self-harming type.'

Poppy nodded slowly as if forming some unspoken opinion about her.

'Lie down on the bed, on your front.'

Bailey obeyed, positioning herself on the lower bunk, her head facing the door.

The chair creaked as Poppy stood up. She pulled the chair over to the side of the bed. On the chair, she placed a home-made contraption which Bailey assumed was the tattoo gun, along with an upturned bottle cap containing a small amount of a dense black liquid.

Poppy picked up the tattoo gun. Bailey eyed it with trepidation.

'Don't worry. It's sterilised,' said Poppy.

Looking closer, Bailey could see that the tattoo gun appeared to be constructed out of a toothbrush which had been cut down and bent or melted out of shape. The lower half of a biro formed the top of the gun, a tiny piece of wire poking out from where the ballpoint had been chopped off. Bailey assumed that was the needle. A small electric motor was taped to the back of the device. Bailey couldn't even begin to imagine where that had come from. Two long thin wires connected the motor to a battery that lay on the chair next to the gun. It was ingeniously constructed and Bailey marvelled at the resourcefulness it entailed.

'Very clever.'

'You have to make do with whatever's available in here.'

Bailey frowned. 'Does that mean you're going to use biro ink?'

Poppy tutted in disgust and shook her head. 'Your flesh'll rot if you use that. The biro tube is just a housing for the needle.' She pointed to the upturned bottle cap with its small amount of viscous black liquid. 'This is what we'll be using. It's my own personal recipe. It basically contains soot, which you get from burning cotton wool, a few drops of baby oil to thicken it and – to disinfect it – a dash of ethyl alcohol distilled from hand sanitiser. So there's no need to worry.'

She gave Bailey a brief thin smile. It was the first time she had smiled.

Without further ado, Poppy got onto the bunk and straddled Bailey. It was cramped and Bailey was acutely aware of Poppy's proximity. It was strangely intimate, to be so close to a stranger. Bailey realised she hadn't been naked and this close to another human being since...

Since her torture and violation at the hands of him.

At the thought of him, her nostrils filled with the phantom whiff of clove smoke, sweet and cloying. That's what he'd smoked – clove cigarettes. And she'd hated the smell ever since.

With some effort, she pushed those painful memories away from the light of day back down into the darkness where they belonged.

She felt Poppy run her fingertips lightly over the scars and burn marks on her back. Bailey flinched at the contact, even though it was fleeting and surprisingly tender.

'Sharp things and hot things by the looks of it. So how did these come about?'

The memories bubbled up again as Bailey flashed back to her previous undercover job. The nightmares. The razor blades. The burning tip of a clove cigarette. The horror.

'I'd rather not talk about it,' she said.

'Suit yourself.'

Poppy fiddled with the wire on the tattoo gun. It buzzed into life. The tiny needle turned into a blur as it went back and forth at high speed.

'Now keep still,' she instructed.

Bailey placed her head sideways on her crossed arms. She felt the needle penetrate the skin of her lower back, at the base of her spine. The pain was acute and concentrated. She winced and tensed.

Poppy immediately stopped. 'Does it hurt?'

It did hurt, although it was nothing compared to what she'd experienced before, to what had given her the scars that she bore. Anyhow, she reasoned that to admit any kind of pain would look weak to a member of a prison gang.

'It's fine. I can hardly feel a thing.'

Poppy gave a small murmur of approval and recommenced the tattooing, pausing from time to time to dip the needle into the tiny pot of tattoo ink.

Eventually, the area began to numb as Bailey's brain released pain-suppressing endorphins. It was an almost pleasurable feeling. She began to relax a little.

'What are you in for?' Poppy asked eventually.

Bailey recounted her cover story about being an accountant and embezzling money, reciting much the same as what she'd told Sharon. She felt the cover story rolling off her tongue easily enough. It felt good to say it out loud. Each time she spoke it, it made it feel a little more real, made it a little easier to say.

'That's interesting,' murmured Poppy.

To Bailey's surprise, she actually sounded sincere. 'Most people find accountancy very boring.'

'Being good at maths is a useful skill to have.'

'How did you end up in here?'

Poppy lifted the needle. The gun still buzzed. There were a few moments of silence.

'It's coming along nicely,' she said, dabbing at Bailey's lower back with a tissue.

Bailey realised she was referring to the tattoo. She guessed Poppy didn't want to talk about her crime, whatever that had been, so she didn't probe.

'The tattoo is more than just an ornament for us,' said Poppy.

'I guessed as much.'

'It's a way for us to recognise each other, to recognise another member, from another prison, if we've never met them before. We see the tattoo and instantly we can trust them. We know they're one of us.'

'What's stopping just anyone from getting one that looks the same?'

'If someone was stupid enough to get one of our gang tattoos without actually being a member of our gang, and we found out... well, we'd catch them, hold them down, and slice it out of their skin.' She paused thoughtfully. 'And then Toni would probably make them eat it. Just to make a point. Because that's the kind of person she is.'

Bailey shuddered at the thought of it.

She lay there in silence, subordinate to the buzzing tattoo gun drilling into her flesh. After a while, the numbing effect of the endorphins started to wear off, so she was relieved when Poppy finally stopped.

Poppy disconnected the battery from the tattoo gun and the buzzing stopped. She placed the gun on the chair.

She dabbed at her work with a tissue and dropped it onto the chair. Bailey saw that the tissue was soaked crimson with her blood.

Poppy got off the bunk and stood up.

'You can get up now.'

'Is that it?' said Bailey. She estimated they had been there for around half an hour.

Poppy shook her head. 'It's going to take several sessions. I don't want to overwork the skin. It'll end up scarred otherwise. Anyhow, after forty minutes or so, the pain tends to get quite uncomfortable. This is just the beginning. No need to rush it. After all, you want something good, don't you? It's going to last you your whole life.'

Bailey put her clothes back on and left Poppy's cell, her lower back tender and sore. As she walked along the landing, she wondered just how much it would cost to get the tattoo lasered off once she was out of this place.

34

'What the hell happened to you?'

Frank Grinham's dead watery eyes displayed an uncharacteristic glimmer of concern when Bailey sat down at his table in the visit hall. Her black eye and bruises were still visible enough to elicit concern.

'It was an initiation,' she said. 'I submitted to it voluntarily. It looks worse than it is.'

'If you say so. I was getting a bit worried I hadn't heard from you.' He paused and scrutinised her injuries. 'Does that mean you're in with them?'

She nodded, glancing around the busy visit hall, grateful that the noise and clamour, mostly from visiting children, was able to mask the sound of their conversation. They were sitting at the same corner table that they'd occupied on Frank's previous visit. This time, Bailey took careful note to keep an eye out for Sharon, but it didn't look like there was any sign of her in the visit hall today, which was a relief.

'And?' he said.

She turned her attention back to Frank.

'It seems that the ABC operate in other prisons besides this one,' she said. 'They recognise each other by means of the distinctive tattoos on the lower back.'

'I see. So they're fairly well-organised. This is good stuff, Bailey. Now we're starting to get a picture of how this drugs ring works.'

'The head honcho here is a psycho called Toni Quinn. She's in for murder and I think she's more than capable of scalping somebody. Her lieutenant is called Keisha Stone. There's another member called Rong Xi and a big one they call Muscles, who they use as an enforcer; her real name is Jane Foot. And then there's their tattooist; her name is Poppy O'Shea.'

'How are they getting the drugs into the prison?'

'I haven't found out yet. I've only just joined, remember? Plus, I've had a three-day unscheduled stay in the hospital. Anyhow, they're not going to start dishing out all their secrets just yet.'

'You need to locate the source. Remember what Alice said about him or her being well concealed.'

At that moment, a prison officer walked slowly by their table, patrolling the circuit of the visit hall.

'Auntie Jean's knitting you a sweater,' said Frank in a normal volume of voice.

'Oh, that's nice,' said Bailey. 'It does get a bit draughty in here sometimes.'

The prison officer passed out of earshot. The brotherly smile dropped off Frank's face, leaving him cold and exacting once more. He leaned across the table towards her.

'Just don't forget the focus of this operation. The drugs squad are the ones funding it, and their priorities are your priorities.'

'And what about Alice's murderer?'

'Follow the drugs and you'll find out who killed her.'

'Drugs or no drugs, I'll find out who killed her.'

35

The Governor was thinking about his yacht. Well, technically it wasn't his yacht just yet. In about six months he'd have enough money to buy it. Sailing was his passion and he'd been wanting to own a yacht for years and now the dream was soon to become a reality. He was a long-time subscriber to *Yachting World* magazine and had done plenty of research to identify the exact model he planned to purchase – a forty-foot Beneteau Oceanis. Once he got it, he'd sail it down to the Mediterranean and take a nice leisurely cruise around the Greek islands—

There was a knock on the door. He looked up, his pleasant fantasy dissipating immediately as he remembered with a sinking heart that he had to do an adjudication. That was the reason he was sitting by himself in this whitewashed room on this uncomfortable metal chair.

The adjudication was just one more thing on his plate that he didn't need right now, what with all the extra work he'd had to take on whilst they found an interim replacement for the Deputy Governor who'd just gone on maternity leave. They'd had someone lined up to fill her shoes, but the person had dropped out at the last minute due to other commitments and they were having problems finding a suitable replacement.

He sighed and opened up the inmate's folder, which was lying on the desk in front of him. He'd lost count of the number of adjudications he'd done over the long course of his career as a prison governor. He generally found them tedious, but they were a necessary part of his job.

An adjudication happened when an inmate committed an offence. If the offence was serious, like being caught in possession of a mobile phone, or assaulting another inmate, then they would be dealt with by an external adjudicator, who could award up to an additional forty-two days of imprisonment for each guilty verdict.

This offence, however, wasn't serious enough to warrant an external adjudication, hence his involvement. It was more of a simple disciplinary action.

'Come in,' he said.

The door opened and one of the male prison officers, Dylan, entered with an inmate. He nodded to Dylan, who left the room, closing the door behind him.

The inmate stood there, head bowed, hair hanging down over her face.

'Well don't just stand there. Take a seat,' he said, nodding at the empty chair on the other side of the table.

She sat down in the chair, hands in her lap, glancing up at him, hanging her head in a funny way as if she was hiding behind her fringe, unwilling to look him directly in the eye. He noticed then that she had a nasty black eye, several bruises on her face and stitches in her lip. All in all, she didn't look in a good way.

He looked down at her file. It contained details of her criminal history, her prison record and any other relevant information about her such as that gathered during her induction. She didn't come across much better in the mugshot which was stapled to the top left corner of the file. Dark rings under the eyes, barely able to look into the camera. He'd seen so many of these files and so many of these criminals had the same look about them.

This one's name was Bailey Pike and according to her criminal history she had been an accountant who'd embezzled money from her employers.

He looked up at her. Her apparent reluctance to meet his gaze only served to contribute to the kind of shifty furtive manner that he would have expected an embezzler to have.

Another one who'd thought she could get away with it but hadn't been smart enough to. He often thought that plain stupidity was the reason that most of them ended up in here. He imagined that she'd probably stolen the money and immediately gone out and bought a Porsche, which she'd then driven to work the next day. And then wondered why she'd got caught.

He scanned over the adjudication sheet in front of him, which contained the set of standard questions that he was required to recite by law. He had conducted so many adjudications that he knew the questions off by heart without any real need to look at the piece of paper.

'Have you received the form DIS1?' he asked.

That was the nicking sheet.

She nodded.

'Have you received the form DIS2?'

That was a record of how the hearing would progress.

She nodded.

'I'm now going to read out the charge,' he said.

She nodded.

He sighed to himself. So far she hadn't said a single word. She must have been terrible in court. One more reason that she'd ended up in prison.

He cleared his throat. 'The charge is one of reckless behaviour and attempted endangerment of your life. According to Shelley, it seems that you were playing some kind of silly game. She's under the impression that you were trying to pull a "fast one" on her. She says you told her that you saw some inmates selling drugs, but then you proceeded to jump off the balcony, much to the amusement of everyone who was there.'

He looked up at her.

'Is that correct?'

She nodded.

'Do you want legal advice or help during the hearing before we proceed any further?'

She shook her head.

'Have you had time to think about what you want to tell me and prepare a defence?'

She nodded.

'Will you be calling any witnesses?'

She shook her head.

'How do you plead? Guilty or not guilty?'

'I just haven't been myself since I've got in here,' she said.

Finally. She was speaking. He smiled.

'Guilty or not guilty?' he repeated gently but firmly.

'Not guilty.'

He made a note on the adjudication paper.

Now that the boring questions and procedure were out of the way, he would give her the talk that he gave them all, especially if it was their first adjudication.

'Look, I understand that things can be difficult in here and I want you to know that I want the best for you. I'm not the hang 'em and flog 'em type. I have an open-door policy, which means that you can request to come and see me in my office any time, within reason, to discuss anything that might be on your mind. Office hours, Monday to Friday.'

She nodded, disinterested.

He sighed and continued, 'I believe that all of you deserve a second chance. I know that many of you didn't have the right opportunities to start with or you may have made bad life choices for whatever reason.' He didn't mention plain stupidity.

She looked bored. She was a proper no-hoper this one.

He put on his most paternal tone. 'I want you to know that I genuinely care. I have three teenage daughters of my own and I certainly wouldn't want them to end up in here.'

They had better not, considering how much their private schooling was costing him. If he hadn't had to pay for that he could have bought his yacht years ago, but he supposed it would be worth it in the end.

The Governor did believe in the power of rehabilitation, but he also believed, from long experience, that it didn't work for all inmates. Some were just too far gone, and he was beginning to wonder if this one fitted into that category. And, by the sounds of things, she was mentally unstable.

'I think that the most productive outcome of this adjudication would be for me to refer you to the prison psychologist,' he said. 'So that's what I'm going to do.'

She rolled her eyes.

'I'm fine,' she said. 'I really don't need to see a shrink.'

'You don't have a choice in the matter.'

He closed her file and took a long look at her bruised features.

'And a word of advice before you go. I'd be careful about the kinds of people you get mixed up with in here. It's a small world and it can be very unforgiving... as it looks like you're already finding out.'

36

For lunch today, Bailey had been veering between the choice of jacket potato or beef goulash. She'd eventually gone for the beef goulash as it smelt particularly appetising.

She was sitting with the ABC at their corner table in the canteen. They were friendly now that they had accepted her as one of their own, but she was still careful to be wary. With people like this, you could never be quite sure. She knew from past experience that criminals could be the most amiable people one minute but then switch to the complete opposite in the blink of an eye. And when they turned nasty, they were capable of doing very bad things indeed.

One thing she had noticed since joining the gang was the marked difference in how she was treated by the other inmates. Now that they knew she was a member of the ABC, they generally made a point of staying out of her way and she caught a few of them looking at her with something approaching fear in their eyes. She had to admit, it felt kind of good.

Bailey casually scanned the canteen and noticed the skinny carrot-haired inmate who had tripped her up and spat on her not so long ago. She was sitting by herself a few tables away. Bailey fixed her with a piercing stare and soon caught the girl's eye. The girl appeared to recognise her, and when she saw who Bailey was sitting with, her eyes widened in fear. She went pale, dropped her gaze and suddenly took a very strong interest in the contents of her plate. Bailey allowed herself a little smirk.

'The last time I had beef goulash here,' said Keisha, eyeing Bailey's plate, 'I got the shits like you would not believe. Sometimes the food here just goes straight through me.'

Bailey looked at her plate of beef goulash. She poked at the brown lumpy stew with her plastic fork and stirred it around a little bit. For some reason, it didn't look quite so appealing any more.

'Did you know that diarrhoea is actually a genetic condition?' said Rong.

Keisha looked at her with mild surprise. 'Genetic condition? Really? I never knew that.'

'Yeah. It runs in the family.'

There was a brief pause, then a chorus of boos at the bad joke.

Muscles was frowning to herself. She didn't seem to get it.

'Man, you had me going there for a minute,' said Keisha, laughing and shaking her head. 'Genetic condition!'

Now that they were laughing and in a relatively good mood, Bailey decided that this would be an opportune moment to test the waters.

'So who am I replacing?' she asked, recalling Toni's mention in the hospital that the gang had been short of one member before she joined.

They all fell quiet and once again dark, cryptic looks passed between them.

Toni turned to look at Bailey with her cold hard gaze.

'Never you mind about that,' she said in a tone that firmly put an end to any further questions on the matter.

'Just remember what we said,' growled Keisha. 'Blood in. Blood out.'

It was an overt warning. More of a threat really. The harsh granite expressions on their faces said it all.

Bailey nodded obediently and went back to poking around in her beef goulash and they returned to talking about more mundane matters.

What Bailey found odd was that so far she hadn't heard the gang talking about the one thing that seemed to be on the lips of every inmate in here – the recent murders. The conspicuous absence of this topic in their conversation seemed somewhat suspicious to her. She decided to probe a little. Seeing as everyone else in the place was gossiping about it, surely it wouldn't sound too odd if she mentioned it.

'So what do you think is going on with these murders then?' she asked.

They all fell quiet and the mood suddenly turned distinctly chilly.

All eyes turned to Bailey. Toni's in particular seemed to bore into her.

Bailey swallowed. Had she overstepped the mark?

'You ask a lot of questions, don't you?' said Toni.

Bailey instantly regretted broaching the subject. The question had been too direct, too blunt. Her eagerness to find out what had happened to Alice had obscured her judgement. But she couldn't unsay it.

'What?' said Toni softly. 'Are you scared? Scared of getting scalped?' There was a taunting, mocking tone in her voice.

Toni slowly began to mimic a scalping, using her jacket potato as an ersatz human head. She sawed the skin off the top of it with the serrated edge of the plastic knife, revealing the white flesh of the potato underneath. All of them watched, transfixed.

When she'd sawn off the 'scalp', she held it up, dangling it between her thumb and forefinger and then she popped it into her mouth and started chewing it.

The others all burst out laughing. Bailey joined in, forcing herself to laugh along, even though she could find no humour in the situation.

Was it just a joke or was there a deeper truth to be uncovered?

'I'm not scared,' said Bailey. 'Just wanted to know if I need to buy any new shampoo in the shop or not. Won't be needing quite as much as normal if I get scalped.'

Toni and the others snorted in amusement.

Any tension that might have been there now disappeared, and the conversation turned to dessert.

Bailey decided there and then to be more careful about pursuing the issue. She didn't want to look suspicious. She'd have to be patient and bide her time. Softly, softly, catchee monkey, as the old proverb went.

She laughed and chatted with them for a while longer, then eventually made her excuses and got up to put her tray in the rack and leave the canteen.

Just as she was sliding her tray into the rack, a voice next to her said: 'I recognise you from somewhere.'

Bailey turned around. Standing next to her was an inmate she hadn't noticed before. She was small, with sallow rodent-like features. It took

Bailey a few seconds to recognise her, but when she did her stomach dropped.

'Yeah. I'm sure I know you,' the inmate continued, her eyes narrowing as she tried to place Bailey. 'Have we met before?'

Her name was Carly Potson and she had been some scrote junkie Bailey had arrested way back in her uniformed days, long before she'd started undercover work. She was surprised at the girl's power of recall, especially considering how many drugs she'd probably ingested over the years. If Carly made the connection, Bailey would be in big trouble as she would likely blurt it out right there in the canteen.

She should have known this might happen. Having arrested as many people as she had done in her career, it was always going to be a possibility that she would encounter one of them in here. She desperately tried to think what she could do to prevent her cover getting blown.

Out of the corner of her eye, she noticed Toni and the others standing up and walking towards her to put their trays in the rack.

Shit.

She could only pray that her appearance was sufficiently different, and that the context of the prison was sufficiently removed, that Carly wouldn't make the connection.

'No. You must be mistaken,' said Bailey.

Carly shook her head slowly. 'I swear I've seen you before.'

'Must be déjà vu.'

Carly peered hard at Bailey. 'No I don't think so... now where on earth was it?'

Toni and the others had now arrived at the rack. They were looking on with interest, hovering next to her. Perhaps because Bailey was new to their gang, they didn't quite trust her completely as yet and wanted to gauge who else she communicated with.

Bailey realised she had to do something right now to make Carly go away. As the undercover training instructor had repeatedly drummed into them, the ability to think on your feet and use your initiative were key attributes of being a successful undercover police officer. And right now she was thinking pretty hard...

She flicked her hair aside to reveal the jagged scar on the side of her face.

'See this?' she muttered.

Carly's eyes widened. She nodded.

'Seen it before?' said Bailey.

Carly shook her head. Bailey had obtained the scar some time after dealing with Carly, so Carly wouldn't have known her with the scar.

'Quite recognisable, isn't it?' She injected a mean tone into her voice.

Carly nodded, staring at the scar.

'I can give you one just like it if you want. Then everyone will recognise you very easily.'

Carly's eyes widened in fear. She shrank away from Bailey.

'Now fuck off and don't bother me again,' hissed Bailey.

Carly cowered and scuttled away out of the canteen.

The rest of the gang laughed and sniggered.

Toni patted her on the back. 'Way to go, champ!'

Bailey breathed a sigh of relief and brushed her hair back down over her scar.

She might have deflected suspicion this time, but that didn't mean this was the end of it by any means. Knowing that there was someone in here who could potentially identify her as a policewoman made her very, very uneasy. It made her situation inestimably more precarious. She couldn't afford to let it eat away at her though. She took a deep breath to calm herself. She'd just have to roll with it and pray that her act just now had done the trick. Hopefully she wouldn't be seeing any more of Carly Potson.

37

Bailey lay awake on her bunk in the darkness of the night, pondering her progress so far. From below came the gurgle of Sharon's snoring and the sporadic creak of the springs in her mattress as she shifted position in her sleep.

Beyond the locked cell, distant sounds echoed through the sepulchral Victorian edifice. The clang of a door opening and closing. The croak of muffled sobbing. The shout of a prison officer barking something to someone.

She'd been in here for almost three weeks, but it felt like considerably longer. She supposed it was good that she had adapted to prison life so quickly, but on the other hand, she had almost forgotten what life was like on the outside. Either way, she felt like she was making good headway in her investigation now that she had succeeded in infiltrating the gang.

It hadn't taken long, of course, for Sharon to notice her bruises and nascent tattoo, along with her new lunch buddies in the prison canteen. Sharon knew exactly who the ABC were and what they did, and apart from a few minor asides, she was uncharacteristically restrained when it came to asking Bailey about her involvement with them. Bailey guessed Sharon held them in the same wary regard as everyone else in the place. At the very least, she was grateful for anything that might help to keep Sharon off her case.

She turned onto her side to try and find a more comfortable posture, wincing slightly as she did so, the aches and pains from her beating a week ago still somewhat tender.

She was afraid, as always, to give in to the pull of tiredness for she knew what the night would bring. But the day's activities had drained her and she felt worn out. Slowly, inexorably, she closed her eyes and succumbed to sleep.

And the nightmares descended upon her, like they did every night, always the same...

She is in a dark cavernous room. A cold bare room with a concrete floor and metal girders for rafters. She is hanging from one of the metal rafters, chained up to a meat hook.

She knows that however loud she screams for help, no one will be able to hear her because this place is too isolated.

Her feet are not touching the ground and she can feel the hard metal chains biting into her wrists. She can feel the stress on her shoulder muscles as they support her body weight. But she knows this discomfort is nothing compared to what is to come.

As she hangs there, she realises that she is at the mercy of the figure waiting in the shadows.

Her torturer.

He is visible only by the red glow of a cigarette tip. Spiced smoke drifting towards her. The smell of a clove cigarette being smoked in the darkness.

Vainly, she peers into the shadows. Always she does this.

She tries to reason with him. Pleads with him. But it is no good. It is never any good. He is silent. He is watching her. He is relishing her discomfort.

He steps forward into the small pool of light cast by the bare overhead bulb. He is dressed in expensive clothes, metropolitan in appearance, very well-groomed, and there is a deceptively affable smile on his face.

He demands the name.

Always, he asks the name.

And always she refuses.

He takes the cigarette he is smoking and grinds the burning tip into her flesh.

She screams and writhes on the meat hook, but to no avail. She can smell her flesh burning. She can hear the sound of it sizzling. The hiss of the fat bubbling.

Once more, he demands the name.

Once more, she refuses.

Again with the cigarette. Again and again.

Still, she refuses to say the name.

Then he takes the cut-throat razor from the inside pocket of his designer jacket. Slowly, he opens it up, brandishing it in front of her, the wafer-thin steel blade sparkling in the light.

The name.

She refuses.

And he begins to slice into her flesh.

The blood running down her body. Slick and wet. Running in rivulets. Dripping off the ends of her clenched toes to drip, splat, splat, splat, onto the concrete floor, forming a crimson puddle beneath her.

The name.

She refuses. Screaming and crying.

The name.

The name.

The name.

The name.

She tries to force the name down. But the pain and horror always win out. In the end, she always succumbs. Please just make it stop. Anything to make it stop.

The name rises to the surface like a bubble of air escaping and there is nothing she can do to stop it bursting from her mouth.

Saying it over and over again.

'Spyros!'

* * *

Bailey jerked awake the next morning, the stench of her burning flesh still strong in her nostrils.

As always, she reflexively checked herself, running her hands over her body, surprised to discover that she wasn't bleeding and her flesh wasn't raw. The scars were now thin hard ridges of flesh and the burns were now coarse discoloured patches.

She rolled off her bunk and put the kettle on, noticing a faint shaking in her hands as she opened her breakfast packet. Not long after, Sharon yawned, stretched and got up to join her for tea.

They both sat there in the cell, drinking tea, neither of them saying much to the other. Sharon seemed uncharacteristically quiet and Bailey got the impression she wanted to say something. Eventually, she tilted her head at Bailey, a faintly quizzical expression on her face.

'You were saying stuff in your sleep last night.'

Bailey felt a burst of panic. What had she revealed?

'What was I saying?'

'You were tossing and turning a lot. That's what woke me up, see. The bed springs creaking. You were murmuring and moaning. You didn't sound happy. And then you started saying stuff.'

She cursed to herself. What if she had given her cover away?

'What kind of stuff?' she asked. She had to know if she'd revealed anything compromising.

'Something about Spyros. You kept saying the word Spyros. What's Spyros?'

Her heart thumped hard.

The name.

She'd said the name.

'Oh nothing.' She tried to sound casual.

'Sounds like a Greek restaurant.'

Bailey tried to emit what she hoped was a casually dismissive laugh.

'Is it a person?' Sharon enquired.

Bailey shrugged. 'I don't know. People say all kinds of stuff in their dreams.'

'I've heard you say it before when you've been sleeping. It must have some kind of meaning. Is it a bloke?' Sharon winked suggestively.

Bailey realised she needed to give Sharon something to sate her curiosity.

'Yeah, it was a bloke.'

'Ahh... thought so. You're a dark horse, Bailey.'

'But I don't want to talk about him,' said Bailey, deliberately flicking her lock of hair aside to reveal the scar on her face.

Sharon's face went serious, almost in a caricature of shock. 'Oh... he did that to you, did he? What a bastard!'

She didn't know the half of it.

38

Doctor Malcolm Bodie winced as he fingered the bruise on the side of his bald head and prayed that his next appointment wasn't the volatile type like the one who'd punched him the day before yesterday.

Still, as a forensic psychologist, it wasn't as if he was blind to these occasional risks of the job. They came with the territory. His particular profession was regarded as one of the most demanding positions within the field of clinical psychology and the circumstances could often be stressful. But, despite that, he never lost sight of the fact that it was necessary to maintain compassion for the inmates. After all, many of them had experienced the worst types of violence, abuse and drug addiction, and had become trapped in the kind of negative life cycles that he was here to help them break out of. The odd mishap aside, he generally enjoyed his job and derived a great deal of fulfilment from it.

His office was located in the administration block, not far from that of the Governor, and the decor was something he had given careful consideration to. On one shelf stood a variety of academic psychology tomes, none of which he actually needed to keep in there as he had read them all already, but he figured their presence lent a certain authority to his words and made the inmates take him more seriously. On another shelf was a ceramic phrenology head with the different parts of the mind traced out across its white glazed surface. Phrenology had been a nineteenth-century fad that was completely discredited these days, but he found that the inmates enjoyed looking at it and, like the books, it hopefully reinforced the clinical setting.

On his desk sat a framed photograph of his two children and a mug that bore the words 'World's Okayest Dad'. These again were calculated props to put the inmates at ease and make them feel able to connect with him as a human being. He knew that many of them had kids and he was happy to talk about his own if they asked. And they often did.

He peered through his wire-rimmed glasses at the file lying open on the desk in front of him. Reading through the notes, it appeared that his next appointment, Bailey Pike, had possible suicidal tendencies. She had been referred to him by the Governor as the result of an adjudication following an apparent attempt at self-harm. Suicide and self-harm were very serious issues and an increasingly prevalent problem inside the prison system. In today's one-to-one assessment, he hoped to get to the root cause of her suicidal thoughts and assess how far she might try to do something similar again.

He leafed through her file and briefly scanned her criminal history. The details were fairly sparse. An accountant who'd embezzled money from her employers. The nature of the crime gave little insight into her personality.

He turned to her intake evaluation – the psychometric tests she'd filled out when she'd been inducted into the prison – and began to study the results.

Interesting—

There was a knock on the door. He looked up. He positioned the mug so that the words 'World's Okayest Dad' would be plainly visible to the person sitting opposite him.

'Come in,' he said.

The door opened and the inmate came in, accompanied by a female prison officer. He smiled and nodded at the prison officer, who left, closing the door behind her.

'Hello, Bailey,' he said. 'I'm Doctor Bodie. Thank you for coming to see me. Please take a seat.'

She sat down on the other side of the desk, crossing both her arms and her legs. Her head hung forward to the left, her hair obscuring that side of her face. He could instantly tell from her body language that she appeared unwilling to engage.

He noticed that she had sustained some kind of beating as her face showed signs of cuts and bruising, not unlike his own, but somewhat worse.

He smiled at her. She smiled a thin perfunctory smile back at him. He knew she wasn't here of her own volition, but he had to find a way to break down the barriers somehow.

'It took me a while to find your file. It had been put back in the wrong place, probably by the Governor himself, I shouldn't be surprised! They keep all the files in these big filing cabinets in the room next door. Quite an antiquated system really. You'd think it would all be on computer these days, but it isn't. This place is so backward, they probably still use ledgers and quill pens like they did in Victorian times, eh?'

She sat there unmoved, looking at him with her grey eyes. So much for his attempt to break the ice.

He changed tack. 'I notice you have some nasty bruises on your face. I myself got punched the other day.' He pointed to the bruise on his forehead and attempted to laugh in an offhand manner. 'I can't say I enjoy being assaulted, especially when I'm just trying to do my job. Can I ask what happened to you?'

She sighed and rolled her eyes. 'I slipped and fell.'

Finally. She'd spoken. Obviously she was lying though. She clearly didn't want to reveal the true reason for her injuries, probably for fear of being perceived as a snitch. He could see that she was unwilling to disclose any further information.

Maybe a more direct approach would be better. He cleared his throat, leaned forward and steepled his fingers under his chin.

'So... you jumped off the balcony. Why did you try and do that?'

She shrugged and looked away, indifferent, unwilling to answer.

A difficult one, he thought. So many of them were like this, reluctant to help themselves.

'Have you attempted suicide or tried to self-harm before?'

'No.'

'Have you had psychiatric contact before?'

'I can't say I've ever found shrinks to be of much use in the past.'

'I see.' He began to scribble some notes on his notepad. 'And have you ever been diagnosed with a psychiatric disorder?'

'No.'

'Are you sure? When it comes to suicide and self-harm, there's often some kind of underlying psychiatric disorder lying at the root of it. Depression, panic, anxiety and post-traumatic stress disorder are among some of the things that can cause people to want to hurt themselves. Or sometimes substance abuse can be the problem. Drugs, alcohol and so on.'

'I feel just fine.'

'People who feel just fine don't usually jump off balconies.'

'Look, I just did it for a laugh, okay.'

'Now we're getting somewhere. Why would you do that? Why would you endanger your life "for a laugh"?' He made quotation marks with his fingers.

She exhaled impatiently and looked at her watch.

'Look, Doctor, I appreciate you trying to help me, but I assure you I'm perfectly okay.'

He was used to inmates being reticent but this one seemed to be particularly unforthcoming. He sighed.

'I'm glad you feel that way, Bailey, but I have to be sure that you're not at-risk. The fact that you conducted a near-lethal suicide attempt means that something's not quite right and I'm determined to find out what it is.'

She rolled her eyes.

He continued with a firm no-nonsense tone in his voice. 'I'm going to place you on the ACCT sheet. That stands for Assessment, Care in Custody and Teamwork and it means I'll be monitoring your mental health very closely. I'm particularly concerned for you because you're a relatively new inmate. Suicide rates are highest amongst those who've been incarcerated for less than thirty days, and you've been in here for just under three weeks.'

'You're wasting your time.'

This inmate's attitude was starting to stretch his patience.

'I'm here to help you, Bailey. But if you want me to help you, you have to want to help yourself. Remember, it's me who advises the parole board on your suitability for release. If you're not willing to improve, then you may be spending longer in here than you want to.'

A small smile flickered across her face.

'I'll leave here when I'm ready to leave,' she said.

'I'm glad you're so confident, but I have to make sure that you're fully rehabilitated and in a suitable mental state to be able to fit back into normal society. That's what I do with all the inmates here and you're no exception.'

He began to write down some further notes in her file, outlining the type of treatment programme he planned to follow with her.

'Rehabilitation's a waste of time,' she said suddenly.

'Really?' he peered at her over the tops of his glasses. There was no denying that there was something intriguing about her. On one hand, she seemed so closed, yet here she was suddenly willing to engage with him. 'Why do you think that?' he asked.

'Some people are bad people and they'll always be that way. Full stop. And there's nothing you or anyone else can do to change it.'

'That's a rather fatalistic view. So what do you suggest we do with these people?'

'Lock them up and throw away the key.'

He frowned. 'That's an odd attitude for an inmate to have. Most inmates in here believe that they've been unjustly imprisoned. Do you not feel that way about yourself?'

She chewed her lip and looked into the distance.

'I'm in here for a very good reason,' she said.

'I see. Well, at least you're being honest. That's a start. Being sent to prison is a big thing to happen to someone, Bailey. It often changes a person's whole approach to their own personal psychology. You can choose to learn from your mistakes. You can look at the path which brought you here. You have the ability to analyse the chain of decisions which resulted in your imprisonment. This is an important thing to do if you want to make progress.'

'Like I said, I'll leave when I'm ready.'

She looked determinedly into his eyes. In the sudden pause in conversation he found himself momentarily mesmerised by her grey unblinking stare. He dropped his gaze to the papers on his desk.

'You took some personality tests when you came in here. They make interesting reading. They indicate that you are intelligent, resourceful and enterprising, but also obstinate and perhaps even a little arrogant. You are self-contained and you place a heavy value on autonomy. You are not averse to taking risks and, in fact, it appears that you almost crave uncertainty and a distinct amount of stress. Is that true?'

She nodded slowly, smiling slightly. 'Spot on, Doctor. I guess I do get bored easily. I get antsy just sitting around.'

'Is that why you embezzled the money?'

She shrugged.

'Strange though,' he said with a frown on his face.

'What?'

'Well, your tests reveal a certain degree of social conscience which just doesn't gel with the nature of your crime, nor with a criminal personality generally. Quite a puzzling contradiction.'

She observed him silently, almost suspiciously, as if he had touched on something sensitive. The fact that she appeared to have clammed up again only stoked his interest in wanting to find out more about how she ticked.

'You have a lot of potential, Bailey. I think you genuinely possess the capability to turn your life around and make something of it. But I sense something else, something which is troubling you. Something lying just below the surface which you're not telling me. Something to do with the reason that you ended up in here.'

She gazed at him coolly with her grey eyes. He could tell she wasn't about to reveal anything further.

She looked at her watch. 'Can I go now?'

'Not just yet. I'd like to administer some further tests. Is that okay? Just to be on the safe side.'

'What kind of tests?'

Again that suspicious look on her face, as if she almost felt threatened by the prospect.

'They're just simple tests which can help me better understand your mental health.'

He took out several sheets of paper from a drawer and pushed them across the table to her, along with a biro. She looked at the long list of questions and emitted a puff of boredom.

The tests were commonly used psychological tools in his profession. One was the Beck Suicide Intent Scale. The other was the Wessex Dissociation Scale. With these two tests, he was hoping to establish the level of her suicidal thoughts and the possible explanations behind them.

'You'll see that each question asks you about how you feel. All you have to do is score each one on a scale of one to ten. Please fill it out honestly. It's in your best interests to do so.'

She sighed and began to fill out the questions. He watched her as she did so, noting for the first time the ugly white scar running down the side of her face and neck. She worked fast and diligently, marking the paper with confident flicks of the pen.

Many inmates needed help with the questions, often due to low levels of literacy, but this one was clearly smart and well-educated.

After a short while, she finished and pushed the completed tests back across the table to him.

She started to stand up.

'We're not done just yet.'

'There's more?'

'I have some homework for you.'

'Homework?'

'I'd like you to keep a daily diary of your thoughts. Positive, negative, however you're feeling at any given point of the day.'

'Sure,' she shrugged. 'Whatever you say, Doctor.'

He had a feeling she wasn't going to bother.

39

As Bailey made her way back to her cell, she reflected on her meeting with Doctor Bodie. She'd encountered his type on numerous occasions during the course of her police work – forensic psychologists often worked with the police on investigations to conduct criminal profiling. He came across as a bit of a do-gooder and she had found it mildly entertaining to toy with him, earnest as he was, but she was also wary of revealing too much of herself. After all, it was his job to be perceptive and she couldn't afford to let him suspect that she wasn't who she claimed to be. A couple of times he had got quite close to the mark and she was conscious of the need to stay on her toes the next time she saw him, that is, if she was still in here by the time her next appointment was due.

Once back in her cell, alone, she decided to examine her tattoo. Pulling her jogging bottoms down slightly to expose it at the base of her spine, she stood in front of the small plastic mirror, awkwardly twisting her head around so she could get a proper glimpse of it.

She touched it gingerly with her fingertips. Although it had scabbed over, it still felt tender and raw. But it looked fresh and sharp and there was no denying Poppy's skill as a tattoo artist. This wasn't some crude prison scrawl. It was an elegant and striking design, and it wasn't even finished yet.

Poppy had completed the outlines of the three fanned-out playing cards and had drawn in the letters 'ABC', but she had yet to start on the skeleton clutching the ace of spades dagger.

The lines were clean and well-defined and the shading had been expertly executed with a finely stippled effect. It was amazing to think that she'd been able to accomplish this with such a basic tool as the home-made tattoo gun and ink.

When Bailey had woken up that morning, she had found that ink had drained out of the tattoo onto her bed linen. She had pulled back the covers to see, imprinted on the white sheets, an exact impression of the lines etched into her back. She wondered what they would think in the laundry.

Later on, when she'd taken a shower, more ink had run out of her, and bits of coloured skin had fallen off and washed down the plughole with the soapy water. It was kind of disgusting, but she guessed that her body was ejecting the excess ink. What remained there beneath the lower subcuta-neous layers of skin would be there forever unless she had it removed, although she was now thinking twice about having it lasered off, so impressed was she with the quality of Poppy's handiwork.

The good thing about the tattoo was that it increased her credibility as a convict, not just in the way that she was perceived by the other inmates but also in the way that she felt about herself – it helped her get into the right frame of mind psychologically to perform this role.

She had found when working undercover that the clothes you wore and the attitude you projected made people respond to you in a particular manner, which in turn reinforced the way you felt about yourself. It might have seemed like a superficial thing, but it was inestimably important when it came to maintaining a credible cover. It was the kind of thing which could mean the difference between gaining someone's trust or not. It could even mean the difference between life and death.

Pretending to be someone else wasn't as easy as it might have seemed though, especially when you had to act like you enjoyed the company of profoundly unpleasant people. Whatever you felt like on the inside, you couldn't afford to let your cover slip for one moment.

Of course, there was always the concern in the back of the mind of every undercover police officer that a situation might arise where they would become so immersed in their role that they would forget who they had once been, that the person who would eventually emerge when the job was over would be someone completely different, someone permanently soiled by the darkness and corruption of that criminal world.

Bailey had never come close to that herself, but she certainly didn't want to be in this prison any longer than she had to.

Natalie Spakes lay asleep on the bunk, her long thick hair splayed across the pillow, her young face banded with shadows cast by the bars of the window, beyond which a sharp crescent moon hung brightly in the clear black sky.

She breathed in and out softly, her chest gently rising and falling, an occasional indecipherable murmur escaping from her lips.

She was the sole occupant of the cell. That was because the cells in the segregation block were each designed to only accommodate one inmate.

The segregation block lay separate from the four main house-blocks over on the northern side of the prison complex. It housed those inmates who could not mix with the general prison population for whatever reason – those who were vulnerable to assault by other inmates, such as snitches and sex offenders, and those who were particularly violent or unstable.

Lying there asleep, it was hard to tell which category Natalie belonged in. She looked deceptively peaceful, with no outward indication of the kind of trouble that might have brought her into this special accommodation unit.

The gentlest of breezes ruffled the hairs on her head.

She stirred a little and rolled over.

The fine hairs on her earlobes swayed imperceptibly.

She inhaled suddenly and her eyes popped open. She lay there looking up at the ceiling, wondering why she had woken up in what seemed to be the middle of the night.

Her mind immediately went to her four-year-old son. His name was Kyle. He was usually the first thing she thought of when she woke up. She missed him a lot. Her boyfriend on the outside was currently taking care of him. All she wanted was to be reunited with Kyle and in an indirect way that was kind of the reason she'd ended up in segregation.

She had originally been imprisoned for handling stolen goods. It had started casually, with a few things here and there – stolen phones and the like – but had eventually escalated to larger-value items from the proceeds of professional burglary. She had been sentenced to two and a half years, but with any luck she'd be out before then, if everything worked out...

She had been in the segregation block for almost a month now and she was in here for her own protection. One thing she did like about it was that it was considerably quieter than the rest of the prison. Its isolated location and the fact that she didn't have a cellmate meant that she usually slept much better, which was why she found it odd that she had woken up all of a sudden.

What the hell had woken her?

She turned her head to the side and slowly scanned the shadows of the cell. Then her eyes widened and her body tensed, awake now.

She squinted and did a double-take. She rubbed her eyes.

She had to still be dreaming surely.

She knew that she must still be dreaming because what she saw defied reality. It defied the reality she knew, that she had become accustomed to in this place.

The cell door was wide open. It was open and unlocked and beyond it lay the dark maw of the corridor.

A shiver ran through her. She blinked again and shook her head, clearing the cobwebs of sleep from her mind.

But the vision remained the same. The door was wide open.

She slowly pulled the covers aside and stepped from the bed, her prison-issue vest scant protection from the chill night air, goose pimples immediately forming on the surface of her skin, on her arms and legs.

She brushed her hair out of her eyes.

Mesmerised by the black rectangle of the doorway, she straightened up and padded towards it, pausing at the threshold.

She had walked in and out of this cell many times before. But that was in the daytime. Now, at night, it was different. This cell was her home, her comfort zone. Out there, it was dark, in shadow.

A primal fear tugged at her, but something else – curiosity – made her tentatively place her foot over the threshold, the black shadow engulfing her toes, then the rest of her foot.

The open door was inviting her to walk through it and she couldn't resist. It was almost as if she was hypnotised by it. The rest of her body was swallowed by shadow as she passed through the portal and left the cell.

Out in the corridor, all was dark and silent. Oblique shards of moonlight cut across the shadow, but everything else was black.

At night it looked much bigger and felt much emptier, like the vast emptiness of space, almost infinite in what it could contain.

She stood there for a moment outside her cell, enveloped in the murk. The concrete floor was cold and gritty beneath her bare feet. She was silhouetted in the doorway by the moonlight entering through the small window in her cell, her figure defined in a square of light cast against the opposite wall of the corridor.

Again, the faintest of breezes ruffled the hairs on her head. It was as if the prison was alive and the corridor a respiratory tract within this vast slumbering beast as it breathed slowly in its sleep.

She inhaled... exhaled. Relaxing now, accustoming herself to this new and unusual situation.

But then a noise...

The tiniest of scuffles... out there in the shadows. Indistinct. A scraping of something across the pitted surface of either the floor or the walls of the corridor.

She froze, her goose pimples rising up even further, the tiny hairs on the surface of her skin standing up. Her eyes narrowed, her pupils widening to let in as much light as possible onto her retinas as she strained to peer into the darkness to make out whatever it was that was out there, because there was definitely something out there.

She strained to listen.

Silence once more. Was she imagining it?

Again, a scuffle. No, there was definitely something out there. There was something moving in the corridor.

The rustle of fabric on fabric.

Her breathing became a little faster now. Her heart beat a little harder. She swallowed and squinted out into the darkness.

Suddenly a movement. Something cut through a shard of moonlight. Out of shadow and back into shadow, so fast that she couldn't make out what it was.

She stifled a gasp as a jolt of fear went through her. She took an involuntary step backwards and bumped into the door frame of her cell. She grasped it for support, her palms slippery with perspiration.

Craning her head, her gaze shifted from one shard of moonlight to the next. But there was nothing.

A rustle of fabric, closer now, just a few metres from her. Something there. Someone there.

She retreated back into her cell, back into her comfort zone, away from the alien darkness of the corridor and whatever lurked there.

But she realised then that she was trapped in here. There was no route of escape and she could not close the door because it locked from the outside.

An intense terror took hold of her, rooting her to the spot. The segregation block, supposedly the most secure part of the prison, offered no protection for her now.

She stood there in the middle of her cell transfixed by the black rectangle of the doorway and what was about to emerge through it, for she knew something was coming.

In the shadows, silence.

Then she saw it...

The glitter of metal.

The glitter of polished steel.

And the figure standing there, wreathed in penumbra, holding the blade in a black leather-gloved hand.

She opened her mouth to scream.

And then the figure came at her out of the shadows. Lightning fast. Faster than she could anticipate. Faster than she was able to draw breath to form a scream.

41

The lockdown was the first sign that something was up. Soon after that there was a cell search, in which a prison officer wearing rubber gloves rooted through her personal belongings. His name was Brian Bunter as Bailey recalled. She'd never talked to him before.

'Hey it's Brian, isn't it?' she said. 'What's going on?'

But Brian wasn't particularly forthcoming, merely issuing a non-communicative grunt. He was somewhat overweight and his bald head had begun to glisten with a faint sheen of sweat from the exertions of lifting up their mattresses to look underneath.

'Looking for murder weapons?' she asked.

He looked up at her sharply, his eyes narrowing suspiciously.

'I thought so,' she said.

'Another murder?!' said Sharon, who was standing in the corner watching him with her arms crossed. 'What's that now? Three? How about bumping up security a bit?'

'What do you want? A personal bodyguard?' he sneered.

'Feeling a little bit safer would make a nice start.'

'Are you scared?' he taunted.

'No!' she said defensively, but to Bailey's ears she didn't sound too certain.

As soon as the lockdown was lifted, Bailey headed down to the prison yard. As she made her way along the landings and descended the stairwells, she couldn't help but catch the dark murmurs of the inmates huddled protectively in their groups. Already they knew about the murder. The guards, too, conversed with one another in low, grave tones, momentarily hushing when she passed. A palpable feeling of fear and suspicion permeated the echoing dingy Victorian structure and she was glad to get outside.

Standing in the sunshine, she peered around the yard. She spotted the gang sitting on one of the concrete picnic benches.

They nodded to her as she went over and sat down amongst them. She was keen to find out what they knew of the situation, but they were midway through verbally abusing the remaining police forensics officers and detectives who were packing their material back into their vans a short distance away on the other side of the chain-link fencing.

They were making the inevitable pig-snorting noises and turning up the ends of their noses in imitation of pigs' snouts.

'I smell bacon!'

'Fucking pigs!'

'Oink oink!'

Bailey played along with them in an attempt to fit in, feeling vaguely embarrassed for herself and for her police colleagues who, if they were in earshot of the taunts, pretended not to hear them.

Eventually the mockery subsided.

'Do you know what they do to pigs in abattoirs?' said Toni, a nasty grin on her face. 'They hang them upside down and cut their throats. That's what I'd do to a pig if I had one all by myself.'

Bailey observed her. Was she making a veiled reference to Alice?

The thought of what Toni might do to her if she ever discovered that she was a police officer was too awful to contemplate. But at the same time she felt exhilarated that she was fooling them.

That was one of the things she loved about working undercover – the adrenaline rush you got from being in dangerous situations, from being around people who'd kill you in the blink of an eye if they knew you were a cop, where even the smallest slip-up could cost you your life. It was a perpetual high-wire act and most of the time there was no kind of safety net. Her non-undercover police colleagues admired her guts but also thought she was crazy. But they'd never understand. No one ever understood until they'd actually done it. The adrenaline was a drug, perhaps the most dangerous drug of all – seductive, terrifying and powerfully addictive. That's what had hooked Bailey in the first place and still now she craved it...

Toni turned to Bailey and met her stare. For a few brief seconds, Toni looked into her eyes. Then she spoke softly, dangerously.

'What would you do if you had a pig all to yourself?'

Bailey tried to think of an appropriate response but all she could come up with in the heat of the moment was: 'I've always been partial to pork scratchings myself.' She imbued her words with what she hoped was a sadistic tone, hoping they'd read something unpleasant into it.

Puzzled glances passed between members of the gang. She cringed inwardly.

Then Keisha nodded and smiled in approval.

'Yeah! Skin them alive and then deep-fry them. I like it!'

They all laughed. Toni looked grudgingly amused.

'So what's going on?' said Bailey, nodding towards the police vans, trying to sound as casual as possible.

'A murder in the segregation block,' said Rong.

'A scalping?'

Shrugs passed around. Bailey couldn't tell if it was because they genuinely didn't know or whether they were just being coy.

'Who was it?' she asked.

'Someone who'll be sorely missed,' said Toni.

From the heavy sarcasm in her voice, Bailey guessed that whoever had been killed wasn't a friend of the gang.

They didn't say anything more about it and Bailey decided not to pursue the matter. For now.

42

Creepers of smoke curled through the air, sinuous and sleek. They twisted and broke, disintegrating into the grey haze which filled the cell. The low bass thump of the dub pulsed softly from the stereo system.

Strings of origami ducks hung from the ceiling, attached to lengths of cotton. They twisted and turned slowly in the layers of grey smoke. Crazy Mel's handiwork was everywhere. It looked like an infestation of brightly coloured origami creatures had overrun the cell.

Kay, Seema and Mel sat slumped in a dope haze.

Seema took a drag of the joint she was holding, the harsh herbal smoke biting into her lungs. She held it down for a few moments then released it, letting it escape upwards from her mouth in a vertical stream.

She pondered on the important matter that they were discussing, listening to Kay as she held forth on it.

'That's when the red warning lights go off,' Kay was saying. 'That's when the alarm bells start ringing. When the price is actually printed on the packet.'

'I agree with you to a certain extent,' said Seema. 'When you see that, you know the quality isn't going to be great.'

'I mean, a pack of custard creams for thirty-five pence? The manufacturers actually feel the need to state that on the packet, to make sure that they're not sold for any more than that. It's like an explicit admission that these are biscuits of an inferior quality.'

'Yeah, but custard creams have never been a high-end biscuit. They've always been a working-class biscuit.'

'I'm just using them as an example. The same can apply to bourbons, Jammie Dodgers, fruit shortcakes...' She counted them off on her fingers.

They were revisiting one of their favourite topics of conversation – biscuits. It was a complex and diverse subject that all three of them were able to discuss for hours on end.

'I think one thing it's important to remember,' said Seema, 'is that it's possible to mitigate the poor quality of any biscuit merely by dunking it in a cup of tea.'

Kay shook her head. She wasn't convinced.

'But even on that level inferior biscuits possess suboptimal dunkability potential. Surely you must have noticed that?' She turned to Mel. 'Mel? Have you noticed that?'

But Mel was just sitting there staring at the opposite wall, her eyes wide open, trapped in some kind of trance, and had clearly not been paying attention to what they had been talking about.

Kay snapped her fingers in front of Mel's face. 'Mel? Earth to Mel. Come in, Mel.'

Eventually, Mel blinked and looked at them. She swallowed. Her eyes rolled fearfully.

'He's a duppy,' she whispered hoarsely. 'He's in here and he's gonna get us. Mi fraida duppy!'

Kay raised her eyes to heaven. 'You and your bleeding duppies. They're nothing but old wives' tales. They're all you ever seem to be going on about since your cellmate got topped.'

It appeared that Mel was still fixated on their previous conversation – about the most recent murder.

'It did happen in the segregation block,' said Seema. 'That place is like a fortress. Big thick walls and permanently locked doors. Yet Natalie was murdered inside her cell. Tell me how that happened. I mean, if you're not safe in segregation, then where are you safe?'

'Locked doors and walls don't mean nothing to a duppy,' said Mel. 'He can walk through walls. If a duppy wants to get you, he'll come and get you wherever you are.'

'What a load of bollocks!' scoffed Kay. 'Natalie was a snitch. That's why she was in segregation. That's why she was killed. End of story.'

'But scalped?' said Seema. 'She was killed just like the others. That's what I heard. All carved up. Like properly fucked up. There's something weird about that. Something evil.'

'Ah duppy killed her,' said Mel, her voice rising an octave.

'Duppies don't exist,' sneered Kay. 'Just like Santa doesn't exist.'

Mel fixed her with a baleful stare. 'Duppies a real! Mo real dan yuh can know! Inna Jamaica everyone knows dat duppies a real! De duppy ah guh fi guh cum inna here an guh fi guh kill wi aal!'

Seema and Kay glanced at each other. When Mel started talking in patois, it meant she was working herself up into one of her frenzies, and once she got going it was never quite certain what the consequences could be. They didn't call her Crazy Mel for nothing.

Seema grabbed the stack of origami paper and shoved it at Mel. Mel started folding furiously, obsessively constructing an origami duck, folding the paper back and forth. Faster and faster. Like a blur. Her eyes wide.

They watched her, strangely fascinated.

The completed duck tumbled onto the floor alongside the other origami creatures. Seema picked it up and began to string it onto a length of cotton.

Mel plucked another sheet of paper and started another creature, the haunted look never leaving her eyes.

Kay and Seema weren't in the mood to discuss biscuits any more.

43

The morning meeting wasn't going well for the Governor. The prison officers, sprawled across the chairs in front of him, seemed to be in a particularly defiant mood today.

'I think I can speak for all of us,' said Terry, 'when I say that security is quite clearly a systemic issue within this prison. There have been three murders now. Three brutal murders.'

'The last one happened inside the segregation block,' said Amber. 'That's maximum security. That's supposed to be one of the safest places in the prison.'

'I'm well aware of the implications,' snapped the Governor. 'This is both completely unprecedented and completely unacceptable.'

He sternly scanned the assembled prison officers.

'I have been talking to the police and we are both of the opinion that a member of staff may have been involved in some way.'

He let his words hang ominously in the air. He scrutinised each of them in turn, hoping to detect a shifty lowering of the eyes or some other physical giveaway indicative of guilt.

The officers themselves were looking around now, regarding each other anew, their perceptions of their colleagues tainted with the seeds of suspicion. The atmosphere was one of unease and uncertainty.

The Governor had them on the back foot now and he was pleased about that. It made him feel like he was in control again.

'The police will be questioning you all in depth and they will get to the bottom of it,' he said. 'And you will extend your fullest co-operation towards them.'

They muttered and groaned and exchanged resentful looks with each other.

'Why are we the ones who are being treated as criminals?' remarked Terry. 'We're just trying to do our jobs the best we can.'

'You will co-operate with the police,' repeated the Governor. 'And you will help them get to the bottom of it.'

'And in the meantime?' said Maggie. 'The inmates are getting jumpy. They're getting scared. They don't feel safe. We have a duty to protect them.'

'Business will go on as usual,' said the Governor. 'Unless you're suggesting some kind of permanent lockdown, you know as well as I do that there's little else we can do beyond what we're already doing.'

They all knew that the prospect of a permanent lockdown was completely unviable. Even just a temporary lockdown caused huge disruption, affecting everything from the processing of new inmates to the operation of basic services such as the canteen. But, more significantly, the Governor knew that that kind of emergency action would signify to those outside, not least to his superiors, that he had lost all control over the situation inside the prison. And he would never permit that to appear to be the case.

'You could hire more staff,' said Terry. 'This kind of thing is happening because we can't do our jobs properly. Because we're understaffed and overworked. Not only is it affecting the safety of the inmates, it's affecting our safety as well. So far it's just been them who've been getting murdered, but I can't imagine it'll be long before it's one of us. We need more staff and we need side-handle batons.'

The Governor rolled his eyes and sarcastically mouthed 'side-handle batons' as Terry was saying it. He'd heard that petition so many times before.

'You'll make do with what you've got,' he said.

'We'll see what the union has to say about that,' Terry huffed.

44

Bailey lay there and tried to focus her mind on something other than the sharp pain in her lower back as the tattoo gun drilled its intricate patterns into her flesh.

Poppy was once again sitting astride her on the bunk, working intently on the design.

'Tell me more about your crime,' said Poppy, pausing to dip the tattoo needle into the tiny pot of ink on the chair beside the bunk.

Bailey was surprised that Poppy was so curious about the reason that she had supposedly ended up in here. It wasn't as if it was a particularly interesting or unusual crime, and she'd already told her a bit about it during their previous session.

It did cross her mind that Poppy might have been tasked with probing her story in a little more depth in order to confirm that she was actually who she said she was.

Either way, Bailey had no choice but to recite her story just the way she had rehearsed it so many times in her head.

'Like I told you before, I worked in the accounts department for a big marketing company. People never suspect that the mild-mannered person in accounts is actually stealing hundreds of thousands of pounds from the company. I guess their mistake was that they had the same person responsible for setting up new vendors, processing invoices, making payments and reconciling the financial statements. That person was me.

'I saw how much the top executives would spend on their business trips, on entertaining top clients, and so on. So I thought I'd take the opportunity to siphon off a bit of that cash for myself. The company was rolling in it and I thought they wouldn't notice if a little bit went missing here and there.

'It was dead easy as there wasn't really any system in place to check what I was doing. It was pretty simple for me to set up a new vendor, a made-up company which appeared on the financial statements as "Corporate Services Ltd". It sounded convincing enough not to raise any suspicions and it sounded suitably bland enough that it could have been providing anything from corporate entertainment to logistics.

'I billed the marketing company for the services provided by this fake vendor, processing the invoices myself and then writing the cheques to be paid directly into their bank account, which happened to be my own personal bank account.'

'Hmm... very clever. So how did you get caught then?'

'How do you think? I got greedy didn't I. You see, no one noticed at the beginning. It was just too easy. I got overconfident and started to increase the amounts. But then all it took was somebody questioning a particularly large payment to "Corporate Services Ltd", and it all began to unravel. They suspected something was up, so they brought in a forensic accountant behind my back to do some digging around. They checked out the vendor and found out it was fake and that was that.

'If I'd have kept it low-key, I'd have gotten away with it. I'd have flown beneath the radar and no one would have been any the wiser. I'd probably still be doing it now.'

'Well, maybe things are meant to happen for a reason,' said Poppy. 'Maybe it was fate that brought you in here.'

There was something slightly cryptic about Poppy's response and Bailey couldn't quite work out what she was getting at.

'Yeah maybe, but hopefully not fated to get scalped though,' she said, steering the conversation in a new direction.

Poppy sighed. 'It's a pity really. I kind of liked her.'

'Who?'

'Natalie.'

'You knew her?'

Apart from her name, Bailey knew next to nothing about the latest victim, save that she had met her demise whilst incarcerated in what was supposedly the securest part of the prison.

'It doesn't seem like that long ago that she was lying right here on this bunk where you are now, getting her tattoo done.'

Bailey perked up, lifting her head. 'You mean...?'

'She used to be one of us.'

'A member of the ABC?'

'Didn't you know?'

Toni and the others had mentioned nothing to hint that Natalie had once been a member of the gang. This was a revelation. This was just the kind of information Bailey had been hoping to find out.

'They don't tell me anything.'

'That's because you're new.'

'Is that why she was in segregation?' Bailey asked.

'She wanted out. But you know how it is...'

'Blood out...'

'Apparently she was going to snitch on us. I guess that ain't going to happen now.'

Now it all made sense. The talk of being one member down and the dark looks that had passed between the gang whenever the subject arose. Natalie was the missing member. Natalie was a snitch. Natalie had wanted to leave the gang. And there was only one way to leave. Blood out.

The question Bailey was dying to ask was on the very tip of her tongue...

'Right, that'll do for today,' said Poppy, wiping the blood and excess ink from the tattoo. 'It'll take a few more sessions to get the details completed, but I want to make sure it's perfect.'

The moment had passed. Bailey felt a rush of frustration. She had been tantalisingly close to finding out the truth, she was sure of it.

She got off the bunk and put her clothes back on before glancing at her watch. Twenty minutes of free association time left. She hoped the queues at the phones weren't too long.

45

'And that's the reason it's called HMP Foxbrook. Because of the River Foxbrook.'

Bailey stood in the queue for the phones half listening to Maggie as she cheerfully regaled the waiting line of inmates with facts and tales about the prison's history.

Maggie was there to clear the queue and make sure that all the inmates went back to their cells when free association ended, which it would in about eight minutes' time. But she appeared to be enjoying the opportunity to explain the etymology of the prison's name to what was essentially a captive audience.

Bailey looked at her watch anxiously and willed one of the phones to become free soon. She had reached the very front of the queue and she was impatient to update Frank with what she had learned.

She glanced behind her. Some of the inmates were making a point of yawning widely, but that didn't seem to deter Maggie from her mission to educate them on the more obscure points of the prison's background. As prison officers went though, Bailey thought that Maggie seemed a good type and she did actually find some of her facts quite interesting.

Noticing a phone become free, she quickly hurried over to it. There were six minutes left within which to make the call. She punched in her PIN number and then dialled Frank's telephone number. Rita answered after two rings.

'Hello, Sullivan Knight Solicitors. How can I help?'

'It's Bailey Pike speaking. I'd like to talk to Mr Knight please.'

'Just putting you through.'

She got to listen to five seconds of Beethoven's 'Moonlight Sonata' before Frank came on the line.

'Have you found out how the drugs are getting into the prison?' he said, bypassing the usual pleasantries.

'I'm still working on it,' she said.

'Well work harder. The drugs squad are on my case. They're the ones ploughing cash into this operation and so far they haven't received any actionable intelligence from you.'

She didn't take his harsh tone too personally. She remembered now that he got like this whenever he was under the cosh.

'Leave it with me, Frank. You know I'll deliver the goods one way or another.'

'Do you have anything that you can tell me?'

'Natalie Spakes was scalped.'

'I already know that. You, on the other hand, as an inmate, are not supposed to know that. We haven't made that information public.'

'Word gets around fast in here. Same signature. Same killer. I'm ninety-nine per cent certain it's the gang. Did you know that she used to be a member? And she wanted out. Apparently she was planning to blow the lid on their activities.'

'Yeah I know. Her boyfriend mentioned it. He's pretty cut up about her death. They've got a kid you know. A four-year-old. The kid's the reason she wanted to leave the gang. She was hoping that by snitching she could get out earlier so she could be with him. I can't understand why she joined them in the first place.'

'Protection. Prestige. Peer pressure. Who knows? You wouldn't understand unless you were in here. Being in here twists your perspective on things.'

'The murder investigation team are working off the possibility that a member of staff may have been involved, if not in actually committing the crime, then at least in facilitating it. She was found dead in a locked cell in a particularly secure and heavily monitored part of the prison. Somebody with access to a set of keys must have been complicit somehow. What's more, the cameras to that part of the prison went down shortly before the murder happened. They thought it was a technical glitch, so they called an engineer out, but he wasn't able to get there until the next morning, by which time the deed had already been done.' He paused. 'It turns out that some wires had been cut.'

'Cut?'

'Apparently there was a small vulnerability in the wiring leading to the segregation block. Anyone who knew about it – staff or inmate – could have cut those wires.'

The fact that the murder had taken place in the segregation block had been a strong hint to Bailey that a member of staff was embroiled in some way, but the news of the wire cutting illustrated just how audacious and determined the perpetrators actually were.

'The whole thing must have been planned out in advance,' she said. 'It looks like the drugs ring and the murders are all tied up together. If a member of staff was involved in Natalie's murder, then I bet that same person or persons is helping the gang get the drugs into the prison. We just need to work out who they are.'

'According to the rota, there were over thirty prison officers on duty that night – Friday the seventh of June. They've interviewed all of them, but no one seems to know anything. Like I mentioned before, the staff aren't particularly co-operative and the inmates even less so.'

'What about forensics? DNA? Surely that must have thrown up something.'

'Inconclusive. Just like with the other two. When it comes to DNA, there's just too much opportunity for cross-contamination to make it a reliable source of evidence. Even in segregation, Natalie's clothes, her bedding, her food, could have come into contact with numerous members of staff and inmates through a variety of means.'

Maggie came over to Bailey and tapped her wristwatch, indicating that her time was almost up. Bailey nodded and smiled, waiting until she'd moved away before continuing.

'The fact that she was murdered in segregation means that they're sending a clear message that no one is safe from them,' she said.

'If a member of staff is involved, then we need to find some way to narrow it down. Currently there are just too many contenders and not enough information to pinpoint any one of them as a feasible suspect.'

Maggie had come back again and was now gesturing for her to tie up the call.

'Look I have to go now,' said Bailey. 'I'll do my best.'

And she hung up.

46

Amber patrolled slowly around the edge of the canteen keeping a watchful eye on the inmates as they ate their dinner. It looked like chilli con carne was on the menu and the smell of it made her mouth water.

Dylan had been in here a few moments earlier, revealing the secrets of his special guacamole recipe to her, a side dish he said he always liked to make when he had chilli. Somehow he'd ended up making her laugh even though it was just guacamole he'd been talking about. Something about putting so much salt in it that you'd have a stroke before you'd even finished eating it. He was a ladies' man, no doubt about that. He had that twinkle in his eye. And she knew when someone was trying to chat her up. Still, she didn't mind. She was kind of flattered. He was quite handsome, she supposed. And, anyhow, it temporarily lightened the grim atmosphere that had been enveloping the prison of late. But now that he'd excused himself to go off somewhere, she was all by herself in here and once again she felt that ubiquitous aura of unease descend upon her.

Although everything seemed outwardly calm, there was an indefinable sense of something else in the air. A tension, like that atmospheric electricity you felt in your skin just prior to a thunderstorm.

She knew what it was of course. The recent spate of murders had really put the wind up the inmates, made them more fearful, more uptight than normal. She had noticed that there had been more flare-ups of late, attributable no doubt to this heightened state of agitation. With each new killing, the tension seemed to ratchet up another notch.

Amber checked her watch. It was 18:35. Just under an hour and a half left on today's shift. She began to run her mind through what she'd do once she got home—

An ear-splitting screech tore through the room. Amber jerked around sharply. A fight had suddenly erupted out of nowhere, two inmates viciously going at it. She'd passed by their table only moments earlier, where they'd been sitting together, just the two of them, chatting in low tones, ostensibly engaged in amicable conversation.

But now, all of a sudden, they were punching and scratching each other, wrenching each other's hair out, screaming and spitting abuse.

A fight.

A slam.

Amber's heart rate immediately tripled as she frantically tried to think what to do. She cast her mind back to her training, trying to recall which control and restraint procedure would be most appropriate.

She looked around desperately for support, but there were no other prison officers present in the canteen. She was all by herself.

'You fucking bitch!' one of them was screaming. 'He's mine!'

'Well now he's mine!' screamed the other one.

She recognised them as Agata and Marlena. They were both Eastern European. Agata was Polish and Marlena was Slovakian. Or was it the other way round? Right now, it didn't really matter.

A tray of food got knocked off the table, clattering noisily onto the floor, splattering chilli con carne over the surrounding inmates, which didn't help to defuse the situation.

There was nothing else for it. Amber took a deep breath and waded straight in.

'That's enough!' she barked, attempting to separate them, but it was like trying to pull apart two very large, particularly vicious cats.

There were whoops of encouragement from the rest of the inmates. They revelled in diversions like this and they had all stopped eating to watch.

'You're nothing but a fucking slut!' shouted Marlena as she swiped at Agata's eyes with her long, painted fingernails.

'He's over you! You don't mean anything now!' hissed Agata as she kicked Marlena in the shins.

Marlena responded with a left hook.

Unfortunately, Amber's face was in the way and she caught part of the blow on her temple, the force of it knocking her glasses right off her head. They skittered across the floor under a table.

She staggered back, momentarily stunned, her head throbbing from the impact.

The two inmates paused, staring at her in surprise as if registering her presence for the first time.

And then a large heavy figure barrelled into Marlena, knocking her to the ground.

It was Terry.

At last. Backup.

He knelt on Marlena's back and bent her arm roughly behind her so she was pinned to the floor. She shrieked in pain, swearing at him.

'Fighting's not allowed!' he growled in her ear.

'That fucking bitch took my man!' she shouted.

Amber gathered herself and turned to face Agata, who backed down, hands raised defensively, a nervous smile on her face.

'It wasn't my fault,' she said. 'She started it.'

'I'm putting you both on the nicking sheet,' said Amber, trying to block out the throbbing pain in the side of her head.

The situation was soon ironed out and the canteen went back to normal. There was a faint air of disappointment – from the inmates, at least – that the excitement was over.

Terry picked up Amber's glasses and handed them to her.

'Thanks. I was wondering where those had got to.' She put them back on. 'And thanks for backing me up.'

He shrugged it off like it was no big deal.

'Are you okay?' he asked.

She rubbed the side of her head. It still stung from the blow.

'I think so.'

'Side-handle batons. That's what we need. Like I'm always saying.'

Amber was much more inclined to agree with him now she'd tasted violence first-hand. It had been her first experience of it in here and she hadn't felt particularly able to protect herself.

She left the canteen.

As she was walking along the corridor, Terry caught up with her.

'Hey Amber,' he whispered, looking around to check that there was no one watching.

'Yeah?' she said.

He pulled something from his pocket and offered it to her. In his open palm was what appeared to be a small aerosol canister.

'CS gas. Technically illegal, but it could save your life if things go tits up in a big way.'

He pressed it into her palm and before she could say anything he was gone.

She looked down at the CS gas. The sight of the small black can sent an illicit frisson through her and she slipped it quickly into her pocket before anyone could notice.

This certainly hadn't been in her prison officer training.

47

Later that evening, Bailey was lying on her bunk doing a cryptic crossword, killing time before lights went out, absently curling her loose lock of hair around her fingers and letting it uncurl as she tried to work out the answers.

Sharon was sitting on the chair, one foot up on the desk, cutting her toenails, the sound of the clippers loud inside the small cell. The toenail clippings were pinging randomly over the desk and the floor of the cell and Sharon didn't appear to be making any effort to clear them up.

'Did you see that fight in the canteen today?' said Sharon. Clip, clip.

'It was hard to miss.'

'It blew up really suddenly, didn't it?' Clip.

'They usually do.'

As a policewoman, Bailey had witnessed a fair number of fights. They mostly followed the same pattern – a sudden explosive outburst of violence that was usually over in a matter of seconds. Today's altercation had been no different.

'Did you see, poor old Amber got her glasses knocked off,' said Sharon. Clip, clip. A toenail clipping ricocheted onto the floor by the bunks.

Bailey had felt bad for Amber, as a rookie, having to deal with a situation like that all by herself. As soon as it had kicked off, her policewoman's instincts had jumped to the fore and she'd had to stop herself from rushing in to give Amber a hand, knowing that she could easily have ended the situation. But she'd been sitting with the ABC at their corner table and it would have looked exceedingly suspicious if she, a mere accountant, had leapt in and applied expert control and restraint procedures, not to mention helping a prison officer, who they more or less regarded as the enemy.

So she'd had to just sit there and watch, wincing inwardly when Amber got hit, feeling secretly relieved when Terry had finally arrived.

'That fight was very revealing,' Sharon continued. She picked a toenail clipping out of her hair and flicked it onto the floor. 'I was sitting at the table right next to them.'

'I didn't exactly get what it was about. I think one of them was accusing the other one of stealing her boyfriend or something.' It seemed pretty standard, run-of-the mill stuff to Bailey.

'I'm surprised no one's noticed it.'

'Noticed what?'

'Knowledge is power.' Sharon tapped her nose.

Bailey realised that Sharon was deliberately obfuscating, being all coy about whatever secret she seemed to know. She appeared to enjoy playing these little games and Bailey guessed it was her way of gaining validation.

Bailey sighed and played along. 'So what are you going to do with this "knowledge"?'

Sharon smiled and rubbed her thumb and forefinger together in the universal sign for money.

Blackmail of some sort.

As Bailey recalled, that was the reason that Sharon had ended up in here in the first place. A leopard doesn't change its spots, she thought.

She watched her cellmate cutting her toenails and reminded herself just how dangerous Sharon was. Bailey was terrified that she would reveal something in her sleep that Sharon could exploit to her advantage, like the fact that she was an undercover cop. Although everything seemed okay for the moment, she knew she would have to continue to tread very, very carefully around her.

48

There was no reason given for the summons, merely an order to come to cell 319 in C-Wing at 2 p.m.

Bailey paced briskly along the second-floor landing of C-Wing, navigating her way through the various groups of inmates who were lounging around. Sunlight filtered feebly down through the begrimed skylights high above, hinting that it might be quite a nice day outside.

She looked at her watch. It read 13:59. She arrived at the cell, pausing for a moment to catch her breath. It wouldn't look seemly to be too flustered. Then she stepped into the doorway, tensed, prepared for anything.

Toni was sitting on the edge of the lower bunk, alone in her cell. She smiled up at Bailey with all the warmth of a crocodile, her gold tooth glinting. She patted the bunk beside her. 'Don't be shy. Come on in. Take a seat.'

Bailey hesitated for a fraction of a second, then went in and sat down next to her, but not too close. She shivered. The cell seemed unusually cold. Or maybe she was just scared.

She glanced around. The decor was relatively sparse. On the desk were an Xbox and a stack of violent video games, along with a copy of *Mein Kampf* and a large academic textbook entitled *Principles of Human Anatomy*.

'I don't think me and you have had the chance for a proper one-to-one catch-up yet, have we?' said Toni.

'Guess not,' Bailey replied, still trying to ascertain if there was a special, and possibly unpleasant, reason for this meeting.

Her eyes settled on a fluffy heart-shaped cushion with the letter 'T' embroidered on it which was lying on the bunk. It looked incongruous in the context of the other items in the cell.

Toni noticed her looking at it. She picked it up and tilted her head wistfully, gazing at the blank wall in front of them. She was silent for a few moments, then she spoke in a soft, almost tender voice, holding the cushion to her chest.

'I miss him you know.'

'Who?'

'My baby.'

Bailey was surprised. Maybe she'd misjudged Toni. But then most of the inmates in here seemed to have kids, so why should Toni be any exception?

'Where is he now?' she asked gently, imagining that he was probably in care or had even been put up for adoption.

'He's dead,' said Toni.

'Oh... I'm so sorry.'

'The police shot him.'

'What?! The police shot your baby?!'

'I'd only let him off the lead for five minutes.'

The penny dropped. 'Oh...'

'My pit bull. His name was Taser. My baby.' Toni looked down at the cushion. 'I made this in craft class so I'd never forget him. The love of my life... gone forever.'

'That's... uh... sad.'

'It was totally unnecessary. He would have let go of that kid eventually.' Her face turned sour. 'Bastards!'

She sighed and shook her head, then placed the cushion to one side and turned to look at Bailey.

'Anyway, down to business.'

Toni glanced around furtively, then beckoned Bailey closer.

'I want to tell you something,' she whispered. Her flint-coloured eyes gave nothing away. They were dead and calm, like the sea before a storm.

Bailey leaned in slowly.

Suddenly Toni grabbed her by the hair and yanked her head backwards so her throat was exposed. She felt the sharp filed edge of a shank pressing into the side of her neck. It had appeared out of nowhere.

Bailey froze, her heart thumping hard, her mouth dry. She swallowed and even that small movement of her throat caused the blade to bite into the skin of her neck. She held her breath, barely gasping, barely able to even speak.

'This is your carotid artery,' whispered Toni in her ear, stroking the edge of the blade up and down the left side of Bailey's neck just beneath her ear. 'It's responsible for carrying oxygenated blood from your heart to your head. If I cut it open right now, your blood would pump out in big jets at five litres a minute. That's a lot of blood. You wouldn't last very long.'

'I see you've been reading up on your human anatomy,' whispered Bailey hoarsely, trying to make light of the situation in an attempt to mask her fear.

She'd only just begun to feel better following her beating from her brutal initiation into the gang. She didn't fancy a whole new set of injuries.

Toni moved the blade slowly across to the front of Bailey's throat, the roughly filed edge of the knife scraping at her skin.

'And this is your trachea,' said Toni. 'Also known as your windpipe. If I was to slice through this, you'd suffocate to death. You'd be flopping around like a fish out of water, possibly for up to three and a half minutes.'

Bailey modulated her breathing, trying to remain calm, trying not to panic, trying not to think about what it felt like to have your throat cut.

Had Toni found out that she was a cop? Was this the reason she had been summoned here? Would Toni try and force her to admit what she really was? Would she lose her nerve and break cover? If she did, that would seal her fate as surely as anything.

Never. Break. Cover.

Without letting it lose contact with her skin, Toni moved the blade up the side of Bailey's face until the point of it rested at the base of her right eyeball.

'Or I could push this shank right through your eye and into your brain. First, your eyeball would puncture and all the liquid inside, which is called the vitreous, would ooze out all down your face. And, of course, your eye wouldn't work any more. But that would be the least of your problems because then the knife would go into the frontal lobe of your brain, and I don't even want to get started on what that would do to you, especially if I twisted it around a bit.'

All Bailey could see out of the corner of her eye was Toni's shark-like leer, and that gold tooth gleaming evilly in her upper jaw.

Gripping her hair even tighter, so tight that it hurt, Toni trailed the knife up the side of Bailey's face, pointedly tracing the tip of the blade along the line of the scar on her cheek, moving up onto her forehead until the cold sharp edge of the shank was sitting laterally across her hairline, poised to slice into her scalp.

Bailey flicked her eyes down and around to try to get an impression of their physical juxtaposition. She thought back frantically to her jiu-jitsu classes, attempting to mentally choreograph the most appropriate move to get her out of this bind. It would have to be *kote gaeshi* – outside wrist twist – accompanied by an elbow strike to the chin, followed by some kind of armlock, like *ude gatame*.

Adrenaline fired through her. She was just about to spring into action when Toni abruptly took the shank away and let go of her hair. She winked at Bailey and patted her amiably on the shoulder.

Although her heart was thumping furiously, Bailey fought hard to appear as unruffled as possible.

Toni nodded and smiled in approval. 'You're good. I like you. You're a pretty cool customer. Pretty cool... for an accountant.' She squinted at her, the smile suddenly dropping off her face again. 'That's what you were, right?'

It had been a test. Toni had just been testing her nerves. She guessed she'd passed.

'Yeah,' she said. 'Just a simple accountant who got in way over her head.'

Toni scrutinised her. 'I like you, Bailey. You're not a pussy. I feel like we're on the same wavelength. We need people like you on our team.' She flipped the shank in her hand so the handle was pointing towards Bailey. 'Here. Take it. It's yours. If you're going to be a member of the Ace Blade Crew, you're going to need a blade, right?'

'Yeah... I guess.'

Bailey took the shank from Toni. She examined it, turning it over in her hands. It was simple and utilitarian – a single piece of metal about seven inches long, one end bound with tape to form a crude handle. The blade was filed razor sharp on both edges and it tapered off to a narrow vicious point. It weighed very little but was clearly capable of doing some serious damage as Toni had been only too keen to demonstrate just a few moments earlier.

'That's the only kind of stiletto you'll be wearing in here,' said Toni.

Bailey loathed the idea of carrying a knife, let alone actually using one, but she knew that this was as much a badge of membership as the tattoo.

'Thanks,' she said, forcing a grateful smile onto her face.

Was that the reason she had been asked to come here? So that Toni could give her a shank?

Toni seemed to read her thoughts. 'Probably wondering why I asked you to come here, huh?'

'It did cross my mind.'

'I think it's time for you to do your first job for us.' She glanced around again even though the cell was quite clearly empty apart from the two of them. 'It's top secret.'

She stood up and walked to the cell door. She turned around and looked at Bailey, who was still sitting on the bunk.

'Well, what are you waiting for?'

Bailey stood up and followed her out of the cell. Toni walked fast, with a purpose, and Bailey hurried to keep up with her. They traversed the length of the landing, the other inmates dissolving rapidly out of their way as soon as they recognised Toni. They descended the metal stairwell at the far end of the landing, going all the way to the ground floor.

From the huge echoing galleries, they proceeded down into the dank basement corridors beneath B-Wing, Bailey getting more and more curious as to the nature of their destination. Judging by her confident stride, Toni seemed to know her way around every last murky recess and cloistered passage of this decrepit Victorian pile.

The sound of machinery and power tools echoed through the corridors as they got closer to the prison workshop. As they passed by it, Bailey glanced through the small window in the door, catching a glimpse of inmates in welding masks manipulating white-hot oxyacetylene torches.

And then they had rounded a corner, Toni trotting fast, constantly looking from side to side to check who else might be around, who else might be monitoring their movements.

Suddenly she stopped, so suddenly that Bailey almost bumped into the back of her. She was standing next to a small, innocuous-looking door.

Toni looked around one last time. The corridor was empty.

She pulled the door open and gestured for Bailey to quickly go inside. It was too dark to see what was in there, but there was no time for debate. She stepped inside and Toni went in behind her and shut the door.

They both stood in the sheer blackness for a few moments. Then there was the click of a light switch and a single bare bulb illuminated what appeared to be a simple maintenance cupboard.

Around them were shelves stacked with bottles of bleach and cream cleaner and packs of sponges and rubber gloves. Mops and brushes were stacked against the walls and on the floor were plastic buckets and big industrial rolls of cleaning tissue.

Space was limited and she and Toni were standing virtually nose-to-nose.

Toni knelt down. She pushed the rolls of cleaning tissue aside to reveal a small metal ventilation grille set into the base of the back wall. It looked innocent enough. She ran her fingers over its chrome surface. Then, sliding her fingernails behind the edges of the grille, Toni pulled at it. It came off the wall quite easily, flakes of paint and dust falling away as it did so. Bailey noted that the screws which would have once secured it to the wall had been removed at some point.

She peered over Toni's shoulder at the rough black rectangular hole that the grille covered. She realised now what this was. It was a stash. Toni wasn't stupid enough to keep anything really valuable or really illicit in her cell where it might be stolen or confiscated so she hid it here.

'Very clever,' murmured Bailey.

'Got a number of these hidden all around the prison,' said Toni. 'Can't be too careful, y'know.'

She reached inside until almost the whole length of her arm was in the hole. She groped around awkwardly and then slowly withdrew her arm. Her hand emerged clutching what Bailey recognised as a rat trap. It was basically a super-sized version of an old-fashioned mousetrap – the inhumane type – with a spring-loaded bar designed to break the neck or back of the rat. These rat traps were littered all over the prison in an attempt to address the rat problem. In this case, it served as a nasty surprise that would easily break the fingers of anyone who might try to get to Toni's stash.

She carefully placed the trap to one side and then reached back inside the hole and pulled out a clear plastic ziplock bag.

Bailey could see that it contained a mobile phone and several large rolls of banknotes. Mobile phones were illegal inside the prison. As she knew well, almost all inmate communication with the outside world was vetted by the prison authorities. Bailey assumed that Toni used this to talk to criminal associates on the outside.

Toni switched on the phone. It took a few moments to bleep into life. She waited until the signal appeared. It was very weak – just one bar.

'That's the problem with keeping it down here,' she said. 'The reception's shit.'

After it was apparent that there were no messages or voicemails for her, she switched it off again and put it back in the bag. She took one of the thick rolls of banknotes out next. The wad was wound tight with an elastic band.

As they had been repeatedly made aware during their induction, cash was forbidden inside prison. Any money the inmates earned from jobs they did was credited to their canteen accounts – money they could use to buy cigarettes or to enhance the meals they had with extra goodies – but that wasn't real money. Not like this. This was money that the inmates paid for drugs with, money that they themselves, or their visitors, had smuggled in.

Toni whipped off the elastic band and expertly flicked through the notes. Observing closely, Bailey estimated that the roll of cash constituted around a thousand pounds in fifties and twenties. Toni reapplied the elastic band, then handed the wad to Bailey without even looking at her. She then reached into the bag and handed Bailey two further rolls.

Bailey took the money from her. It wasn't often that she got to handle this much cash. She quickly ran her eyes over it, calculating that she was holding around three grand in total.

Standing there in the cupboard, she held the bundles of cash while Toni re-sealed the bag and pushed it back into the hole. Toni carefully replaced the rat trap and then affixed the grille back into its former position. Finally, she pushed the rolls of cleaning tissue in front of the grille and then stood up.

She turned to Bailey, their faces only centimetres apart.

'In case you're wondering, that isn't a present,' she said.

'I guessed as much.'

'That's for you to pay our contact. It's who we get the drugs off. It's very simple. You'll just deposit the money and collect the drugs.'

Bailey felt a tingle of excitement. Finally she was gaining some traction. This was the next step up the chain. This had to be the source that Alice had mentioned. Just before she'd been killed.

'Sounds straightforward enough,' she said.

'It is. But, of course, if anything should go wrong, then the consequences for you will be dire,' said Toni with a death's-head smile. 'So you'd better not fuck up. For your own sake.'

And she switched off the light.

49

The chapel was cool and dim. Bailey stood at the top of the aisle, rows of empty wooden pews stretching out on either side of her down to the front of the room. There, atop the altar stood a painted statue of Jesus hanging on the cross, his face frozen in an expression of pious agony.

She was keenly aware of the bundles of cash secreted just beneath her waistband, and had been so ever since Toni had given them to her.

She scanned the room again. There was no sign of anyone else in here. Yet.

As for Father O'Malley, his office door was closed and she had no intention of disturbing him.

As soon as Toni had informed her that the chapel was to be the rendezvous point, the possibility had crossed her mind that Father O'Malley might be the contact. But it seemed unlikely. He was a drunk and drunks just weren't reliable enough for this type of thing. More probable was that the chapel had been chosen for the very reason that he was too inebriated most of the time to pay proper attention to what was going on in there. At any rate, it explained why Toni had come here that time that Bailey had covertly followed her. She had been making a pick-up.

Bailey padded down the carpeted aisle to the front of the chapel and, as per Toni's instructions, headed for the right-hand of the two confessional booths. She stepped inside the small wooden cubicle and sat down on the narrow seat. It was the first time she had been inside a confessional. It was cramped, very dim and it smelt faintly of varnish.

To her immediate right there was a wooden grate to enable communication between the two booths. And it was when she peered through this that she became aware of someone occupying the other booth. It was too indistinct to make out anything other than a shadowy outline sitting there in silence.

A jolt of anticipation went through her. This must be the contact she was supposed to meet.

The person shifted impatiently, their clothes rustling. Whoever it was, they were aware of her presence and waiting for her to say something.

'Forgive me Father for I have sinned,' she said.

'A sin is not a sin if no one sees it,' came the response. A man's voice. A cockney accent. Definitely not Father O'Malley. It had to be one of the guards, but she wasn't able to make out which one.

'What the eye doesn't see, the heart doesn't grieve over,' she said, completing the script that Toni had told her to recite.

There was a pause. The silhouette leaned closer to the grate.

'It's under the seat,' he said.

She reached between her legs and groped around under the wooden seat of the confessional, her fingers closing around a large package wrapped in polythene. She picked it up. It was fairly heavy. It must have weighed around a kilogram.

'Leave the money in the same place,' he said. She could smell cigarettes on his breath. He was a smoker.

She pulled the bundles of cash out from her waistband and placed them beneath the seat. She then tucked the drugs into her tracksuit top and zipped it up, hoping that it was baggy enough to disguise the bulky package.

If only she could see who was on the other side of the grate. It was frustrating to be so close and yet unable to make a positive ID.

'The money's there,' she said.

'Say ten Hail Marys and piss off.' He laughed sarcastically.

She took one last squint through the grate.

'Well, what are you waiting for?' he growled. 'Business is done for today.'

'Thank you, Father,' she whispered. She stood up, exited the confessional and scurried out of the chapel.

But once she was outside she didn't go straight back to Toni's cell as she'd been instructed to. It was imperative that she identified the contact and this could be her only opportunity.

The weather wasn't bad, so the yard was relatively busy, unlike before when she'd followed Toni to the chapel. Not far away she noticed a group of inmates playing football, being cheered on by a few bystanders. She pulled her hood up and headed over to them, attempting to mingle with the spectators as inconspicuously as possible while maintaining an eye on the door of the chapel.

It took a long five minutes before the door opened and someone emerged.

It was Terry.

So Terry Brinkle was the source. He was definitely well concealed, or at least made an effort to be that way.

He stood by the door for a few moments, his eyes narrowed, scanning the yard to see if anyone was watching him.

She dropped her head, hiding her face beneath the hood, and made some cheering gestures at the footballers. Glancing up, she saw him walking briskly in the direction of the administration block. She imagined he was probably going to deposit the money in his locker or something like that.

A feeling of elation sparked within her. It was all starting to make sense now. Finally.

* * *

When she got back to Toni's cell, the whole gang were there sitting around glaring at her. She felt an arctic chill of hostility and suspicion emanating from them.

'What took you so long?' hissed Toni, her eyes bulging in a scary fashion.

Bailey scrambled for an appropriate lie.

'There were some screws hanging around in the yard by the entrance to the house-blocks. I was worried they might search me, so I took a detour to avoid them.'

Toni eyeballed her for a few moments, then nodded slowly, apparently satisfied with her explanation.

'You can never be too careful,' she said.

Bailey unzipped her tracksuit top and pulled out the package. She handed it to Toni, who hefted it in her hand, a satisfied smirk crossing her face. She tossed it to Keisha, who was sitting on the bunk. Keisha began to peel off the polythene.

The drugs consisted of two bars of what Bailey recognised as cannabis resin.

'Each of those blocks of hash is five hundred grams,' said Toni. 'Each one has got twenty grams of smack and twenty grams of coke embedded in it. It's the most efficient way of delivering it.'

Bailey nodded, carefully memorising the information.

Toni continued, 'Once we split that up and sell it, it'll net us in the region of forty grand or so. We can charge up to four times the street value in here, sometimes more. It's all about supply and demand, see. And demand for that is at a premium.'

It was a lucrative business indeed and Bailey was eager to find out more about quantities and frequencies of deliveries so she could get a sense of the scale of their operation, as well as any insights into the nature of the organised crime group on the outside who were supplying the drugs. However, not wanting to appear too interested, she contented herself with an obedient nod.

Toni clapped her on the back and smiled, her gold tooth sparkling in the corner of her mouth. 'You did good. You're one of us now. And soon you'll be reaping the rewards.'

50

Bailey closed her eyes and savoured the dreamlike piano chords of Beethoven's 'Moonlight Sonata' through the earpiece of the phone receiver.

'Hello, Bailey,' said Frank, the music cutting off abruptly.

Her eyes blinked open.

'I've located the source of the drugs,' she said, without any preamble. 'It's a prison officer by the name of Terry Brinkle.'

She then proceeded to recount the nature of the transaction in the chapel, the cash and the drugs involved.

'Excellent work,' he said when she had finished. 'This is exactly the kind of information the drugs squad want to know.'

'Alice must have been on the cusp of identifying Terry when she was murdered.'

'Let me check something quickly,' he said.

She heard the sound of computer keys tapping in the background.

He came back on the line: 'I just looked at the prison officers' rota. I got a copy off the murder investigation team. It says here that Terry was one of those who was on duty the night that Natalie was murdered.'

'What about Alice and Poodle?'

'Just a sec...'

She waited tensely as he checked, listening to his ragged breathing – he was evidently as excited as she was.

'According to this,' he said. 'Terry was on duty when Alice was killed but not when Poodle was killed. He had a day off.'

'Well, assuming that he just facilitated where necessary, he only actually needed to be on duty when Natalie was murdered as that required the most facilitation.'

'I think we've narrowed it down sufficiently to point to Terry as their agent on the other side of the bars. Do you think he's working alone, or do you think there are other members of staff involved? By the sounds of things, it's quite a slick and well-organised operation with fairly significant quantities involved. I'd be surprised if he isn't getting some kind of assistance.'

'The gang haven't mentioned anyone else and he's the only member of staff I've conducted business with so far.'

'Well, we'll just focus on him for the time being. You've done excellent work in managing to identify him.'

'Alice said he was well concealed. And he certainly makes an effort to be that way.'

'He can't afford not to be. Have you heard what they do to ex-screws inside?'

'No. What?'

'They chuck a cup of boiling water over them. Except that they put sugar in it. That makes it stick to you like napalm, so it melts your skin.'

'Nice.'

'And I'm sure he's well aware of that. Which means when we catch him, he'll do anything to avoid a custodial sentence. He'll give up the gang in the blink of an eye if he thinks it'll get him off. We'll have much more leverage over him than we would over your average inmate. Once we've got him in an interrogation room, we'll make him spill the beans on everything, including the organised crime group who are behind the supply of drugs to the prison.'

'And then we can finally find out exactly what happened to Alice.'

'Sure. We've just got to catch him. The important thing is to get him in the act. We need you to find out exactly when the next delivery is going to take place.'

51

It was raining outside, a soporific patter which threatened to lull her to sleep even though it was only three in the afternoon. Lying face-down on Poppy's bunk, Bailey would almost have felt cosy in here, were it not for the persistent jabbing pain of the tattoo needle drilling its patterns into her flesh.

Poppy knelt astride her, concentrating intently on the intricacies of the design, pausing occasionally to dip the needle in the pot of ink that stood on the chair beside the bunk.

'It's like the penthouse suite up here,' said Bailey. 'You're lucky – you've got a nice view. You can see over the walls.'

Poppy lifted the whirring tattoo gun from her back for a moment.

'Sometimes when I'm bored I look out of the window and try to count the sails of the windsurfers on the reservoir. On hot days, I wish I could swim in there. It's so close... yet so... you know.'

'Well, actually, taking a shower in here is kind of like having a swim in the reservoir. That's where the prison pipes in all its water from apparently.'

'How d'you know that?'

'Maggie cornered me and some others while we were waiting to use the phone. She's a veritable fountain of knowledge about the prison.'

'Oh god, I should have known! That woman is so bloody tedious! She always manages to pin you down and then she talks at you and you just have to stand there and listen to her.'

'So I guess that means you're not interested in hearing about the meaning of the name. I thought it was kind of interesting.'

'It's named after some river or something. Yeah I know all about that.'

'She told me that when this place was built in the 1800s it used to draw its water directly from a subterranean tributary of the River Foxbrook. But the river dried up in the thirties after they dammed it in order to build the reservoir.'

'I find history so boring. It's all in the past. What's the point of knowing about it? Who cares?'

'Don't they say those who forget history are condemned to repeat it? History helps us to learn from our mistakes. And mistakes are the reason we're in here, aren't they?'

'I'm not sure that knowing about the local reservoir is going to make much of a difference.'

Bailey laughed. 'Yeah, maybe you're right.'

'Talking of mistakes, though... How exactly did you get those scars? I know you said you don't like to talk about it...'

As part of her undercover role, Bailey knew that she needed to have a plausible explanation for her scars. However, because people often felt awkward broaching the subject with her, she was generally able to avoid having to go into too much detail.

'It was...' Bailey paused to choose the appropriate words, '...an abusive partner.'

She knew how many of the women in here had been in abusive relationships of one form or another and that this answer wouldn't sound particularly unusual.

'He did that to you for no reason?' asked Poppy.

'I guess he had his reasons.'

Poppy's fingertips traced the ridges of the scars on Bailey's back, moving in a feather-light pattern across the disfigured flesh.

'You flinched the first time I touched you. Before I'd even started tattooing you. Like it hurt you.' She paused. 'Did he...?'

'Did he rape me?'

There was a silence between them. A long silence.

'You don't have to let it ruin your life, you know,' said Poppy.

Bailey was faintly concerned that Poppy's probing of this sensitive area would cause her to inadvertently lose emotional control and reveal everything. So she decided to change the subject.

'That French writing on your chest,' she said. 'What does it say? I've been wanting to ask you ever since I saw it.'

'It says "je meur de soif aupres de la fontaine". Translated, that means, "I die of thirst next to the fountain". It's medieval French.'

'I die of thirst next to the fountain,' echoed Bailey. 'Very poetic.'

'That's because it's from a poem. The poem's called "The Ballad of Contradictions". It was written by a poet called François Villon in 1451. Have you heard of him?'

'No.'

'He lived in France in the fifteenth century. He wrote this earthy but incredibly beautiful poetry about the Parisian underclasses in the Middle Ages. He was kind of a proto-punk and also a lyrical genius. He disappeared from the history books in 1463 and no one knows what happened to him.'

Bailey was surprised. She'd imagined it saying something crasser and much more banal.

'I thought you said you hated history.'

Poppy laughed. 'I'll make an exception for François Villon. He was a bit of an outlaw and he was always getting thrown in prison. He wrote some of his greatest poetry whilst he was in prison.'

'Does the library here have any?'

'Nah. I already checked. He's a bit too obscure unfortunately.'

As she lay there on the bunk, Bailey reflected on how different Poppy was from the rest of the gang. She was more cultured for one thing, but she also seemed to have a sense of humanity about her that they quite blatantly lacked. Bailey realised that she was actually starting to like Poppy. But she had to be careful. Those kinds of feelings could sometimes be a dangerous thing when you were working undercover.

52

Bailey was impatient for something to happen, but she knew she couldn't rush things. And what she definitely couldn't do was to force something to happen, however great the temptation was to steer events in the direction she desired.

One of the most important things she had been taught as an undercover police officer was not to be an agent provocateur. It was expressly forbidden to actively incite criminals to commit a crime in order to catch them, because if it ever came to light when the case went to court, then the case would immediately be scuppered. Not only that, it would in itself constitute an illegal act.

Her training had required her to learn the law inside out when it came to this area, so she knew exactly where the boundaries for acceptable action lay. The true art of being an undercover police officer instead resided in being able to insinuate oneself to the degree that one became part of the planning without actually getting the criminals to do anything they wouldn't have done by themselves.

So she channelled her restive feelings into a clandestine observation schedule, secretly shadowing Terry over the course of several days as he performed his duties around the prison. Her aim was to build up a picture of his activities and gather any information that could be of use in constructing a case against him. Where she was able to, she eavesdropped on the conversations he had with other prison officers, learning in the process that he was a union representative and appeared to hate the Governor, and vice versa. Most of his dialogues seemed to revolve around various issues with 'management', such as overwork, personal safety and government cost-cutting.

One thing that did puzzle her, and one thing that she was unable to ascertain from just watching him, was the method that he was using to smuggle the drugs into the prison. She knew that the guards were subject to random bag checks when they entered and exited the prison. So maybe he just took a gamble each time and had always been lucky. But that seemed like a risky way of doing business. And given that it had been going on for a while, surely he should have been caught out by now. There had to be something else to it...

She was certain all would become clear soon enough. She had a good feeling about this job. She had succeeded in cracking the drugs ring and she sensed that the operation was now drawing to a successful close. More than anything, she was determined to make sure that Terry and the gang would pay the price for Alice's death.

In many ways, Terry was more despicable than the gang in her eyes. As a corrupt prison officer, he was betraying the trust that had been imbued in him by the state and by the public, all for the sake of lining his own pockets. At least the gang were relatively frank about their criminality, but him, he was devious and dishonest. There was something low-down and dirty about what he was doing and it quite literally turned her stomach.

The more she watched him, the more she wondered how he'd been corrupted. When had he taken that first step down that dark road that had brought him to this current place?

As an undercover cop, she understood the lure of corruption all too well. One of the dangers of working undercover was letting yourself fall prey to the benefits of the criminal life. When you infiltrated a criminal gang, you were exposed to that kind of life, day in day out – the designer clothes, the high-performance cars, the posh restaurants, the respect and fear of virtually everyone you encountered. For a police officer who didn't get paid a great deal, relatively speaking, the temptation could be very strong. And for some it was too much to resist.

For her, though, it had never been much of an issue. The fancy lifestyle – she could take it or leave it. What she'd always been more worried about was the mental contamination. Hanging about with criminals all the time meant that you started to pick up their habits and their fucked-up logic. Their mindset became your mindset and you became tainted with their twisted morality, or their complete lack of it. But sometimes you had no alternative. Because when it came to surviving in their world you had to think like them in order to be one step ahead of them.

Maybe that's what had happened to Terry. He'd been contaminated. Working in the prison system, being around criminals all day long, he had at some point gone native.

53

The vegetarian lasagne was of a remarkably good quality – creamy béchamel sauce, a tender aubergine filling and a crispy brown cheese topping.

Today the lunch choice had been between that and chicken tikka masala. Bailey had never been a big curry fan, so she'd opted for the lasagne.

Sitting there by herself, her tray of food in front of her, with little else to occupy her attention, she idly observed the other inmates in the canteen as they ate their lunch. The various cliques sat at their tables, hunched conspiratorially over their food, gossiping furiously amongst themselves, no doubt speculating about Natalie's murder. From what Bailey had eavesdropped, it appeared to be the sole topic of conversation at the moment. The demise of yet another inmate had inevitably cranked up the general sense of paranoia among the prison's population.

Over in the queue, she noticed the three stoners – Kay, Seema and Mel – debating over the menu options, all of them eventually going for the chicken tikka masala. She watched them walk to a table holding their trays, Mel limping along behind the other two, her tangled afro bobbing up and down. Bailey had noticed on previous occasions that Mel had a gimpy leg which gave her a distinctive lopsided gait.

They had hardly sat down at the table before Kay began teasing Mel. Bailey was sitting a bit too far away to make out what she was saying, but the subject was quite clear – Kay was making exaggerated gesticulations miming the action of scalping and making horrible faces. Mel was twitching nervously, her eyes rolling, shaking her head and giving out sporadic low moans.

Bailey felt a twinge of pity for her. It was quite evident that she was mentally unhinged. She was what was referred to in here as a 'fraggle' – a headcase. Crazy Mel.

As for the cause of her mental health issues, who knew? Perhaps Doctor Bodie did. But all the drugs she smoked probably didn't help.

Mel suddenly emitted a loud shriek and stood up sharply, her chair falling over behind her. She stormed out of the canteen, limping furiously to the exit and pushing the swing doors open so hard that they banged violently against the wall.

Everyone fell quiet to watch the scene, which was over almost as soon as it had started. Conversation drifted back to normal with shakes of the head, indicating that this was nothing to be particularly surprised about when it came to Mel.

Her tray of chicken tikka masala lay untouched on the table. Kay was shrugging innocently as if to say 'what did I do wrong?'

Reflecting on the scene, Bailey wondered if she herself wasn't too far off becoming a fraggle. After all, hadn't Kay said that you had to be a bit crazy to want to be an undercover cop, let alone one who'd agreed to infiltrate a prison?

54

Leanne was scared. A cold sweat prickled across her skin and a nauseous dread filled her guts.

One minute she'd been in her cell enjoying a game of Connect4 with her cellmate. The next minute, the ABC were all standing there and they didn't look too happy. Her cellmate had been told to make herself scarce, which she had done so in short order, leaving Leanne all alone with them. And that wasn't a good situation to find oneself in.

She knew them all by name – Toni, Keisha, Rong and the big one they called Muscles, who was now blocking the doorway, her only avenue of escape. Not that escaping would have done much good. It would only be prolonging the inevitable.

She knew exactly why they were here.

'I'll get you the money,' she stammered. 'I promise. Just one more week. I promise.'

'You said that last week,' growled Keisha.

'I mean it! Really.' Against her will, a whiny pleading tone had entered her voice, which she knew would only increase their contempt for her.

'The time for excuses is over,' said Toni.

Leanne glanced desperately from one to the next, trying to eke out some glimmer of sympathy or understanding. But their faces were stony and unforgiving. She cowered before them and laughed nervously, as she was prone to do when things weren't looking good.

'What are you laughing at?' snapped Rong, glaring at her cross-eyed.

'Nothing.'

'Are you laughing at me?' Rong's voice had taken on a low dangerous tone and she leaned in menacingly.

'N... no.'

'I don't like people laughing at me. You laughed at me.'

'No I didn't.'

'Are you saying I'm wrong?'

'No, you're right.'

'No, I'm Rong, right?'

'Right.'

'So am I right or am I Rong?'

Leanne knew that whatever answer she gave would be incorrect. She let out a sob of despair.

They all burst out laughing. Keisha punched Rong playfully on the upper arm to congratulate her on her wordplay.

Toni stepped forward and looked at her watch. She turned to address Keisha.

'Where is she?'

'I told her to meet us here at three,' said Keisha.

Leanne wondered who they were talking about, her sense of dread growing even more pronounced.

At that moment, Muscles stepped aside to let someone into the cell. It was a member of the gang Leanne hadn't seen before. She was slender, with brown hair, pale skin and a distinctive scar down the left side of her face.

Toni turned to her. 'Just wondering where you had got to.'

'What's up?' said scar-face, surveying the scene with interest.

'Get your shank out.'

Scar-face hesitated a moment, then reached behind her and pulled out a shank.

Leanne eyed it and gulped. This was just what she had been fearing. They weren't called the Ace Blade Crew for nothing. She had been stupid enough to obtain drugs from them without having the means to pay and now she was going to suffer the consequences.

'This cunt owes us money,' said Toni. 'And you know how we feel about unpaid debts. We thought we'd let you do the honours.'

'The honours?'

'A nice little reminder if you know what I mean.'

Scar-face nodded. An unpleasant sneer came over her face.

'With pleasure,' she said, stepping towards Leanne.

Leanne retreated as far into the corner of the cell as she could manage, her back pressed right up against the wall.

This new member of the gang looked really mean, a proper nasty bit of work with those dead grey eyes and that horrible scar. She looked like the quiet type and they were always the worst, and she had that thousand-yard stare that all the real nutters had.

Scar-face stopped. She held up her shank and examined the edge of the blade, running her thumb along it.

'You know I don't know if this is sharp enough for what I've got in mind.'

'Oh god... no...' whispered Leanne. 'Please...'

'But then maybe blunt is better. It'll take longer that way, give you more time to think about why you should pay your debts on time in the future.'

She took another step forward.

'Please don't hurt me,' whimpered Leanne.

She had always had a low pain threshold. And she had a feeling this was going to hurt in a big way.

'Now, where shall I start,' said scar-face, licking her lips.

She was really stringing this out. What a sadist. She obviously enjoyed wallowing in the suffering of others.

Leanne's mind was turning over all the horrible possibilities of what was about to be done to her. The terror grew and grew, enveloping her totally and thoroughly in its icy grip. Eventually it reached such a pitch that she didn't think she could bear it any more. She felt her bowels loosen and then give way completely.

The stench of her defecation immediately filled the cell.

'Phwoar!!'

The gang all put their hands over their faces with expressions of disgust.

'That's revolting!'

'Have you got no self-control?'

Leanne sunk to the floor, a sobbing wreck, the warm brown goo oozing through her tracksuit trousers.

Scar-face looked down at her with contempt and shook her head. She put the shank away and turned to Toni. 'I think she gets the point.'

55

Bailey breathed a sigh of relief as she left the cell with the rest of the gang. That had been a close call. Her heart had dropped when she'd realised what they expected her to do. She'd stalled as long as possible, frantically trying to think of some way to avoid having to physically harm the inmate. Thank god the poor creature had soiled herself. Fortunately, that appeared to have been enough to sate the sadistic urges of the gang. She just prayed that she wasn't put on the spot like that again.

Toni moved alongside her so they were walking abreast along the landing.

'Impressive. You made her shit herself. Not bad... for an accountant.'

Once again Toni was scrutinising her closely and Bailey couldn't quite work out if she was completely convinced by her cover story.

'Mental scars can be just as effective.'

'Fear means power, and that's all up here.' Toni tapped her head. 'And you seem to understand that.'

She placed a hand on Bailey's upper arm.

'Here, hold back a minute.'

They both waited for the rest of the gang to walk off along the landing.

Toni pressed something into Bailey's palm. 'This is for you.'

Bailey looked down. It was a roll of cash. It looked like several hundred pounds.

'What's this?'

'Earnings.' Toni flashed a gold-toothed smile at her. 'I told you you'd soon be reaping the rewards.'

Drug money. It figured. That's why they were doing it after all.

It technically counted as a criminal payment, which Bailey wasn't allowed to spend. But she could hardly refuse it. That would just look downright suspicious.

She looked at the cash in her palm, unsure of what to do with it. Toni seemed to read her mind.

'Use it in here to buy stuff, the kind of things you can't get in the prison shop. Or, if you'd rather, we can get our contact in here to pass it to trusted associates on the outside who'll invest it for you, if you know what I mean.' She winked at Bailey, no doubt referring to some money-laundering scheme. 'A little nest egg for you for when you get out of here. We can chat personal finance in more detail at some point if you want. All you need to remember is that there's plenty more where that came from. Talking of which...' She glanced around furtively. 'We've got another delivery coming in next Saturday. Same arrangement as last time. Can I count on you?'

* * *

'Are you certain?'

'That's what she said. Next Saturday. Saturday the twenty-second of June.'

Bailey glanced over her shoulder, discreetly tucking herself even further into the phone booth.

'We'll have to apprehend Terry outside the prison,' said Frank. 'Presumably he'll either have it on his person or in his car. Because of the highly secretive nature of the operation, we will not be informing the prison authorities in advance.'

'And me?'

'Carry on as normal for the time being. We'll stay in close contact. If all turns out as expected, then I can see us pulling you out within a matter of days.'

'I just want to make sure we nail Alice's killer.'

'And we will. Don't doubt that for one moment. You've done a sterling job, Bailey. I knew it wasn't a mistake getting you back on board.'

56

Doctor Bodie reflected with some rancour on how the hard-faced police detective running the murder investigation at the prison had dismissed his offer of help with nary a consideration for the fact that he had a PhD in forensic psychology.

The police had refused to share any kind of official information about the murders with him despite the fact that had they done so, he might actually have been able to give them insight into which of the inmates could potentially have been responsible for committing such horrendous crimes, because from what he'd heard, the murders had sounded particularly gruesome.

But if that's how the police wanted to play it, then so be it. They were just cutting off their noses to spite their faces.

He took a sulky slurp of tea from his 'World's Okayest Dad' mug and placated himself with the knowledge that probably the reason they'd excluded him from the investigation was because they were treating him as a potential suspect in the case, as they were just about everyone else in the place, inmates and staff alike.

There was a knock on the door. He sighed and made himself forget about the police and their murder investigation. Composing himself, he put on a welcoming smile.

'Come in,' he said.

The door opened. It was Bailey Pike.

Her follow-up appointment was due today and he was pleased to see her. At least he had something interesting to focus his skills on. The more he found out about this particular inmate, the more intrigued he was by her.

She sat down opposite him. Once again she had her head tilted away from him, her hair hanging down over one side of her face, her arms and legs crossed – her overall demeanour giving the impression that being here constituted something of an inconvenience for her.

He had analysed the tests that she had done the last time she was here and the results had proved to be most interesting. Her answers indicated a level of pathological dissociation indicative of some kind of traumatic experience. What he hoped to achieve today was to gain some insight into the nature of that trauma.

But first things first. He smiled at her.

'Have you done your homework?'

She frowned in puzzlement.

'Your thought diary?' he said.

'Oh that. Sorry, I completely forgot about it.'

He sighed. This didn't come as a total surprise to him.

'Like I said in our previous meeting, Bailey, if you want to get better, then you have to want to help yourself.'

'I'm sorry, Doctor. It genuinely slipped my mind. I got sidetracked with some other stuff.'

He gestured at the sheets of paper on the table in front of him. 'These are the tests you did last time you were here. Remember? The results are quite revealing.'

'Revealing?' A wary look.

'Yes,' he said. 'You were referred to me because you threw yourself off a balcony. An attempt at suicide or self-harm tells me that you're clearly troubled in some way. Looking at your test results, I'm wondering if this is down to a traumatic experience which happened to you in the past.'

He saw a flash of something in her eyes. Raw emotion. Pain. Fear. But then, just as quickly, it was gone, the grey eyes staring at him cool and calm once again.

'You can tell that just from this test?' she said, a sceptical tone in her voice.

In truth, he didn't need a test to know that something unpleasant was locked up inside that head of hers. With her mannerisms and her scar, which he guessed was the outcome of some violent encounter, it was hardly an outlandish assumption to make. And with almost twenty years' experience as a forensic psychologist he had become particularly attuned to reading people like her.

'Would you like to talk about it?' he asked.

'Not particularly.'

'Traumatic experiences, if unaddressed, can be the cause of major mental health issues. They can lead to suicide attempts, self-harm and other highly detrimental behaviour.' He paused. 'Have you heard of something called post-traumatic stress disorder?'

She nodded and looked away.

'When we undergo a particularly traumatic experience, the mind can compartmentalise that experience. It's like a defence mechanism in order to help us preserve a functional sense of self and prevent emotionally unacceptable material from entering our consciousness. But because those memories aren't properly integrated, they're not anchored in any context of time or place like normal memories are. That means that when they intrude, which can happen quite suddenly, it feels like—'

'Like they're happening right now,' she said in a quiet voice. 'Like you're re-living them. Like you're actually there all over again, seeing the same things, feeling the same feelings, smelling the same smells.'

Excitement gripped him. At last, he was getting somewhere! He had finally broken through that defensive shell of hers.

'Yes, Bailey! That's precisely it! I'm so glad you understand what I'm saying. You see, talking about it, although it might be painful, can help to reintegrate those traumatic memories into your consciousness and thus get rid of those unpleasant intrusions.'

He saw the shutters come down – a tautening in her jaw muscles, a sudden frostiness in her eyes.

'I don't want to talk about it,' she replied.

'Why not?' He was genuinely puzzled by her unwillingness to discuss the issue. After all, it sounded like she was well aware that she had a problem.

'I just can't,' she said. 'So please don't ask me about it again.'

57

It was a bright fresh Saturday morning and there was a definite crispness in the air. Amber loved being outside on days like this. She was on her way to start her morning shift and she was walking across the prison car park in the direction of the gatehouse.

Even the bruise on her temple couldn't dent her positive mood. It had gone down considerably since the fight in the canteen, but it was still a little bit on the tender side. She would definitely be more careful from now on when it came to intervening in prisoner-on-prisoner disputes. At least now, though, she had a little extra insurance in the form of the CS gas Terry had given her. So saying, she kept it in her locker most of the time as she didn't feel completely comfortable with the idea of using it.

As she drew closer to the gatehouse, she fell within the shadow of the huge perimeter wall that towered up above her. Even on a nice sunny morning like this, the place still looked incredibly draconian and unwelcoming. But then she guessed that was supposed to be the idea – it was a prison, not a five-star hotel.

As she made her way through the car park, she recognised Terry's maroon S-type Jaguar pulling into a nearby bay. Presumably he was due to start work on the same shift that she was on. She looked at his car in admiration and wondered, not for the first time, how he had managed to afford such a nice vehicle on a prison officer's salary.

She'd almost reached the entrance to the gatehouse when the howl of a police siren cut through the tranquillity of the morning. She jumped in shock, startled by the loud noise, and spun around to see what was happening.

At least three police cars and one police van had suddenly appeared from different directions, seemingly out of nowhere, their blue lights flashing. They skidded to a halt, their doors swung open and a torrent of uniformed and plain-clothes police officers poured out.

Amber stood rooted to the ground, watching in astonishment, completely taken aback by this sudden frenzy of activity. What the hell was going on?

At the epicentre of the commotion was Terry's Jaguar. He had just opened the door and stepped out and he looked just as bewildered as she did. Their eyes met for a fraction of a second before he was overwhelmed by a squad of police officers and roughly manhandled into a face-down position on the bonnet of his car, where he was handcuffed and read his rights.

At that point she thought it best to continue on into the prison, if only for the reason that hanging around outside any longer would have made her late for work. She went through gatehouse security in a semi-trance, her mind still processing what she had just witnessed. Terry had obviously done something very wrong to be the subject of such a furore, but what exactly?

By the time they were sitting down for the morning briefing, the news of his arrest appeared to have spread throughout much of the prison and speculation was rife.

Dylan had sat down next to her. He seemed to have been making a habit of doing that recently in the morning briefings. Not that it bothered her particularly. She could smell his cologne and she couldn't deny that he smelt quite pleasant. He smiled at her, observing her appreciatively with his pale blue eyes. She adjusted her bun and straightened her glasses.

'I hear you witnessed the big drama,' he said.

'I've never seen so many police in all my life. What do you think it was all about?'

He shrugged in an offhand manner, a humorous slant to his mouth. 'I heard his wife was a bit of a shrew. Maybe she tipped him over the edge.'

Amber emitted a giggle. 'What? You think he did her in?'

'Probably with a side-handle baton.'

The two of them promptly stopped their joking as soon as the Governor entered the room. The assembled officers all fell silent, hoping to get a definitive explanation.

The Governor looked solemn. He cleared his throat.

'As many of you are probably aware by now, Terry has been detained by the police.'

He paused to look over the room. They were all sitting forwards on their seats in anticipation of what he was about to say next.

'In case you're wondering why he's been arrested, that information hasn't yet been disclosed to me, so I'm as much in the dark as you are.'

There were a few groans of disappointment.

'I heard drugs were involved,' said someone.

'Do you think he's on the take?'

'He has got a gambling problem.'

'And that wife of his...'

'That's enough speculation!' barked the Governor. 'Now there's no reason why this should affect your work. So it's business as usual, understand?'

Amber knew how much the Governor detested Terry, and vice versa. They locked horns in almost every briefing. But if the Governor was pleased at the misfortune that had befallen his enemy, he made no outward show of it.

The prison officers all stood up to begin their day's work. As Amber got to her feet, she noticed something lying on the floor next to her chair. She frowned and leant down to pick it up. It was a black leather glove.

She held it up and examined it. The leather was soft and supple and it felt expensive.

'Hey, Dylan,' she said to his departing back. 'Did you drop this?'

He turned around. At the sight of the glove, his face broke into a surprised smile.

'Whoops! Must have fallen out of my pocket.' He took it from her. 'Thanks.'

'Looks like it's designer,' she said.

He pulled the matching glove from his trouser pocket and held them together in a pair. 'They're Italian,' he said. 'I find I drive better when I'm wearing them. I guess I should go and put them in my locker.'

He winked at her and walked off, casually slapping the pair of black leather gloves into the palm of his hand.

What a nice pair of gloves, thought Amber. Perhaps she should buy herself a pair.

58

From the second Bailey woke up on Saturday morning, her insides had been twisted in apprehension at the prospect of what today would bring.

She kept her ears open, subtly monitoring the murmurings within the cliques hanging about on the landings, and it wasn't long before she became aware of the news she'd been hoping to hear. Terry had been arrested as he'd arrived at work that morning. No one seemed to know the reason why, and she felt an almost smug sense of superiority that, not only did she know, she was the very person who'd engineered it.

Things were moving fast now. A turning point had been reached in the operation, and now it was almost at its end. She felt simultaneously elated and also extremely jittery. If things went to plan she'd be out of here very soon indeed.

At lunchtime, she went down to the canteen. The ABC were all sitting at their customary corner table – Toni, Keisha, Rong, Muscles and Poppy.

She could instantly tell that they were preoccupied with Terry's arrest. They seemed unusually subdued, picking disinterestedly at their food, muttering in low tones amongst themselves.

They acknowledged her arrival with only the slightest of nods. She sat down opposite Toni, who fixed her with a long, piercing stare. Bailey forced herself to remain calm, modulating her breathing. *Act normal*, she thought. *Carry on as usual.*

'Today's pick-up is not going to happen,' said Toni in a quiet voice. 'Our contact has been arrested.'

'Terry was our contact?' said Bailey, trying her best to sound surprised.

Toni nodded slowly. 'This really fucks things up.'

She glanced around the canteen murderously, then turned to address the gang.

'Let's tone it down for the next few days. No dealing. Let's keep a low profile until we know exactly what's going on.'

They all nodded and murmured their approval.

Bailey watched Toni as she ate her lunch, noting the way she kept glancing over her shoulder as if someone was going to get her. She seemed to have a hunted look about her, her animal instincts telling her that the net was closing in. The tables were now turned. The predator had become the prey. It was only a matter of time before Terry gave them all up and Alice would be avenged.

But Bailey tempered her sense of jubilation with the knowledge that a cornered animal could be the most dangerous. Right now was the time that she needed to be more vigilant than ever. She prayed for this limbo state not to last for too much longer.

59

The cell was dark and silent, moonlight casting a shadow of the bars across one wall. Lights had gone out two hours earlier, but Bailey was still wide awake. She lay on her bunk unable to sleep, unable to stop herself brooding over all the possible turns that events might take from now on.

Sharon's voice drifted up from the bunk below. 'Are you still awake?'

'Yes.'

'Can't get to sleep?'

'I suppose not.'

A pause.

'Do you like stories?'

'Yeah, I guess.'

'My nan used to tell me stories to help me get to sleep when I was a kid.'

'That's nice.'

'Do you want me to tell you a story?'

'Sure, why not?'

Bailey didn't imagine she had much of a choice anyhow. Sharon seemed determined to talk and Bailey might as well have something to fill the silence other than her own thoughts.

A pause.

'Okay,' said Sharon. 'Well... once upon a time, there was this criminal gang, see. They stole cars. High-end motors. BMWs, Mercedes, Maseratis...

that kind of thing. They'd steal them and then they'd sell them abroad. Lots of money involved. Big operation.'

Bailey lay there breathing in and out, listening, an unpleasant feeling growing inside her. This wasn't the sort of story she'd been expecting.

'But one day they found out, somehow, that they had an undercover police officer in their midst. A woman. She was posing as a secretary apparently. Fairly low-level in their organisation. But she was spying on them, feeding information back to the cops, setting them up for a bust.'

Bailey felt herself stiffening. Sharon's voice tinkled along casually as if this was just some kid's fairy-tale.

'They ran a very tight outfit so they were pretty sure that she'd only been able to infiltrate them with the help of someone inside their organisation, someone high up who had turned snitch. And they wanted to know the identity of this traitor. So instead of killing her immediately, like they wanted to, they decided to torture her until she gave him up.'

Bailey's mouth had turned dry. Her heart was pounding against the inside of her chest.

'So that's what they did. Tortured her horribly. And raped her. But she didn't break. She didn't give him up. She refused to even admit that she was a cop. I guess she must have been a pretty tough cookie.'

Sharon paused as if she was listening, trying to gauge Bailey's reactions. Bailey lay there frozen, barely breathing now.

Sharon resumed: 'As soon as the traitor heard they'd caught her, he panicked and fled. Went straight to the police. Now he's in a witness protection programme apparently. He's a dead man if they ever find him. He's got a massive contract on his head.'

Prone on her bunk, Bailey stared straight up at the ceiling, saying nothing, the atmosphere in the cell pressing down on her with a suffocating pressure.

The meat hook...

The burning cigarette...

The straight razor...

The blood...

The pain...

The violation...

'And the undercover cop?' said Sharon. 'She managed to escape. Somehow. Lucky for her.'

Bailey forced herself to breathe. Steady. Even. In. Out. In. Out.

'The traitor, the one she refused to give up,' said Sharon. 'Do you know what his name was?'

Bailey said nothing.

'His name was Spyros,' said Sharon.

Silence in the dark cell.

Spyros.

She'd refused to say the name at the time, knowing that if she had done so, then they would have killed her just as surely as they would have killed him.

Now she repeated it night after night in a fruitless attempt to give her torturer what he wanted, to just make him stop, to make the nightmares go away...

Sharon knew. Somehow she had found out. She must have heard about the contract – it was the kind of thing that was common knowledge in underworld circles.

'What a coincidence,' said Bailey, trying to keep her voice level. 'Must be some other Spyros.'

'Sure,' said Sharon. 'Must be a plain old coincidence...'

* * *

The next morning no mention was made of the previous night's conversation, but as she was getting dressed, Bailey noticed Sharon paying more attention than usual to the lattice of scars which adorned her upper body. She self-consciously pulled on her tracksuit top to cover them up and began to prepare breakfast.

As they sat there drinking tea, Sharon was infuriatingly and uncharacteristically quiet, a smug knowing glint in her eyes.

There was no way that Bailey was going to acknowledge that Sharon had come anywhere near the truth, regardless of how plain the connection might appear. If confronted outright, she would deny it completely. She had no other option.

Never. Break. Cover.

Although they shared an ostensibly friendly relationship as cellmates, Bailey felt a deep ambiguity about Sharon's motives. She was well aware by now of the reason that Sharon was in here and was under no illusion as to the possibility that she would stitch her up if it served her purposes to do so.

'Up to anything exciting today?' asked Bailey in an attempt to puncture the awkward silence.

Sharon smiled enigmatically and tapped the side of her nose.

Bailey knew Sharon was dying for her to ask more, but she decided to deny her the satisfaction of doing so. Today in particular she was in no mood for playing her mind games.

Instead she finished her tea and started on a cryptic crossword, impatient for free association time to start so she could escape the claustrophobic atmosphere in the cell.

60

The ABC were out in force in the atrium, sprawled across one of the plastic picnic-style benches. During free association time they were usually engaged in some form of criminal enterprise but, since Toni's edict to tone down their drug-related activities, they were sitting idle.

Keisha and Rong were playing 'I spy', Poppy was lounging languidly across the top of the table, Muscles was sitting motionless as a block of stone, her huge hands resting on her knees, just staring straight ahead, and in the centre was Toni, a scowl on her face, grinding her teeth, scanning the atrium back and forth relentlessly.

Bailey walked over and sat down amongst them. There wasn't really much else to do apart from sit there and project the appropriate air of casual menace, which is what she did.

Rong had made a little telescope with her hands and was looking around the atrium.

'I spy with my little eye, something beginning with... ugly.'

'That's not a letter,' said Keisha.

Rong removed the telescope from her eye. Her lip curled in an expression of disgust. Bailey followed her gaze. Amber had just entered the atrium with an inmate who Bailey didn't recognise.

'Yeah, I see what you mean,' muttered Keisha, peering at the inmate who Amber was accompanying.

Despite her long black hair, large breasts and tall, relatively slender figure, the inmate had an unfortunately masculine-looking face, at odds with the rest of her figure.

'Looks like a bloke,' said Rong.

'Probably got a cock,' said Keisha.

The rest of the gang snickered.

As Amber and the inmate passed the gang, Rong and Keisha began to chant a little taunt.

'U-G-L-Y, you ain't got no alibi, you're ugly!' Clap clap-clap 'Ugly!' Clap clap-clap.

The inmate cowered self-consciously behind her long hair, hiding her face from them.

Amber shot them an angry glare, placing a protective hand on the inmate's shoulder as she escorted her past the gang and out of the atrium. Bailey got the impression the inmate was relatively new to the prison and unused to the harshness of the place. She'd soon learn.

The gang burst into cackles of laughter and then proceeded to banter about other things.

'Uh-oh,' muttered Rong about ten minutes later.

She had spotted Amber marching towards them, her eyes blazing with anger.

Amber was alone now, having delivered the inmate to whatever destination she'd been taking her. She halted in front of them, standing there with her hands on her hips. Her gaze rested on Bailey for a fraction of a second and in that brief look Bailey detected both disapproval and disappointment that she was now sitting with the gang. Bailey would have liked to explain to her that it wasn't what it seemed, that she was doing this for a very good reason, but her hands were tied and instead she just dropped her eyes in shame.

Amber then proceeded to reprimand Rong and Keisha.

'It's not very nice to sing nasty little chants like that.'

'We were just having a bit of fun,' said Rong.

'You're little better than playground bullies,' chided Amber.

'So why don't you put us in detention,' hissed Keisha.

'I'll put you on the nicking sheet if you don't watch your tongue.'

Keisha sneered at her and said nothing. Bailey watched them face off and knew that Amber's intervention was partially for her benefit. She was making a point to Bailey that she was hanging out with the wrong type of people.

Bailey made a mental note that someday, when this was all over, she would catch up with Amber, buy her a drink and explain the truth of the situation.

But for the time being she couldn't break cover.

61

Sharon thought about her cellmate as she walked through the prison. She was an odd one, that Bailey. She kept her cards close to her chest that was for sure, but could she really be an undercover police officer? The very idea of it seemed beyond belief.

But then Spyros was an unusual name. And that contract on his head... there were plenty of people chasing after that. And those scars... Sharon had never been a big one for coincidences.

If she was an undercover cop, then what exactly was she doing here? If she was an undercover cop... well, that offered up a whole realm of delicious possibilities, the prospect of which filled her with relish. She could think of plenty of people who would be very interested in knowing that kind of information. All for a price, naturally.

It would require a little more probing of course, just to be certain. A little more teasing and tormenting to worm open those cracks in the facade that she was so diligently trying to maintain. And then Sharon would have her trapped like a fish on a hook, ready to reel in at her leisure.

But Bailey would have to wait for the time being. Today Sharon had a slightly bigger and more immediate fish to fry. She glanced at her watch and quickened her pace, keen to get to the rendezvous point ahead of time.

Pushing open the door to the canteen, she stood there motionless for a few moments, glancing around at the empty tables and then up at the CCTV camera fixed to its bracket directly above her. She pressed herself up against the wall, keeping within the blind spot of the camera, and edged along until she reached the door to the prison kitchen. Easing it open, she slipped inside, relieved to be in a camera-free zone.

Just like the canteen, the kitchen was silent and deserted. The hobs were cold. All the pots and pans were hanging up on the rails. The extractor fans were silent. The stainless-steel work surfaces were scrubbed clean, ready for the next set of meals to be prepared.

The inmates ate breakfast in their cells, having received a breakfast pack the night before with their evening meal, and so lunch was the first meal of the day to be prepared in the kitchen. Sharon knew they wouldn't start making lunch until 10.30 and that gave her a good forty-five minutes or so until anyone would begin to turn up here, more than enough time for what she needed to do.

Sharon spent several hours each day working in the kitchen. That's why she knew the schedule so well. She worked there because it meant the added wage put a little more money into her canteen account, enabling her to buy extra goodies each week. But also, occasionally, she liked to slip laxatives into the inmates' food just for a laugh.

She had chosen the kitchen as a meeting point because she knew it would be empty at this time of day. For a sensitive issue such as the business she was about to conduct, a little privacy was likely to be necessary.

She looked at her watch. The person she was due to meet would be here in just a few minutes' time. Leaning against the counter top, she crossed her arms, carefully adjusting her poise so she looked composed and self-assured. She always liked to be early to meetings; she felt it gave her the psychological upper hand in any subsequent 'negotiations'.

Nonchalantly surveying the empty kitchen, her eyes came to rest on the open storeroom door at the back. She knew the rules of the kitchen well and she knew that particular door shouldn't have been left open. One of her sloppier colleagues had obviously neglected to close it the previous night. The storeroom door had to be kept shut because that's where all the non-perishable foodstuffs were kept and if the door was left open then the rats might get in, and that just wouldn't do.

Sharon pushed herself off the counter and walked over to the door in order to close it. But as she got there, she was suddenly seized by the irrational notion that maybe someone was in there. Quite why anyone would be in there was beyond her, but there was something about the crack of darkness behind the partially open door that ignited a tiny ember of uncertainty.

She paused in her tracks, her hand wavering a few centimetres from the door handle. Should she close it or should she check inside? And if she did look inside, what would she find?

She took a deep breath and, with a firm shove, she pushed the door wide open.

Inside it was dark, dry and cool. She reached in and switched on the light. Nothing but the shelves stacked high with big sacks of rice, pasta and sugar, and industrial-sized drums of cooking oil. There was no one in here.

She breathed a sigh of relief. Switching the light off, she pulled the door firmly shut behind her. What had got into her all of a sudden? Probably all these damn murders, secretly eating away at her nerves without her noticing. And now she was all keyed-up for no reason. She cursed under her breath. *Get a grip, Sharon*, she told herself. *You're not some chicken-hearted scaredy-cat.*

She turned around and made her way back to where she had been standing before. As she did so, she noticed a motion out of the corner of her eye. She looked around sharply.

On the far side of the kitchen, one of the shiny steel saucepans was swinging on the hook from which it was suspended, as if someone had knocked it whilst walking past. It certainly hadn't been her.

Was there someone else in here? Another one of the workers? That's all she hoped it was. Just another one of the workers.

Turning in a slow three hundred and sixty degree circle, she scrutinised the kitchen. Apart from the swinging saucepan, there was no motion and no noise.

But then, on the glass surface of one of the oven doors, she caught a flicker of movement.

She spun around. There was no one there.

Maybe this was a set-up.

She glanced around anxiously, her gaze coming to rest on the knife rack. One of those would come in handy. Unfortunately, however, all of the knives were locked and tethered behind reinforced glass in a special cabinet and only the kitchen supervisor had the key. She cursed again under her breath and looked around for a suitable means with which to arm herself.

The cheese-grater? No.

The garlic crusher? No.

The skillet? Yes.

She eased the heavy iron skillet off its hook. Brandishing it before her, she padded warily along the kitchen aisle feeling slightly more at ease.

'Don't be afraid,' she uttered. 'I'm not going to hurt you.'

Suddenly someone was right next to her. She jumped back in shock, holding the skillet up in front of her, but then she realised that it was just her own reflection in the steel door of one of the refrigerators, warped by the slightly bowed surface of the metal into a grotesque caricature.

She sighed in frustration, lowered the skillet and turned away. She didn't like this game any more. It was starting to make her feel almost... frightened. She tightened her grip on the handle of the skillet, her palms sweating.

Suddenly, it became obvious who was in here. It must be the person she was supposed to meet. They had got here even earlier than she had with the aim of trying to unnerve her, trying to get the upper hand. Well, she wasn't that easy to rattle.

'I know your secret,' she said. 'I know what you're up to. Sharon knows exactly—'

A pair of black leather-gloved hands shot out from underneath the kitchen counter and wrenched her feet away. She crashed forwards onto the tiled floor. The skillet flew from her hand and clattered away out of reach.

She lay there stunned for a moment. Then she tried to get up. But whoever had tripped her up now rolled out from under the counter and jumped onto her back, their weight pinning her to the floor. She gasped, winded.

A hand grabbed her hair and viciously yanked her head back. Then she felt a sharp biting sensation at the top of her forehead as a blade began to slice into the flesh, cutting its way upwards.

The sharp burning pain was beyond anything that she had ever experienced. With a colossal lurch of horror, she realised what was happening to her. She was being murdered. Just like the others!

Still too winded to scream, she could only flail and struggle as the knife sawed away at her scalp, scraping over the bone of her skull, making a ghastly scratching noise unlike anything she'd ever heard before. Blood poured down her face, hot and wet, getting in her eyes, running into her gasping open mouth, filling her throat with its iron tang, making her choke. And then the blade sliced through the last remaining shreds of flesh, severing her scalp completely.

Her bleeding head jerked forward, released from the grip, and finally she managed to catch her breath. Evacuating all the pent-up terror inside her, she ejected a shrill penetrating scream. She drew her breath to scream again, but before she could do so the knife sliced deep into her windpipe, severing her vocal cords and silencing her forever.

Crazy Mel's bloodshot eyes popped wide open at the sound of the scream. She clenched her fists, her entire body stiffening in response to the awful sound that had just ripped through the smoky cell.

Kay and Seema snapped out of their stupors a few moments later, vaguely disconcerted, puzzled as to what they had just heard. But Mel knew what it was. Oh yes, she knew all right.

'It's him,' she gasped. 'Him cum bak again. Cum bak to kill. Come bak fi Mel!'

Her face had morphed into an ashen mask of pure dread. She pushed herself along the bunk into the corner of the cell as far as she could go until she was hunched into a ball, staring petrified at the open cell door.

'De duppy ah guh fi guh kill wi aal,' she panted. 'Everi lass one of wi...' Then, with an awful realisation, she lifted up a clenched fist and slowly uncurled her fingers.

The three of them stared transfixed at her outstretched hand as it became apparent that lying there in her palm was a crushed origami duck.

Amber had just about finished berating the gang when a scream echoed through the prison, instantly stopping them all in their tracks.

High-pitched and agonisingly drawn-out, it hit Bailey like an icicle jammed down her spine.

'What on earth?' exclaimed Amber, looking up and around, trying to locate its source.

The gang perked up like meerkats, their ennui instantly dissipating. It sounded like something highly unpleasant had just occurred. In other words, it sounded like it could be interesting.

There was one other prison officer in the atrium. Bailey recognised him as Brian. He had been standing over on the other side.

'Canteen!' he barked, his eyes bulging in alarm. 'It came from the canteen!'

He beckoned furiously at Amber and she sprinted after him in the direction of the prison canteen.

A fraction of a second later, all of the inmates in the atrium followed suit in a ghoulish stampede to see what had happened. A red-faced Brian led the way, panting with the effort, his bald head shining with perspiration.

Bailey raced along with them, hot on the heels of the prison officers, starting to form her own uneasy ideas about what they might encounter.

They burst into the canteen, scattering the chairs asunder in their mad rush, looking around wildly but seeing nothing amiss.

'The kitchen,' panted Amber. 'Must be in the kitchen.'

En masse, they piled into the kitchen.

And stopped dead. Silent. Struck dumb by the gory tableau which confronted them.

The stainless-steel surfaces were splattered with blood. Everywhere.

At first, Bailey didn't recognise that it was Sharon who was lying there on the floor. Her head was covered in blood, the glistening raw surface of her skull clearly visible where her scalp had been hacked off, her eyes half-open in the dull vacant stare of death.

She lay on the floor between the counter top and a row of steel cupboards. One arm was stretched out before her in a final plea for escape, the splayed fingers of her hand dripping red.

Amber, who was standing right over the body, had visibly blanched. Even Bailey, who had become relatively inured to the sight of dead bodies as a policewoman, was shocked by what she saw, not least because the victim was her very own cellmate.

'Stand back!' shouted Brian, ineffectually trying to shoo the inmates away. 'There's nothing to see here!'

The inmates ignored him, jostling for position, trying to get a better look.

'Fuck me!'

'Holy shit!'

'Is that Sharon?'

There was a retching sound as one of them threw up.

Bailey looked at Toni and the others as they craned their heads to take it all in. They seemed just as surprised as she was. Her mind raced, reassessing everything she'd come to believe up until this point.

Sharon had quite obviously been scalped, yet the gang appeared to have had nothing to do with it. When this had occurred, they had been upstairs with her getting scolded by Amber. Likewise, Terry couldn't have done it because he was in police custody.

It begged the question – who had done it? If the perpetrator of this crime was the same one who'd killed the others, then she'd have to re-evaluate her entire theory around who'd murdered Alice.

She peered closer and noticed that something was scrawled crudely in blood on the steel door of one of the cupboards close to Sharon's head. It seemed that her dying act had been to write something in her own blood, hence her outstretched arm and fingers.

Bailey pushed her way to the front of the crowd and bent down to take a closer look. Four letters, jagged and uneven, but legible all the same.

First, the vertical line and two crossbars of a capital 'F'. Next came the straight downward slash of an 'l', the tail of which then jerked sharply to the right to become the inner curl of a shaky lower-case 'e', itself followed by a separate, even wobblier lower-case 'e'.

'Flee,' she murmured, forming the four letters into a word.

Amber noticed what she was looking at. She knelt down on her haunches and squinted at it in puzzlement.

'Flee? What does that mean?'

'It's almost like... like some kind of warning,' said Bailey.

The sight of that single word sent a chill through her. There was something deeply ominous about this stark and fatalistic call to action.

Flee.

Get out of here now.

There is no hope.

Just get out while you can.

Unfortunately, most of them didn't have that option.

Bailey was starting to get the nasty feeling that there was a whole other dimension to these murders, something much darker and more frightening than she had previously been aware of.

64

The mournful opening piano arpeggios of Beethoven's 'Moonlight Sonata' tinkled away down the earpiece of the phone.

'Hello, Bailey,' said Frank, the music cutting out. 'I'm glad you called.'

Bailey opened her eyes.

'She was my cellmate, you know.'

'Who?'

'Sharon Finn. The one who just got scalped.'

'Oh... I'm sorry.'

'I wasn't close to her. In fact, I didn't really like her one bit. And I think she was onto me. I guess I should almost be glad that she's no longer a threat in that respect. But I wouldn't wish her fate on anyone. It was pretty unpleasant.'

'That's an understatement. I saw the crime scene photos.'

'How are her family taking it?'

'Well... it turns out she's estranged from most of them. We spoke to an aunt, who seems to be the only one who was on speaking terms with her. Reading between the lines, she screwed over most of her close relatives at one point or another, they all hated her and none of them are particularly surprised that something like this has happened to her. Still, I thought it best to recommend a closed-casket funeral all the same.'

'Please tell me the canteen CCTV captured something useful.'

'I'm afraid not. You can just see the edge of the kitchen door opening but you can't see who went in because they were outside the camera's cone of vision. Whoever did it is well aware of the limits of CCTV coverage within the prison.'

'Shit!' She chewed on her knuckle. 'This messes up everything, you know. If we assume that it was the same person who scalped and murdered all of them – Alice, Poodle, Natalie, Sharon – then it can't have been the gang because they were with me when Sharon was killed. We were being told off by one of the prison officers. And Terry can't have been involved because he was in police custody.'

'Like I said, I'm glad you called when you did because I've got some news for you on that front.'

'What news?'

'We're going to have to release him.'

'What?! Release Terry? Why?!'

'No evidence. We didn't find any drugs on his person, in his car or at his house. He's not saying anything and there's very little we can do about it. Either your intel was wrong or he's much more careful than we gave him credit for.'

'Fuck! I saw him delivering the drugs with my own eyes. He's guilty as hell!'

'As you well know, without a wire we can't prove anything.'

She sighed in frustration. She understood how it worked.

'It just doesn't add up though,' she said. 'Something else is going on here. It's not the gang who have been doing the killings. These murders... I'm getting the feeling they may not even be drug-related at all.'

'It doesn't matter. Forget about it. We're pulling you out.'

'What?! Why?!'

'Like I said at the start, the funding for this operation is coming from the drugs squad, and that's the primary reason that you were inserted – to uncover the drugs ring. But the problem is that Terry and the gang will be much more careful from now on, now that they know they're being watched. There's no telling how long it'll be before they resume their trafficking operations to the extent where it makes sense to monitor them properly. So it's been decided that it would be a waste of time and money to keep you in there any longer. It's therefore been decided to terminate the operation due to budgetary restraints.'

'But what about Alice?'

'What about her?'

'Don't you want to find out who killed her?'

'Of course I do. That's why the murder detectives are there.'

'But they aren't any closer to finding out who did it than they were at the beginning. I'm the best shot you've got at finding out who killed her and you know it.'

'Look, Bailey, it made sense for you to investigate the murders if it seemed like they might tie into the drugs. But now that's finished for the time being, there's no reason for you to be in there any longer. The operation is over. We're pulling you out.'

'I'm not leaving,' she said bluntly.

'You're what?' She could visualise the disbelieving expression on his face.

'You heard me. I'm staying.'

'That's insubordination.'

'I have to find out who killed Alice. And the other girls. And I have to find out why. I owe it to her.'

'You're letting it get personal. That's not professional.'

'You could have used someone else instead of me, but you knew Alice was my friend and you knew that because of that I'd be much more motivated to get to the bottom of whatever was happening in here. And now you want me to forget about her?'

'I'm worried about you, Bailey,' he said gently. 'You're in there all alone with no backup and I'm worried that the psychological pressure of working undercover is getting to you. Maybe I made a mistake in asking you to come back. Maybe you weren't ready.'

'You didn't make a mistake. And I appreciate that you care about me. I know that you cared about Alice in the same way. And I know that you're itching to find out what happened to her just like I am. You owe it to her almost as much as I do. She was one of us, remember?'

There was a silence on the other end of the phone. She knew she had him on the fence.

'Bailey, I don't have any choice in the matter. The drugs squad own this operation and they're the ones who—'

'Tell them I'm working a new angle,' she said. 'Tell them anything. Just stall them until I've found out a bit more information. Something's going on in here, Frank. Something very odd. And I'm determined to get to the bottom of it. It killed Alice. And it killed Poodle, Natalie and Sharon. And if I'm not mistaken it's going to kill more inmates before we're through. And we don't want their blood on our hands, do we?'

'Nice to know you care about them even if they'd likely kill you if they found out who you really were.'

Ignoring him, she pressed on. 'You'll do it won't you, Frank? You'll stall the drugs squad for me. You'll buy me a little more time.'

There was another silence, a longer one. And then an audible sigh.

'All right, Bailey. You win. I forgot just how stubborn you can be. I guess that's one of the reasons you're so good. You never give up.' He paused. 'You've got two weeks, maximum. If you can't establish anything solid by then, we're pulling you out. End of story.'

65

Bailey lay on her bunk staring up at the ceiling, counting the cracks in the paintwork, speculating with a slight tinge of guilt that it was kind of nice to have the cell to herself for the time being. Privacy was at such a premium in this place. But, of course, for Sharon's sake, she would have wished for different circumstances in which to have obtained that privacy.

An orange light filtered through the small window as the sun went down outside, the bars casting long shadows against one wall. She was now locked in for the evening and activity within the prison had died down to the sporadic clang here and there of a distant door opening and closing, the odd shout, the odd cry.

With Sharon's demise, the overall sense of claustrophobia in the prison had grown even more cloying. Now as night fell, it began to impinge on Bailey more than ever. She lay there, acutely aware that, all alone, she was that much more vulnerable to someone sneaking in when she was asleep pulling out a knife and—

She shut off the thought. She couldn't afford to let herself succumb to the fear that was enveloping the rest of the inmates otherwise she'd be no good to anyone.

Maybe Frank did have a point about her mental state. After all, here she was insisting on remaining locked up in this miserable and oppressive place surrounded by people who'd happily do her in without a second thought if they knew she was a policewoman. On top of that she was trapped in here with a killer who appeared to have a penchant for scalping and it wasn't wildly unrealistic to suppose that she herself could be the next victim.

Maybe that last job had sent her round the bend. Maybe she should be paying more attention to Doctor Bodie...

Screw that.

She reminded herself why she was still here. She was here to find out who killed Alice and make sure that they faced the appropriate justice.

It was all about justice at the end of the day.

Justice was the spur that drove her onwards from deep within. Jennifer. An eight-year-old child standing permanently on the periphery of her consciousness, demanding justice, ever since she'd gone missing all those years before. Bailey couldn't let her down.

She'd told Frank that she was their best shot. But was she really? Now that she knew it wasn't the gang, she was right back at square one. The murder squad, with their team of dedicated detectives and their fancy technical resources, had been working on this since the beginning and had made little progress in their investigation. Did she really believe that she could do better than them just by herself, all in the space of the next two weeks? Doubts were starting to creep in...

She forcibly quashed them and turned her thoughts again to the evidence, rolling it over and over in her mind, trying to establish a new perspective from which to approach it.

She needed to think like a homicide detective.

She needed to think in terms of offender profiling.

What could she infer about the characteristics of the offender based upon their crime scene behaviour?

There was obviously one blatant element that linked all of the murders – the victims had all been scalped. And that was really all that she had to go on right now. So that had to be where she started.

She'd assumed that this mutilation had just been a gory way for the gang to strike fear into the inmate population. But if the murders weren't connected to drugs and power, then it would seem that the scalping formed a reason in and of itself.

But who would do such a thing and for what reason? It made little sense, but whatever the motive, the perpetrator was clearly a very sick and dangerous individual.

There had to be some clue somewhere in this huge dilapidated dump. She lay there on her bunk and thought about everything that she'd seen and experienced over the past few weeks, raking over her memories for any salient details. There had to be something. There had to be.

66

The Governor stood by the window in his office and watched the inmates trudging around in the prison yard on their morning exercise. It was at times like this that he was pleasantly reminded that everything he could survey, from horizon to horizon, fell under his domain. Admittedly, the horizon stopped dead at the huge perimeter wall that blocked out the rest of the outside world. But still, it felt good to be the one in charge, the one to whom all here had to defer. He wasn't just the Governor, he was the Guv'nor and this was his manor. There was just one thing which gnawed away at this feeling of potency and that was the nagging issue of these blasted murders.

Of course they were shocking and tragic occurrences. But it really didn't do to have these policemen here all the time. Not only was this his turf and he resented their infringement upon it, but they didn't even seem to be doing their job very well as they still hadn't caught anyone.

Moreover, his real worry was that this whole situation was in danger of drawing attention to the place. More specifically, he was worried that it would draw attention to him. It would make him look inept. And that wasn't good for his career. Or for his knighthood. Because that's what he was angling for – to make it onto the honours list next year. And an OBE wouldn't cut it. No way. It was a knighthood or nothing as far as he was concerned. And he didn't see why not. He had spent years running various prisons up and down the country, doing his bit for society. He had quite literally served his time and now he felt that it was only fair that he was rewarded for that.

That's why he wished the murders would just go away. At least they hadn't been plastered all over the media. Not yet. His strategy of containment appeared to be working so far. No one outside the prison seemed to be paying too much attention to what was going on inside. He just hoped that it would stay that way. Otherwise it could really damage his credibility with the Home Secretary.

He turned away from the window and stopped for a moment to admire a framed photograph that hung on the wall of his office. It had been taken at an official function and it depicted the Governor smiling broadly whilst shaking hands with the Home Secretary. The Governor had been working hard to make a good impression on him and he felt that he was getting close to the point where he could almost call him a friend.

With the Home Secretary behind his nomination for a knighthood, he knew that it would be a shoo-in, so he'd been progressively grooming him, slipping him hints here and there whenever they met at official functions and the like, with the hope that he would submit a nomination on the Governor's behalf. The important thing was to appear humble and selfless and committed, which he was quite good at doing.

He looked at his watch. It was eleven o'clock. He felt a little buzz of pleasure. The Governor had a ritual which he meticulously stuck to every day. At eleven o'clock, he would sit down at his desk with his Danish pastry and coffee, with strict instructions not to be disturbed, and read through the latest issue of *Yachting World*. He often advised the inmates that having some form of daily routine would help them to deal with doing their time. Well, they had their routines and he had his.

He sat down at his desk, opened up the magazine, took a sip of his coffee and chewed on a mouthful of Danish pastry. He leafed through the reviews section, eagerly absorbing the technical specifications of the newest models, thinking again about the Beneteau cruiser he was planning to buy – a sleek white forty-footer with that tasteful wooden decking at the aft that you could turn into a bathing platform once you were anchored somewhere.

Maybe once he'd got his yacht, he'd invite the Home Secretary on board. After he'd got his knighthood of course. It wouldn't look very humble to be swanning around on an expensive yacht before then. They would sit on the deck and drink fine brandy, maybe smoke a cigar, and chat like the patrician men that they were, about things like the state of the nation and the damn difficulty in finding a decent tailor these days.

He smiled to himself, lost in his fantasy, when the phone on his desk rang, jerking him out of his reverie. It was the prison switchboard.

He sighed in irritation. Didn't they know better than to disturb him between eleven and eleven thirty? He could choose to not answer it. But then again... it might just be the Home Secretary returning one of his calls.

Better safe than sorry. He picked up the phone.

'Yes, what is it?' he said brusquely.

'I have a journalist here on the line,' replied the switchboard operator. 'Shall I put her through?'

'A journalist?' He felt a bite of anxiety. 'What does she want?'

'She wants to know if you have any comment on the story that's in today's paper.'

'Story? What story?'

67

Sitting by herself in the corner of the canteen, Bailey absently pushed the spaghetti carbonara around on her plate and reflected on how quickly they'd cleaned up the mess in the kitchen after Sharon's death. The scene of crime officers had finished their business with admirable speed and minimal disruption to the inmates' feeding routine. It was impressive, if rather clinical.

She looked up from her pasta to see Mel limping along holding a tray of food, her frizzy hair bobbing up and down, her big brown eyes rolling nervously from side to side.

A feeling had started to grow in Bailey that Mel wasn't just some headcase. Sure she was unhinged, but there was something more to her, Bailey was certain. Mel knew something. She knew something about the murders. Any mention of scalping seemed to set her off, like that time she had suddenly stormed out of the canteen. Of course, Alice – her cellmate, who she'd liked – had been murdered in a particularly brutal fashion, and Mel did smoke way too much dope, but Bailey sensed that her reactions stemmed from something deeper and more significant than either of these things. Locked inside that crazy head of hers was some vital piece of information and Bailey was determined to find out what it was.

Someone sat down next to her, breaking her train of thought. It was Keisha. Then Rong sat down. Then Muscles. And then Poppy.

They bantered for a bit, distracting her from her observations of Mel.

After a short while, Toni came and joined them. She looked tense and preoccupied. They all fell silent. They knew better than to speak up when she was in a mood like this.

She looked like she was going to say something. They waited expectantly.

She scanned the canteen suspiciously then, turning her attention back to them, spoke in a very low voice, almost a whisper. 'Turns out that fucking bitch was Old Bill.'

A preliminary chill shot through Bailey.

'Who?' said Keisha.

'Remember that one who got it in the laundry a while back?'

'She was a cop?!' exclaimed Poppy.

'No shit!' growled Rong.

'A fucking pig?!'

'That fucking bitch!'

'How did you find that out?' asked Bailey, attempting to keep her voice level.

'It was in today's paper,' said Toni. 'Apparently the police tried to cover up her death, so her family went to the newspaper. Turns out that she was undercover right here in this prison.'

'An undercover cop,' muttered Keisha, glancing around apprehensively. 'If there was one, there could be more. Sitting in here right now. We could be surrounded by them.'

Bailey took a deep breath and kept her calm. She scowled and looked over her shoulder in a similarly paranoid fashion.

'Maybe that's why Terry was arrested,' said Rong. 'What do you think, Toni?'

All eyes turned to Toni. She grimaced, her gold tooth glinting.

'Stay vigilant and look out for anyone who's acting suspicious.'

Her eyes rested on Bailey for what Bailey thought was a fraction of a second longer than they needed to. Or was she just imagining it?

* * *

At the first opportunity, Bailey made her way to the phones, where she waited impatiently in the queue for a booth to become free.

She was on edge, acutely aware that, thanks to the newspaper story, many of those around her now had their eyes open to the possibility that there could be an undercover police officer in their midst. It lurked there in every glance in her direction, every veiled whisper. But she knew that it was mostly just in her head and she fought to keep those negative thoughts at bay. No one knew who she really was and she was going to make sure it stayed that way. So long as she kept her cool, she would be fine.

A phone became free. She scurried over to it and hurriedly punched in her PIN, followed by Frank's number.

'Hello, Sullivan Knight Solicitors,' said Rita in her customary sing-song tones.

'It's Bailey Pike speaking. I'd like to talk to Mr Knight please,' said Bailey, reciting the words as if by rote.

'Just putting you through.'

She got to listen to less than two seconds of Beethoven's 'Moonlight Sonata' before Frank came on the line. He dived in immediately, clearly expecting her call.

'Bailey, it's as much of a surprise to me as it is to you. The first I knew of it was this morning's paper, but there was no way for me to get hold of you. Is your cover still intact?'

'I think so. I can't tell for sure. But either way, this revelation is something I just don't need right now.'

'I'm really pissed off with the family,' he huffed. 'I thought I made it quite clear to them that this kind of action could endanger ongoing police operations.'

'Well, what's done is done. I'll just have to be that bit more careful.' She paused. 'One thing it did prove though is that up until this morning the gang had no idea that Alice was an undercover police officer, which only serves to reinforce my belief that they didn't kill her, or any of the others for that matter.'

'But are you any closer to finding out who actually did do it and why? I told the drugs squad you'd found a new angle and that seemed to satisfy them for the time being, but time is running out, Bailey.'

'You don't need to remind me.'

68

Bailey stood just outside the cell, to one side of the open door, eavesdropping on their conversation, trying to ascertain what they were saying above the soporific bass beat of the dub.

'You know, I see him as a chocolate digestives man,' she could hear Kay saying. 'Dark chocolate, obviously. There's something classic about them which I think would appeal to him.'

'No way,' said Seema. 'He'd be into something Belgian, like those butter waffle-style ones that they like to eat over there. Or no, actually, the more I think about it, he'd probably go for Oreo cookies. All those years in Hollywood, he surely would have gone native by now, certainly in terms of biscuits anyway.'

'You're missing my point. We're not talking about what he actually eats in real life. We're talking hypothetically here. We're imagining a biscuit as an embodiment of man and man as an embodiment of a biscuit. There is a human spectrum and a biscuit spectrum and we are trying to establish, in his case, where those two spectrums intersect.'

'I see... okay. We're getting kind of metaphysical here.'

It didn't take long for Bailey to realise who they were talking about. After all, their conversations appeared to revolve around a fairly limited set of topics.

She turned into the cell and leant against the doorway.

'I think he'd probably go for Garibaldi,' she said. 'As biscuits go, they possess a certain masculine quality, don't you think? And that definitely makes them worthy of a world-class kickboxer.'

Kay, who was sitting on the desk chair, looked up slowly, squinting at her through the miasma of dope smoke that filled the cell.

'Oh... it's you again. Haven't seen you for a while. Got any more gear?'

Bailey reached into her tracksuit pocket and pulled out the original bag of weed she'd purchased from Keisha several weeks earlier. Not having touched it since the last time she'd been in this cell, she still had a fair amount left over.

She tossed it over to Kay, sitting at the table, whose eyes flared in appreciation as she eagerly pulled open the little bag and began to construct a new joint.

Seema peered up at Bailey from the lower bunk. Her face creased in thought.

'Garibaldi, huh? A controversial choice.' She turned to Mel who was slumped next to her. 'What do you think, Mel?'

Mel was just staring vacantly into middle space. She hadn't demonstrated the slightest awareness of Bailey's presence. Seema nudged her.

'Uhhh?' said Mel, blinking and shaking her head clear.

'Garibaldi? Jean-Claude? Yes? No?'

Mel looked slowly at each of them in turn with her big bloodshot eyes, befuddled as to what they were talking about.

Bailey sat down on the edge of the bunk next to Mel and waited for Kay to finish making the joint. After a minute or so, Kay held up the completed spliff with a flourish.

'I think that's definitely a nine out of ten.'

She lit it, took a few deep drags and then passed it to Bailey.

Bailey once again pretended to participate, being careful not to inhale. She needed to be on the ball for the next stage of this little plan.

As soon as it looked like they were relaxed with her presence in the cell, she yawned and spoke casually as if she was just starting a random conversation.

'You know, me and you have got something in common now, Mel.'

Mel frowned in puzzlement. 'Uh?'

'Yeah. Both of us had cellmates who were murdered. Your one, Ally, was first. Then my one, Sharon just the other day, in the kitchen.'

Mel convulsed slightly, eyeing her warily.

'Then there were those other two as well,' continued Bailey. 'Poodle and Natalie. That makes four in total.'

Mel twitched reflexively at the mention of the murders. She tried to suppress her agitation, but her fingers drummed against the surface of the bunk. Bailey observed her reactions closely.

'Aren't you all a bit worried?' asked Bailey, addressing the question to the three of them. 'I'm a bit worried that the next time it could be me or you.'

'I am totally shitting myself,' said Seema, looking around fearfully. 'The prison is supposed to protect the world from us. But who protects us from the prison?'

'No one's going to protect us,' Kay scoffed. 'The more of us that get killed the better. Don't you see? It's all part of their plan. Each one of us that dies, it's one less mouth for the taxpayer to feed.'

'The weird thing is that they were all scalped,' said Bailey. 'Don't you think that's weird?'

Mel tensed. Her eyes rolled even more. Her knuckles turned white as she gripped the bedspread, the material bunching up around her. The tendons stood out on her arms, hands and neck.

'What do you reckon, Mel?' Bailey asked, leaning in a little closer to Mel. 'Why do you think they were scalped?'

'Uh-oh,' muttered Seema. 'I don't think you want to be asking her about that.'

'Ah let her...' said Kay. 'This could be interesting.'

'What do you think, Mel?' said Bailey, trying to probe a little further without sounding too much like a policewoman. 'Why on earth were they scalped?'

A low guttural moan came from Mel. Bailey shuddered, genuinely disturbed by the torment and horror which she detected in the depths of those bloodshot brown eyes.

'You've done it now,' said Seema, edging away from Mel on the bunk as if she were a bomb about to explode.

Mel swung her head round to skewer Bailey with a deranged stare. Bailey recoiled slightly.

'Him a duppy,' hissed Mel. 'Duppies always get yuh inna de end! De duppies gwine kill wi aal!'

'Duppy?' said Bailey. 'What's a duppy?'

'Jamaican folklore bullshit,' said Kay.

'Mi told yuh,' uttered Mel to no one in particular. 'Mi told yuh him was bak. Mi told yuh! Ah him. Him ah bak! AH HIM!'

Her entire body began to twist in anguish while a subdued moaning issued from her throat.

Mel's shaking hand shot out, her fingers scrabbling for a sheet of paper from the bed beside her. She started folding it without even looking at it, making neat precise creases. She knew what she was doing.

Bailey leaned closer to Mel, who was staring into middle space whilst simultaneously folding the paper. She appeared to be mumbling something.

'...ertresorertresorertresorertresor...'

Bailey couldn't make out what it was. She leaned in closer still.

'What's that, Mel?'

Mel ignored her, the paper rustling. Seema and Kay were now sitting as far back away from Mel as their respective corners of the cell would allow them.

Mel burbled the same noise over and over again like a Buddhist mantra while the paper rustled, a small origami animal beginning to take form.

'...ertresorertresorertresorertresor...'

'I can't hear you, Mel,' said Bailey getting closer, close enough that she could feel Mel's hot breath on her face. 'Speak up.'

'If you know what's good for you,' whispered Seema. 'You'll stop right there.'

But Bailey pressed on. 'Mel. Why do you think they're scalped?'

Mel suddenly stopped folding the paper. A half-completed origami duck fell between her legs. Both Kay and Seema watched it drop in horror. They had never seen Mel not complete a duck.

Mel's eyes suddenly focused on Bailey. She spat a single word at her.

'HAIRDRESSA!'

Then like a banshee Mel was up and had her hands around Bailey's throat, wrestling her to the ground.

Before she had time to react, Bailey was off the bunk and on her back on the concrete floor with Mel sitting astride her, screaming and throttling her.

Bailey gasped and tried to speak but she could hardly even breathe. 'Uhhh... Mel... ughhh... puh-lease...'

Mel's mouth was wide open, yellow teeth bared, emitting a wail like an air-raid siren that just would not stop. Her bloodshot eyes stared into Bailey's with the force of industrial lasers.

Bailey wasn't weak, but she was no match for a strength drawn from a deep reservoir of madness.

'MI KILL HIM! MI FUCKING KILL HIM!' screeched Mel.

'Go for it, Mel!' Bailey heard Kay shout in encouragement. She was enjoying the spectacle.

Mel's fingers were like metal rods bending into the soft flesh of her neck, squeezing her windpipe, cutting off the blood in the arteries in her neck. Bailey tried to lever her fingers under Mel's hands, but it was no use. It was as if they were welded to her neck.

With a horrifying finality, Bailey suddenly realised that Mel would kill her unless she did something fast. She had unleashed something beyond her control.

She clenched her fists and put them together and, with all the force her fading strength could muster, she punched Mel in both breasts.

Mel's wailing suddenly went off-pitch with a high squeak of pain and, for just a moment, her grip weakened on Bailey's neck and that was all Bailey needed. Using a jiu-jitsu counter she had learnt in defensive groundwork training, she pushed Mel's right elbow outwards, causing her to lose balance and topple sideways. She then got her knee up underneath her and kicked downwards hard, knocking Mel's leg away.

She flipped Mel over on her back, wrenching her hands from her throat. Suddenly their positions were reversed. Bailey pinned one of Mel's arms down with her knee and the other down with her hand and used her remaining arm to shove an elbow across her neck to force her head back against the floor.

Bailey caught her breath. God, it felt good to be able to breathe. She leaned in close to Mel's contorted face.

'Mel, I'm not the killer,' she panted. 'The killer is out there. Not in here.'

Mel gasped and wheezed. Her eyes rolled. Once again Mel wasn't there. She was in some other place.

Bailey braced herself and then jumped off Mel as fast as she could, lurching to the far side of the cell and into the doorway. But Mel just lay there on the ground panting, gibbering, tears running from her eyes, her energy spent.

'Bor-ing,' said Kay.

'Now you know why we call her Crazy Mel,' said Seema.

69

The tattoo gun whirred as the tiny needle etched its marks into the flesh of her lower back, Poppy pausing intermittently to dip it into the pot of ink beside her.

Coming here was still a necessity for Bailey if she realistically wanted to maintain her cover. Although the focus of her investigation had now shifted away from the gang, she couldn't just decide to part company with them unless she wanted to discover exactly what 'blood out' entailed, and she was in no rush to do that.

Anyhow, she'd grown to look forward to these sessions, having become accustomed to the pain, and found it satisfying to witness the gradual completion of what was shaping up to be a beautiful and intricate tattoo, even if ultimately she might have to get rid of it.

She heard Poppy suddenly gasp.

'What's the matter?' said Bailey.

'You've got a nasty bruise on your neck.'

'It's nothing. I had a run-in with one of the more unbalanced inmates.'

'Who?' asked Poppy, a dangerous tone in her voice. 'I'll sort her out.'

'Really, it's nothing. It looks worse than it is. I honestly can't feel a thing.'

'If you say so...'

Bailey felt Poppy's fingertips tenderly brush across the bruised tissue.

They lingered there for a short while, then they trailed down to the hard ridges of scar tissue and cigarette burns which adorned her neck and upper back.

'Tell me about him,' said Poppy.

'Who?'

'Your ex. The one who did this to you.'

Bailey was silent for a few moments. She desperately craved the catharsis of being able to spill the truth to Poppy, but there was only so much she could reveal.

'I should never have got involved with him in the first place.'

'How did you meet him?'

'It was through work.'

It had all started when the police arrested Spyros Scafidi, a Greek national who occupied a key logistical role in the car theft ring.

The ring was operated by a notorious and well-established London crime family who had their tentacles in many places, car theft being one of their more lucrative enterprises.

They targeted top-of-the-range vehicles, premium brands, which they acquired through all manner of means, from keyless theft to straightforward carjacking. The stolen cars were taken to a network of scrapyards and lock-up garages which the gang owned around the country, where the necessary work was done on them to obscure their dodgy provenance. Then they were sold abroad in the kinds of places where law enforcement was slack, corruption was rife and wealthy people wanted nice cars without asking too many questions about where they came from.

And that's where Spyros entered the picture. He was in charge of getting the cars to their destinations without anyone realising they were stolen. He worked out the routes, manipulated the paperwork and conducted the necessary liaisons with crooked customs officials.

It was largely thanks to him that the operation was so successful, netting the gang tens of millions of pounds a year. But Interpol had been tracking him for a while, suspecting his involvement in the movement of stolen cars. And so it was that, following a joint surveillance operation with the UK National Crime Agency, they finally pounced on him. On his laptop, they found material that incontrovertibly linked him to the theft of a large number of vehicles in the UK. To save himself a heavy jail sentence, he turned informant and agreed to help the authorities infiltrate the gang's operation so they could gather enough hard evidence to nail the ringleaders. With his help, a sequence of undercover police officers were inserted into the organisation, each one vouching for the next. Bailey was fourth in the chain, infiltrated as a secretary into their modern, airy west London offices.

The place was clean, slick, open-plan. It resembled the offices of any successful mid-sized business. On the surface, the people there were operating a bona fide business focused on the sale and export of prestige cars. They talked in terms of revenue projections and market penetration, pricing strategy and supply chain, lead generation and sales pipelines. They took it seriously. It almost sounded legitimate.

Her job was mundane – answering the phone, taking minutes of meetings, making travel arrangements – routine administrative tasks that she diligently performed whilst carefully fostering a meek and obedient demeanour.

But beneath the boring clerical work, she was quietly gathering evidence against them: secretly recording their conversations, copying computer files onto a memory stick, taking down details of names, places, dates and transactions – constructing a picture of how they operated and who did what, with the aim of reaching that critical point where the police could swoop in and arrest them all.

Despite the run-of-the-mill, almost anodyne, nature of the office, she didn't let herself get complacent for one second. She was under no illusions as to what would happen to her if the gang sussed her out. She was aware of just how ruthless they were and knew that for them murder was a necessary tool of the business when circumstances dictated.

The day it all went wrong had started out just like any other day there – typing up agendas and sorting out air tickets, followed by a meeting with a prospective client from South Africa. The meeting was supposed to be held in the lobby of an upmarket central London hotel. Meetings were often held there because it impressed clients and promoted the image of the gang as trustworthy, respectable businessmen, which is how they liked to see themselves.

It was whilst she was in the back of the car, on the way to the meeting, sandwiched between two particularly brawny members of the gang, their muscles bursting out of their Savile Row suits, that she realised that something was amiss.

Instead of driving into central London, she noticed that they were in fact on the A12 heading eastwards out of the city in the direction of Essex. At that point a bad feeling began to gnaw at her.

'Just got to make a little detour first,' was the answer when she casually enquired where they were going.

If a problem arose while she was working undercover, she would send a coded text message to her police colleagues to let them know that something was up, and if need be they could triangulate her position from her mobile phone signal.

She reached into her bag. But her phone wasn't there. A bolt of alarm shot through her. She rooted further. It definitely wasn't in there.

'Lost something?'

'My phone.' She sighed, playing ditzy. 'Silly me. Must have left it on my desk.'

But she knew they must have taken it from her bag when she wasn't looking. They were one step ahead of her. Something was definitely up.

But she couldn't afford to panic, or to show any kind of fear. That would have given the game away for sure. So she sat there, quietly trying to anticipate, with a mounting dread, what lay in wait for her when they reached their final destination.

The traffic thinned out as they entered a bleak industrial estate situated just beyond the north-eastern outskirts of the city – big grey warehouses, empty units, vacant weed-strewn lots... and the location of one of their scrapyards.

The scrapyard had big concrete walls with broken bottles set into the cement along the top. The metal gate rolled back to let them in and then clanged shut behind them. The place was filled with stacks of rusted cars, towering five or six high – write-offs destined for scrap. All around, among the dirty puddles in the pitted ground, lay bits of engines and other car parts. Over to one side was a row of grim-looking concrete workshops, outside of which were two huge, slavering Rottweilers chained to a metal post.

It was when the car stopped that they started on her. Within the tight confines of the vehicle, they grilled her relentlessly, two in the back on either side of her, and two in the front, all of them aggressively firing ques- tions and accusations at her.

They alleged that she was an undercover cop, claiming they had it on good authority from a source inside the police who'd tipped them off to her presence. But whether that was true or whether they were bluffing, she wasn't going to admit that she was anything other than an innocent secretary.

Never break cover. Whatever they might say. Whatever they might claim.

Never. Break. Cover.

They knew an informant must have been involved in her infiltration and they wanted to know who this traitor was. They wanted her to give up Spyros. But she couldn't afford to do that. She denied all knowledge of what they were talking about.

But these weren't the kind of people who took no for an answer.

So they hauled her out of the car, dragging her through the puddles into one of the workshops – a cold, bare room – where they chained her up and hung her from a meat hook suspended from one of the metal rafters.

And they left her to him.

Her torturer.

She hadn't seen him before. Perhaps they'd brought him in especially. A professional sadist with a taste for designer labels and clove cigarettes. He was methodical and systematic in his infliction of pain. And up close, in his face, it was plain to see that he derived pleasure from her every gasp of agony.

They established a strange twisted intimacy revolving around the name that he wanted from her... the name that she steadfastly refused to give him... and the pain and violations which inevitably followed her denials.

At some point, she spat in his face. Fuck you. He didn't like that. Made her pay. But she knew that the longer she resisted, the longer she would stay alive, for as soon as she caved in, they would have no further use for her.

She lost track of how long they kept her hanging there, chained up from the rafters, caked in her own blood. All she knew for sure was that if it kept on going the way it was going, then she'd eventually die. But chained up as she was, escape was impossible. And in a place this out of the way, her screams would go unheard.

It was while she was being held there that Spyros caught wind of the fact that they'd captured an undercover cop. Fearful that she would expose him under the pressure of their brutal methods, he panicked and fled. He ran to the police for protection, taking his wife and two children with him, knowing full well that the gang would not only kill him but them as well if they knew he was an informant.

The problem, however, was that neither Spyros nor the police had any idea where the gang was holding Bailey, so they were powerless to help her. She was all by herself.

As soon as Spyros split, the gang realised that he was the traitor they were looking for and that they therefore no longer needed Bailey. So they unchained her with the intention of disposing of her.

Teetering on the verge of consciousness, weak from loss of blood, dehydrated, she knew that the end had come. Regardless of whether they knew she was a policewoman or not, she knew that they couldn't risk keeping her alive after what they'd subjected her to.

Pretending to have passed out completely, she let them drag her out of the workshop, all the while forcing her shattered mind to desperately try and fathom some last way out of this.

They threw her in the boot of a knackered old Toyota sedan and slammed the lid shut, leaving her in darkness. Lying there, she could overhear them talking, discussing the best way to get rid of her. And what she heard confirmed the worst rumours she'd heard about them. They were going to throw her in the crusher.

According to gangland hearsay, this was how they liked to dispose of their enemies – by putting them in a car which then went into a giant industrial baling press to be crushed into a compacted cube of scrap metal. That was to be her fate.

She listened to them arguing about who was going to do it, and as she lay there in the boot of the car, she knew that she had an ever-decreasing window in which to try and make her escape.

Eventually one of them was nominated to drive the forklift truck and take her to the crusher. She squirmed around desperately in the cramped blackness, probing in vain for some means of escape. A short while later there was a loud crunching sound as the prongs of the forklift truck smashed through the side windows of the car. She felt the car being lifted up and carried along.

Summoning up her last reserves of energy, she pushed with all her might at the lid of the boot... but it was locked shut. Then she remembered that, with some cars like this, it was possible to push down the back seats in order to create extra storage room. So she turned her attention to the back seats, feeling for some kind of lever or latch that would push them down. But she couldn't find anything. In the end, brute force sufficed. She dug down deep inside herself to find the strength in her weakened legs. Squeezing herself into a position of maximum leverage, she repeatedly slammed her feet into the back seats until something finally snapped and one of them went down.

Peering through the gap, she could make out the stacks of rusted cars passing by as they trundled through the scrapyard on their way to the crusher. Eventually they came to a halt, and with a jerk and a crash, the car was dropped to the ground next to the crusher.

From her vantage point in the boot, Bailey could just about see what it looked like – a giant metal box-shaped contraption which had a booth at one end with a huge hydraulic arm with pincers that would pick the car up and drop it into the opening at the top.

She pushed her head out a little further and saw that the forklift truck driver had parked the truck and was now walking over to the crusher. By the looks of it, fortunately, he was now the only person in the vicinity. This was her only chance.

She watched him begin to climb up the metal ladder into the crusher's control booth. As he was doing so, while his back was turned, she furiously squirmed out of the boot, into the back of the car and then wormed her way out of one of the broken passenger windows. She rolled away through the mud and the puddles, scrambling for cover beneath a towering stack of rusty cars.

From her concealed position, she watched as he operated the hydraulic arm, lowering the metal pincers onto the car's roof, clamping them shut with a metallic crunch, lifting it up and then dropping it into the crusher. She saw him smiling to himself as he methodically worked the levers in the control booth, the crusher wheezing and groaning as it chomped the car one way and then the other with the deafening sound of rending metal.

She didn't stick around to watch the cube pop out the other end. Instead, she slipped rapidly away through the piles of cars, limping through the dirt as fast as she could, exhausted beyond all belief, willing herself onwards, searching for a way out of this metal graveyard.

But the place was like a maze, with many paths leading to dead-ends among the chaotic mounds of scrap metal. Turning a corner, she suddenly found herself out by the workshops. There they were, standing around outside, smoking, chatting and joking amongst themselves like nothing was amiss, like they hadn't just decided to throw a woman into an industrial car crusher.

The Rottweilers noticed her and starting barking their heads off and straining at their leashes, trying to get away from the metal post they were chained to. But the gang members didn't cotton on, couldn't understand why the dogs were barking. They shouted at them to shut up.

Bailey drew back sharply, retreating into the forest of rusted metal, and eventually managed to navigate her way to the concrete wall which enclosed the place. She determined that her best bet was to clamber up a precarious stack of rusted cars next to it, and then haul herself over the top. So that's what she did, slicing her hands on the jagged glass of the broken bottles, dropping down on the other side into the weeds and gravel of an empty lot.

She staggered away through the backstreets, eventually getting to a main road, where she managed to wave down a supermarket delivery lorry. The driver, aghast at her blood-covered appearance, wanted to take her straight to the hospital, but she insisted on going directly to the nearest police station.

The gang were eventually sent down on the basis of the evidence that she'd gathered, along with the testimony of Spyros, and most of them were now serving long sentences. She in turn had been commended for her courage and her professionalism.

As for the supposed source inside the police who'd betrayed her, nothing had ever come to light despite Frank's best efforts to get to the bottom of it. One of these days she'd find out who it was though, no doubt about that. And when she did, her justice would be unforgiving.

And her torturer? He had never been caught, or even identified. He was out there somewhere. But she would never forget his face, never forget the smell of his clove cigarettes, never forget the pleasure he took in violating, hurting and maiming her. She would get him too at some point, that was for sure, and when she finally caught up with him, she would make him pay dearly for what he'd done to her.

He'd given her the scar on her left cheek, carved it slowly into her face with his straight razor and a lascivious grin. She'd been offered plastic surgery to deal with it. Maybe she'd take up the offer one day. But not until she'd found him. Until then she'd wear the scar like a badge of faith, along with all the others across her body – a commitment to never give up in her quest to track him down and punish him.

A surge of raw emotion threatened to overwhelm her. For a brief moment, she thought she might break down and cry. Only Alice would have understood. If only Alice was still around.

Poppy must have sensed her disquiet. She gently stroked Bailey's shoulder.

'Bad memories, huh? Forget about him.' Her fingers began to trace a slow path down Bailey's spine. 'Just forget all about him.'

Her voice was husky and soothing, her caress tender and healing. The tattoo gun had been switched off and the cell was silent but for their breathing.

'I've got a plan,' said Poppy softly. 'For when I get out of here.'

'It's good to have a goal to work towards.'

Poppy sighed, a soft melancholy sound injected with desire. Her fingertips continued their ever-so-gentle route down Bailey's spine. Her touch sent electrical tingles up her back. The atmosphere was suddenly charged with a sexual tension that had caught Bailey wholly by surprise.

'It's like a dream of mine,' said Poppy. 'And I want you to be part of it.'

'Uh... you do know I'm straight, don't you?'

Poppy's fingers paused their progress. 'Sure. I know you are.'

'But we can still be friends, right?'

'Sure.' Poppy's voice was colder now, more businesslike.

She climbed off Bailey.

'We're done for today,' she said.

'But we've only just started.'

Bailey sat up. Poppy was standing by the window, gazing out at the distant reservoir. Bailey could see that she had been hurt by her rejection.

'Tell me about your plans,' she said gently.

'Some other time maybe.'

Bailey shrugged and put her clothes on. She genuinely liked Poppy and didn't enjoy seeing her upset, but she had a feeling that whatever she now said would only aggravate her mood.

As she turned to leave the cell, she paused for a moment in the doorway and glanced over her shoulder in regret, hoping for a reprieve. But it was clear from Poppy's demeanour that she was hoping in vain. So she continued on her way, annoyed with herself for feeling so perturbed.

70

The inmates sat in the canteen eating lunch whilst the prison officers made their rounds, taking down their applications. Applications were any requests that the inmates might have for particular items or things that they wanted to do, such as arrange a visit or purchase a new computer game.

Bailey sat alone in the corner of the canteen, watching the inmates and the prison officers as they interacted with each other. She had her eye on one particular inmate:

Mel.

She was sitting, as always, with Kay and Seema.

Ever since their recent near-calamitous encounter, Mel's hysteric utterance had been playing on Bailey's mind.

Hairdressa.

What did that mean exactly?

Mel hadn't been in any state to answer further questions, but Bailey's instincts told her that she was onto something and that she should dig a little more. This time she'd try and catch Mel when she wasn't with the other two. She just had to remember to play it careful.

Bailey had observed that Mel had a routine of sorts. Directly after lunch she usually went for a walk in the yard by herself, after which she would go and get stoned with Kay and Seema.

Bailey had decided that Mel's post-lunch walk presented the best opportunity to catch her alone for a second approach.

A shadow fell across the table.

'Any applications to make today?'

She recognised that voice.

She looked up. It was Terry standing there. So he was back at work again. A shudder of revulsion went through her.

She smiled a fake smile.

'No. Not today,' she said.

He nodded slowly, his gaze lingering on her. Did he suspect her or was she just imagining it? She watched him walk off, once again feeling the icy grip of paranoia. She glanced around the canteen. It suddenly felt like the walls were closing in on her. She needed to get out of here.

She looked back to where Mel had been sitting. Her seat was now empty. Bailey stood up, put her tray in the rack and walked out of the canteen.

* * *

Mel sat on the ground by herself at the edge of the yard, staring down at the dirt with wide-open eyes. Her lips moved furiously as she conducted some intense debate either with herself or with some party invisible to all but her. Her face flitted wildly from expression to expression – puzzlement, anger, surprise, humour and back to anger – punctuated frequently by a pointed finger, a conciliatory palm, a clenched fist.

On the far side of the yard, Bailey stood and watched her, attempting to gauge the best way to approach her. As she did so, she reflexively massaged the red bruises on her neck that she had sustained from Mel only too recently.

Bailey wondered if Mel had a shank. She looked paranoid enough to carry one and unbalanced enough to be capable of sticking it into anyone who might upset her. And, as Bailey knew, it wasn't that hard to upset her.

Sod it, she thought. *Let's just get on with it.*

She set off across the yard towards Mel, skirting the groups of inmates standing around in the afternoon sun. As she neared Mel, she slowed to the kind of cautious, guarded pace that you might use to approach a large, dangerous-looking dog.

'Hey,' she said quietly, as she stopped a few feet away from her, the closest safe distance from which to conduct a conversation.

Mel blinked up at her, frozen in mid-gesticulation. Her bulging eyes showed no recognition as she looked Bailey up and down blankly.

'It's me, Bailey, remember?'

Mel eyed her warily.

Hoping to appear less threatening, Bailey squatted down on her haunches so she was facing Mel on the same level.

'I wanted to have a little chat with you,' said Bailey gently. 'Is that okay?'

'Mel just wants to chill out... chill out, yeah.'

'Sure, Mel. I'll let you chill out. Just one thing though. When we were... uh... chatting the other day, you said a word. You said...' Bailey braced herself. '...Hairdressa.'

At the sound of the word, Mel visibly tensed and her eyes narrowed in suspicion. Again, Bailey felt the bite of certainty that she was onto something, that Mel knew something. She was determined to find out what it was.

'I was just wondering what you meant when you said that.'

Mel blinked and shuddered. 'Mel doesn't want to talk about it.'

'It's something to do with your past, isn't it?' said Bailey. 'Is that why you take so many drugs, Mel? To forget about something that happened in the past?'

Mel rocked gently, staring back down at the dirt, her voice now wobbling unevenly. 'Friends... all my friends... all gone now.'

'Tell me what you meant, Mel,' Bailey persisted. 'What did you mean when you said Hairdressa? Is it a person?' She paused. 'Is it the killer?'

Mel stared at the ground mutely, trembling, her eyes open wide.

'If you're scared, Mel, I can protect you,' said Bailey. 'Tell me who the killer is and I can protect you. Tell me and we can all be safer. Do you know who the killer is? I think you know.'

But Mel was now lost in some trance of memory. She seemed to have forgotten that Bailey was there.

Bailey snapped her fingers in front of Mel's face. Mel jerked her face up at Bailey, her teeth bared in a snarl. Bailey flinched, almost toppling over backwards. She recovered her balance and fixed Mel with a firm gaze.

'I think you know something, Mel. I think you know something very important. I think you know who the killer is.'

Mel's demented bloodshot eyes bored into Bailey. 'Mel knows... Yes... Mel definitely knows...'

Bailey's breathing quickened. Excitement seized her. She was almost there.

'Tell me what you know, Mel,' she whispered. 'Tell me who the killer is.'

Mel opened her mouth, ready to speak and spill whatever she knew. Bailey leaned forward in anticipation.

Then Mel abruptly closed her mouth. The derangement in her eyes had receded slightly to be replaced by a sly and calculating look.

'What's it worth?'

Bailey did a double take. 'Sorry?'

'I said what's it worth? Ain't nothing for free in here.'

Bailey sighed. 'Okay. How much money do you want?'

Mel shook her head and licked her lips hungrily.

'I don't want no money.'

71

In the open palm of Bailey's hand were three cling-filmed rocks of crack cocaine. As a member of a drug-dealing gang, getting hold of them hadn't presented her with too much of a problem.

Mel sat entranced on the edge of her bunk, staring at them with a slavering hunger.

The two of them were alone in Mel's cell. Mel's current cellmate, the one who practised yoga, didn't appear to be around at the moment and Bailey was hoping she'd remain absent until Bailey had finished her forthcoming business with Mel.

Mel's eyes were wide, like a kid in a toyshop. She reached up greedily. Bailey closed her hand and lifted the drugs out of reach.

Mel's face turned sullen.

'Gimme the rocks!' she said petulantly.

'When you've told me what you know.'

Mel sat back on her bunk, arms crossed, looking away. She wasn't going to say anything.

When Mel had demanded crack cocaine in exchange for answers, Bailey had been dubious, to say the least, about supplying someone who was already pretty strung out with a drug that was renowned for inducing severe paranoia. But she had no choice if she wanted to find out what Mel knew.

Bailey plucked a single rock from her palm and tossed it into Mel's lap.

Mel looked down and furiously scrabbled for it as it fell onto the bedclothes.

She looked up wildly at Bailey. 'The others!'

'When you've told me who the killer is.'

'I want them now! No rocks no killer!'

Bailey walked backwards a few steps until she was standing above the small toilet in the corner of the cell. She held her hand up over the toilet and placed her other hand on the flush.

'I'll just flush these away. I promise I will. I've got no use for them.'

Mel's face morphed into an expression of alarm and she leant forward, her arm outstretched. 'Nooo... don't do that! I'll tell you.'

Bailey moved forwards and sat down on the chair by the table, positioning herself so she was facing Mel.

Mel scowled at her, huffed and then reached beneath her bunk and groped about under there for a few moments. Her hand emerged holding a plastic bottle with an empty biro tube taped to a hole in the top. A dark cloudy liquid slopped around inside the bottle. Wrapped across the mouth of the bottle was a piece of blackened foil punctured with small holes. The inside of the bottle and tube were encrusted with a brown residue.

Bailey realised that it was a home-made pipe.

Mel reached into a pocket and, after a bit of fumbling, pulled out a small plastic lighter. She carefully unwrapped the rock and placed it on the foil on top of the pipe.

The routine was meticulous and deliberate. Bailey watched her with a grim fascination.

Mel lifted the pipe and placed the tip of the biro tube in her mouth. A brief glance at Bailey and then she flicked the lighter and lowered the flame towards the rock. She sucked in and the flame curled downwards into the foil.

The rock glowed red and crackled as it burned. Dense white smoke filled the inside of the bottle. Mel sucked furiously, her eyes closed, her chest expanding and expanding and expanding. The murky water inside the pipe bubbled as the smoke passed through it, cooling it on the way into her mouth. Then, when she couldn't inhale any more, when she had reached her full lung capacity, she stopped, her mouth tightly closed, her eyes clenched shut.

A few moments passed. Then she exhaled a long stream of white smoke which instantly suffused the cell with a sharp chemical odour. It seemed to take ages for her to empty her lungs of it.

Bailey coughed and waved the smoke out of her face.

Mel slumped back against the wall and emitted a deep orgasmic moan. 'Oh god!'

Bailey watched her, emotionless, tapping her fingers gently against the side of the chair, waiting...

Mel lay there for what may have been a few minutes, bathed in drug bliss. Then, without opening her eyes, she started speaking. To Bailey's surprise, her voice was measured and quite sane-sounding. This was a completely different Mel...

'I used to work the streets around Walsall and Wolverhampton. That's where I'm from. The Midlands. Know it?'

'I've passed through it on the train a few times.'

'I worked in the red-light district there. All Saints it's called. Me and my friends. We did good business. When I came down to London, I did the same thing because that was the only thing I knew how to do. It's what I was best at.'

She sighed and opened her eyes a crack and looked at Bailey, who was listening intently.

'The men are rank and the sex is shit. And it's dodgy as hell. But it's easy money. And if you're desperate for cash because you need to buy drugs, then you do it. You just close your eyes and get on with it.'

Bailey stared at her, saddened that someone could live their life in such a way.

Mel's glazed eyes stared back into the past. 'But then it gets to the point where you're taking the drugs just so you can deal with the sex, which you're doing just so you can buy more drugs. And that's how it goes...'

Bailey didn't want to seem insensitive, but right now she needed to get the name of the killer.

'Yes, Mel, that's, er, interesting, but how does it relate—'

'They found the first one dumped in a car park in Walsall.'

Bailey leaned in closer. Mel had her full attention.

'He'd killed her with a knife. Stabbed her. Cut her throat. But he'd also done... an odd thing.'

'What kind of "odd thing"?'

'He cut her hair off.'

'Cut her hair off?' Bailey frowned, puzzled.

'Yeah. Chopped off a load and took it. Don't ask me why because I don't know.' Mel sighed – a soft sad sound. 'I knew her. She was my friend. They were all my friends. He killed a whole load of them. They were just trying to get by... just like me. We were all just trying to make a living the only way we knew how.'

Her face twisted now, bitter.

'But he didn't care. He killed and killed and killed... girls like me. Easy prey. Girls that had nothing... who had nobody... nobody who cared about them. Maybe that's why they never caught him... because no one really cared enough about us.'

Mel looked distant, lost in the same kind of trance that Bailey had seen her in earlier.

'The Hairdresser. That's what they called him in the newspapers. The Hairdresser... because he took their hair. Killed them and took their hair. Silly name. But he wasn't silly. No no. Not silly at all.'

'When was this?' said Bailey with a frown. She didn't recall hearing about it.

'2014,' said Mel. 'That was the year all my friends were killed. I'll never forget it.'

Mel paused, breathing heavily, her eyes wide, but she was calm. Not manic and paranoid like before, but more collected.

'It got to the point where I was carrying a razor blade for self-protection. Kept it up here.' She rubbed her hand through her tangled afro. 'It's the only place you can keep it when you don't have any clothes on.'

She reached up into her hair and pulled out a razor blade. She held up the rectangular sliver of steel between her forefinger and thumb. It had been smuggled into the prison somehow.

'So what happened?' Bailey was breathless. She felt there was some climax to Mel's story and she was desperate to know what it was.

'It was a freezing winter night when I met him, when he came for Mel. I was standing there naked when he got out the knife and that's when I knew it was him. All I remember was seeing that blade shining like... like a star.'

She shuddered, lost in a haze of memory.

'I jumped straight out of the window. Smashed through the glass. A second-floor window. That's how I fucked my leg up. Landed on the cobblestones. Freezing-cold cobblestones. But I managed to get away. Mel got away. Mel survived.'

The gravity of what she was saying suddenly hit Bailey.

'So you're saying that this Hairdresser killer who killed your friends in the Midlands several years ago has now come back... has come here to this prison... to continue killing?'

Mel nodded gravely, her gaze never leaving Bailey.

'When I heard about the scalps I knew it was him. Taking their hair.'

Bailey was sceptical. 'Hair's one thing. Scalps are something else.'

'Don't you see?' hissed Mel. 'He's getting worse. Getting badder. It's like an addiction with him. With an addiction, you start small but you always end up needing more. It's not enough just to take their hair any more. Now he needs their scalps.' Mel was breathing hard now. 'I always knew he'd come back... come back for Mel!'

Her voice had gone up an octave. She shuddered and hunched up into a ball.

'I thought I'd got away from him when I came to London but no... he's back!'

Mel was returning to her normal self. The effects of the drug were wearing off.

'Tell me what he looked like,' said Bailey.

'I didn't see his face.'

'But you said you were close.'

'It was dark, I was off my head, he had a baseball cap pulled down low.'

'Surely you must remember something.'

Mel unhunched herself and leaned forward, staring into Bailey's eyes with a full-on intensity.

'He's a duppy. That's what he is. He ain't no normal killer. He's a duppy. And that's why Mel's scared of him.'

'I'm sorry, hold up a sec. Can you explain just what a duppy is exactly?'

'Duppies are evil. They come from the land of the dead to hunt the living. Bad, very bad,' whispered Mel. 'My grandmother used to tell me about them when I was a kid. Stories from Jamaica, old stories from way back. She believed in them, thought they were real, as real as you and me. When I grew up, I left those stories behind, thought they were nothing more than fairy tales for kids and old women, just spook talk of evil spirits. But when I met the Hairdresser, that's when I knew that duppies were real.'

She started to breathe harder. 'Dem ah real. Aal along mi grandmoda was rite...'

The cast-iron conviction in Mel's voice sent an eldritch chill through Bailey. She shook it off. She had never believed in the supernatural and she wasn't about to start now.

'I don't believe in the supernatural,' said Bailey. 'I think your cellmate Ally—'

Mel cut in with a sharp hiss. 'Mi friend Ally, shi dead cuz shi neva believe inna duppies! Dem all dead cuz dem nuh believe!'

She pointed a long bony brown finger at Bailey.

'An yuh wi dead eff yuh nuh believe.'

Bailey couldn't help but shiver at Mel's pronouncement. She needed to get the conversation back in the world of the real.

'After you met the Hairdresser, did you go to the police and tell them about him?'

Mel shook her head vigorously. 'Mel hates the police. Mel would never go to the police.'

Of course, she'd been a prostitute and they weren't renowned for having the greatest relationship with the police. Bailey sighed and chewed her lip. She still hadn't got what she'd come here for.

'If he's a bloke, like you say, then he must be one of the prison officers. You must remember something about him. Even just the smallest detail?'

Mel rolled her eyes and bared her teeth.

'Mi told yuh aredi. Him ain't nuh bloke. Him a duppy.'

'That's no good to me. I need to find out who he is!'

'Him de Hairdressa!' screeched Mel. 'Fuck yuh!'

She slumped back on the bunk and started sobbing, long painful whiny sobs.

'Mi friends... aal ded... bess friends mi eva had...'

Bailey stood up. She looked down on the sobbing Mel with pity. She tossed the rocks of crack onto the bunk next to Mel, who ignored them and continued sobbing. Bailey turned and left the cell, feeling now more than ever like she was chasing a shadowy mirage.

72

The prison library appeared to be completely deserted. Bailey stood there, looking around, wondering where the librarian had got to. She wasn't sitting at her usual position at her desk by the door. She was probably off shelving books somewhere.

Bailey had been to the library a few times before. Inmates were allowed to visit it once a week and borrow up to six books. The selection of books wasn't great, but the tranquil atmosphere made for a pleasant retreat from everyday prison existence.

She turned her head and jumped in surprise to see the librarian suddenly standing there right next to her. For someone so muscular and bulky, she was remarkably light on her feet.

Her name was Jacqui Sigmundsen and Bailey had learned from other inmates that she was a former biker serving an eighteen-year stretch for armed robbery and murder. Probably in her late forties, her thick arms were etched with tattoos of lightning bolts and daggers which were now starting to blur with age. She peered at Bailey over the top of a pair of half-moon spectacles which seemed incongruous with the rest of her look.

'Gosh! I didn't hear you at all,' said Bailey.

'On edge, are we?' said Jacqui in her thick raspy smoker's voice. 'I guess everyone is these days, what with everything that's been going on.'

'I was wondering if you could help me out.'

At that point, seeing that she had a captive audience, Jacqui held up her hand to signal Bailey's silence. She opened a small slim volume that she had been holding and began to read aloud from it:

> 'Stone walls do not a prison make,
> Nor iron bars a cage;
> Minds innocent and quiet take
> That for an hermitage;
> If I have freedom in my love,
> And in my soul am free,
> Angels alone, that soar above,
> Enjoy such liberty.'

She closed the volume and raised one eyebrow archly at Bailey.

Bailey wasn't quite sure how she should respond.

'Er... that's nice.'

'Robert Lovelace. He was an English poet from the seventeenth century. "To Althea, from Prison" is the name of the poem. He wrote it in 1642 while he was imprisoned in London during the English Civil War. Do you understand what he's saying?'

Bailey hadn't been expecting an impromptu English examination and certainly not from the likes of Jacqui, but seeing as she needed Jacqui's assistance today she gamely attempted to play along.

'It sounds like he's saying that because his mind is free the walls and the bars can't imprison him.'

Jacqui nodded, impressed with Bailey's analysis. 'Exactly. The poem is a paradox. The imprisoned man is actually free. He's free to think and dream of anything he wants to. And not only that, he believes that because he's innocent the prison has actually been transformed into a hermitage – a haven – for him to concentrate on what's important to him, like his love for the woman Althea to whom he's dedicated the poem.'

'Reframing,' said Bailey. 'It's a psychological trick to help you make the best out of a bad situation, to look on the bright side.'

'This poem has got me through many hard times over the eleven years that I've been in here and it'll get me through many more. I actually know it off by heart. I always find it helps to read it when I'm down. And so should you.'

She offered the book to Bailey.

'Thanks. But I'm not that into poetry, to be honest with you. I was actually looking for a book in your true crime section.'

Jacqui sighed, a little disappointed. 'Well, that is the most popular bit of the library. Unsurprisingly. What book are you looking for?'

'Any book that might have something about the Hairdresser.'

Jacqui nodded. She seemed to know what Bailey was talking about. 'Follow me.'

Bailey followed her along the aisles to the true crime section.

Jacqui peered over the tops of her half-moon spectacles and scanned the spines of the titles on the shelves.

'I've read almost every book in this library and...' she reached past Bailey to pull out a small paperback, '...I think this should cover what you're looking for.' She handed it to Bailey.

It was a dog-eared paperback printed on cheap paper, its black cover embossed with a large silver title that read *Cold Cases Vol. 3*.

Bailey wasn't a big reader, but even she could see that this was from the trashier and more salacious end of the true crime spectrum. She flicked through it, pausing briefly at the photo sections – black and white images of blood-spattered crime scenes, discarded murder weapons, body dump sites, smiling graduation photos of unsuspecting victims and the inevitable police mugshots of killers who seemed to carry a universal expression of mild indifference.

She leafed through to the section on the Hairdresser. She began to read to herself. This was exactly what she was looking for.

She glanced up to see that the librarian had disappeared as silently as she had appeared.

Bailey glanced around the visit hall, leaned forward across the table and lowered her voice.

'How's it going with the drugs squad?'

'They want to know what your new angle is,' said Frank. 'They're really breathing down my neck on it.'

'You said you'd give me two weeks, right?'

He sighed and rolled his eyes.

She forced an optimistic smile onto her face.

'I think I might be onto something interesting,' she said. 'The Hairdresser. Heard of him?'

Frank creased his brow as he tried to recall the significance of the name. 'Vaguely. A serial killer who murdered prostitutes up in the Midlands. That was quite a few years back. He was never caught. I think he got his name because he used to—' He stopped and stared at her in disbelief. 'Wait a minute, you don't really think...?'

'He used to cut their hair off, didn't he?'

'And you think he's now graduated to scalping?'

'It's well-documented that serial killers often start out on small animals before eventually moving onto humans. What I'm saying is that as they grow older their tastes evolve. And their methods change accordingly.'

Frank stroked his chin thoughtfully as he mulled over the idea. 'I see your point. But it's a little tenuous though. What put you onto this?'

'There's this inmate, Mel. She's what they call a fraggle...'

She proceeded to tell him what Mel had told her, leaving out any mention of duppies. When she had finished, he fixed her with a faintly amused look.

'A claim about a serial killer coming from an ex-crack whore who you yourself said is a bit...' he made the 'crazy' gesture with his finger. 'It's not exactly the strongest of sources to go on. But then again... it would be remiss to disregard it completely.'

'I did some research on it.'

She took out the book that she had borrowed from the library. A book was one of the few items that inmates were permitted to bring to a visit. She looked around surreptitiously. No one appeared to be paying them any attention.

She put it on the table and slid it over to him.

He picked it up and looked sceptically at the tacky cover with its embossed silver lettering.

'*Cold Cases Volume Three*? Looks like the kind of thing some hack knocked out in five minutes.'

'It was all they had in the prison library. Listen...'

She took it from him, opened it up and started to read to him in a low voice.

'The Hairdresser. A serial killer who preyed on sex workers in the red-light districts of Wolverhampton and Walsall. He was dubbed the Hairdresser by the local media because of his obsession with cutting off and taking his victims' hair. Six prostitutes fell prey to his cruel knife. The killings all happened within an eight-month period during 2014 and then stopped abruptly and were never repeated. He was never captured. What happened to the Hairdresser? Did he die? Did he give up? Did he just get tired of it? Or is he waiting for the ruckus to die down so he can strike again?'

'Cold cases are usually cold for a good reason,' said Frank. 'I remember when all that was going on. They had a shitload of police on the investigation. And they didn't manage to solve it. It turned out to be one big dead-end.'

'I remember once when I was a kid,' said Bailey in a soft voice, 'we went to stay with some friends of my parents who had a smallholding in the countryside. One night we woke up to the most godawful squawking noise.

The next morning, we went outside to see what had happened. It turned out that a fox had managed to get inside the chicken coop. There were white feathers and blood everywhere. And dead chickens. Lots of dead chickens. Torn to pieces. Once the fox had got in there, they were...' She grasped for the right word.

'Sitting ducks?' suggested Frank drily.

'The women in here fit his victim type exactly – ex-hookers... lost women. But this is a group of victims with a difference. They're all enclosed like chickens in a coop. They're easy prey.'

'Are you saying what I think you're saying?' he said, eyeing the prison officers making their slow circuit of the visit hall.

She followed his gaze and nodded. 'Maybe the heat got too much in the Midlands so he decided to move away somewhere else, to lie low for a bit.'

'And he just conveniently decided to get a job as a prison officer?' Frank raised one eyebrow doubtfully.

'It's a perfectly viable explanation. Decent salary, financial security, and the chance to have access on a daily basis to exactly the kind of women he likes to hunt. Plus he has the protection of a uniform. He's in a position of trust and authority. It would also explain how he manages to get around the prison so easily and so elusively – he has his own set of keys.'

'Prison officers are vetted before they can work in a prison. They have to undergo fairly detailed background checks, criminal record checks, that kind of thing.'

'You know as well as I do that if he was never caught for anything before, then nothing untoward would have shown up in any checks. And even if he had, I'm sure you're also aware that any dedicated criminal can quite easily source a new identity, a clean identity, which means it'd be no problem getting around those background checks.'

Frank conceded her point with a nod and a raised eyebrow.

'Still,' he said, 'the Hairdresser is a cold case, which means it's an angle that's only worth pursuing if you can find something new, something solid, to go on. And at the moment you don't appear to have anything of the sort. Cheap crime books and crazy ex-hookers don't make the cut. You should know me by now, Bailey.'

She did indeed know only too well the kind of stringent standards by which Frank insisted on operating.

'Something solid,' she sighed. 'Sure...'

'And don't forget,' he added, tapping his watch. 'You're running out of time.'

74

Bailey lay on her bunk ruminating, listening to the pipes gurgle, staring at the wall watching the shadows grow longer as the sun went down. She curled her hair around her fingers and let it uncurl...

Frank was right. Time was running short and she desperately needed something more to go on than the unsubstantiated assertions of one of the less sane inmates in the prison. The idea of the Hairdresser was enticing but ultimately futile if she couldn't establish anything concrete.

She swung herself off the bunk and began to pace the cell impatiently, back and forth like a caged animal, willing some kind of solution to come to her.

But nothing did.

She sighed in frustration and sat down heavily on the bare mattress of the lower bunk, Sharon's former bunk. Sharon hadn't yet been replaced with a new cellmate and Bailey supposed that in the meantime she could switch her bedding from the upper bunk to the lower bunk. After all, in prison the lower bunk was regarded as the more preferable bunk to possess – you weren't right up by the glare of the ceiling light and you didn't need to climb up and down all the time.

Bailey ran her hand over the mattress and decided against switching. She'd kind of got used to the upper bunk and, if truth be told, despite her professed lack of superstition, she felt slightly uneasy about sleeping in a bunk whose previous occupant had been brutally murdered.

Poor old Sharon.

Bailey hadn't particularly liked her, but no one deserved a fate like that.

She recalled the gruesome scene and that single cryptic word that Sharon had scrawled in her own blood as she lay dying.

Flee.

A chilling warning.

There was something eerie about it. It brought to mind Mel's duppies.

A momentary wave of goosebumps rippled across her flesh. She instantly quelled those thoughts. The supernatural did not constitute a feasible explanation.

But now, the more she thought about it, the more Bailey was sure that the answer lay there, locked within that single scrawl, just beyond reach.

What exactly had Sharon seen in the kitchen? Why had she even been in the kitchen? Bailey knew that she worked there, but the murder had taken place outside of work hours, so she must have gone there for some other reason.

She lay down on Sharon's bunk, placing her hands behind her head, hoping to absorb by osmosis some new insight. She cast her mind back to Sharon and her schemes. Had she had some kind of blackmail scheme going? Had she been murdered because of it? If so, it must tie into the other murders somehow.

On the morning that Sharon had been murdered, Bailey had asked her what she was doing that day. Sharon had tapped the side of her nose. A secret.

As a police detective, Bailey had become accustomed to observing and memorising the minutiae of people's behaviour. And, as she recalled, Sharon had done that same gesture one time before...

It had been when she'd been talking about that fight in the canteen.

Knowledge is power.

That's what she'd said as she'd tapped the side of her nose.

Maybe it was just a mannerism. Maybe the connection was too tenuous.

Or maybe not.

75

Agata looked attractive from a distance with her blonde hair and exaggerated pout, but up close it became apparent that she had bad skin and poorly maintained teeth.

Bailey hovered nearby in the yard, covertly studying her as she stood alone in the shadow of the east wall smoking a cigarette.

Of the two inmates who'd been fighting in the canteen, Agata was the only one Bailey had been able to locate. She'd followed her around for a bit, picking up her name in the process, waiting for an opportune time to make an approach. And right now looked ideal, seeing as she was all by herself.

Bailey pulled out a cigarette and put it between her lips. She made a show of patting her pockets and frowning.

She then sauntered casually over to Agata, the cigarette hanging out of the corner of her mouth. Agata eyed her guardedly – as far as she was concerned, Bailey was a complete stranger.

'Got a light?' asked Bailey.

Agata held out a pack of safety matches. Bailey smiled, took them, struck one and lit her cigarette.

She handed the matches back.

'Thanks,' she said.

Agata nodded in acknowledgement.

Bailey sucked in a lungful of smoke, immediately feeling dizzy from the head rush. It had been at least five years since she'd last smoked a cigarette.

'You sure beat the shit out of that girl in the canteen the other day,' she said. 'That was you, wasn't it?'

Agata threw back her head and laughed, blowing out a stream of smoke.

'Yeah that bitch had it coming.' Her accent was strong. Bailey guessed Polish.

'Come to think of it I haven't seen her around recently.'

'She got transferred to another prison.'

That explained why Bailey hadn't been able to find her. She took another puff on the cigarette.

'She was accusing you of stealing her boyfriend or something like that, wasn't she?'

'I can't help it if he preferred me to her.' Agata puffed up a little, like she was bragging.

'Fair dues. Although... surely it's pointless to argue over someone who's outside the prison?'

'Who said he was outside the prison?' Agata smiled slyly.

The implications of what she was saying sunk in. If he was inside the prison, then this boyfriend had to be a member of staff.

Bailey knew that conducting sexual relationships with inmates was highly forbidden for prison staff. The legal term was 'misconduct in public office'. It was the kind of offence that resulted in jail time. They always dished out heavy sentences in order to deter future offenders. And like Frank had said, it wasn't a nice experience to be a former prison officer behind bars.

Was this the knowledge that Sharon had acquired during the course of the fight? She had been sitting very close to them at the time, at a neighbouring table, and so she could have overheard something to that effect. It was exactly the kind of juicy secret she would have relished holding over somebody.

Had she been attempting to blackmail a member of staff?

Had that person murdered her?

Was that same member of staff responsible for the other murders?

Had Sharon unwittingly picked a vicious killer as the subject of her extortion attempt? Surely she would have been a bit more careful had she known the true nature of the person she was trying to blackmail.

The unanswered questions tripped over and over in Bailey's mind.

'So who is it?' she said in what she hoped was a jokey conspiratorial whisper. 'Let me in on your little secret.'

Agata laughed and shook her head. 'I'm not going to tell you that. If everyone knew about it then it wouldn't be fun any more.'

Bailey wanted to grab her by the lapels and shake the identity out of her but instead she smiled and shrugged like it was no big deal.

Agata crushed her cigarette underfoot, winked at Bailey and walked off.

76

It was just past midnight and the monolithic prison slumbered beneath a bright full moon. Not everyone was asleep however...

Mel cowered on the floor in the far corner of her cell. Her eyes were wide open. A low keening moan of fear issued from the back of her throat.

Nighttime was when duppies liked to come out. That was when she had to be most vigilant. Sometimes her cellmate would wake up and tell her to be quiet. But her cellmate didn't understand. Mel envied her ignorance as she lay there snoring lightly.

She looked around the cell, peering up at the window, squinting once again into the shadows by the door, alert for any possible intrusion, her paranoia sharpened and amplified by all the dope she had smoked the previous day.

The prison might have big thick walls and locks and bars, but these were no obstacle for a duppy. Duppies could walk straight through walls and locked doors. Or sometimes they liked to transform themselves into animals, like a fly or a rat, and get into a place through some unprotected crack.

That was the thing with duppies. They could be anything. They could be anywhere. You never knew for sure. That's why she was so scared.

When she was a child, her grandmother had told her plenty of stories about the duppies which haunted the hills and jungles of rural Jamaica. Rollin' Calf, Whooping Boy, Bubby Susan, Ol' Higue...

There was a whole host of them to be scared of, all of them grotesque-looking and frightening, and each with their own horrible method of killing you. If you were foolish or unlucky enough to be walking around at night when one of them was around, then they would hunt you down and kill you for sure.

'Who are they? What are they?' she would ask her grandmother.

'Dem be de duppies of a people dere long 'fore our people.'

The evil souls of the ancient dead wandering the earth...

But her grandmother had warned her that it was your run-of-the-mill duppy that you had to be most careful of, because those were the ones that looked human. These were most often the angry souls of wronged people seeking vengeance or the malevolent souls of particularly bad people who couldn't bear to give up their twisted ways.

More worryingly though, her grandmother had told her that duppies weren't just limited to the realm of the dead. In fact, you could even be a duppy yourself and not know it. Her grandmother had explained that when you fell asleep your soul wandered off and did things. You woke up and remembered those things as dreams. But maybe, in some cases, you actually did them for real...

Either way, all Mel knew was that duppies existed and they were something to be very, very afraid of. The only real way to get rid of a duppy was to get an obeah man – a witch doctor – to carry out a special ritual. But there were no obeah men in here to do that. That was the problem.

Whether the Hairdresser was the soul of a living person or a dead person, or whether he was some kind of ancient demon, she didn't know. But the way he got around like he did without ever getting caught and the nasty things he did to his victims put her in no doubt that he was quite definitely a duppy.

A small movement on the floor suddenly snagged her attention. She froze. Something had scuttled out from under her bunk.

A cockroach.

She stared petrified as it crawled along the edge of the cell towards her.

The Hairdresser...

At any moment he would change back into human form and pull out his knife and then... and then...

She whimpered and swallowed, barely able to draw breath, so constricted was her throat by the raw fear which gripped her entire body.

The cockroach paused in a beam of moonlight, its long black antennae wavering. She braced herself for the transformation. But it didn't happen. The cockroach just sat there. She could feel it watching her.

'Mi duh nah fear duppies,' she whispered hoarsely, but she had no faith in what she was saying.

The cockroach edged forward to within a few centimetres of her big toe. She jerked her foot back.

She reached into the tangle of her afro and pulled out her razor blade. It was deceptively light and insubstantial, but it was deadly if used in the right way. And she knew how to use it.

She held it out in front of her between thumb and forefinger, the dull steel glinting in the moonlight.

'Guh wey evil duppy,' she hissed.

The cockroach twiddled its antennae a little more, then it turned and scuttled away underneath the cell door and out into the prison.

She breathed a sigh of relief.

No duppy was going to get Mel tonight.

No way.

No. way.

77

Bailey looked at her watch. In forty minutes' time she was supposed to meet up with Toni and the rest of the gang out in the yard. No reason had been given for the meeting, only that it was of crucial importance that they all attend.

Forty minutes. That should hopefully give her enough time to do what she needed to do.

Casually lounging against the banister, she turned her attention back to the second-floor landing of C-Wing which she had been observing from her position at the juncture of the four house-blocks.

Her concentration was focused specifically on the fourth cell on the right, the one she had been staking out all morning.

After a few minutes more, Agata finally emerged, walking in the direction of the central stairwell. She passed by, oblivious to Bailey's presence. As she did so, Bailey noticed that she appeared to be wearing make-up – a hint of mascara and a touch of lip gloss, if she wasn't mistaken.

Bailey waited a few moments, then pushed herself off the banister and followed her down the metal stairs, keeping at a safe distance. Agata descended all the way down to the ground floor and made her way across the atrium, looking at her watch as if she had an appointment to keep. She disappeared down the stairwell which led to the prison basement. Bailey sped up her pace, determined not to lose her.

In the basement it became much harder to follow her discreetly. Ahead of her, Agata padded rapidly along the poorly lit corridor, the bulbs flickering unevenly overhead. She walked past the workshop up to the far end of the corridor.

Agata halted and glanced behind her. Bailey stopped sharp and drew back behind a corner. She peeked around and saw that Agata was standing by the door to a room of some sort. With one last glance around, she opened the door and entered the room, closing the door behind her.

Bailey waited a few moments, then walked up to the door. It had a sign on it saying 'ELECTRICITY 2'. Presumably it was some kind of maintenance room which contained fuse boxes and the like.

She needed to find some sort of concealed vantage point close by. There was a door opposite. She tried the handle. The door opened. The room beyond was small, dark and musty and it appeared to be stacked full of metal bunk-bed frames. It was a storage cupboard. Bailey squeezed in and pulled the door almost closed, so it was just open a crack.

She stood there, peeking through the crack across the corridor. She waited for what felt like ages. What was Agata doing in there? Was she waiting for someone to arrive or was that person already in there?

She squinted at her watch in the darkness. She had been standing there for just over ten minutes. Just then, the door opposite creaked open. She looked up.

Agata stood there in the corridor, barely a metre away from Bailey. Up close, Bailey could see that she looked flushed and she had a light sheen of perspiration across her skin. Her hair was ruffled and her make-up was slightly smudged. She brushed a loose strand of hair out of her eyes and walked off up the corridor the way she had come, but at a jauntier pace.

Bailey waited there, tense.

About thirty seconds later, a second figure emerged from the dimness of the electricity room.

A prison officer.

Dylan.

She'd seen him around but had never conversed with him in anything more than the most cursory manner. In his early to mid-thirties, he was handsome in a rugged way, with sandy-coloured hair, a tanned complexion and very light blue eyes.

He stood there for a few moments adjusting the cinch on his belt, softly whistling some tune that she didn't recognise. *Well, well*, she thought. Dylan had clearly been engaged in a bit of 'misconduct in public office'.

As Bailey had suspected, Agata had been dolled up because she was going to meet her boyfriend. And her boyfriend was Dylan. Presumably, he was who the two inmates had been fighting over in the canteen. In fact, now that she thought back, Bailey recalled that Dylan had been in the canteen chatting to Amber just before the fight had kicked off. His presence there had probably triggered the outburst between his two rival lovers.

Had Sharon been blackmailing Dylan? Had Dylan killed Sharon? If so, did that mean he had also killed the others?

Bailey felt something crawl across her foot. She looked down. It was a rat. Its thick fleshy tail dragged across the top of her trainer. She reflexively jumped back in revulsion, bumping against the bunk-bed frames as she did so.

Dylan froze and stopped whistling. He turned to the storage cupboard. His eyes narrowed as he peered at the crack of the door. She felt like he was looking straight into her eyes.

He started forward towards her.

Panic spiked through her. She immediately retreated backwards, squeezing herself behind the stack of bunk frames, managing to conceal herself just as he pulled open the door.

Light flooded in. He stood there silhouetted in the doorway.

Bailey crouched, squashed behind the metal frames, holding her breath. What would he do if he discovered her? Would he put her on the nicking sheet? If anyone should be on the nicking sheet, it should be him. Having sex with the inmates was unprofessional, unethical and illegal.

He stood silently in the doorway. She could hear his breathing and smell the musky tang of his sweat infused with the odour of his cologne. She could virtually smell the sex on him.

The rat scurried out between his legs. He jumped backwards in surprise.

'Fucking rats!' he muttered in disgust.

He kicked at the rat. It squealed and ran off down the corridor.

He stood there for a fraction longer, then he shut the door, leaving Bailey in the blackness.

She heaved a sigh of relief. That had been close.

She listened and waited a few minutes until she was sure that he was gone. Then she navigated her way through the blackness to the door. She felt for the door handle. With a mounting sense of panic, she realised that there was no door handle on the inside. She was locked in.

Shit. She was locked in and due to meet Toni and the others in ten minutes out in the yard.

78

After a certain amount of banging on the inside of the door, someone eventually opened it. It was the small tubby inmate with glasses who worked in the laundry. Bailey was grateful that she had attracted the attention of an inmate rather than a guard, who might have disciplined her.

She made some feeble excuse about looking in the wrong place for something and hurried back up to ground level and out into the yard. She looked at her watch. She was fifteen minutes late.

She spotted Toni and the rest of the gang assembled on one of the concrete picnic tables. Keisha and Rong were playfully punching each other. Muscles sat there like a statue, staring straight ahead. Poppy looked bored, idly filing her nails.

Toni was sitting in the middle. When she saw Bailey approaching, her face twisted into a sneer.

'Where have you been?' she said. 'You're late.'

'I got held up.'

'Where?' Toni's eyes bored into her.

They had all fallen silent and were now staring at her. She remembered her undercover training. Stick to the truth where possible.

'I accidentally got locked in a room in the basement.'

'And why did you get locked in a room in the basement?' said Toni slowly, her brow creasing quizzically.

And now the lie. Bailey took a deep breath.

'I was checking out possible alternative locations to keep a stash. You know... what with what's been going on. I thought it might be a good idea.'

Toni eyed her for a few moments, then nodded. An acceptable excuse it seemed. She turned her attention back to the rest of the gang.

'The reason we're having this meeting is that I wanted to let you know that we're going to resume operations fairly soon.'

'I thought you said it was too risky,' frowned Keisha. 'I thought you said it was too soon.'

'Our contact is confident he can get it in without being found out.'

Bailey wondered how Terry was doing it. Surely, in light of what had happened recently, he wouldn't want to risk spot checks at the prison entrance.

'How's he bringing it in?' she asked.

Toni shrugged. 'I don't know and I don't care. All I know is that every minute we're not working, we're losing money.'

She rubbed her thumb and forefinger together and smiled, her gold tooth glinting, a venal look in her eyes.

79

'Dylan Prince. Dylan spelt D-Y-L-A-N.'

'As in the Welsh poet?' said Frank. 'Just checking right now...'

She stood in the phone booth listening to the tapping of computer keys as Frank checked the prison officers' rota. She glanced over her shoulder at the busy queue for the phones. Nobody seemed to be paying her too much attention.

Frank came back on the line. 'According to this... Dylan was on duty when Alice was killed, when Poodle was killed, when Natalie was killed and when Sharon was killed.'

'All of them?' Even if Bailey had her suspicions about Dylan, she was still somewhat surprised.

'That's right. Who exactly is this Dylan Prince?'

'That's what I'm trying to work out.'

Having had minimal interaction with Dylan before, and having never spoken to him properly, Bailey had very little sense of the kind of person he was. Although she'd noticed him around the prison, he had been fairly elusive so far in terms of making any kind of specific impression on her.

'Well, you'd better work it out soon. I had a meeting with the drugs squad yesterday and they can't understand why this operation's still going. They're giving me all kinds of flak about it. With each day that goes by it's getting harder and harder for me to justify your presence in there.'

She could sense the stress in his voice and she knew from previous experience that he wasn't nice to be around when he got stressed. Being in this place, she couldn't have been further removed from him physically, yet here she was feeling the pressure from him more than ever.

'I was summoned to a meeting with the gang just now. Toni said they're planning to resume operations pretty soon.'

'Did she give a date? Any specifics? Quantities? Pick-up points? That kind of thing.'

'No. Nothing yet.'

He sighed. 'I don't think that's going to satisfy them.'

'Look, just stall them for a bit longer so I can check out Dylan,' she said. 'Have faith in me. I've always delivered before, haven't I?'

80

Dylan stood with his arms crossed, leaning against a pillar, softly whistling that same tune she'd heard him whistling down in the basement.

While he was monitoring free association activity on the first-floor landing of A-Wing, Bailey was covertly monitoring him from a short distance away. Compared to some of the other prison officers, he took evident care in his appearance – his shirt glowed white and clean, his black shoes were buffed to a mirror shine and his trousers were neatly ironed with a sharp crease.

With his sandy-coloured hair and pale blue eyes, he bore more than a slight resemblance to Mark, the detective she'd dated for two years before they'd split up over the issue of kids and marriage. Quite why she was drawn to the 'Teutonic look', as Sharon had put it, she didn't know; it just seemed that most of the guys she'd been out with had looked like that. However, the crimes she suspected Dylan of committing somewhat took the shine off any outward appeal he might have had for her.

After a few more minutes of watching him, she worked out what seemed to be the best way to break the ice. She walked up to him.

'What's that tune you're whistling?' she asked.

He stopped whistling and hit her with a long piercing stare as he sized her up. He looked somewhat guarded and a little wary, in the way that the prison officers often were if you approached them unawares. It was generally the case that inmates didn't approach them out of the blue unless they wanted to extract some favour from them.

'It sounds familiar,' she lied.

'I can't imagine you'd know it unless you're into military marching music.'

'Actually that's my favourite genre,' she said.

The tanned skin around his eyes crinkled into a smile at her sarcasm.

'We used to drill to it when I was in the army,' he said. 'It's stuck in my head ever since.'

'You were in the army?'

That explained the smartness of his appearance. Old habits die hard. The army had probably taught him to bull his shoes to a shine with melted shoe polish, just like she had been taught to in police training at Hendon.

'Royal Marines. Forty Commando. 'Sarie Marais' is the name of the song. It's the official marching tune of the Royal Marines.'

Her knowledge of the Royal Marines extended little further than the recruiting adverts they showed in the cinema before the main feature came on.

'I take it you like jobs with uniforms then?'

He plucked contemptuously at his tie. 'This clip-on tie, this polyester shirt... this uniform's shit. Army kit's much better quality.'

'Why did you leave it then... the army?'

He paused for a few moments. 'I was invalided out. I got injured.'

'How?'

'IED blast in Afghanistan.'

Improved Explosive Device. She'd heard the term on the news many times.

She looked him up and down. 'You look fine to me.'

He pointed at his head. 'I've got a metal plate in my skull.'

'No shit.' She peered at his head. 'The surgeons did a good job. I can't tell it's there.'

He leant forward and pushed his sandy hair aside to reveal a long white surgical scar running around the right-hand side of his head.

'It's made of titanium,' he said. 'It's moulded exactly to the same shape my head was before. It's fitted on with four screws. They had to remove almost a quarter of my skull to let my brain recover from the injury. I spent the whole of 2014 in a medically induced coma in a military neuro-trauma unit in Plymouth while they fixed me up.'

'Wow,' she murmured. 'It must be weird having that much metal in your head.'

'I can sometimes pick up shortwave radio through it.'

'Really?'

'Nah,' he smiled.

'Does it hurt?' she asked.

'Occasionally. They got most of the shrapnel out, but there's still a small piece lodged deep inside my brain. It would have been too risky to remove it so they left it in there.'

'Any side effects?'

He smiled blankly at her.

Then something across the landing appeared to catch his attention. She followed his gaze. A female prison officer was standing there pointing at her watch. Dylan nodded to her, mouthed something and turned back to Bailey.

'I'm due to be relieved so I can go on my lunch break. Have a good day now.'

He nodded politely to her, turned and walked off down the landing.

'Bon appétit,' she murmured to his departing back, thinking absently to herself that she kind of liked the way his eyes crinkled when he smiled. She tried to shake the thought away.

Following their exchange, she felt slightly frustrated at having been unable to properly fathom his capacity as the potential killer. He was just too unreadable. On the surface he seemed perfectly pleasant, but then there was that bit of shrapnel lodged in his brain, and who knew what strange and unpredictable effects that could have on someone's behaviour? The upshot was that she couldn't yet tell if she was on the right track with him or not, although there was nothing so far to make her explicitly doubt her theory either.

The key takeaway from their encounter, however, was the date.

2014.

As she walked back to her cell, she reflected on its significance. At the same time that the Hairdresser had been murdering prostitutes up in the Midlands, Dylan had been lying comatose in a military hospital in Plymouth.

If Dylan did turn out to be a viable suspect then she could completely dismiss the idea of the Hairdresser because there was quite clearly no connection between the two of them.

And given the lack of hard evidence to support the Hairdresser theory, she really only had one option to follow: Find out more about Dylan.

81

Bailey lay face-down on the bunk, her chin resting on her forearms, enjoying the sensation of the tattoo needle puncturing the skin of her back. There was a strange kind of pleasure in the pain and she put it down to the endorphins that her brain was releasing as a response to it. She'd heard in the past how people got physiologically addicted to having tattoos. Now she was beginning to understand why.

The last session had ended awkwardly and she had been a little apprehensive about how this next one would turn out. But so far it seemed to be going fine, both of them acting like nothing had happened.

'What do you think of Dylan?' Bailey asked, breaking the silence.

Poppy lifted the needle momentarily. 'The guard?'

'Yeah.'

'Hmm... I always got the impression he was the happy-go-lucky type until I saw him lose it once. He lost it big time. And it was over something really minor. A girl had her feet on a chair in the canteen, but he completely flipped out. He was shouting and screaming. He actually had to be restrained by the other screws. That can't be right, can it?'

Interesting, thought Bailey. It certainly suggested that there was another side to him, one that she hadn't seen yet.

'Did you know he's got a metal plate in his skull and a piece of shrapnel lodged in his brain?'

'Guess that explains it,' said Poppy. 'Why are you so interested in Dylan all of a sudden?'

Bailey decided to change the subject. 'You told me last time you had a plan for when you got out of here, but we never got to talk about it.'

Poppy didn't respond immediately and Bailey wondered if she had upset her again. But it seemed she hadn't, as Poppy started to speak, softly at first, then with a growing ardour in her voice.

'Toni and the others… this place is their life. It's all they have. But prison isn't the be-all and end-all. You might be king in here, but what's the point of being cock of the roost in what amounts to little more than a glorified brick box. Me… I want more. It started as a dream, but the more I've been thinking about it, the more I think I could make it a reality, ever since I met you actually…'

'Tell me about it.'

'When I get out of here, I want to open a tattoo shop. I've got it all worked out. I'm going to call it "Ink-ubus".'

'I like the sound of it,' said Bailey, with a genuine sense of sincerity. 'Not sure what it means though.'

'It's a pun on the word "incubus", which is spelt with a C. An incubus is a mythological demon who has sex with sleeping women.'

'Sounds charming!' laughed Bailey.

'I've even designed a logo of a naughty little demon,' said Poppy. She paused and swallowed. 'But the thing is, I'm really bad with numbers. I've always been good at art, shit at maths. I need someone to help me on the business side. You told me you used to be an accountant, right?'

'Yeah, that's right.'

'And when you get out of here you want to go straight, right?'

'Sure. I just want to go straight. No more trouble.'

'So you could help me out with my shop. I could do the tattoos and you could do the numbers. I know you must be good at it if you managed to embezzle all that money.' And then she added with a laugh, 'although I'd obviously prefer it if you didn't get up to that kind of thing in our business.' She paused, serious once more. 'How does that sound?'

Now it made sense why Poppy had shown so much interest in the accounting aspects of her cover story. She'd seen long-term potential in their relationship.

'I'm really touched that you're asking,' said Bailey. 'I'd love to help you out.'

For once, Bailey wasn't lying. Although she found it unlikely that she would actually go into business with Poppy, she was certain that once they were both out of this place she could find a way to lend her some sort of assistance with her business without ever needing to reveal that she was a policewoman. After all, she did possess the requisite skills.

'That would make me really happy,' said Poppy. 'I get out in six months. Good behaviour and all that. I know you're in here for a bit longer, but I can come and visit you and we can work on the business plan together. And who knows, maybe you'll get out early with good behaviour as well.'

Bailey frowned. 'But what about the ABC?'

'What about them?'

'It's blood out, right? Even when you're outside prison, you're still a member, aren't you?'

'Sure, there's stuff you're expected to do for them now and then. But it's not going to stop me from opening my tattoo shop. And it doesn't have to interfere with your plans for going straight either. I reckon we can probably get out of doing anything too serious.'

'I guess that sounds fine,' said Bailey. 'I admire your determination and I'm looking forward to helping you.' She paused a moment. 'But we're just doing this as friends, right?'

'Sure,' said Poppy. 'Friends.'

82

The ringing bell jolted through Bailey's head and woke her from her night-mares. She lay there breathing heavily, relieved to be awake. Leaning over, she reached to switch off her alarm clock. And then she remembered that she didn't have an alarm clock. And then she realised that the ringing was way too loud to be from an alarm clock anyway.

It was a fire alarm.

Bailey had no idea what time it was, but the sky was still dark outside. She fumbled for her watch and squinted at the little screen. It was 3.10 in the morning.

And then she smelt the burning smell and she knew it wasn't a drill. Acrid, sharp, biting into the back of her throat and nasal passage. Something was definitely on fire.

She sat up sharply. She pulled back the sheets and jumped out of the bunk. With a surge of panic, she realised that she was locked in the cell. She could burn to death or die of smoke inhalation if she was trapped in here.

She ran to the door and heard the commotion outside. Other inmates were panicking in the same way, banging on the doors and shouting.

Then there was the sound of a key rattling in the lock. Her door was flung open. A female prison officer stood there.

'This is not a drill,' she announced. 'Go to the end of the landing and follow the fire evacuation procedure.'

Bailey faintly remembered the fire drill instructions she'd been given when she'd been inducted into the prison, something about stairwells and meeting points.

She walked out of the cell. The burning smell was a lot stronger out here and the landing had a thin layer of smoke filling it. All of the other cells were open or in the process of being opened. The inmates milled about chaotically, both jittery and befuddled, coughing at the smoke, some pushing each other aside in an attempt to get out faster. The prison officers were barking instructions, trying to get them to evacuate in an orderly fashion, but the feeling was one of barely contained panic and Bailey was worried that it would degenerate into a stampede. Fortunately, it didn't and she joined the crowd as they descended to the atrium and made their way out into the prison yard.

Outside, a spattering of stars twinkled across the clear black sky. The inmates clustered in a large groggy mass, the prison looming over them like a shapeless stone behemoth. In the semi-darkness, she couldn't immediately make out anyone she knew.

The murk of night seemed to amplify the general mood of dread that shrouded the prison and the inmates huddled together instinctively for self-protection, casting fearful glances into the huge black triangles of shadow cast by the corners of the giant house-blocks, whispering amongst themselves, speculating perhaps... was this something to do with another murder?

The prison officers herded them around, shouting at them to line up according to wing and landing, so they could count them off floor by floor.

Not too far away, she noticed Dylan moving the inmates into line, walking up and down, eventually coming to a halt in the shadows by the wall.

He presented an enigma to her. And the thing about enigmas was that she was never satisfied until she'd solved them.

He seemed affable enough, but he was a little too closed for her to get a proper sense of what he was really like. He came across as smart-looking and professional, yet he was breaking the law by having an affair with at least one of the inmates. On top of that there was the intimation of mental instability and the circumstantial possibility that he was a vicious and sadistic killer.

She needed to find out more about him, and now was as good a time as any.

She sidled up to him.

'What's going on?' she asked.

He looked down at her blankly for a few moments, then a twinkle of recognition lit up in his eyes.

'Satpal set her mattress alight. Again. This is the third time this year. She's in for arson. Guess the rehabilitation's not working.'

'How long before we can go back in again?'

He looked at his watch. 'Probably be here quite a while. We've got to wait for the fire brigade to get here and declare it safe. At least it's a warm evening.'

He was right. There was a definite balmy feel to the air. She lit up her digital watch to look at the date. It was 2nd July. It was getting into summer. The idea of being cooped up in this place over sunny summertime didn't hold much appeal for her.

'Jesus,' she muttered to herself.

'What is it?' he said.

'I've been in here a month and a half already.'

'Time flies when you're having fun,' he said with a smile, his eyes crinkling in that way she liked. She couldn't help but smile back.

She studied him for a few moments. Perhaps here in the darkness he'd have less inhibition about talking to her. Maybe he'd open up a little. She drew closer to him.

'What was Afghanistan like?' she asked.

He looked at her silently for a few moments. In the shadows it was hard to make out the expression on his face.

'You don't want to know,' he muttered.

'You fought the Taliban, right?'

At her mention of the Taliban, he made a derogatory spitting sound and looked away. But she persisted.

'They sounded pretty barbaric from what I saw on the news.'

He turned to face her again. 'That's an understatement. They didn't take no prisoners, that was for sure. And when they did capture our guys...' he paused, his jaw clenching and unclenching, '...they did some terrible things. Tortured them. Mutilated them. Cut bits off them. They hung body parts in the trees to provoke us, to taunt us. Legs, arms, heads. All booby-trapped so you couldn't do anything about it.' He shook his head in disgust. 'You didn't hear about it back home. Bad PR if you know what I mean.'

'Urgh! I had no idea,' said Bailey.

She was horrified by the images he was conjuring up, found it shocking to think that the man standing right in front of her had seen and experienced these terrible things. As a policewoman, she'd seen her fair share of unpleasant scenes. It was to be expected to a certain extent when you signed up for that kind of job. However, she'd seen nothing remotely as gruesome as what he was describing.

She looked at him as he gazed off into the distance at the prison towering above them. He inhaled and exhaled slowly, then turned to look directly at her, his face taking on a steely set.

'To fight an animal, sometimes you have to become an animal. You've got to give back what you get, and more... if you want to survive. No room for the Geneva Convention in a place like that. They didn't abide by it and neither did we.'

Her curiosity was piqued now. 'Like what did you do exactly?'

'Nothing they wouldn't have done to us.'

His blue eyes flickered with a cold harsh emptiness. He turned to look away, up into the black void of the night sky.

Now he made more sense to her, at least in terms of his past. Not only had he killed in the service of Queen and Country, it sounded like he'd also been driven to participate in some pretty brutal atrocities. Dylan certainly didn't seem quite so happy-go-lucky any more.

She suddenly noticed Toni and some of the others standing together a short distance away. She didn't want them to think she was too friendly with the prison officers for fear of being perceived as a snitch, so she moved away from Dylan, melting back into the crowd of inmates.

He turned as if to talk to her, then saw that she was gone. He glanced around, puzzled by her sudden disappearance. He looked a little crest-fallen. Or perhaps that was just a trick of the light.

83

Doctor Bodie reflected on how surprising it was to see Bailey Pike back in his office. Considering her general reticence on previous occasions, the fact that she had voluntarily booked an appointment with him marked a significant turning point in her progress.

'You know, I'm over the moon to see you here, Bailey. To have decided to come here of your own accord, that's a big deal.'

She was sitting opposite him, arms crossed, her hair hanging down in its customary way over the left side of her face. She smiled thinly at him in that impenetrable way of hers.

'I've been thinking about what you were saying last time,' she began, 'and I thought it made sense to come and chat to you about it.'

'I'm glad you finally feel ready to open up. Talking is the best form of therapy after all.'

'Last time I was here, you mentioned post-traumatic stress disorder. I just wanted to understand a bit more about it.'

At last, she was taking steps to acknowledge her condition. Maybe today he'd get to find out how she had got that nasty scar. He flexed his knuckles with relish.

'I'm very pleased you asked, Bailey. Post-traumatic stress disorder, or PTSD as it's commonly known, happens to be one of my specialist areas. It can affect anyone who's undergone a particularly traumatic experience.'

'Like a combat veteran, for example?'

He sensed that she was deflecting, not quite wanting to talk about her own situation just yet.

'Yes. Precisely. They often suffer from the symptoms. Nightmares, amnesia, flashbacks...'

He paused and studied her for a few moments. He spoke gently.

'If you're suffering from these kinds of symptoms, Bailey, and I suspect that you are, based upon what you said in our last session, then the first step in getting rid of them is to try and talk about the experiences which caused them. Shall we do that?'

She dropped her head and chewed her knuckle. She appeared to be thinking about something. Then she looked up at him.

'Could a person do something in a flashback that they wouldn't normally do, perhaps even be unaware of?'

'By all means. Flashbacks are dissociative by their very nature.'

He wondered what she was getting at.

'In cases of really serious trauma,' he added, 'people can even fall subject to conditions such as dissociative identity disorder.'

'Dissociative identity disorder?'

'Sometimes known as split personality. A most fascinating condition, from a clinical viewpoint, but not so pleasant for the person experiencing it.'

She moved closer, onto the edge of her seat. He could see that she was very interested, but he wasn't sure why because he was fairly certain that she herself didn't suffer from dissociative identity disorder.

'Tell me more about it,' she said.

'I feel we're moving off-topic here, Bailey. This session is supposed to be about you.'

'Doctor, I'll get round to talking about myself soon enough. I promise.'

'Well... it's not unknown for the personality structure to fragment as a result of particularly traumatic experiences.'

'Fragment? How?'

'It breaks into two or more sub-personalities – distinct identities with their own individual patterns of thinking and behaviour. All the bad stuff that the person experienced or did during the traumatic experience is compartmentalised into one of these sub-personalities.'

'And that sub-personality could suddenly take over?'

'Yes. It's like a severe form of flashback. It would probably be triggered by some kind of environmental cue or stressor. During this state, the sub-personality takes control of the person's behaviour.'

'Is the person aware that this is happening?'

'Sometimes they are, sometimes they aren't.'

He watched her as she sat there digesting what he'd just told her.

'Thank you, Doctor Bodie,' she said. 'That's very interesting. You've been most helpful.'

She started to stand up.

'Wait a minute!' he said. 'You said you'd talk about yourself.'

'I will, Doctor. Next time.'

She turned and left the office, closing the door behind her.

He clenched his fist in frustration. Why did he get the funny feeling she'd been using him in some way?

She truly confounded him. Doctor Bodie had seen hundreds, if not thousands, of inmates over the considerable time he'd spent as a psychologist in the prison system, but, out of all of them, Bailey Pike had to be one of the most puzzling he'd ever come across.

84

Bailey watched Detective Superintendent Frank Grinham as he observed the controlled chaos of the visit hall. His customary cold detached look was accompanied today by a slightly clenched jaw and agitated twitching fingers. These signs, she knew from experience, meant that he was nearing the limits of his patience with her. She'd only just sat down and already she was feeling apprehensive about talking to him.

They were sitting in their usual seat in the far corner, their conversation conveniently drowned out by the bawling of children and the intermittent barking of the prison officers as they reprimanded both inmates and visitors for infringing visiting guidelines by sitting too close or touching each other.

'That's him,' said Bailey. She nodded at Dylan, who was currently standing on the other side of the visit hall.

'That's Dylan?'

Frank surreptitiously studied Dylan, sizing him up with a professional policeman's eye.

'Go on then,' he said. 'Convince me. And it had better be solid.'

She glanced around to check no one was listening and leaned forward across the table. She laid out everything in a low urgent voice, explaining how she'd progressed from Sharon to Agata, and then from her to Dylan, describing in detail her subsequent encounters with him, along with a summary of her chat with Doctor Bodie.

Frank listened without interrupting, occasionally nodding as he did so. When she had finished, he sat there looking down at the table, mulling over what she had said. She waited tensely for his approval. He finally looked up at her.

'So you're basically saying that he's this Jekyll and Hyde character who's reliving some kind of battle trauma when he's committing these crimes?'

'I think he's capable of doing very bad things. When he talked about Afghanistan, he implied that he did the same things to the enemy as they did to his fellow soldiers. He mentioned mutilation and cutting off body parts.'

'Did he explicitly state that he took scalps?'

'No, but I think it's highly plausible that he did.'

Her most recent conversation with Doctor Bodie, combined with her insights into Dylan's military past, had reinforced her belief in his culpability.

'You're just speculating now,' said Frank. 'Like you were before, with the Hairdresser.'

She found his scepticism frustrating but not unexpected. Frank had never been a fan of hunches.

'But you have to admit it makes perfect sense when you consider his background and the nature of the crimes being committed in here. And it's all backed up by Doctor Bodie's explanation. And you yourself checked the rota – he was on duty when all four of them were murdered.'

'I find it hard to accept that someone who has been committing these kinds of crimes would also be able to sustain what is basically a regular sexual relationship with one of the inmates.'

'That's my whole point. One part of him is conducting a normal relationship with Agata, but another completely different part of his personality is doing the murdering and the scalping.'

Frank frowned and chewed on one of his fingernails. She could tell that he wasn't convinced.

'I don't think he's completely aware that he's doing it,' she said. 'That's because this other sub-personality takes control of his behaviour when he—'

She felt Frank suddenly kick her under the table. She broke off and glanced around. Dylan was approaching their table on his circuit of the visit hall. He walked slowly past. As he did so, she looked up at him. He smiled pleasantly at her, the tanned skin around his pale blue eyes crinkling in that distinctive way. He nodded politely at Frank and continued past their table.

They waited until he was out of earshot.

'I think he likes you,' said Frank, a faint smirk briefly piercing his harsh demeanour.

'Are you taking me seriously or not?'

'Sorry. You were saying?'

'The whole reason the sub-personality exists in the first place is because of the traumas that he underwent in Afghanistan. And his brain injury has probably exacerbated the whole problem. I'm sure it can't have helped.'

'I don't buy it.'

'What about Sharon then?'

'What about her?'

'Remember I only got onto Dylan in the first place because I was trying to work out if anyone might have had a good reason to kill Sharon. And he's the most likely contender. If she was blackmailing him.'

'For misconduct in public office?'

'Yes. She probably thought she could extract money or some kind of privilege from him, but she obviously didn't realise the kind of person she was trying to blackmail.'

'So you're saying she somehow unleashed this crazed sub-personality...'

'Maybe it comes out when he's under duress... like when he's being threatened with blackmail.'

Frank was shaking his head. 'Maybe this. Maybe that. It's all maybes. You need to find some evidence. Hard evidence. Body parts. Scalps. A weapon. Anything that explicitly connects him to the crimes. Either that or you've got to catch him red-handed. And soon.'

'I'm doing my best.'

He grimaced and shook his head slowly and she knew with dismay that for him, right now, her best just wasn't good enough. Sometimes he could make her feel so isolated, but that was just the way he was.

'The drugs squad are demanding to see some kind of intel from you.

From this "new angle" I told them you were working on. If they don't see something soon...'

'Just string them along for a little bit longer,' she pleaded.

He fixed her with his arctic watery stare.

'I'm under pressure, Bailey. And when I'm under pressure,' he pointed his finger at her, 'you're under pressure.'

85

As she walked through A-Wing, Bailey looked up through the mesh of the anti-suicide netting which was strung across the balconies and noticed Crazy Mel standing by herself on the landing above. She was swaying slightly, staring vacantly into space, her hands jammed in the pockets of her jogging top, her hair sticking up in its usual chaotic tangle. She glanced downwards and for a brief moment their eyes met. But there was no recognition there, only a frazzled blankness.

Bailey lowered her head and continued on her way, weaving deftly between the groups of inmates lounging outside their cells, making sure that she didn't lose sight of Dylan. He was striding along about ten metres ahead of her and by the looks of it he was headed towards the stairwell at the end of the landing. She had been covertly following him around all morning in the increasingly desperate hope that she would uncover something tangible that linked him to the murders.

As far as she was concerned, she was sure that she was on the right track with him. She just needed some sort of confirmation. The more she thought about it, the more she had become convinced that his experiences in Afghanistan had unleashed a mental trauma of some sort. Suffering as she did from PTSD, she could identify with him to a certain degree for they both lay on the same spectrum, he was just at the most extreme end of it. And that was the reason he also scared her, not just because of what he might have done, but because of what he represented – a human being lost to madness, the same kind of madness that nipped at the edges of her own mind in the greyness of the pre-dawn.

He began to descend the cast-iron stairwell, whistling to himself as he did so. She caught a snatch of it, that same military marching tune he'd been whistling before. What was the name of it again? She couldn't remember. It didn't matter.

She followed in his footsteps, hopping down the metal stairs, trying to keep up with him whilst also trying to remain as inconspicuous as possible.

When he reached the ground floor, he made his way towards the stairwell that led down to the basement, and at that point it occurred to her that he might be on his way to another rendezvous with Agata. But then again he might be up to something completely different. She wouldn't know unless she followed him down there. So she did.

Once down in the basement, she hung further back, keeping behind the corners where possible to remain out of his line of sight should he suddenly turn around. There was just the sound of his soft whistling echoing back up the dingy corridors that told her that he was still somewhere up there ahead of her.

Then suddenly the whistling stopped.

Coming to a halt, she peeked cautiously around the next corner. The corridor was empty. He must have gone into one of the rooms. But which one and why?

She decided to wait where she was, reasoning that he would emerge eventually. If he doubled back up the corridor in her direction, she would have enough of a head-start to make it back up to the atrium before he reached her position.

It was perhaps three minutes that she had to wait there before the door to the workshop opened and Dylan emerged. He set off down the corridor in the opposite direction, away from her. The question now on her mind was whether his visit to the workshop had been part of a routine patrol or whether he'd gone in there for some other, possibly more sinister, reason.

She weighed up whether to continue following him or whether to check out the workshop. In the end, she decided on the workshop.

Waiting until he'd disappeared around the next corner, she stepped out and made her way to the workshop. She peered in through the wire-reinforced glass window. It didn't look like there was anyone in there. She tried the door handle. The door opened. That was odd. She would have expected the room to have been locked when it wasn't occupied. Maybe he'd forgotten to lock it. She pushed the door open and went in.

When in use, the workshop was probably one of the noisiest rooms in the prison, resounding with the racket of power tools drilling and grinding, but right now it couldn't have been quieter. All the machinery sat dormant, switched off, and the only sound was the faint crunching of metal shavings beneath her feet as she paced slowly along the centre of the room between the rows of workbenches.

As she walked along, she looked around the room, taking in the racks of drills and woodworking tools hanging on the walls, the oxyacetylene tanks with their red and green rubber cables, the industrial lathe... the tiny reflections of herself in the chrome handles of the clamps on the benches.

The problem was that she didn't know what she was looking for exactly. Something out of the ordinary. Something that didn't quite fit. She figured she'd know it when she saw it.

She stopped and sniffed the air. Beyond the smell of sawdust and oil there was some other odour which she recognised, distinct and out of place in here...

The smell of cologne.

She spun around.

Dylan was standing right behind her. She jumped back in surprise. He had somehow snuck up on her.

'You were following me,' he said softly, his blue eyes boring into her.

'No I wasn't.'

'I'm not stupid. Why were you following me?'

That was why he'd left the door unlocked – to lure her in here and trap her. The question was, what was he going to do next? A bolt of fear spiked through her.

She swallowed and forced an expression of casual innocence onto her face. 'It's just a coincidence that I'm down here the same time as you.'

He shook his head and smiled as if he found something amusing. 'You suddenly come up to me out of the blue and start striking up conversations, wanting to know all about me. Why would you do that? Inmates are never friendly unless they want something... and I think I know what you want.'

His tanned face crinkled into a knowing smirk.

Realising what he was getting at, she felt herself relax a little, relieved that his intentions at this stage didn't entail attacking her.

'You're getting the wrong end of the stick,' she said.

'Am I?'

He took a step towards her. She took a step backwards.

'You're an attractive woman,' he said.

She studied his handsome face, trying to ascertain at what point the psychotic sub-personality might emerge and how she would know when it did.

'What about Agata?' she asked, in an attempt to deflect his advances.

'You know about Agata?'

'I know all about you.'

'She doesn't get me. Not like you do. You're different from the others here. There's something about you. I don't know what it is.'

'You're breaking the law by sleeping with the inmates.'

'It's a stupid law.'

He took another step towards her. She tried to retreat but found herself backed up against a workbench.

'Keep your distance,' she said calmly.

'I'm not going to hurt you.' He reached up and brushed her hair aside to reveal the scar on her face.

She raised one eyebrow. 'I'm warning you.'

'I have to have you.'

The tanned skin crinkled around his eyes. Good-looking as he was, she certainly wasn't going to surrender to him. But how would he take her rejection? Would it tip him over the edge? Better not to take that chance. Better to act pre-emptively and deal with the consequences afterwards.

He reached up with his other hand.

As he did so, she grabbed his forearm, simultaneously twisted to the side of him and pulled him across her outstretched leg. *Tai otoshi* – body drop. He crashed to the floor.

He lay there in stunned surprise.

'What the—?!'

But she wasn't done yet.

She squatted down behind him, slipped her thumbs into the collar of his shirt and yanked it hard so the top two buttons of his shirt popped off, along with his clip-on tie, then she pulled it tight across his throat so the stiff fabric was biting into the flesh of his neck. *Okuri eri jime* – sliding collar strangle.

He flailed and batted at her hands as he tried to twist out of her grip. She tightened her hold on his neck, torqueing the material of his shirt so it constricted his neck even further. He coughed and gasped, his eyes wide with shock.

'If I apply just a bit more pressure here,' she twisted his collar a fraction tighter, 'I'll be cutting off the flow of blood to your brain. In twenty seconds you'll be unconscious, in under a minute you'll have permanent brain damage, and not long after that you'll be dead.'

He stiffened and then went slack, passive in her grasp.

'Jesus...' he stuttered in a choked gurgle, 'I thought... I'd met... some... nutters... in the army... but you're... one crazy bitch!'

She was stuck now. She'd passed the point of no return. She had no option now but to get him to admit it. And as for what she'd do after that, she'd cross that bridge...

Still keeping a firm grip, she slightly loosened her hold on his neck so he could speak without restriction. He let out a wheeze of relief.

'I understand your problem,' she said. 'I know you're not completely in control.'

'Problem? My only problem right now is you.'

'Post-traumatic stress disorder. Afghanistan. Flashbacks.'

He was silent for a few moments, his chest rising and falling.

'What would you know about that?' he said softly.

'More than you think,' she replied, trying to get him onside. 'Trust me, I know where you're coming from.'

'Let go of me.'

'Not until you admit it.'

'Admit what?'

'Killing them,' she hissed in his ear.

'They were Taliban. I had no choice.'

'I'm not talking about the Taliban. I'm talking about Sharon. I'm talking about Alice. Poodle. Natalie.'

'You what...?' He sounded genuinely puzzled.

'You killed them and you scalped them.'

'No I didn't. I didn't do anything of the sort.'

'Maybe you don't think you did, but you did. During some kind of flashback.'

'I wasn't even here when Sharon was killed. I had the day off.'

'You're lying,' she growled. 'I don't like liars.'

She squeezed his neck tighter again, causing him to cough and twitch. Then she eased off again to let him speak. He took a gulp of air.

'I had to go to a veterans group meet-up. It's normally on Sundays, but they switched it to Tuesday because of a transport strike. So I had to arrange a last-minute shift swap.'

'Rubbish!'

'You can look at my rota if you don't believe me.' He nodded downwards with his chin. 'It's in my top pocket.'

'Get it out. Slowly.'

He reached up carefully and pulled a folded piece of A4 paper from his top pocket. He unfolded it and held it up for her to see.

It was a printout that listed the names of all the prison officers and the dates that they were scheduled to work.

She scanned the rota for the date that Sharon had been murdered: the twenty-third of June.

On Dylan's printout, that particular date had been ringed in biro with an arrow pointing to the twenty-fifth of June next to the name of Brian Bunter.

'You swapped shifts with Brian?'

'That's right. I worked the twenty-fifth for him. Ask him if you want.'

She didn't need to. She remembered now that it had been Brian who had led the mad rush to the kitchen in the immediate wake of Sharon's murder. He had definitely been working that day even though this rota stated that he was supposed to have had the day off. That meant therefore that Dylan was likely to be telling the truth about the shift swap. And if he was telling the truth about the shift swap, could he be telling the truth about the murders? He had an alibi for Sharon's murder at least.

Had the murder investigation team been aware of this informal shift swap arrangement when they'd been interrogating the prison officers? If they had, then the information hadn't filtered down to either her or Frank.

Shit!

She let go of him. He dropped the rota and wrenched himself away from her.

They both stood up. He massaged his neck and eyed her warily.

'I'm sorry,' she said. 'I was wrong about you.'

He gazed at her curiously and shook his head. 'Just what kind of weird game are you playing?'

Suddenly the door to the workshop creaked open. They both spun around. Maggie was standing there in the doorway, eyeing them both suspiciously. Bailey could see her register Dylan's open shirt collar.

'What's going on here?' she said.

'Er... nothing,' said Dylan, trying to pull the top of his shirt closed.

Bailey noticed the rota lying on the floor just behind the workbench. She quickly bent down, picked it up and slipped it into the back pocket of her tracksuit trousers.

'There's no reason for either of you to be in here,' said Maggie, her arms crossed, tapping her foot.

She jerked her head at the door for Bailey to leave. Bailey dutifully scurried past Dylan and made her way out of the workshop.

As she did so, she heard Maggie say to Dylan: 'I think it's time you and me had a little word.'

She guessed that Dylan had somewhat of a reputation and that his colleagues were well aware of it. She left him to be reprimanded by Maggie, feeling a tiny twinge of guilt at leaving him to take the blame, especially now that it looked likely that he wasn't the murderer.

'Hello, Sullivan Knight Solicitor's. How can I help?'

'It's Bailey Pike speaking. I'd like to talk to Mr Knight please.'

'Just putting you through.'

The familiar strands of Beethoven's 'Moonlight Sonata' played for a few seconds and then Frank came on the line.

'Made any progress?'

'It's not Dylan,' she said. 'He wasn't here when Sharon was murdered. He had a day off. He did a last-minute shift swap with another prison officer. And if he didn't kill Sharon then that means he probably didn't kill the others either.'

Frank was quiet for a few moments.

'So all that stuff with Sharon blackmailing him...?'

'Mistaken conjecture. I was barking up the wrong tree. She was just in the wrong place at the wrong time.'

'You realise this puts you right back at square one,' he said. 'First, there was the Hairdresser and that didn't come to anything. And now the Dylan angle has fallen through. It feels to me like you're grasping at straws. Things aren't looking too promising, are they, Bailey?'

'Not quite.'

'How's that then?'

She glanced around and tucked herself further into the phone booth.

'I was looking at Dylan's rota and it got me thinking about the dates. Sharon was murdered on the twenty-third of June. Right?'

'Yeah that's right.'

'Go back sixteen days before that to the seventh of June – that was when Natalie was murdered. Go back a further sixteen days and we're on the twenty-second of May – that was when Poodle got murdered. And go back sixteen more days and it's the sixth of May – that was when Alice was murdered.'

'Hmm... Every sixteen days, huh? Interesting. No one else spotted that.'

'I'm angry with myself that I didn't spot it earlier, but then time passes strangely in here – you kind of lose track of it. And also it's not as if sixteen days is an immediately obvious pattern to notice.'

'Is it connected to the rota?'

'Not that I can ascertain. At least, I couldn't make out any clear correlation between the dates of the murders, the locations of the murders and the shift patterns of the prison officers.'

He sighed. 'So the upshot of all this is that you still don't have anything.'

'The whole reason I'm mentioning it is because we now know when the next murder is due to take place.'

'If there is a next murder. If the killer sticks to this pattern.'

'The ninth of July,' she said. 'That's when it's going to happen. In five days' time.'

'A date by itself is not enough to justify taking any kind of action. You need to provide me with—'

'Something solid. Yeah I know.'

87

No sooner had she got back to her cell than Bailey turned around to encounter the gang filing through the door, crowding into the small room. Toni. Muscles. Rong. Keisha. No sign of Poppy. She hadn't noticed them hanging around outside, but then she'd been so deep in thought about the significance of the sixteen-day pattern that she hadn't really been paying attention to anything else.

An unannounced visit. They didn't look happy. This wasn't good. A knot of fear immediately formed in Bailey's stomach.

They moved into the cell so they were all standing around her. Toni nodded to Keisha, who pulled the cell door shut behind her. This definitely wasn't looking good.

'Hey guys, what's up?' She tried to sound light-hearted. But they weren't smiling.

'Muscles,' said Toni.

Muscles grabbed Bailey from behind, pinning her arms behind her back. Bailey squirmed in her grip, but Muscles was far too strong.

'I don't understand. What's going on?'

'What's going on is that we think you're a cop.'

'A cop?' said Bailey, evincing an expression of shock. But inside, her heart rate had suddenly gone up exponentially.

'Yeah. A fucking pig!' spat Toni.

'Just admit it,' said Keisha. 'It'll make things a whole lot easier.'

A whole lot easier for them to kill me, thought Bailey.

'I don't know what you're talking about,' she said.

'It's so obvious,' growled Toni. 'You come in here. You join our gang. Terry gets arrested. All a little bit too convenient.'

'You've got it all wrong.'

'No, I think we've got it all right.' Toni eyed her with a nasty leer. 'You see, Keisha here happened to be talking to someone called Carly Potson, who swore on her grandmother's grave that she was arrested by you one time.'

Fuck.

Bailey's heart sank at the mention of Carly Potson. She realised now that she had made a fatal error in hoping that Carly would forget about her following their encounter in the canteen. Bailey had seen Carly around the prison, and Carly hadn't approached her again, so Bailey had assumed that she had moved on, but apparently that wasn't the case.

'Now, normally we wouldn't place much stock in the say-so of a worthless parasite like Carly Potson who could just be trying to ingratiate herself with us to get off the hook for money she owes us.' Toni paused and tilted her head thoughtfully. 'But then I did some thinking... of the mathematical kind. The two-plus-two kind. And it all suddenly adds up. You're. A. Fucking. Pig.' With each venomously hissed word, she poked Bailey hard in the chest with her forefinger.

This was exactly the kind of situation where the prime rule of working undercover was put to the test.

Never break cover.

However sure they were that she was a serving police officer, whatever evidence they had, however convincing, Bailey had to deny it to the hilt.

Because if she didn't, she was dead.

Sure, there was that little perverse itching temptation that every undercover cop had in a situation like this, which was to give in and admit it, to free oneself of that horrible weight of pressure caused by the constant need to conceal and deceive.

She fought it back.

She remembered her training. The life-saving mantra.

Never. Break. Cover.

'That's absolute bullshit,' croaked Bailey, her mouth dry with fear. 'She's got me muddled up with someone else.'

Rong fixed her with a bulging cross-eyed stare. 'Don't try and wriggle out of it.'

'You're always making all these phone calls all the time,' said Toni.

Keisha leaned in with an aggressive grimace. 'Like you were just now.'

'Who are you talking to exactly?' snarled Toni, prodding her hard in the chest with each word.

'My lawyer.'

'And who's that who comes in to visit you?' said Rong.

'My brother.'

'Not much of a family resemblance.'

'Yeah. His nose is too big,' grunted Keisha.

'He's my half-brother. Same father, different mothers.'

'Bullshit!' hissed Toni, leaning in close so their faces were almost touching.

Bailey swallowed and tried to maintain her composure.

She cursed herself for underestimating how closely they had been watching her.

'And you're always trying to get out of hurting people,' said Keisha. 'There's definitely something wrong with you.'

In any other situation Bailey would have laughed at Keisha's logic, but there wasn't much to laugh about right now.

Toni reached behind her and pulled out her shank. She held it up to Bailey's face so she could absorb every tiny detail of the home-made blade – the roughly filed edge, the vicious point.

She brushed back Bailey's hair from the left side of her face to reveal her scar.

'That's a nasty scar you've got there. I think we'll start by giving you one on the other side of your face to match it. They always say symmetry is an important factor in physical beauty. Shall we make you beautiful?'

Bailey tried to writhe away from the blade, but Muscles was holding her too firmly. Toni grinned in her signature shark-like way, her gold tooth winking from the corner of her mouth as she pressed the sharp tip of the shank against Bailey's right cheek.

'I'm not a cop!' gasped Bailey. 'You have to believe me!'

'Too late for that,' growled Toni, dismissing her protests.

Bailey closed her eyes and gritted her teeth, bracing herself for the pain, feeling the beads of sweat rolling down her face, her heart hammering inside her ribcage.

The flashback hit her right there and then.

...Hanging chained up from the rafters... the burning cigarettes... the smell of her toasting flesh... the razor blade... the blood dripping...

The name...

The name...

The name...

'No!' she screamed, her eyes popping wide open.

Toni recoiled in surprise.

'Well, well... a little more squeamish than I'd bargained on.'

She lowered the shank.

'Don't worry. I wasn't planning on giving you a scar. Too messy. And inconvenient. And anyhow, we're beyond all that now.'

What did she mean exactly? Bailey's bad feeling got that little bit worse.

Without breaking eye contact with Bailey, Toni smiled and held out her hand. 'Rong?'

Rong stepped forward and held up a hypodermic syringe. She depressed the plunger slightly to make a small squirt of liquid come out of the top.

The syringe must have been stolen from the medical facility or smuggled in somehow.

Bailey hated needles at the best of times. And this was far from the best of times. This didn't bode well at all.

'What's that?' she whispered, trying to buy herself a precious few extra seconds. She had a horrible feeling, though, that she didn't want to know what it was.

Toni took the syringe from Rong and held it up in front of Bailey's face. It was filled with a sandy-coloured liquid in which tiny impurities floated. The needle glistened, a droplet of liquid oozing from its tip.

'This is a hundred quid's worth of ninety-three per cent pure Pakistani heroin.'

Ninety-three per cent.

Bailey knew from her police experience that most heroin that drug addicts took was twenty per cent pure, if that. With a black sinking dread, she realised that they were intending to give her what junkies fearfully referred to as a hot-shot – a deliberately lethal injection of smack designed to kill the victim by overdose.

'Much as I'd love to carve you up personally,' said Toni, 'it's a lot less trouble for us if you're just found here in your cell dead of an overdose with a needle sticking out of your arm. No one will bother investigating your death and therefore no one will interfere with our business. They'll just think you were some sad junkie who OD'ed.'

Bailey squirmed and struggled in Muscles' iron clutch.

'Hold her tight, Muscles,' said Toni.

Muscles gripped her even tighter whilst Rong took hold of Bailey's left wrist and yanked up the sleeve of her jogging top to expose her left fore-arm. She wrenched it forward. Toni hunched over it and aimed the tip of the syringe downwards.

'Hold her still! I've got to get it into the vein.'

'No please! Please don't do it! I'm not a cop! I'm not a cop! I swear!'

The sinews in Bailey's arm stood out as she twisted and wriggled against them but she couldn't escape. Their fingers bit harder into her flesh as they held her immobile. She felt the sharp tip of the needle scrape the skin of her forearm.

'Hold her still, damn it!' said Toni, trying to line up the needle with the vein.

Bailey closed her eyes, clenched her teeth and braced herself for the massive hit that would put her into a coma within seconds from which she would never awaken.

'She's not a cop.'

Bailey opened her eyes.

Poppy was leaning against the doorway, her arms crossed, her black fringe hanging down across her face, calmly observing the situation with her large kohl-rimmed eyes.

Toni paused, a grimace on her face, the needle poised just a few millimetres from Bailey's forearm. She twisted her head around slowly.

'How do you know?' she growled.

'She told me stuff.'

'What stuff?'

'Accountancy. She knows too much about accountancy to be a cop. No pig would ever know that much about spreadsheets.'

Bailey felt an overwhelming surge of relief at Poppy's intervention. Her life was hanging in the balance and Poppy was now all that stood in the way of certain death. All those conversations they'd had together and all those interactions during the tattooing sessions now converged upon this single crucial moment.

'She could have been lying to you,' said Toni, with a sceptical sneer. 'That could just be her cover story.'

'I never let anyone lie to me.'

Toni sighed, faintly dismayed. 'Are you vouching for her, Poppy? Because if you are, you'd better be sure.'

'I vouch for her. If I find out she's lying, I'll kill her myself.'

Toni straightened up slowly. She looked at Bailey and then at the syringe. Her eyes narrowed. An idea seemed to have occurred to her.

Still clutching the needle, she reached into her back pocket and took out a mobile phone.

'Just to be sure, I want you to call your lawyer right here in front of us, right now. I want to listen to his voice. I want to know that he actually exists.'

The phone sat there in Toni's outstretched palm, shiny and menacing.

Muscles let go of Bailey's right arm.

Bailey reached out and took the phone. They all stood there silently watching as she dialled Frank's number with a shaking finger. As soon as the ringtone started, Toni reached across, took the phone from her and put it on speakerphone so they could all listen in. She held the phone in front of Bailey's mouth.

Rita's nasal sing-song voice answered. 'Hello, Sullivan Knight Solicitors. How can I help?'

Bailey could visualise Rita sitting there in the office with her head-phones on, probably filing her nails at the same time. Bailey swallowed and took a deep breath.

'It's Bailey Pike speaking. It's really important that I talk to Mr Knight.'

'He's just with a client at the minute. If you hold just a moment I'll see if he can come to the phone.'

Beethoven's 'Moonlight Sonata' came on. But this time it seemed to play for ages, longer than the usual five seconds or so.

The gang glared at her silent and stony-faced as the melancholy chords tinkled from the phone's small speaker. In what could be her last moments, Bailey made an effort to savour the beauty of the music, noting ironically that it sounded more funereal than ever under the current circumstances.

It stopped abruptly as Frank came on the line.

'Hello Bailey. I'm glad you called. No doubt you're wanting to know where I am with your appeal. Well, I'm just putting together the last few bits. In a nutshell, I think we've got a good chance of the appeal working on the basis that the key prosecution evidence used against you was way too flimsy. I'll be in court this afternoon with some other cases, but I should have everything related to your appeal completed by lunchtime tomorrow. Do you want to call me back then?'

Toni was staring fiercely at Bailey, the phone in one hand, the syringe in the other.

'Bailey?' said Frank. 'Is everything okay?'

'Everything's fine. Just fine. Tomorrow sounds great. Thanks for everything.'

'No problem. Talk to you soon. Take care now.'

'You too.'

He ended the call.

Toni lowered the phone and slipped it back into her pocket.

For what seemed like aeons, they all stood there in silence, Toni scrutinising her with her flint-grey eyes.

Bailey started to feel dizzy and then realised she had been holding her breath as she awaited the verdict.

Toni's face broke into a smile. She handed the syringe to Rong, patted Bailey on the shoulder and straightened her tracksuit top which had got rumpled in the altercation.

'Guess it was just a case of mistaken identity after all. Had to be sure though. No hard feelings, eh?'

Then she and the rest of the gang filed out of the cell as promptly as they had entered.

Only Poppy remained, standing there with her arms crossed, leaning against the wall.

'Thanks for sticking up for me,' said Bailey, rolling her left sleeve back down, massaging her forearm from where they had been gripping it.

Poppy said nothing, and just stood there studying her for a few moments.

'Just remember our deal,' she said.

And then she turned and left the cell.

Bailey stood there all alone, her heart beating hard. She felt weak and shaky all of a sudden now that the adrenaline had run its course. She slumped down onto the bunk.

As she sat there, she reflected on the wisdom of having previously set up a special code with Frank. As part of the security protocol they'd agreed that if she prefaced the call to the switchboard with 'It's really important that I talk to' instead of the usual 'I'd like to talk to' then it was a signal to Rita that she should prompt Frank to answer in character as there might be other people listening in.

Once again she'd scraped through. Just.

88

Bailey stood by herself in the canteen queue, impervious to the clatter and chatter going on around her, lost in thought about the murders. She knew the answer was lying there right in front of her, tantalisingly close, almost within her grasp. It resembled a particularly difficult cryptic crossword clue, except that in this case someone would die in five days' time if she didn't work it out.

She sighed in frustration and shuffled along with the rest of the queue. She momentarily ceased her introspection to tune into the conversations around her, hoping to detect some elusive fragment of information that would solve the mystery. From what she could overhear, the fear of being viciously mutilated and murdered was still foremost in the minds of many of the inmates. After all, quite a few of them had witnessed first-hand the aftermath of Sharon's slaying and if they hadn't fully comprehended the gory reality of it before, then they certainly did now. An edgy pall of impending doom hung in the air – even if they weren't consciously aware that one of them would die in five days' time, it seemed like they could almost sense the inevitable butchery that was to come.

So saying, not everyone was talking about murder...

Directly in front of her stood two white inmates who were squinting up at the lunchtime menu that was written in messy black marker pen on the whiteboard propped next to the serving counter.

'Lamb wokra?' said one of them. 'Never had wokra before. What do you think it is?'

'Wokra?' said the other one. 'Sounds like some kind of stew.'

Bailey listened in with mild interest. She too had never heard of wokra before. She looked at the whiteboard. It took her a few moments to realise that the messy writing was actually referring to lamb with okra. The 'with' had been abbreviated by 'w/' but the '/' was too faded to be visible so instead it just looked like 'wokra'. She chuckled to herself.

'Excuse me, but I think you'll find it's supposed to be lamb with okra,' she said.

They both turned and looked at her quizzically.

'Okra? What's okra?'

'It's a plant,' she said. 'It's kind of like a green pod with gooey seeds in it. It's used a lot in African cooking.'

They both swapped glances and wrinkled their faces in distaste.

'Gooey green pods. Yuck! Don't like the sound of those,' said the first one.

'I think I'll go for the sausage and mash,' said the other one.

When it came to Bailey's turn to be served, she also opted for the sausage and mash, not because she disliked okra but because she'd never been that keen on the flavour of lamb.

She sat down and started to eat, smiling to herself as she reflected on their misinterpretation.

Wokra.

She supposed that if you didn't know what you were looking at then it was quite easy to mistake the abbreviation for—

It suddenly triggered a flash of insight within her.

Could it be...?

Thinking back, she visualised Sharon's bloody scrawl in her mind's eye. With mounting excitement, she took her fork and spread the mashed potato out on her plate, and with the tip of her knife she traced the letters in exactly the way that she recalled they had been written by Sharon's dying hand.

First a capital 'F'. Then the downwards stroke of an 'l', the tail jerking sharply to the right to lead into the first lower-case 'e', which was followed by a further lower-case 'e'. It was the 'l' that niggled at Bailey though. There was something ambiguous about it. She'd assumed that it was a lower-case 'l' with a wonky tail joining it to the following 'e', but what if it had actually been a capital 'L'? Maybe it was just written so closely to the following 'e' that it looked like it was joined up when in fact it wasn't supposed to be. After all, the two 'e's weren't joined up. And if Sharon had meant to write the word 'flee' then surely she wouldn't have used a capital 'L' in the middle of the word. Of course, when she'd written it, she'd been scalped, her throat had been cut and she was dying – not exactly the best condition to be in when attempting neat legible handwriting – but still... had she actually been trying to communicate something completely different? Had she deliberately intended to write it as a capital 'L'? And if she had, then did that mean that the capital 'F' was actually an initial of some sort?

Bailey peered into her mashed potato, trying to unlock Sharon's true intent. She smeared it smooth and started again, this time separating the first two letters: F Lee.

Maybe she hadn't written 'flee' at all.

89

Amber was patrolling the third-floor landing of C-Wing, stopping here and there to chat to the inmates lounging on the balconies.

Bailey watched from a short distance away, waiting for Amber to disengage from her current conversation. As soon as she did, Bailey stepped forward and made her approach.

As she drew closer, Amber recognised her and her face tautened with that same whiff of censure she'd expressed towards Bailey ever since she'd discovered that she'd become a member of the Ace Blade Crew.

'Hello, Bailey,' she said stiffly. 'What brings you to C-Wing?'

'You, actually.'

'Oh?'

Bailey glanced around and lowered her voice slightly. 'I was wondering if you could help me out with something.'

Amber seemed to soften slightly. 'I'm always happy to be of assistance.'

'I've been thinking about what Sharon wrote in her own blood when she was murdered.'

'Oh... right. Most unpleasant.'

'What did you see?'

Amber hesitated, shuddering at the memory. She looked at Bailey with a puzzled expression.

'Why were you thinking about that?'

'I have a funny feeling that there's more to it than meets the eye.'

Amber frowned as she tried to recall. 'Well... I saw the word "flee". At least that's what I think it said.'

'What did you make of it?'

'It seemed like... like a warning maybe. Who knows? She was dying. People probably think and do all sorts of crazy things when they're dying. It doesn't necessarily mean that it signified anything.'

'I'm not so sure.'

'What are you getting at?'

Bailey took a piece of paper out of her pocket, on which she had replicated in biro what she had drawn in her mashed potato. She showed the piece of paper to Amber.

'It looked like this, didn't it?'

Amber peered at the piece of paper. 'Yes... yes, I believe it did.'

'What if it didn't say "flee" but "F Lee"?'

Amber frowned. 'You mean... like a name?'

'Exactly. I needed to talk to you about it because you were there and you clearly saw it. And you're smart.'

Amber nodded slowly as she turned the idea over in her mind. 'Hmm... you could have a point. But who does "F Lee" refer to?'

Bailey shrugged. 'I have no idea. That's the problem.'

'I'm not sure I can help you, Bailey, and if I'm to be honest, it sounds a little dubious to me.'

Bailey nodded glumly, downhearted. She wasn't about to give up just yet though.

'You wouldn't happen to know anyone in here by that name, would you?' she asked hopefully. There were over six hundred inmates in the prison, and a good number of prison staff on top of that. Bailey didn't know the names of all of them by a long stretch, but she was hoping that Amber might be able to provide some insight on that front. As a prison officer, Amber was probably acquainted with many more of them than Bailey was.

Amber sighed, eyeing Bailey with a mixture of pity and reproach, then her kinder side seemed to get the better of her. She tilted her head and pondered for a few moments. Then she shook it.

'I'm afraid not. I can't think of a single inmate or member of staff who goes by that name. It could be someone who was in here before my time though. I only started working here quite recently.'

'Okay. Thanks anyway.' Bailey was disappointed, but Amber had just sparked an idea in her mind of who she might ask next.

Bailey folded up the piece of paper and tucked it back in her pocket.

'Why are you so interested in this all of a sudden?' said Amber.

'It was my cellmate who got murdered.'

'Of course,' replied Amber. 'I forgot Sharon was your cellmate.' Amber nodded sympathetically. 'Well... stay out of trouble, okay?'

90

'SILENCE' read the sign above the librarian's desk. It stated what was quite clearly apparent. The place was completely dead. The librarian was nowhere to be seen and there didn't appear to be anyone else in here.

Bailey stood there by the entrance briefly and then ventured down one of the aisles in search of Jacqui. She trailed her fingers along the spines of the books, inhaling the musty smell, thinking to herself that it was a pity this tatty collection of texts wasn't better funded.

She turned down another aisle. Still no sign of the librarian. It was quiet, too quiet...

She stopped, turned around to retrace her footsteps... and jumped in surprise.

Jacqui was standing just a few centimetres away from her, peering at her over the tops of her half-moon glasses. How did she do that?

'Change your mind about wanting to borrow that poetry book?' rasped Jacqui, a vague undercurrent of menace in her voice.

'Er... not exactly. Although I was wondering if you could help me with something.'

'What are you looking for?'

'It's not a book I'm looking for exactly.'

Bailey tried to think of the best way to phrase it without causing possible offence.

'Last time I was here, you mentioned that you'd been in here for quite a while.'

Jacqui nodded slowly. 'That's right. Eleven years. Got a further seven to do. Why?'

'So you probably have a good knowledge of who's been locked up here in the past?'

'Not really. I keep myself to myself. I find it works better that way. I'm barely acquainted with anyone in here. I'm like a hermit. The only people whose names I'm familiar with are those who use the library. And that's not many people, as you can see. Why do you ask?'

Bailey felt disappointment weigh down upon her. Maybe it had been a waste of time to come here. 'Well, it's a bit of a long shot really, but do you know any inmate who would have had the name F. Lee?'

Jacqui pondered for a few moments, tapping her lip with a large tattooed finger.

'There is one name that springs to mind.'

'Who's that?'

'Felicia Lee.'

'Felicia Lee?'

'Anyone who's been in here longer than two years knows the name of Felicia Lee, even a recluse like me.'

'Why? What's so special about Felicia Lee?'

'Well, when she was in here, no one paid her much attention. She kept herself to herself. If you asked me what she looked like, I wouldn't be able to tell you. It's what she did subsequently which made her famous. Or perhaps "infamous" is a better word to use.'

Bailey found herself seized with a sudden excitement. She was onto something. She knew it.

'What did she do?' she asked breathlessly.

'She escaped. It's prison legend. One day she just disappeared without trace. And they never figured out how she did it. And she's never been caught. She's still a fugitive to this day, I believe.'

Bailey racked her mind as to what possible connection there could be between Felicia Lee and Sharon and the murders, if indeed there was any kind of connection...

'What was she in for?'

'She murdered her baby.' Jacqui wrinkled her nose. 'Bashed its skull in apparently.'

'Jesus!'

'Why are you so curious about Felicia Lee?'

'You know Sharon who was murdered in the prison kitchen? She wrote the name "F Lee" in her own blood as she lay dying. And I'm wondering if she was referring to Felicia Lee.'

'How odd.' Jacqui paused. 'Well, I suppose it's not completely random. After all, they did use to be cellmates.'

91

On the way to the phones, Bailey observed Dylan patrolling in her direction. He noticed her at almost exactly the same time that she noticed him. At the sight of her, he appeared to recoil slightly, an almost fearful expression on his face.

As they passed each other on the landing, he gave her the widest possible berth and refused to meet her eyes, keeping his gaze fixed firmly on the ground in front of him. She couldn't help but smile to herself at the effect she had on him. No doubt he was still convinced that she was 'one crazy bitch' as he'd called her.

Clearly he hadn't been suspended though. Not yet. It looked like Maggie hadn't reported his misdemeanours with the inmates this time around, although Bailey got the impression that she'd probably given him a pretty stern telling-off. She hoped he'd learnt his lesson for the time being. At any rate, she couldn't imagine he'd be coming onto her again. And she was pleased, at least, that she hadn't ended up on the nicking sheet as a result of the whole incident. She contemplated reporting him if and when she got out of here, but decided that it probably wouldn't be worth her while. Anyhow, there were slightly larger problems plaguing this prison and getting those ironed out was her main concern.

The queue down by the phones was thankfully short and she didn't have to wait longer than a few minutes before one became free. She tapped in her PIN number and waited for Rita to answer.

'Hello, Sullivan Knight Solicitors. How can I help?'

'It's Bailey Pike speaking. I'd like to talk to Mr Knight please.'

'Just putting you through.'

Several seconds of Beethoven's 'Moonlight Sonata', then Frank.

'Hello?' he said, a cautious tone in his voice.

'It's okay, Frank,' she said. 'No one's listening in this time.'

'Good. What happened? Is everything okay?'

She heard the worry in his voice, and it reassured her that he still cared for her as her boss.

'Yeah. Just a little hiccup with my cover. I think I managed to straighten it out though.'

She glanced over her shoulder. She couldn't spot any of the gang in the vicinity. Even so, she tucked herself further into the phone booth.

'I want you to check something out for me. A name. A person.'

'Who?'

'Felicia Lee.'

'Who's that?'

She outlined the meagre amount of information she knew.

'I thought you said Sharon was just in the wrong place at the wrong time,' he said.

'She wrote that name for a reason.'

'Why would she write the name of her former cellmate in her own blood?'

'Beats me. That's why I want you to try and track her down.'

'You said she escaped two years ago. That's a long time. She could be anywhere by now.'

'We've got four days until the next murder.'

'I'll do what I can but don't get your hopes up.'

'Felicia Lee is the key to this whole thing. I'm sure of it.'

The razor blade lay on the table between the stack of coloured paper and the ashtray. On the edge of the ashtray balanced a half-smoked joint waiting to be relit.

Long brown bony fingers skittered like two spiders mating as they expertly folded a red piece of paper. Mountain fold... valley fold... reverse fold... pivot fold... sink fold...

The fingers manipulated the paper with expert dexterity, twisting and creasing it into the desired shape. Gradually it took form...

Bailey sat outside in the yard on one of the concrete benches, her eyes closed, her face to the sky, savouring the sensation of the warm July sun on her skin on this bright fresh morning, taking the opportunity to absorb a bit of vitamin D before she was locked up back indoors again.

With her eyes closed, she could almost pretend that she wasn't in prison but on some beach somewhere, tanning herself. She certainly didn't need to be looking at the prison. Even nice summer weather like this couldn't do much to soften its oppressiveness.

As she sat there, she became aware, all of a sudden, that something was blocking out the warm light of the sun. She opened her eyes and blinked.

A figure stood over her, silhouetted against the sun, the features not immediately visible. But that distinctive frayed afro was enough to tell her who it was.

A brown hand placed something on the table in front of her.

It was a small red origami creature.

Crazy Mel moved out of the sun and looked down at Bailey with her manic bloodshot eyes. Bailey guessed she was stoned, as usual.

Mel nodded at the origami creature.

Bailey took a closer look at it. It had a rectangular body, four triangular legs, a head with two tiny ears, and a pointed tail. She marvelled at the intricacy of it. It was evidently supposed to be some kind of animal, but which one, she couldn't tell.

'That's fabulous, Mel. What is it?'

'It's a tiger.'

'For me?'

Mel nodded. 'Protection.'

'Against what?'

'Him.'

Bailey picked up the origami tiger. It was insubstantial, almost as light as a feather. Some protection! She looked up at Mel and smiled.

'Why thank you, Mel.' She spoke in the manner that you would to a child or a mentally handicapped person.

'Be careful,' said Mel. 'It bites.'

Bailey examined the tiger's tiny head.

'I don't see any teeth, Mel.'

Mel nodded sagely and winked at her. Then she turned and limped off across the yard. Bailey watched her jerking along awkwardly in her weird lopsided gait until she disappeared around the corner of B-Wing.

She turned over the little origami tiger in her fingers. It didn't exactly look like a tiger, but there was no doubt as to the level of craftsmanship which had gone into its construction. She contemplated leaving it there on the table. But then in a moment of superstitious panic she carefully pressed it flat and slipped it into her back trouser pocket. Mel had met the Hairdresser and survived. Maybe some of that survival instinct would rub off on Bailey. Perhaps the little tiger would offer her some kind of talismanic protection, if nothing else. At this point in her investigation she needed whatever luck she could get.

94

If only Doctor Bodie would get rid of that stupid 'World's Okayest Dad' mug he insisted on using, Bailey thought, as she sat there in his office. In her eyes, it came across as a feeble and slightly condescending ploy to try and appear more approachable to the inmates. And it didn't seem to be working, because from what she'd overheard, most of them thought he was a patronising middle-class wanker. Still, she couldn't fault him for trying.

He scrutinised her earnestly through his wire-rimmed glasses.

'If you remember, Bailey, you promised that the next time you came to visit me you would talk openly about yourself.'

'Yes, Doctor. I remember. And I don't break my promises. That's why I'm here today. I think I am finally ready to tell you everything.'

He grinned and rubbed his hands in anticipation.

She felt slightly guilty as she did have an ulterior motive for coming here today. But she knew she couldn't string him along for too much longer.

She put on a pained expression. 'Just one thing first though.'

'Is there something the matter?' he asked, concerned.

'I really need the toilet,' she said.

He frowned. 'You should have gone before you came here.'

'I know. I'm sorry. It's all that coffee I drank for breakfast. I should cut down on it really. Can I use the toilet here?'

'Technically I should call a prison officer to accompany you.'

She sighed. 'To use the toilet? It's just a few doors down the corridor, isn't it? It's hardly like I'm going to be able to escape.'

It was true. The administration block was situated well within the prison security perimeter.

He sighed. 'Okay, better make it quick though.'

'Thanks!'

She got up and left his office, closing the door behind her. But instead of turning left and going to the toilet, she turned to her right and went directly to the room next door, which was marked 'Filing Office' on the frosted glass.

On previous visits, she had noticed that there was a staff toilet situated at the end of the corridor, but that had just provided a convenient excuse for her to get out of Doctor Bodie's office for the few minutes that she needed in order to do what she wanted to do.

The real reason for her visit today was to access the inmates' files. As Doctor Bodie had mentioned in passing during her very first appointment with him, they were stored in the office right next door to his.

To get inside the administration block, a magnetic key swipe was required and that meant that inmates couldn't just walk in. The only way for her to get in, to get to the filing office, had been to make an appointment with Doctor Bodie.

She looked both ways, up and down the corridor. There was no one around. But she had to act fast. She tried the door handle of the filing office. It was unlocked, as she expected it would be during office hours while people needed access to the files.

She took a deep breath and hoped that no one else was already in there.

She pushed the door open. The filing office was unoccupied.

It was a barren room with drab grey walls lined with row upon row of large green filing cabinets containing the prison records of all the inmates incarcerated at HMP Foxbrook. By the considerable size and number of cabinets, it looked like the records probably went back a while. Or at least that was what she was hoping.

She gently closed the door behind her.

She looked at her watch. She had no more than two or three minutes at most to try and find what she was looking for.

She prayed that no one would come in and catch her. It would result in serious disciplining, a long stretch in segregation for sure. And that would mess up things in a big way, especially in regard to the forthcoming murder.

She went to the first cabinet and gently eased the top drawer open. The files were arranged in alphabetical order. She was at the 'A's.

She closed the drawer and moved to the top drawer of the third cabinet along. The 'H's. She moved to two drawers below it. The 'M's. She moved up a drawer. The 'L's. Bingo! Kneeling down by the drawer she began to leaf through the files, going slower now.

She heard the sound of voices outside, two people getting closer, talking to each other. Male voices. It sounded like two prison officers. She froze, her mouth dry, her heart beating hard. There was no time to move, or to hide, not that there was anywhere to hide in here anyhow. All she could do was wait and hope. She watched as their outlines passed by on the other side of the frosted glass. The conversation faded into the distance as they continued up the corridor. She breathed a sigh of relief. But she knew she needed to act fast.

She turned her attention back to the files. She didn't have much time. Maybe a minute or so left.

She leafed through them, one by one, going through the surnames.

Lane...

Lansbury...

Laughton...

Ledoux...

Lee

There were quite a few Lees.

Abigail...

Anna...

Barbara...

Denise...

Felicia.

There it was.

She slid the manila folder out of the drawer, her hands shaking with excitement.

She opened it quickly to check.

Her attention was immediately drawn to the photo that was stapled to the top inside corner of the file. It depicted a pale-skinned girl with dark eyes and a tangle of punky-looking black hair staring vacantly back at the camera.

So that's what the infamous Felicia Lee looked like.

For a moment, they stared into each other's eyes. Bailey felt an odd inexplicable shudder go through her. There was something about this girl. Bailey knew instinctively that she had hit the nail on the head.

She was sorely tempted to read through the file right now, but she didn't have time. Instead she closed it and tucked it beneath her jogging top which she then zipped up tight.

She gently pushed the drawer closed and stood up. She figured it would be a long time, if ever, before anyone noticed that the file had gone missing. After all, why would anyone want to look at it? Felicia Lee was no longer here. It was a dormant file.

Bailey stepped up to the door and once again hoped that she didn't bump into anyone in the corridor. She opened the door a crack and peeked out.

There was no one there.

She slipped out of the filing office and walked back into Doctor Bodie's office. Sitting down, she was conscious of the large stiff cardboard file concealed beneath her clothing. Hopefully it wasn't too obvious.

'Feeling better?' said Doctor Bodie, looking pointedly at his watch.

She nodded.

'So where were we?' she said.

'You were about to tell me all about your traumatic experiences.'

'Where shall I start?'

'Let's try the beginning.'

'The beginning? Sure.' She took a deep breath. 'It all started with this guinea pig I owned when I was a little girl. His name was Squeaky. I used to adore that little guinea pig. But then one day my father came home drunk...'

95

Bailey waited until later that evening, until after she had been locked in her cell for the night, before taking out the file from underneath her mattress, where she had concealed it immediately after getting back from Doctor Bodie's office.

Now, at last, she had the time and the privacy to peruse it at her leisure and she was both nervous and excited about what she might discover. Sitting on the edge of the lower bunk, she laid the file across her knees and opened it up.

Once again she was drawn to the small photograph at the top. She examined it in more detail. By the looks of it, Felicia Lee couldn't have been older than her mid-twenties when the picture had been taken. It had likely been done on her induction to the prison.

She wasn't unattractive, but it was quite clear that, at least in this photograph, her appearance was the least of her concerns. Her punky hair stuck up in messy black tufts and her pale skin contrasted sharply against the dark rings around her eyes. She seemed to be looking back at the camera from some distant, cold place where the sun never shone. There was something unmistakably damaged about her, but Bailey couldn't quite put her finger on what it was. Maybe it was the absence of something rather than the presence of something that unnerved her as she studied the photograph.

Shaking off the feeling of unease, Bailey leafed through the file. As well as information relating to her incarceration, the file contained details of Felicia Lee's criminal record, a variety of psychiatric assessments and a number of reports made by social workers. This was exactly the kind of information that Bailey was looking for.

Outside, the sun had gone down and the sky had turned dark blue with the first twinkles of stars beginning to appear.

Sitting there on the bunk, Bailey started to read through the file...

96

'She's off the radar completely,' said Frank. 'Seeing as she's still on the run, my guess is that she's been lying low somewhere for the past few years. She might have changed her identity. She could even be abroad for all we know. Either way, the trail's dead.'

Bailey stood in the phone booth listening to him break the bad news. It didn't come as a complete surprise to her.

'My luck was slightly better,' she said. 'I managed to gain access to her prison record. I was up all last night reading it.'

'Prison records? I thought that kind of thing was confidential.'

'"You need to be able to use your initiative". Isn't that what you told me that very first time I started working for you?'

He chuckled. 'So I did. What did you find out then?'

'She grew up in an abusive environment. She was eventually removed from her birth parents and placed into care, and that was basically where she spent the rest of her childhood, in various foster homes and the like.'

'Sounds like the typical background of your average prison inmate.'

'Yeah, but there's something else. The social worker reports mention something called "The Family", spelt with a capital "F". It relates to the abusive environment that she was in prior to being placed into care, but they don't elaborate on what it actually meant. Does it mean anything to you?'

'The Family? Hmm.... doesn't ring any bells.'

'Okay. Anyhow, as an adult she got pregnant and gave birth to a child, which she then subsequently murdered by smashing its head against a wall. And that's what brought her in here.'

'Why did she do it?'

'In her defence she claimed it was down to post-natal depression. That didn't manage to get her off but it played a mitigating factor in her sentencing.'

'What about the father?'

'No mention of him in the file. I'm guessing she probably accidentally got pregnant by some random bloke and couldn't handle the responsibility of raising a child by herself.'

'Well, that's all fascinating, Bailey. And depressing. But it still doesn't explain how she's tied into the murders, does it?'

'I know she's connected somehow. I can feel it. Just looking at her picture, I know it.'

'The trail is dead, as I told you. There's nothing more I can do to help you. And what's more, the drugs squad have lost patience with your "new angle". I think they're starting to suspect that I'm bullshitting them, but they don't know why. Either way, I can't stall them any longer, Bailey, we're going to have to pull you out.'

'The next murder is in two days,' she pleaded.

'And you're no closer to finding out who's going to do it.'

She sighed in frustration. He was right. But she wasn't going to give up. Not now. Not yet.

'That "Family" thing is niggling at me,' she said. 'Can you look into it? Just do this one last thing for me. Please?'

The other end of the phone was silent.

'Frank?' she said.

'It's the last roll of the dice, Bailey. But I'll see what I can do.'

And he hung up.

97

The tattoo gun ceased its buzzing. The sudden silence broke Bailey's trance of concentration.

'Have you been listening to anything I've been saying?' said Poppy from behind her.

Poppy had been speaking for the past few minutes, but Bailey hadn't been paying attention to any of it, so preoccupied was she by thoughts of how she could progress her investigation.

'Sorry? What were you saying? I was totally zoned out.'

'I was saying that I'm really excited about opening our tattoo shop. About going into business together. About our future.'

'I'm excited as well,' said Bailey. 'It'll be great. I know that whatever you do, it'll work out just fine.'

'All I ever needed was someone to believe in me. Someone like you.'

Poppy switched the tattoo gun back on again and resumed her work on Bailey's lower back.

A short while later, she switched off the gun and placed it on the chair by the bed. She dabbed at her handiwork with a tissue.

'There. It's almost done. One more session and it'll be finished.'

She climbed off Bailey and stood up.

Bailey got off the bunk and pulled her vest on. She turned to face Poppy. Poppy's face went serious as she realised Bailey had something important to say.

'What is it?' asked Poppy.

'I want you to be careful,' said Bailey.

Poppy looked confused. 'Why? What's wrong?'

'This Tuesday...' started Bailey, but she didn't know how she could explain it to Poppy without telling her everything.

'What about this Tuesday?'

She started again. 'These murders that have been happening... I want you to be careful.'

Poppy's face broke into a smile. 'You don't need to worry about me.' She patted the back of her waistband, presumably where she was carrying her shank. 'I can handle myself just fine.'

'I'm sure you can. But... just watch out, okay?'

Poppy placed both hands on Bailey's shoulders and looked deep into her eyes. 'It means a lot to me that you care though. You're a true friend.'

Right at that moment, Bailey was hit by a powerful urge to tell Poppy the truth about everything, about who she really was and the reason she was really in here. It would take just a few words to forever remove that invisible one-way barrier that lay between them. Almost involuntarily, she felt the revelation move up to her mouth.

She took a deep breath and braced herself to speak. She would confess everything. Right now. And damn the consequences. She suddenly couldn't bear to deceive Poppy any longer. For people she didn't care about, she embraced the duplicity as part and parcel of the job, but when it came to someone she actually had feelings for, someone who trusted her, it pressed down on her like a heavy weight. These situations did arise every so often when working undercover, and when they did, Bailey always found them challenging to deal with.

She looked into Poppy's eyes. She moistened her lips. She opened her mouth to speak...

Poppy slid her hands along Bailey's shoulders and placed them gently around the back of her neck, cradling her head. She gently pulled Bailey's head towards her and Bailey knew she was going to kiss her. She knew she didn't want it to happen but she knew if she didn't let it happen, then she'd spill everything to her.

Never break cover.

Never. Break. Cover.

So she let it happen.

Poppy's lips locked onto hers, preventing Bailey from speaking, thus saving her from herself. Poppy pulled her close into a tight embrace and for a while they stood there entangled in intimacy.

Eventually the urge to reveal herself receded to a safe distance. Bailey broke off and drew away.

'I'm sorry,' said Poppy, looking a little guilty. 'I couldn't help myself.'

'That's okay. I'm glad you did.'

'Business partners,' said Poppy.

'That's right. Business partners.'

And it all was just business at the end of the day, thought Bailey as she left Poppy's cell. That's what she had to remember when it came to this game. That's what she couldn't afford to forget. All of it was just business. And nothing more.

98

Monday morning came. And still Bailey had nothing that she could act on. Felicia Lee's file had made fascinating reading, and Bailey had learnt a good deal about her messed-up background, but she couldn't work out for the life of her how it related to the murders in the prison. If it did at all. And that was the problem. If she was correct in her assumptions, then someone in here would die tomorrow and she was powerless to prevent it from happening. And then she would be pulled out of here and she would never find out who had killed Alice.

As soon as they unlocked her cell, she made her way to the phones. She didn't have particularly high hopes that Frank would have managed to find out much in the short space of time since their last call. But what else was she going to do?

The queue for the phones seemed particularly long today. She waited impatiently in line, cursing every minute lost as a minute wasted. After what seemed an aeon, she reached the front of the queue and when a phone finally became free she marched over to it and furiously punched in the numbers.

'Hello, Sullivan Knight Solicitors,' said Rita. 'How can I help?'

'It's Bailey Pike speaking. I'd like to talk to Mr Knight please.'

'Just putting you through.'

Beethoven's 'Moonlight Sonata' was on for less than a second before Frank came on the line.

'What took you so long to call me?' he said.

There was an urgent tone in his voice. Did he have bad news or did he have good news? She couldn't tell.

'You found out something?' She was almost too scared to ask.

'You bet I found out something.'

'Well...?'

'I looked into The Family.'

'And...?'

'Turns out that it was a religious commune. It was kind of notorious at the time. They held rather extreme views.'

'Like a cult?'

'Yeah kind of, I guess. Mind control. Physical deprivation. And so on and so forth. They kept all the children locked up in cages. Anyhow, when they shut it down all of the kids were rescued and put in care.' He paused. 'Both Felicia Lee and her brother.'

'She had a brother?'

'The same age. They were twins.'

'It didn't say anything about a brother in her file!'

'His name was Leonard.'

'Leonard Lee?'

'That's right.'

'We have to find him.'

'I'm one step ahead of you, Bailey.'

'Of course you are.'

'Same deal as her. Off the radar. No trace of him.'

There was a pregnant pause on the line.

'Why do I get this funny feeling you're about to pull something big out of the hat?' she said.

'Leonard's trail went dead at his last known address. Hilden Close, Wolverhampton.'

He let the news sink in.

'Oh shit,' she whispered. 'The Hairdresser is Leonard.'

'I cross-checked with West Midlands Police homicide files. The Hairdresser murders ceased at around the same time that Leonard stopped living at the Wolverhampton address.'

'So that's who Mel met,' murmured Bailey. 'She must have met Leonard. And it's him who's killing the inmates.'

'If Leonard is the Hairdresser, and he's not one of the prison officers, then how's he getting into the prison?'

'He's getting in the same way that his sister got out.'

'But no one knows how that is.'

'That's what I have to find out. By the end of today.'

99

Bailey stood in the yard and gazed at the huge perimeter wall and the gate-house that was situated partway along its eastern length. The gatehouse was the only official way into the prison and, with its X-ray machines and electronic double-door entry system, security there was pretty tight. And elsewhere in the prison the sturdy Victorian fortifications weren't exactly designed to make it easy to get in and out of this place. But somehow Leonard was managing it, like his sister had done.

But just how had Felicia Lee escaped? Had she dug some kind of tunnel that lay undiscovered somewhere in the prison? It seemed unlikely that she had assiduously burrowed her way out of here. Bailey was certain that the breach took some other form. But without knowing what this was or where it was, there was nothing that she or Frank, or anyone else, could do.

She looked at her watch. Time was ticking down. She had around an hour or so of free association time left before she was locked in her cell for the rest of the day, and once that happened she might as well give up for good.

A hand grabbed her upper arm, breaking her reverie. She spun around. It was Toni, accompanied by Keisha. They both closed in on her.

'We've been looking for you,' said Toni.

'Oh?' She tensed and assumed a defensive stance.

Since her close call with them a few days earlier, Bailey had been actively trying to avoid Toni and the others. And in the meantime, she'd been so consumed with trying to work out the Felicia Lee connection that she'd forgotten to consider that they were probably wondering where she'd got to.

Toni leaned in menacingly. 'I hope our little misunderstanding the other day didn't make you forget that you still work for us, remember? And there's business to be conducted.'

Shit.

This was not what she needed right now. She just didn't have the time for it.

With a mirthless smile, Keisha pushed a plastic bag full of drugs into the pocket of Bailey's jogging top.

'I want you up on the fourth-floor landing of A-Wing,' said Toni. 'Pronto.'

'Sure. No problem,' she said, silently berating herself for getting caught up in the gang's activities. She knew there was no excuse that she could make so she headed indoors. Glancing over her shoulder, she saw Toni give her the 'I'm watching you' gesture.

Up on the fourth-floor landing, Bailey leant on the balcony, her head hung in despair as the sounds of the prison echoed around her. She reflected that her chances of finding out anything by the end of today had now grown slim to the point of being almost non-existent.

'Got any speed?'

Bailey looked up. A lank-haired inmate with sallow skin and twitchy-looking eyes was standing beside her, fidgeting nervously and looking around in a shifty manner.

'Sure,' said Bailey.

She eased a small bag of amphetamine powder from her pocket.

The inmate opened her palm to reveal a handful of screwed-up banknotes.

Bailey gave a cursory glance around her before conducting the transaction—

—And froze as she spotted the uniform of a prison officer walking in her direction along one side of the fourth-floor landing.

She gestured for the inmate to hold off for the moment. They both smiled falsely at each other in a pretence of conversation.

As the prison officer got closer, Bailey saw that it was Terry. She relaxed slightly. If there was one prison officer who wouldn't be disrupting her business, it was him.

As he passed by, he shot her a sly knowing look. He knew exactly what she was up to and it served to line his pockets handsomely. He strolled slowly past.

She waited until his back was turned and he was walking away from her down the other side of the landing before completing the transaction with the lank-haired inmate. The inmate wandered off, leaving Bailey once again by herself, leaning on the balcony.

She glumly fingered the bag of drugs in her pocket. Despite her efforts, despite Alice's efforts, the drugs were flowing back into the prison in much the same quantities as before, all thanks to Terry. Somehow he was getting them in. Somehow...

A thought started to take form in her mind...

She looked up sharply at Terry's receding back as he walked off down the landing.

Terry had found a way to evade gatehouse security and the random checks which that entailed. How else did it explain the fact that he'd never got caught? How else did it explain the fact that he felt confident enough to continue smuggling drugs in despite being under suspicion so recently?

He must be exploiting some kind of hidden gap in the prison's security. Could this be one and the same gap that Felicia Lee had used in order to escape?

Terry had the answer to what Bailey was looking for, but she could hardly go up and ask him.

She stood there on the landing, furiously analysing the situation, examining it from every angle, going back, right back, to the beginning...

Terry... the drugs... the killer... they all intersected with one person.

Alice.

Alice had been investigating the drugs ring and Alice had been murdered by the killer.

She thought back to Alice's original text message: Source well concealed in prison. Investigating today. Will update later.

Could it be possible that Alice had been referring to the breach rather than to a person?

The breach quite obviously had to be well concealed because if everyone knew about it then everyone would try and escape through it.

But as part of her investigation into the drugs ring, Alice had somehow worked out where it was, identifying it as the source point of the drugs flowing into the prison. She had gone to investigate the breach and she had encountered the killer getting into the prison. And that's how she'd ended up dead.

The breach was located in the laundry.

100

Bailey looked at her watch. Sixteen minutes of association time left. She still had time.

She scanned the landing for signs of Toni and the others. She couldn't see them anywhere. Now was her chance; she couldn't leave it any longer.

She headed for the stairwell, gripping both banisters, launching herself downwards, two or three steps at a time, her trainers clumping hard on the metal beneath her feet.

'No running on the landings!' she heard one of the prison officers shout from somewhere up above her. Bailey slowed temporarily until she was out of his line of sight, then resumed her frantic pace.

When she reached the bottom of the stairs, she bolted across the atrium – getting a few surprised looks as she did so – and made her way once again down into the basement.

She sprinted along the dingy corridors, panting hard with the exertion.

And then she was at the laundry.

She halted outside the door, trying to catch her breath while she peered in through the small glass window.

It was full of inmates working, pushing laundry trolleys, loading and unloading the washing machines and dryers, folding linen. She noticed a prison officer standing on one side of the room conversing with one of the inmates.

Bailey cursed to herself. She couldn't just go in and start poking around. But she needed to know the specifics of the breach. To know that it was in the laundry wasn't good enough. She needed to know exactly what form it took if Frank was to have a solid basis on which to launch a police operation and liaise with the prison authorities to lock down the prison.

She looked at her watch. Twelve minutes left.

She stood outside the door of the laundry, gnawing her lip and tapping her foot, trying to work out what to do, trying to work out what form the breach could possibly take. It was something in the fabric of the prison. Something which had been overlooked.

She stared at the big heavy door in front of her. The metal plaque riveted just beneath the window panel looked like it had been there since the prison was built.

'WATER SUPPLY ROOM'.

These days, the water was piped in from the reservoir. That's what Maggie had told her.

But back in the old days...

...The prison used to draw its water directly from a subterranean tributary of the River Foxbrook.

But the river had dried up when the reservoir was built.

Drawn directly...

...from a subterranean tributary...

...which was all dried up...

...which must lead out to a dry river bed somewhere to the north of the prison.

Source well concealed in prison.

And then it hit her.

The source was a well which was concealed in the prison.

A well.

The breach was a well. The well had drawn water from the subterranean river, but it had fallen into disuse when that had dried up. And the well was in the laundry – the 'Water Supply Room'.

Alice had been telling them exactly that in not-so-plain English. The answer had been there right in front of them all along.

She had gone to the laundry that day to try and locate the well and confirm its existence. But it hadn't been Terry who'd climbed out of it carrying drugs. It had been the killer.

It all fell into place now in a white-hot rush of revelation.

Bailey prayed it was enough to go on. It had better be. She had no choice now. She had no time left. She ran back along the corridor and up the stairs, heading for the phones. She still had time to call Frank.

When she saw the massive queue at the phones, she swore aloud. She looked at her watch. There were nine minutes of association time left before they were all locked back in their cells. She knew she would never get to the front of the queue in nine minutes' time.

She suddenly remembered. Toni kept a mobile phone in her stash down in the basement.

Bailey hurried back down to the basement, this time making her way to the small maintenance cupboard beneath B-Wing where the stash was located.

She pulled the door shut behind her, turned the light on and knelt down among the cleaning products. She pushed the industrial rolls of cleaning tissue aside to expose the small ventilation grille set into the bottom of the wall. Levering it off with her fingernails, she placed it on the floor.

She put her hand in carefully. Very carefully, remembering the rat trap...

But there was nothing in there.

She reached in further, putting almost her whole arm in. Nothing.

Shit!

Toni must have moved the location of the stash.

Bailey pulled her arm out and looked at her watch. Six minutes left.

She had no choice but to resort to the nuclear option.

101

'Come in,' said the Governor.

Shelley pushed the door open and nodded at Bailey to go in.

It was the first time Bailey had been in the Governor's office and the decor immediately put her in mind of one of those old-fashioned private members' clubs. The walls were lined with dark oak panelling and there was one of those fancy-looking leather sofas with buttons on it.

The Governor was sitting behind a huge wooden desk, lounging back in a large throne-like leather desk chair, his hands steepled in front of him.

'Shelley here tells me you wanted to see me urgently,' he said.

'That's right,' said Bailey. 'It's very important.'

He looked up at the antique-style carriage clock on the mantelpiece. 'Couldn't it have waited until tomorrow? I know I said I had an open-door policy, but you've only got two minutes of association time left.'

'I'll keep it brief.'

He sighed and gestured for her to sit down.

Bailey sat down facing him across the desk. She looked up at Shelley and then at the Governor.

'It's private,' she said.

He waved at Shelley to leave.

Shelley left the office and closed the door behind her. Bailey and the Governor stared at each other in silence for a few moments.

'Well?' said the Governor.

She took a deep breath.

'My name isn't actually Bailey Pike. My real name is Bailey Morgan and I'm an undercover police officer.'

The Governor's brows slowly knitted in perplexity. 'An undercover police officer?'

'I was placed here in order to investigate the activities of a drugs ring which has been operating inside this prison. What I've uncovered is almost as shocking as it is unbelievable. But you must believe what I'm about to tell you because if we don't act on it immediately, then lives will be lost. I would have gone through official channels, but there just isn't time. That's why I've come to talk directly to you.'

There. She'd said it. She'd finally done it. She'd broken cover.

It had been a momentous decision to make. And it went against everything she'd been taught. But she'd really had no choice in the matter. She now felt a vertiginous sense of apprehension at what the next few moments would bring.

The Governor sat there, staring at her over his steepled fingers. It was hard to tell what he was thinking. Then he raised his eyebrows in realisation.

'I thought I recognised you. You're the one who jumped off the balcony.' He nodded slowly. 'I believe there were certain issues surrounding your... uh... mental stability.'

'I assure you I am completely mentally stable. I jumped off the balcony for a very good reason. I did that in order to infiltrate—'

'I think you'd be better off talking to Doctor Bodie than to me,' he said. 'Why don't we—'

'Listen to me!' she hissed.

He recoiled, taken aback. He suddenly looked a little bit scared.

'There isn't much time,' she whispered. 'There is a drugs ring operating inside this prison. They are using a breach in security to smuggle drugs in.'

'That's a ridiculous assertion! We follow security procedures extremely rigorously in this prison.'

'There's an old disused well in the prison laundry. One of your prison officers – Terry – is using this well as a conduit through which to transport drugs into the prison.'

'If you're a police officer then why wasn't I told about you?'

'We had no idea how deep the rot went. We couldn't risk letting on about this operation to anyone who worked here.'

The Governor bristled a little and frowned.

'These are very serious allegations.' He looked up at the clock. 'And they're not something that we can adequately address in the next sixty seconds or so. Come back and see me tomorrow and—'

'No! We have to act now.'

'I'm starting to lose patience with you, Bailey. Now as I said—'

'Inmates are being murdered in this prison, in case you hadn't noticed! They're being scalped and murdered. One of them was an undercover policewoman and she was also my friend.'

The Governor went silent.

Bailey continued, 'The murders are being committed by a killer known as the Hairdresser. You may have heard of him. He gained notoriety for murdering prostitutes in the Midlands some years ago. He started off by taking the hair of his victims. Now he's taking their scalps.'

'The "Hairdresser"?' said the Governor, rolling the name off his tongue sceptically.

'His real name is Leonard Lee. He's getting inside the prison via the same breach of security which is being used to bring the drugs in.'

'This disused well?'

'That's right.'

He looked at the clock, then smiled pleasantly at her. 'You're out of time.'

'We're all out of time. Leonard Lee kills on a sixteen-day cycle and the next murder is due to take place tomorrow. We have to call the police, lock down the prison and locate the well, so we can catch him. If we don't take action now then someone will die.'

'Out of the question. It's time for you to go back to your cell, Bailey.'

Desperation overwhelmed her. This wasn't working.

'If you don't believe me, then at least call my boss. His name is Detective Superintendent Frank Grinham. He'll confirm who I am.'

She leaned forward and grabbed a fountain pen from the brass stationery holder on his desk. She looked around for a bit of paper. All she could see on his desk was a glossy magazine entitled *Yachting World*. She flipped it over and tore off a small corner of the back cover.

'Now just a minute...' said the Governor, starting forward in his chair.

'This is his direct line,' she said, scribbling down Frank's number on the piece of paper. She thrust it across the desk towards him. 'You can call him right now.'

'We'll do nothing of the sort.'

'I can call him myself.' She stood up and reached for the telephone on his desk.

He snatched the receiver from her grasp and slammed it back down. 'That's quite enough!' he barked. 'Shelley!'

The door opened and Shelley came in.

'It's time to take Bailey back to her cell,' said the Governor.

'No! You must believe me! You have to believe me!'

Shelley gripped her by the arm. Bailey tried to pull away.

'If you don't behave yourself, then Shelley will place you in segregation,' said the Governor. 'Now, it seems quite clear to me that you still have some mental issues to resolve and to that end I'll be recommending that you attend a further course of treatment with Doctor Bodie until you get better.'

Bailey sagged in Shelley's grip.

She'd failed.

She let Shelley march her out of the Governor's office and prayed to herself that the Hairdresser wouldn't strike until after she'd had the chance to call Frank first thing tomorrow morning.

102

The Governor stared at the piece of paper with the telephone number on it. He picked it up off his desk and noticed that his hand was shaking. Screwing it up into a tiny ball, he dropped it into his wastepaper basket.

He stood up and walked over to the antique wooden cabinet by the window, opened it up and took out a bottle of sixteen-year-old Lagavulin and a tumbler. He poured himself a generous shot and knocked it back. The whisky burned a trail down his throat and instantly made him feel better.

He held out his hand. The shaking seemed to have subsided.

How the fuck had this inmate found out about the well? Weren't they all supposed to be stupid? Isn't that why they were in here?

But then this one had claimed that she was an undercover police officer. And if that was true, then he had even more cause to be worried.

Of course he knew about the well. He'd known about it for years. He'd learnt of its existence not long after he'd started working at the prison. The well had lain unused in the basement ever since the prison changed its means of water supply in the 1930s. Close inspection of the original blueprints of the prison revealed how it connected to the outside world and he had realised that it constituted a small but potentially serious chink in the prison's security. He had thus made plans to get it sealed up completely.

But then one day, in the gatehouse, one of the prison officers had been caught in a random bag check trying to smuggle drugs into the prison. To his surprise, it had been Terry, the union rep. The Governor had always detested Terry for the way he constantly criticised and undermined the Governor's policies and he had relished the opportunity to finally destroy this thorn in his side.

But a cunning notion had then occurred to the Governor. This situation presented a means by which he himself could fulfil plans of his own, plans which would otherwise only ever have remained dreams. So rather than turn Terry over to the police, the Governor had suggested a secret partnership. He had proposed it right here in this office. He would make the criminal allegations go away and he would permit Terry to continue smuggling drugs into the prison under the condition that half of all proceeds would go back to him. Terry had little choice but to agree to his offer. However, to ensure that he didn't get caught again, the Governor had explained to him how he could use the well.

Of course, so as nothing should seem amiss, they both kept up their antagonistic act of prison governor versus union rep. That way no one would ever suspect that they were in cahoots.

The money had been rolling in for a while now, slowly filling up an offshore bank account. Soon he would have enough to retire and buy his yacht. Soon his dreams would come true. It had all been working so well.

Up to now.

Now everything had been thrown into jeopardy. His yacht. His knighthood. God forbid, even he himself could end up on the other side of the bars and that was not something he was even willing to consider. Can you imagine it? A prison governor, behind bars?

And what about his family? His wife? His daughters? Their private schooling. The skiing holidays in Verbier. Their five-bedroom house. The neighbours. What the hell would the neighbours think? And the Home Secretary? My god, the Governor would never live it down! The Home Secretary would never talk to him again.

He shuddered at the thought of it all. He poured himself another large shot of whisky and downed it in one.

If it wasn't already calamitous enough that this inmate knew all about the drug smuggling, she'd also managed to somehow tie it into these recent murders. Whether or not she was right about that, he didn't know and he didn't care. All he did know was that if any of this got out, he was well and truly fucked.

Something had to be done about it.

His hand was shaking again. He clenched it into a fist.

He knew what to do. He knew exactly what needed to be done.

103

The bite of cold steel against her throat jerked her out of slumber. Bailey opened her eyes to see the dim outline of a figure standing over her in the darkness.

'I could have shanked you while you slept,' hissed Poppy.

She sniffed back a sob and pressed the sharp edge of the knife harder into Bailey's flesh.

Bailey swallowed with difficulty and kept very, very still.

'Now let's not do anything silly,' she whispered.

'You betrayed me. You lied to me. You're nothing but a worthless fucking cop!'

'I don't know what you're talking about.'

'Don't lie to me!' Poppy pushed the blade in harder, the sharp, filed edge starting to cut into Bailey's neck. 'I said if you were lying to me, I would kill you. And I meant it.'

A tear fell from Poppy's cheek onto Bailey's bare shoulder.

Bailey tried to work out how Poppy had got into her locked cell in the middle of the night. She tried to work out how Poppy knew she was a cop. And that was when she realised just how high the corruption went.

'The Governor,' she gasped.

Poppy sniffed angrily. 'What are you talking about?'

Bailey realised now that she had a choice to make. She could either continue to deny that she was a police officer, or she could break cover for the second time in as many days and try to explain everything. Either choice could prove to be fatal. She swallowed, feeling the bite of the blade at her throat, and took the plunge.

'I'm here for a reason,' she said in a slow and measured tone. 'A very good reason.'

'So you are a cop!' Poppy's voice went up an octave.

'I was sent in to investigate the drugs, but now I'm here to stop the murders.'

'I vouched for you. I saved your life.' Another hot tear fell onto Bailey's shoulder. 'I can't believe I trusted you and you turn out to be a pig after all.'

'The Governor,' whispered Bailey. 'He's the only person who knew I was a police officer. And that's only because I told him yesterday. He's in on the drugs racket. He must have told Terry, because it was Terry who let you in here, right? He's waiting outside right now, isn't he?'

Poppy said nothing, breathing hard, biting the tears back.

'The Governor needs to silence me,' said Bailey. 'And he's using you to do his dirty work.'

'Everything you told me... your crime... being an accountant... that was all just lies. You used me to get information. I feel so stupid.'

'I didn't lie to you about everything.'

'The plans we made. They meant nothing to you.'

'I was an accountant, before I joined the police. And when I said I'd help you, I meant it.'

'I hate you. I should kill you now.'

'So why don't you?'

Bailey could feel the vibrations of Poppy's hand shaking with emotion as she held the shank to her neck.

'You can't do it, can you?' whispered Bailey. 'I know you, Poppy. You're not some cold ruthless killer. It's not what you are. You're different from them. Just like you told me.'

Poppy sniffed back a sob.

'Help me,' said Bailey. 'I need your help. Right now you're the only person who can help me. I know who the killer is and I can stop him. I tried to tell the Governor but it was no good. But now I've got a chance, if you help me. If I don't stop him, then more of us will die.'

'Us? You're not one of us. And why do you care about us anyway?'

'Because it's my job. And he killed my friend and I want to catch him.'

'Your friend?'

'Her name was Alice. Alice Simms. That was her real name. She was the first one who was killed. In the laundry. Back in May. She was a policewoman too.'

Poppy was silent for a few moments. Another tear fell onto Bailey's shoulder.

'They'll kill me if I don't kill you,' she whispered.

'Come with me,' said Bailey. 'I'll take you out of here. Away from them. I can protect you. And I'll help you, like I said I would. I'll help you with your shop. I promise.'

'Promises!' spat Poppy. 'A cop's promises don't mean anything!'

Bailey reached up ever so gently, ever so slowly, and ran her fingers lightly along the smooth surface of Poppy's arm. She could feel the muscles quivering with tension as Poppy held the knife against her throat.

'There's a special connection between us, Poppy,' she said, softly stroking Poppy's arm. 'I knew it from the first time I met you. I knew it when I kissed you. And I know it now. And you know it too.'

Poppy's large eyes stared down at her, the green irises black in the dimness of the unlit cell. Bailey felt the pressure of the knife against her neck begin to falter.

'There's a way out of here,' said Bailey.

'There's no way out of here,' replied Poppy in a small voice. 'Not for me. Not for you.'

'There's a disused well in the basement. That's how the killer's getting into the prison. It's how Terry's bringing the drugs in. It's also how we can get out of here. Right now. Tonight. Come with me. My job here is done. I know all that I need to know. I'll explain everything to you once we're out of here.'

Poppy was silent. Breathing hard. The pressure of the shank gradually eased off. After a while she spoke.

'A disused well?'

'I need to get out through the well and make contact with my boss. All we need to do is get down to the laundry because that's where it is.'

'You'll help me with my shop?'

'I promise. I told you I would and I meant it.'

104

Terry waited, tapping his foot impatiently, looking apprehensively up and down the darkened landing. It was half past two in the morning. All was silent. Just the rows of locked cells stretching away into the shadows.

What the hell was taking her so long?

Surely it was a case of just sticking the knife between her ribs and that was that.

Fucking copper. Served her right. The sooner she was out of the picture, the better. The last thing he needed right now was some interfering policewoman jeopardising his illicit revenue stream. He had considerable gambling debts to pay off and the loan sharks were pretty unforgiving when it came to late payments. That's how he'd got mixed up in this whole affair in the first place – to subsidise his gambling habit: the horses, the dogs, a bit of poker, a bit of blackjack, in fact just about anything that you could place a bet on he did. He blamed his wife, to be honest. If she'd have just stopped bloody nagging him about his spending, he'd probably never have got involved in any of this.

Anyway, here he was and he had a job to get done. The policewoman had to die.

Of course, it went without saying that the main reason she had to die was because if he got caught he knew that a spell behind bars for an ex-screw would be an exceedingly unpleasant experience. He felt sick with fear at the very thought of it.

He shook off the nausea and peered around anxiously. He eyed the CCTV camera situated by the stairwell at the end of the landing. He wasn't too worried about that though. He knew that no-one was watching them. That was because he was the one who was supposed to be manning the control room tonight.

'Hey!'

He spun around. It was Poppy, peeking from the open door of the cell he had just let her into.

'Get a move on!' he hissed.

'Come here!' she whispered.

'What is it?'

'Just come here. Quickly!'

He swore under his breath and ran to the cell.

He stopped in the doorway. Poppy stood at the far end of the cell pointing at something on the floor in the corner.

'Look,' she said, beckoning to him.

He stepped inside the cell to take a closer look.

And then something hit him hard over the back of the head.

105

Amber didn't mind working the night shift. Some of the others found it a bit spooky patrolling the prison at night, especially down here in the basement. But she had never believed in ghosts or anything like that. And what didn't exist couldn't hurt you, right?

She padded down the dingy corridor, idly trailing her fingers along the wall, causing tiny flakes of dry paint to chip off and flutter to the floor. Looking down, she noticed that her shoelace was beginning to come undone. She stopped and knelt down to retie it.

And that was when she heard the noise.

She froze and tilted her head to listen.

It had sounded like a whisper.

But that was impossible seeing as no one but her was supposed to be down here at this hour.

She knelt there motionless for a few moments longer, straining to listen. But all was quiet.

It must have just been her imagination.

She finished tying her shoelace, stood up and continued walking, rounding the corner...

...where she bumped straight into two inmates.

She gasped and jumped back in surprise. They did exactly the same thing.

She recognised them immediately. Bailey and Poppy. Both members of that nasty gang. This didn't look good.

'What are you doing out of your cells?! How did you manage to get down here?!'

A guilty glance passed between them.

'This isn't what it looks like,' said Bailey, taking a step forward.

Amber assumed a defensive stance. She saw the bunch of keys in Bailey's hand. Those were prison officer's keys.

'Where did you get those keys?' she demanded.

Bailey looked down. 'Oh these? I can explain—'

Then Amber noticed that Poppy was clutching a shank in one hand.

This was not a good situation to be in. Alone in the basement, outnumbered two-to-one by armed inmates who were quite clearly in the process of trying to break out of the prison.

'Don't come one step closer!' she said in a low firm voice.

She reached for her walkie-talkie which was clipped to her belt. She brought it up and pressed the 'transmit' button.

'Please don't,' whispered Bailey desperately. 'They'll kill us.'

Amber frowned. There was something exceedingly odd about this situation.

She paused, her finger on the button, the noise of the static hissing in the otherwise silent corridor. The tone of Bailey's voice and the look of fear in Poppy's eyes told her that she needed to listen.

Slowly, she lifted her finger from the 'transmit' button.

Bailey visibly sagged in relief.

Amber clipped the walkie-talkie back onto her belt but didn't relax her defensive posture.

'Okay, you'd better tell me what's going on. Right now.'

106

Bailey exhaled slowly. Thank god it had been Amber who'd caught them as opposed to some other guard. Although she was uptight and she did things by the book, she possessed that thin margin of empathy that many of her colleagues lacked. In this situation, it could make the critical difference between life and death.

'I'm a serving police officer, acting in an undercover capacity.'

Amber's eyes widened. She raised her eyebrows. A faint smile crossed her face as if this was some bad joke. 'You expect me to believe that?'

'You have to, because it's true.'

'I'm not an idiot, Bailey.'

'I know you're not. You just need to know a little bit of background.'

And with that, Bailey launched into a full, unexpurgated account of her activities at the prison – Alice... the gang... Terry... Crazy Mel... the Hairdresser... Felicia Lee...

It was the first time Poppy had heard the complete story, and both she and Amber listened in wide-eyed silence as the words gushed out in a frenetic unbroken torrent.

Bailey finished and they both just stared at her, astounded.

Amber blinked and shook her head. 'That is one hell of a story, Bailey. A killer getting into the prison through a well which is used for drug smuggling.'

'It's the only explanation. So, as you can see, we've got no choice. If we go back upstairs, there's no telling what might happen. We know the Governor's set the gang on us. And it's only a matter of time before Terry manages to raise the alarm. I'm fairly certain we'll both be killed. We don't have much time.'

'Terry I can accept. I always thought there was something dodgy about him. But the Governor as well?' Amber screwed up her face and shook her head.

Bailey sighed in frustration. 'It's true. I swear.'

'I'm sorry, but this all just sounds a bit too far-fetched.'

'She's telling the truth,' said Poppy.

'A ringing endorsement,' remarked Amber, drily.

'Please give me a chance,' said Bailey. 'You're not like the others. You're better than them. That's why I trust you. Just give me this one chance.'

'As I recall, you were locked up for committing fraud, which means, basically, that you're very good at deceiving people. How do I know you're not deceiving me right now?'

'That was just my cover story!' blurted Bailey, feeling like she was floundering. She reflected how ironic it was that she'd conned them for so long, and yet now she was telling the truth they didn't believe her.

'It was pretty convincing,' murmured Poppy, shooting her a faint sideways smile.

'Look at it from my perspective,' said Amber slowly. 'If I go along with you, I could get into big trouble.'

'I understand that,' replied Bailey. 'But if we don't do something tonight, someone will die tomorrow. The killer is due to strike tomorrow. We have to get out of here through the well and inform the police so they can stop him.'

'Look, why don't the three of us go upstairs and sort it out up there? It'll be fine. Even if what you say is true, they won't dare to do anything to me.'

Bailey raised her eyebrows. 'Are you willing to take that chance? Haven't you been listening to anything I've been saying? The Governor knows I'm onto him. He can't afford to let me live. Neither can Terry. Neither can the gang. And if they know that you know as well, who knows what they'll do to you?'

Bailey held her breath as she waited on Amber's judgement. She could see the cogs turning as Amber anxiously clenched her jaw trying to weigh up the ramifications of believing Bailey versus not believing her. She felt terrible for putting her in such a quandary.

Out of the corner of her eye, she noticed Poppy give her an ever-so-subtle look as if to imply that maybe they should both jump on Amber and subdue her in much the same way they had done with Terry. Bailey gave an infinitesimal shake of the head. Not just yet...

Amber sighed in frustration.

'On the job advert they said this job would be challenging and they were certainly right about that.' She took a deep breath. 'Okay, you're sure this well is in the laundry?'

'Ninety-nine per cent,' said Bailey.

'And if you're wrong?'

Bailey gave a grimace that made it quite clear what the consequences of her mistake could be. She looked down at the keys in her hand, the ones she had taken from Terry. She held them out to Amber.

'Take them. This is how much I trust you, Amber. I'm putting our lives in your hands.'

Amber gave Bailey a nod of respect, took the keys and pocketed them. She turned to Poppy and held her hand out for the shank.

'I'll have to confiscate that, I'm afraid. If what Bailey's saying is true and we can find the well, then you won't be needing it anyhow.'

Poppy hesitated. She looked to Bailey for confirmation. Bailey nodded and Poppy reluctantly handed the shank to Amber, who put it in her pocket.

'Okay,' said Amber. 'Let's go to the laundry and get this mess cleaned up.'

107

All was dark on the other side of the small glass window. Bailey stood in the corridor and peered into the laundry alongside the other two. She was glad she'd managed to convince Amber, but the three of them still had a long way to go if they wanted to get themselves out of here alive.

Amber gave Bailey a sceptical glance. She looked at her watch.

She began to fiddle with the large bunch of keys that were attached to her belt by a chain. They clinked as she went through them one by one.

'I think this one should do it,' she said, holding up a long old-fashioned copper-coloured key.

She inserted it into the lock and turned it.

Click.

Clack.

She twisted the door handle, pushed open the door and stepped inside.

Reaching to her right, she flicked the light switch. The halogen strip lighting flickered on down the length of the room, filling it with a harsh artificial light.

Bailey and Poppy stepped inside. The door swung closed behind them.

Amber turned to face Bailey and folded her arms.

'The ball's in your court now.'

Bailey surveyed the laundry – the silent rows of washing machines and dryers... the canvas-sided trolleys piled with mesh bags full of dirty items... the bed sheets hanging up by the racking... the tangle of pipes and ducts running along the walls and ceiling... the clumps of lint which dotted the tiled floor...

She breathed slowly in and out, detecting the faint acrid smell of detergent.

Suddenly she didn't feel so sure any more.

'I don't see any well in here,' said Poppy in a quiet voice, as if reading Bailey's thoughts.

'It has to be in here,' she said, gritting her teeth.

She scanned the room again, from the doorway right down to the far end, scrutinising every detail, but nothing jumped out at her.

'What are we looking for exactly?' asked Amber.

'It's an old disused well. Like it says on the door, this place used to be the water supply room for the prison. The well supplied the water.'

'I've been in here on numerous occasions and I've never noticed anything which resembles a well,' said Amber.

'It's not going to be obvious,' replied Bailey. 'So we need to be methodical. Let's split up. We'll find it more quickly that way. I'll do this side and work my way down to the back of the room. Poppy, you can look over there to the right, by the racking. And, Amber, how about if you cover this part over here by the doorway? That way you can also keep an eye on anyone who might disturb us. You're our best protection against them now.'

They both nodded and the three of them went their separate ways.

Bailey paced slowly down the length of the laundry, the scattered granules of detergent powder crunching beneath the soles of her trainers. She looked from left to right and up and down, trying to detect any feature that might have once been a well or that might now conceal a well. But, just as before, there was nothing, just a lot of machinery and a great deal of dirty linen.

She reached the end of the room and halted next to the bank of top-loading washing machines that lined the back wall. She turned around and looked back the way she had come. Was there any clue in the layout of the laundry? She tilted her head one way and then the other, as if the difference in perspective might yield some insight. But it didn't.

She was starting to get worried. She had been staking everything on the well. Maybe she had been wrong. Maybe there was no well. In which case...

She didn't want to think about it.

There had to be a well. And it had to be in here somewhere.

She wondered how the others were doing.

'Any luck?' she called out.

There was no answer.

She walked forward a few steps in the direction of the door and then stopped. She peered around for the other two, but they were nowhere to be seen. And she couldn't hear them either. The laundry was completely silent.

'Found anything yet?' she said in a loud voice.

But still there was no answer.

Apprehension rippled through her.

'Poppy?' she said.

No answer.

Bailey walked forward slowly.

'Amber?' she called.

No answer.

The silence was now heavy and oppressive. She could hear her heart thumping in her chest.

Unsettled, she headed over to the racking. The hanging sheets billowed ever so slightly as she made her way between them, pushing them aside.

Something was wrong. Something was very wrong. She could feel it in her gut. As a policewoman she'd learned to trust her instincts and right now an alarm bell was going off in her head.

Ahead of her a sheet briefly billowed aside and she got a partial glimpse of a trainer-clad foot lying sideways on the floor.

A sinking feeling of dread came over her.

'Oh shit,' she whispered.

She hurried forward, pushing the sheets aside, her mouth dry, her heart hammering harder than ever.

And then she stopped. The white sheet hanging directly in front of her was stained bright red with what looked like an arterial spray pattern.

She swallowed hard and wrenched it aside.

Poppy was lying on the floor, her large green eyes wide open, staring sightlessly upwards. Her throat had been cut. The wound gaped like a second mouth, a pool of thick crimson blood ebbing slowly outwards across the tiles.

'Oh my god!' gasped Bailey, reeling backwards.

She felt dizzy. She thought she was going to faint. She took several deep breaths and tried to look away but she couldn't tear her gaze from the dead staring eyes. They seemed to be accusing her. Poppy had trusted her. And now Poppy was dead.

A surge of emotion forced an involuntary sob from her lips. Only now did she realise just how close she'd grown to Poppy over the course of the past few weeks. Those feelings wrenched at her like painful barbs. First Alice and now Poppy. Why did her friends have to die?

She inhaled sharply to try and compose herself. Her scattered thoughts began to regroup. She dropped into a combat poise. She was in mortal danger right now. This had happened without her hearing a single thing, and whoever had done it was very close by indeed.

What about Amber? Was Amber okay?

'Amber?' she stammered, stepping backwards.

'Yes?'

Bailey spun around.

Amber was standing just a few metres away, leaning casually against an industrial steam press. Her bunch of keys dangled from her hand, swinging gently back and forth on their chain like the pendulum of a stage hypnotist.

Bailey stared at them clinking softly, temporarily mesmerised.

And then she noticed Poppy's bloody shank lying on the floor by Amber's shiny black shoe. It was the shank that Amber had confiscated only a short time earlier.

She looked up at Amber. Amber smiled faintly.

Bailey felt as if her insides had been sucked out of her.

'Why?' she gasped. 'Why did you kill her?'

'She was dead weight,' said Amber with a dismissive shrug.

'You bitch.'

'That's not a very nice thing to say,' said Amber with a mocking smile on her face. 'I could put you on the nicking sheet for saying that.'

Bailey was panting hard now, fighting to control the anger that was overtaking her. 'I can't believe it's been you all along, working with them. With Terry and the Governor and the gang. Secretly helping them.'

Amber frowned, puzzled. 'Me? A drug dealer?' She spoke the words with disdain. 'You've got to be joking. You are so off-track, it's almost funny.'

Now Bailey was confused. Really confused. Questions tumbled chaotically through her mind, looking for answers that weren't there.

'But... then... then why...?'

She stared at Amber, confounded. And that's when it hit her.

The realisation surfaced in its entirety. She gasped, almost unable to draw breath. She gazed transfixed at Amber's face as the elements clicked into place and the recognition was complete.

'Felicia Lee,' she whispered hoarsely.

'How very observant of you. But then you are a police officer and the police are supposed to be observant, aren't they?'

The metamorphosis was uncanny – the unkempt tangle of black hair had been dyed blonde and drawn back tight and smooth into a neat bun; the dark brown eyes had been cleverly masked by blue contact lenses; and the facial structure had been deliberately obscured by the large pair of thick-rimmed glasses. On a cosmetic level, the transformation was relatively simple, but crudely effective, and probably enough to fool most people.

But what really completed her disguise was the way that she carried herself. With her pressed uniform and prim demeanour, she seemed worlds away from the nihilistic punked-out girl in the file photo. Now Bailey knew why the picture of Felicia Lee had elicited such a strange feeling of unease in her – she must have on some level subconsciously recognised Amber.

But now, the Amber she'd known was evaporating before her very eyes, casting off the layers of primness and virtue like a snake shedding its skin. And to see it happening unnerved Bailey like nothing she'd ever encountered before.

What disturbed her the most though, was how completely she'd been taken in by the caring and conscientious facade. For Amber to have been able to so successfully conceal her true character served to illustrate just how dangerous she really was. Even just a short while earlier when Bailey had convinced Amber to help, Amber had played her part to perfection.

Assimilating everything before her, Bailey now understood what Amber was doing here.

'You're bringing him into the prison, aren't you?' she said. 'Through the well. Your brother.'

'For a policewoman, you're quite smart. Smarter than your friend anyway. She wasn't half as good as you at concealing her identity. I only realised you were a cop just now when you told me out there in the corridor.'

The breath caught in Bailey's throat. 'You knew Alice was a police officer?'

'I caught her using her mobile phone one day. You do know they're illegal in here? I plucked it right out of her hand before she knew what I was doing. Confiscated it there and then. She hadn't had time to lock it, so I took the opportunity to read though the messages and listen to the voice-mails. It didn't take me long to work out that she was much more than just your ordinary inmate.

'When I put it to her that she was a policewoman, she went ahead and admitted it. Guess she knew I had her bang to rights. Made me promise not to tell anyone. Confided in me that she was investigating some drugs ring, told me that she was trying to work out how the drugs were getting into the prison. So I gave her back her phone and told her about this well in the laundry, how I'd seen some suspicious stuff going on down there. I told her to go down and check it out when no one else was around. Unfortunately she bumped into Leonard...'

Bailey stared at Amber with a growing hatred in her guts. 'You deliberately served her up to him.'

Amber shrugged and smiled. 'I've never liked the police. Besides, she had nice hair. Strawberry blonde. I knew Leonard would like it.'

'She trusted you.'

'She was stupid.'

'She was my friend.'

'Get over it,' sneered Amber.

'You're history,' growled Bailey.

Amber pouted in an exaggerated expression of concern. 'Okay, officer. I suppose you'd better arrest me.' She held out both hands, fists clenched, for Bailey to cuff.

Bailey flexed and reasserted her fighting stance. It didn't matter that she had no handcuffs. With her police training and her martial arts background, she was confident that she would be able to subdue and restrain Amber.

Sizing up her opponent, she took a careful step forward.

She hesitated. There was something wrong. Amber was too relaxed.

Amber's gaze flickered momentarily over Bailey's left shoulder. It was a microscopic tell, but it was enough.

There was someone behind her.

Bailey spun around.

There was no one there.

She spun back to face Amber and found herself looking directly into the nozzle of a small black aerosol canister which Amber had been concealing in her clenched fist. It seemed to have appeared out of nowhere, like a coin produced from thin air by a conjurer.

Bailey realised that Amber's glance over her shoulder had been a feint just as Amber depressed the aerosol nozzle. A thin cold jet of white liquid squirted into her eyes. A fraction of a second later, she felt an intense burning sensation and her eyes began to water furiously. It was some kind of debilitating gas spray.

She coughed and spluttered, temporarily blinded. She lashed out wildly but Amber had the advantage. Amber stepped to one side and then stamped hard on the side of Bailey's right knee. Bailey felt her leg give way with a tearing sound accompanied by an excruciating pain. She shrieked in agony and collapsed forward. Amber then karate-chopped her hard on the back of the head and blackness descended upon her.

108

Consciousness heralded its return with a nausea-inducing headache and blurred vision.

Things gradually swam back into focus and, as soon as they had, Bailey was greeted by the sight of Poppy's dead eyes staring back into her own. The gaping throat wound had now congealed and the pool of blood on the floor had settled into a dark viscous puddle, reflecting the halogen strip lighting above.

Bailey struggled to move but found that she couldn't because she had been tied, hands behind her back, to one of the cast-iron legs of the antique Victorian mangle. She wrenched hard, but the heavy mangle refused to budge. By the feel of the material biting into the flesh of her wrists, an empty plastic mesh bag had been used as the bond.

She pushed herself into a sitting position, prompting an involuntary gasp of pain due to her badly damaged knee.

Turning her aching head slowly, she looked around.

Amber was sitting on top of a nearby dryer. Her feet were crossed and she was swinging them lightly so that her shiny black shoes bumped softly against the side of the machine. She was looking down at Bailey with an expression of detached interest.

'Awake? Good. For a horrible moment I thought I'd put you in a coma or something. But I guess I did pay enough attention on that control and restraint course after all.'

'Why didn't you kill me?' croaked Bailey.

'That would have defeated the point. At least one of you has to be alive. For him. He likes them to be alive... for a little bit at least.'

'Why didn't you didn't scalp her?' Bailey nodded over at Poppy's corpse.

Amber screwed up her face.

'Yuck! I don't do that! What a thought! The scalping... that's Leonard's thing. No... I just plain old killed her because she was in the way. And her hair isn't as nice as yours. Leonard's never been into undercuts,' she said, referring to Poppy's hairstyle. 'Yours is much more up his street.'

'You choose them for him?' Amber's depravity nauseated her.

'Sometimes,' she shrugged. 'And sometimes he just likes a bit of pot luck.'

'Where is he?'

Amber looked at her watch. 'Oh, he'll be here soon enough. He's usually pretty punctual.'

'I thought it was tomorrow that he was due to come in.'

'It is tomorrow, silly. It's gone three o'clock.'

At the mention of timings, a niggling unanswered question re-emerged in Bailey's mind.

'Why does he kill on a sixteen-day cycle?'

Amber frowned as if the answer was obvious. 'Well, that's the way the rota works here. Every sixteen days I'm scheduled to be down here in the basement. Getting him in and out and around the prison requires a certain amount of facilitation shall we say, so it helps if I'm here to welcome him in.'

The rota. Bailey wanted to kick herself for not noticing it earlier. She hadn't spotted the connection between the dates on the rota and the scheduled locations of the prison officers because she'd been too busy looking at the locations of the murders themselves, only one of which – Alice's – had actually occurred in the basement.

They lapsed into silence. Bailey took the opportunity to study Amber more closely, marvelling once again at her chameleonic transformation from Felicia Lee into Amber White.

'How did you manage to get a job here?' asked Bailey.

'Fake references and "good interpersonal skills". It's a lot easier than you think.'

'You'd have made a good undercover police officer,' Bailey admitted.

'People see what they want to see. They take stuff at face value. If they're expecting to see a prison officer, that's what they'll see.'

'Sharon recognised you though, didn't she? That fight in the canteen. You got your glasses knocked off and that's when she recognised you. She knew you better than most because you were cellmates. She was trying to blackmail you, wasn't she?'

'I never really got on with Sharon to be honest. She always thought she was smarter than she actually was. And look where it got her. She was swimming way out of her depth.'

'Seems like a lot of trouble to go to though.'

'What?'

'Getting a job here, in the same prison where you were an inmate. Risking being discovered.'

Amber smiled. 'That's all part of the thrill. That's what I get off on. Knowing that I'm fooling everybody. Laughing at them secretly. The stupid mugs. I've never played such a fun game in all my life. You wouldn't know just how fun it is unless—' Her eyes suddenly widened. 'Oh, well actually you probably would know, wouldn't you, Miss Undercover Cop?'

Bailey grimaced. Sadly, Amber was right on the button. They were more alike in that respect than Bailey cared to admit.

'But I still don't get it though,' said Bailey.

'What is there to get?'

Bailey shook her head in puzzlement. 'Why are you both doing it?'

'Why?' Amber looked baffled, as if what she and her brother were engaged in was the most normal thing in the world.

'Yes. Why?'

A smile spread across Amber's face like an oil slick across water. Her eyes now glittered with an alien coldness. She threw her head back and laughed a low husky laugh. The sound chilled Bailey to the bone.

Amber dropped her head and fixed Bailey with a piercing stare. 'It's all about needs. Leonard's got needs. Special needs.'

'You're telling me.'

Amber's face hardened.

'That's the mistake you people always make,' she snapped. 'You think people like us are stupid, like we've got learning difficulties or something. Well we're not! Anyhow, you're the one who was stupid enough to let herself get tied up.'

'I don't think you're stupid. I just think you're fucked up. You're sick. You need help. I can help you. I can help both of you.'

Amber raised one eyebrow.

'I think you're the one who needs help.' She sighed. 'But sadly it looks like you're not going to get any.'

She looked at her watch and began to hum a jaunty little tune to herself.

'Tell me about "The Family",' said Bailey.

Amber stopped humming and looked at her with surprise.

'My, my… you have been industrious.'

'They had extreme religious views, didn't they?'

Amber snorted a laugh. 'That's an understatement. They had a rather puritanical ethic, shall we say. Anything denoting beauty or sensuality was forbidden. We were kept in cages, forced to wear sackcloth, that kind of thing. Long hair was forbidden. We all had our heads shaved.'

She paused in reminiscence. 'Leonard developed quite a thing for it. For hair. For women's hair. So much so that when he got a bit older they let him do the shearing once in a while. He used to love that. Shearing the girls in the cages. His special treat. I guess he was at a particularly impressionable age. But then it all got taken away from him when social services came along and "rescued" us. He tried it on the outside for a bit – taking women's hair – but it was never quite the same. But when I told him about this place – all the women in cages just waiting to be sheared – he was beside himself. He couldn't wait to get stuck in.'

'He's doing a little more than shearing them,' said Bailey. 'He obviously has a deep-seated hatred of women.'

'He's working through some stuff.'

'What? Mummy issues?' Bailey was unable to repress her scorn. Then a thought occurred. 'Is she the one who locked you in the cages?'

Amber raised one eyebrow. 'Cute analysis. And not far off the mark. But ultimately trite. You'll never understand what my brother and I went through.'

'You're right. I don't think I ever will.'

Amber shrugged indifferently.

Silence once again occupied the space between them.

Despite her current predicament, Bailey wasn't about to give up just yet. She had a job to do and she was determined to extract as much information as possible from Amber.

'Where's the well?'

'You'll know soon enough.'

'How did you find out about it?'

'So many questions...' Amber tutted.

'The mysterious escape of Felicia Lee is prison legend in here.'

Amber puffed up proudly. She looked at her watch.

'Well, I suppose we do still have a few minutes to kill. And I guess telling you is not going to make a difference either way. Are you sitting comfortably?'

She looked at Bailey tied to the mangle and smiled amiably.

'I guess not. Still, never mind. So... not long after I got locked up in here, I decided I needed to earn some extra cash for my canteen account so I got a job in the laundry. Pretty boring, but pretty easy.

'The day I escaped, I'd had a really bad night the night before. Nightmares. No sleep. That kind of thing. Know what I mean?'

'Only too well.'

'Anyhow, the upshot was that by the afternoon the only thing I felt like doing was taking a nice long nap. But I had to go and do my annoying job in the laundry.

'So there I was, pushing this big trolley full of nice clean sheets along and I was looking at it thinking how inviting it looked. It looked so inviting, in fact, that when the laundry supervisor wasn't looking I climbed in and pulled the sheets over me and took a little nap.

'The next thing I knew was that this noise had woken me up. When I opened my eyes, I realised that all the lights were off and the place was empty. No one had noticed me asleep in the trolley. They'd all finished up for the day and left the laundry and locked me in. That was the first thing I realised.

'The second thing I realised was that the noise that had woken me up had come from someone else who was in the laundry with me. To tell you the truth that got me a little scared. I hardly knew if I was still dreaming or not. So I stayed in the trolley hidden under the sheets and peeked out at whoever was in there. Just like a little kid hiding in their bed from monsters.

'Who should it be in the laundry with me? Yep, you guessed it. It was

Terry. The noise that woke me up was the sound of him coming out of the well. I could barely believe what I was seeing. I instantly knew he was up to no good. Why else would a prison officer be entering the prison secretly?

'Anyhow, I held my breath and stayed as quiet as possible and waited until he'd left the laundry and locked the door behind him. I waited a few more minutes, just to be on the safe side, then I climbed out of the trolley and went to investigate. And that's how I found out about the well. I escaped, right there and then.'

She grinned at Bailey.

'Nice story don't you think?' she said.

'Beautiful,' muttered Bailey.

Amber's face soured.

'Be as sarcastic as you want. It won't make any difference. You're going to die soon, in a really unpleasant way. And it'll serve you right.'

Bailey shifted position to try and ease her discomfort. She winced as her injured knee sent an agonising jolt of pain up her leg.

'Why did you kill your baby?' she said.

Amber fixed her with a long look. 'I'm not the nurturing type.'

'So you bashed its brains out?'

'I don't want to talk about it.' Amber crossed her arms defensively.

'Was it retarded?'

'Fuck you!' she spat, looking away.

'It was, wasn't it?' Bailey paused. 'That's why incest is illegal.'

Amber jerked her head around sharply, and Bailey knew her guess had been correct.

'What would you understand about me and my brother?' hissed Amber. 'You don't know what we went through.'

'Let me guess, you went through the care system separately, then reunited as adults. Fell into a relationship. You're the only one that understood him and vice versa.'

'You don't know shit! I'm going to enjoy seeing him rip your fucking scalp off!'

'But an illegitimate mentally handicapped child. That just wouldn't do.'

'Shut up!' shouted Amber.

'Mind you, with parents like you two, it's probably better off dead.'

Amber jumped off the dryer, strode over to where Bailey was sitting on the floor tied to the mangle and kicked her hard in the stomach.

'Shut the fuck up!'

Bailey gasped, winded. It took a minute or so for her to recover her breath.

'So what if you both had problems. That's no excuse.'

'Don't get high and mighty on me. Right now you're in no position to judge us.'

'I just want to understand you.'

'Why? What's the point? You'll be dead very shortly.'

A muted thumping sound echoed through the laundry.

Amber tilted her head to listen. She smiled coldly at Bailey.

'As if on cue.'

Bailey peered around trying to work out where the noise had come from. She couldn't see any sign of him. Yet.

Again the muted thump.

It was coming from the far end of the laundry.

Then a movement from one of the top-loader washing machines by the back wall. It was the one with the sign taped over its control panel which read: 'OUT OF ORDER – ELECTROCUTION HAZARD!'

The lid of the washing machine began to lift up, seemingly of its own accord. Then black leather-gloved fingers emerged to grip either side of the rim, pulling upwards...

Bailey watched, transfixed, marvelling at the simple ingenuity of the deception. The well was concealed beneath the washing machine, which itself was conveniently out of order, no doubt to deter casual investigation. No wonder it had been impossible to find.

A head appeared. It was the head of a woman with long black hair. The hair hung down over her face, concealing her features. As she levered herself up out of the well, the hair fell aside to reveal her face, and that was when Bailey recognised her.

U-G-L-Y, you ain't got no alibi. You're ugly! Clap clap-clap. Ugly! Clap clap-clap.

The schoolyard taunt rang out in her head.

It was the inmate who Amber had been escorting across the atrium just a short while before Sharon had been killed and who, Bailey now realised, she had never seen since.

No wonder she'd looked like a man. She had been a man. In drag.

That had been the killer. That had been Leonard.

Amber had been taking him to the kitchen so he could kill Sharon.

Their modus operandi now became apparent – Leonard had been making his way around the prison disguised as a female inmate in the custody of Amber. The disguise had served him for the short periods that he had needed to traverse areas of the prison in view of other inmates and staff.

Calmly, he pulled himself out of the washing machine, swung his legs over the rim and jumped to the floor. Straightening up, he stood there, looking across the room at them. He flexed his fingers, the leather gloves creaking as he did so.

Lifting his hand, he brushed the long dark hair back to reveal a clean-shaven male face wearing a hint of lipstick and a dash of mascara. Without the make-up it could have been quite a handsome face, but right here, right now, under the harsh light of the halogen bulbs, it looked utterly grotesque – the freakish visage of a perverted monster.

He started to walk towards them, his trainers crunching lightly on the detergent powder scattered on the tiled floor.

And that was when the fear kicked in. A sudden blind terror arising from the primal depths of Bailey's brain. He was coming to scalp her and kill her and each step he took brought that horrible fate a little closer.

She squirmed in vain against the heavy cast-iron mangle, the mesh bag cutting into her wrists, but she was held firm, sitting there helplessly on the floor with her hands tied behind her back, tethered immobile like a sacrificial lamb.

She suppressed a reflexive urge to scream at the top of her voice. Better to conserve her energy.

He stopped next to Amber. She turned to him and draped her arms over his shoulders. He placed an arm around her waist and pulled her close to him. They kissed, long and passionate.

Bailey watched in disgust and fascination.

Amber broke off and spoke in a low voice into her brother's ear: 'She knows all about you. She's a policewoman, you know.'

Leonard looked at Bailey over Amber's shoulder. Their eyes met and a shudder of revulsion went through her.

'A policewoman?' His deep male voice sounded bizarre, incongruous, coming from him dressed as he was.

'She's investigating you,' said Amber.

'I'm flattered,' he murmured.

He disengaged himself from the embrace. Amber stood aside obediently. Reaching behind him, he pulled out a knife with a long shiny Bowie-style blade. He tested the edge with his thumb. It looked sharp. Raising his eyes, he grinned at Bailey.

'She has nice hair,' he said, peering at her scalp appreciatively. He glanced at his sister. 'You chose well.'

'She kind of chose herself,' said Amber.

Bailey felt her guts twist in dread. She writhed and struggled, but to no avail. Her bonds were too tight.

This was it.

This was the end.

She cursed her bad luck.

So much for Mel's tiger protecting her.

Be careful it bites.

Those words returned now, washed up like flotsam on the shores of her panicked mind. What had Mel meant? Had she meant anything at all? How could the tiger bite? It was only made of paper.

For protection.

Mel liked to protect herself because Mel was paranoid.

They don't call her Crazy Mel for nothing...

Be careful it bites.

Protection.

Now Bailey understood.

She prayed that the origami tiger was still in her back pocket where she'd put it after Mel had given it to her. She'd forgotten all about it up to now.

Stretching and twisting herself, she managed to poke her fingers into her back pocket. With the tips of her fingers, she could feel the edge of the folded paper. Thank god it was still there.

If only she could get a grip on it. She didn't have much time. A matter of seconds, maybe a minute, if that.

Amber looked down at her squirming. She gave Bailey a look of mock pity.

'Don't worry it'll all be over soon.'

Bailey got a grip on the origami tiger between her thumb and forefinger. She eased it carefully out of her back pocket. If she dropped it now all would be lost. She pressed her finger against the folded ridge which formed its back. She felt a sharp jabbing sensation as it sliced into her fingertip. Never before had she felt so pleased to feel pain.

It was just as she had suspected. Mel had hidden a razor blade inside the origami tiger. A razor blade – Mel's favourite form of self-defence.

Gripping the tiger firmly, Bailey began to awkwardly saw through the mesh bag which bound her wrists.

She glanced up at him from her sedentary position on the floor. Leonard was beginning to walk towards her, the knife dangling loosely at his side.

She needed to stall him somehow. She needed to think of something to say. Anything.

'Is that just a normal wig or is that a scalp you're wearing?' she stammered, trying to force a conversational tone into her voice.

'Just a wig,' he said, looking faintly amused.

He was getting closer. Four metres away... three metres away... two metres away...

Bailey sawed furiously at her bonds. With her hands tied behind her, she was working blind, but she could feel the individual strands of mesh giving way beneath the edge of the razor.

'The Hairdresser, huh?' Her voice shook. 'I bet you would have preferred to be called something like the Hunter or the Ripper. Hairdresser sounds kind of... effete, don't you think?'

'You're only making it harder on yourself,' said Amber.

And then he was there standing astride her. From her perspective, sitting at his feet, he seemed huge, like a silent colossus, blocking out the light.

He looked down at her and adjusted his grip on the knife, placing his thumb on the back of the blade so he could apply more pressure when cutting.

Bailey's heart pounded uncontrollably in her chest as she desperately sawed through the bonds.

Amber seated herself back on top of the dryer, swinging her feet in anticipation like an excited child.

'This is a rare treat,' she said. 'Normally I don't get to watch.'

Leonard bent down over Bailey's seated form and grabbed a handful of her hair. He viciously yanked her head at an angle and began to wind her hair around his fist, tautening her scalp. She winced and gasped, feeling the roots popping out. He eyed her hairline in the detached manner of a surgeon gauging the best angle from which to make a cut.

She frantically sawed away, feeling just a final few strands remaining.

'Stay still,' he said. 'I don't want to ruin it.'

He bent down closer to her level. She felt his warm breath on her face.

He placed the cold steel edge of his knife horizontally across the top of her forehead. She felt him tense as he prepared to slice her scalp off.

The final few strands of mesh gave way. In that instant, she brought up her left hand and knocked his knife away from her forehead. With her right hand, in a single transverse swipe, she drew the origami tiger across the side of his neck. It left a thin red line in its wake.

Leonard jerked upright and reeled backwards in surprise.

Amber jumped off the washing machine, a puzzled frown on her face.

He put his hand up to the cut on his neck, then looked at his gloved fingers. He grunted dismissively.

The three of them all looked at the little origami tiger, which she was holding up in front of her. It looked pathetic, crumpled, mangled by her efforts to break free. It was barely recognisable as a piece of origami.

'It's a tiger,' said Bailey. 'And it bites.'

Leonard snorted in contempt and his face twisted into an angry sneer. He hefted his knife with relish. She'd pissed him off and he was angry now. He was going to finish what he hadn't quite started, and he was going to make sure it hurt. Except he wouldn't get the chance to...

Bailey tilted the origami tiger so that the razor blade was visible protruding from the crumpled paper.

And at that exact moment the thin red cut on the side of his neck suddenly opened up into a large gaping gash. A geyser of blood sprayed up the side of his face.

She had severed his carotid artery.

He took a step backwards, a disbelieving expression on his face. He clamped a hand to the side of his neck in a vain attempt to stem the flow. Bright red blood now squirted between his fingers.

'Leonard!' gasped Amber, rushing to his side.

She pulled his hand away to get a look at the wound and a gout of blood jetted across her face. She recoiled in shock.

'That's coming out at five litres a minute,' said Bailey.

Using the mangle for support, she pushed herself upright from her sitting position to her feet, gritting her teeth against the excruciating pain from her knee.

Leonard tried to lift his knife hand, but with his life force pumping so rapidly out of him he was unable to. The knife fell from his limp grip and clattered to the floor. He staggered backwards and sat down sharply against the dryer.

Amber stood there aghast, her face dripping with his blood.

'Leonard!'

The jets of blood were weaker now, as his heart slowed down, pumping feebly over the surface of the dryer, getting smaller and smaller until they lapsed into nothing more than a faint trickle.

Leonard's eyes glazed over and his head fell to one side.

Amber screeched a feral cry of torment. She spun around to face Bailey.

Bailey brandished the razor blade before her.

'Want to try that little trick with the gas spray again?' she growled.

Amber hissed at her. Even with her damaged knee, Bailey knew she could take her.

Amber looked down at her dead brother, then she glanced over her shoulder at the far end of the laundry. Bailey realised what she was planning and lunged for her.

But Amber was too fast. She bolted for the well. Bailey threw herself into pursuit, but her injured leg prevented her from catching up. She half-limped, half-ran, every step an agony, gasping and cursing to herself.

Amber wrenched open the lid of the washing machine which concealed the well. She climbed inside and disappeared completely from view, the lid clanging shut on top of her.

Bailey arrived a few moments later, panting hard. Pocketing the razor blade, she pulled open the lid and peered inside. The bottom of the washing machine drum had been modified to be opened from beneath, like a trapdoor. And it now hung open, revealing a mouldy brickwork shaft into the side of which were set ancient rusted rungs. The shaft disappeared down into darkness – a black maw that smelled of soil and dampness.

She listened. Silence.

Then, she climbed into the washing machine and began her descent. She gripped the rusty rungs, making her way stiffly downwards, impeded by her injured knee.

Soon, darkness had enveloped her completely. She wondered how long it would take to reach the bottom. She wondered if when she got there she would encounter Amber waiting to attack her, but she had no choice. For one thing, she was determined to apprehend Amber, and for another, she needed to escape from this place in one piece.

As she descended the shaft, bits of dirt and mould fell into her hair and at one point something scuttled across the back of her hand. And then suddenly there were no more rungs. She hung there in the blackness. Lifting her left foot from the bottom rung, she probed downwards into the void.

The tips of her toes brushed a surface of some sort. It must be the bottom of the well. Letting go of the rungs, she dropped downwards, crying in pain as she landed on her damaged leg. She fell to the ground, feeling rough, dry dirt beneath her face.

Wincing, she pushed herself to her feet and stood there, totally disoriented. The absence of light was complete and she had no idea which direction to go in. In the darkness, she could end up getting forever lost in some underground cave system, never to see the light of day again.

She heard a scratching noise. She froze, and then braced herself for an attack. It got closer. It passed by, down by her feet. A rat.

Silence once again. No sound of Amber.

If she wasn't mistaken, she could detect a very faint air current, the smallest of breezes blowing on her face. It must be coming from outside. It was ever so slight, but it was enough to tell her which direction to head in.

She began to edge her way along the dried-up subterranean riverbed, wary, as she moved forward, that Amber could be lying in wait around the next bend. Pulling the razor blade from her pocket, she once more clutched it defensively in front of her. The ground was thick with sediment, and the stony ceiling of the passage was low and uneven, sometimes causing her to stoop down in order to continue. She limped along, grasping the walls for support, every other step sending a bolt of pain through her.

She willed herself onwards, pulling herself along with her hands. In the sheer blackness, she soon lost track of how long she had been stumbling along, but eventually, after what seemed like ages, she noticed the gradient changing slightly, moving upwards. The passage seemed to be opening up, getting wider, light beginning to filter in imperceptibly. So far Amber had not materialised, and Bailey came to the conclusion that she must have fled.

Finally she reached the mouth of the passage, the point at which the tributary had gone underground. She emerged to find herself standing outside on the rocky dry riverbed of what had once been the River Foxbrook.

All around her were trees and she realised that she was deep in the woods that lay to the north of the prison. The night sky was clear and a bright crescent moon shone down over the gently swaying branches, transforming all colours into a monotone palette of greys and blacks. There was no noise but for the rustling of the leaves in the breeze and her own soft panting.

Bailey peered around. She could neither see nor hear any sign of Amber.

She cursed to herself. She'd lost her. Amber had gone. She'd escaped. She'd had too much of a head-start. If only Bailey hadn't been held back by this blasted knee.

She limped forward and sagged against a tree for support. Exhaustion now overwhelmed her. As she leant there, it suddenly struck home that this was the first time she'd been out of the prison since... since being incarcerated. She was finally free of the place. And it felt weird.

She stood there listening to the rustling of the leaves around her, savouring the tranquillity of nature, cherishing the feel of the rough bark under her hands.

Thoughts of Alice flooded through her mind, filling her with warmth and sadness. Bailey had done all she could to give her friend what she owed her. She reflected too on Poppy with a bittersweet pang of remorse. On an emotional level, Bailey was totally and utterly spent.

She started to think about what she should do now, how she could best contact Frank and what their next course of action should be.

But then a noise penetrated her thoughts... a long sibilant hiss carried on the breeze.

Her hackles went up. It was an eerie spectral sound.

Bailey spun around, one way and then the other, looking for its source.

And then she saw it. A figure in the woods, standing about fifty metres away, barely more than a silhouette in the shadows.

Although she couldn't make out her face, Bailey knew Amber was looking straight at her.

'This isn't over, Bailey!' came the howl. 'I'll come for you one day!'

Bailey took a step forward. She blinked and squinted.

But the figure was no longer there. It had melted away into the woods, leaving only the branches swaying in the breeze.

110

The debriefing was finally over and Bailey needed some fresh air. Her right leg was still painful and stiff as she limped slowly along the corridor to the lifts and went down to the ground floor.

She walked out of the building, passing its iconic revolving 'New Scotland Yard' sign, and found a spot to stand on the pavement. It was a hot muggy July afternoon. London traffic roared past, whilst crowds of people streamed around her in all directions. The scene was reassuringly noisy and busy.

The debriefing had been in front of a tableful of the drugs detectives who had been overseeing and funding the undercover operation, along with members of the National Crime Agency, who were poised to pursue any links to large-scale organised crime, as well as detectives from the murder investigation team who had been investigating the prison slayings. Bailey had taken them through the whole affair exhaustively from beginning to end. It had been a draining but also cathartic experience.

After she'd escaped from the prison through the well and lost Amber in the woods, Bailey had limped to a nearby 24-hour petrol station and called Frank. He and a slew of detectives and uniformed officers had arrived not long afterwards and picked her up. Despite the excruciating pain in her leg, she had waved aside medical attention to accompany them directly to the prison, eager to identify the key players involved.

It hadn't taken them long to locate and arrest Terry, but not before he'd managed to alert the Governor to the situation. Then she'd taken them down to the basement, where they'd recovered the bodies of Leonard and Poppy from the laundry and transformed the whole area into a crime scene for further detailed forensic analysis.

By the time they'd got to the Governor's five-bedroom detached home in Hampstead, he had his solicitor there waiting with him in his drawing room. But his pleas of innocence had fallen on deaf ears. With some satisfaction, Bailey had personally read him his rights, cuffed him and taken him into custody.

For the time being, HMP Foxbrook had been put under the direction of an interim governor, who had sealed up the breach in the laundry and launched a complete review of prison security.

'Bailey.'

She turned around. Frank had just emerged from the building behind her. He smiled.

'That went well. They're really pleased with you. This has worked out great for everyone. And I think your testimony will seal it for good.'

Bailey sighed at the thought of it. It wasn't over yet. The Crown Prosecution Service were planning to prosecute the Governor, Terry and the members of the Ace Blade Crew, and Bailey's testimony was going to be key to securing their convictions.

The Governor and Terry had each been charged with wilful misconduct in public office as well as serious offences related to the supply and distribution of illegal drugs. Both were currently being held on remand in the same prison on a secure wing for their own protection. Terry was being extremely co-operative as expected, in the hope of getting a lighter sentence and, much to the satisfaction of the NCA, had already begun to give up details about the organised crime group who were behind the supply of drugs to the prison. The Governor, on the other hand, was in denial about the whole affair.

Frank chuckled. 'The last I heard, the Governor was demanding to talk to his "friend" the Home Secretary. He's claiming that it's all some kind of big misunderstanding.'

'However much he's paying his lawyer, I doubt it's going to be enough to pull that off.'

'I reckon he'll be spending most if not all of his retirement at Her

Majesty's pleasure. Probably not quite what he was expecting when he signed up to the Prison Service.'

As for the Ace Blade Crew, they had been split up and were in the process of being moved to separate prisons around the country. They were facing prosecution for a gamut of offences, ranging from possession of offensive weapons, possession of mobile phones and possession and supply of psychoactive substances. But Bailey was sceptical that any further convictions would have much effect on their behaviour, particularly for someone like Toni who would no doubt just hook up with whatever chapter of the gang existed in whichever prison she was placed in.

'They've sworn revenge on you,' said Frank, his face darkening, 'and they have associates on the outside who'll be looking to get even with you. So it's probably a wise idea to keep one eye over your shoulder from now on.'

Bailey shrugged it off. 'I'll be fine.'

Frank eyed her in admiration. 'I don't doubt that you will.' He paused and snorted an ironic laugh. 'You know, the drugs squad are under the impression that this whole outcome was part of this "new angle" that you were working on. I thought it better not to tell them that we were just stringing them along for most of the time. After all, they're over the moon with the results, so why shatter their illusions?'

Bailey allowed herself an amused smile. She liked to see Frank looking happy. It was such a rare occurrence normally.

He leaned in conspiratorially. 'This whole thing is certainly not going to do your career any harm, and... between you and me, I've heard whispers that a commendation might be in the works for you.'

'I'm not interested in awards,' said Bailey, shrugging indifferently. 'I just want to catch Amber. As far as I'm concerned, the job's only half done. She's as much responsible for Alice's death as Leonard was.'

A review of the forensic analysis from the prison would likely confirm the connection between the murders there and the original Hairdresser slayings. Leonard's involvement now looked to be beyond doubt and his death tied up that investigation from a cold case perspective. But there was still the painfully outstanding issue of Amber. As Felicia Lee, Amber had already been a fugitive in her own right, but now she was also wanted for assisting Leonard and for directly murdering Poppy, and Bailey was determined to catch her, not least because of her complicity in Alice's death. It really stuck in her craw that she'd let Amber get away and she knew she would never feel satisfied until she'd got her locked up, back on the right side of the bars. For Bailey it was a personal mission.

But it seemed that Amber had gone to ground. There was absolutely no sign of her anywhere. She had been clever enough to evade detection once before and she was no doubt putting those skills to good use again right now. She was a dangerous and devious individual and Bailey had killed the only person she'd ever been close to. Recalling Amber's parting threat, Bailey now wondered if she herself had more to fear from a vindictive and vengeful Amber than from the ABC's numerous affiliates.

She looked around her at the crowds of pedestrians, at the cars and buses whizzing past, at the windows of the office blocks overlooking her and she felt a chill go through her. She had a feeling that somewhere out there Amber was watching and waiting. Waiting to get her.

Unless Bailey got her first.

'What's on your mind, Bailey? You look perturbed.'

'Oh nothing,' she said.

Frank paused for a few moments.

'How do you feel about coming back and working for me again? Undercover. On a more regular basis. I've got some interesting opportunities lined up. We make a good team you and me.'

Bailey reflected on his proposition. Like all undercover jobs, this one had taken it out of her and the last thing she wanted to do right now was plunge back into the extreme stress of that double life. But for how long would she be able to tolerate humdrum normality? That was one thing that really would drive her up the wall.

'I'll think about it,' she said.

He nodded slowly. He knew when not to push her. He adopted a lighter conversational tone.

'So what are you up to for the rest of the afternoon? Back to the office? Back to your sergeant's exams?'

'I've got to make a little detour to the tattoo shop first. I got this tattoo in prison. It's ninety-nine per cent done. There's just one last tiny bit to fill in and then it'll be complete. I think the person who did it would appreciate me having it finished.'

111

They were now locked in for the evening and Crazy Mel sat at the desk in her cell completely absorbed in the process of making an origami animal.

Her long brown fingers intricately manipulated the piece of paper, folding it one way and then the other, shaping it into the desired form.

Lying to one side on the desk was the letter from Bailey. She'd received it in the post earlier that day. In the letter, Bailey had told her that the Hairdresser was dead, that the duppy was gone. She'd thanked Mel for the origami tiger. It had indeed protected her, just like Mel had said it would.

Mel's fingers deftly creased the paper. First the ears, and then the legs, and now a tail. Fold by fold, it slowly took shape...

Hairdresser? Dead?

When it came to duppies, dead didn't always mean dead. That was the thing with duppies. Yuh neva knew fah sure...

ACKNOWLEDGMENTS

All of the team at Boldwood Books who worked so hard and expertly to bring this novel to publication.

Dorie Simmonds, my agent, for her astute advice, boundless enthusiasm and unwavering faith in this novel.

Sarah Cox, formerly of the Metropolitan Police, for her help in answering several questions I had around the structure and operations of the police.

Claire, my wife, for her immeasurable support and encouragement, and her perpetual willingness to listen to new ideas.

I read a number of factual books in order to try and understand the psychology and methodology of undercover policing. One which particularly stood out, and which is a fantastic read, is *The Infiltrators* by Philip Etienne and Martin Maynard with Tony Thompson.

MORE FROM CARO SAVAGE

We hope you enjoyed reading *Jailbird*. If you did, please leave a review.

If you'd like to gift a copy, this book is also available as an ebook, digital audio download and audiobook CD.

Sign up to Caro Savages's mailing list for news, competitions and updates on future books.

http://bit.ly/CaroSavageNewsletter

Villain, the second instalment in the Detective Constable Bailey Morgan series, is available to order now.

ABOUT THE AUTHOR

Caro Savage knows all about bestselling thrillers having worked as a Waterstones bookseller for 12 years in a previous life. Now taking up the challenge personally and turning to hard-hitting crime thriller writing.

Follow Caro on social media:

 twitter.com/CaroSavageStory
 instagram.com/carosavage
 bookbub.com/authors/caro-savage

ABOUT BOLDWOOD BOOKS

Boldwood Books is a fiction publishing company seeking out the best stories from around the world.

Find out more at www.boldwoodbooks.com

Sign up to the Book and Tonic newsletter for news, offers and competitions from Boldwood Books!

http://www.bit.ly/bookandtonic

We'd love to hear from you, follow us on social media:

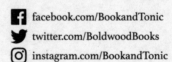

facebook.com/BookandTonic

twitter.com/BoldwoodBooks

instagram.com/BookandTonic